To John,
Very best,
L M Banyan

Phantom FUTURE

L.M.
BANYAN

ISBN: 0692968652
ISBN 13: 9780692968659

Library of Congress Control Number: 2017908877
L. M. Banyan

ACKNOWLEDGEMENTS

I have so many people to thank for helping me on this long journey.

First, to Gaston Leroux for writing about Erik—a tortured genius rejected by society because of his deformity—who still dares to hope for love. Leroux's timeless classic has been reinterpreted by each generation for the past hundred years, often focusing on the gothic aspects of the story. But Leroux's writing and imagery are so much deeper, implying the human paradoxes of wealth and poverty, acceptance and rejection, as well as the ugliness of mortality contrasted with timeless beauty. The hallmark of his writing is not only chilling detail, but also witty humor and insightful irony.

Next, I wish to thank Leonard Wolf who graciously consented to my quoting passages from *The Essential Phantom of the Opera*, his quintessential translation of Gaston Leroux's book, and all quoted passages are from his book. The historical data and lore in Mr. Wolf's insightful annotations were also appreciated.

My heartfelt, special thanks to my two dedicated co-conspirators, who were with me each step of this long and winding road. Although lay editors, they contributed their invaluable insight and support along with infinite patience and untold numbers of hours:

To *Anna Krebs*, my deep admiration for her endless patience during all the edits. Anna is legally blind, so I often read the book to her as she gave her perceptive comments regarding plotlines and characters. Reading the book aloud to her aided in keeping the dialogue realistic and natural to the individual characters. Using a special computer which greatly enlarges the print, she also gave her input in pruning and honing the text. To Anna, I dedicate Chapter Two.

To *Karmen de Lune*, my deep appreciation for her dogged persistence in making each passage true first-person, present tense. As my "narrative police," she hounded me to keep the dialogue and stream of consciousness in natural flow. Her artistic sensibilities were given unselfishly to refine the text, book cover design and website. And she has the heart of a poet and musician, so she assured that aspect of Erik was well represented in the story and prose. To Karmen, I dedicate the book cover and all the passages with Erik's sardonic wit.

Then, through serendipity, a gifted professional editor, Gretchen Stelter, crossed my path. She provided valuable feedback on my plotline and characterizations, then copyedited the book for publication. I wish to clarify that because of a subsequent reedit, any errors are mine. My profound thanks for all her encouragement and valued work.

I owe special thanks to Donna Rion who gave perceptive advice about Erik and the story flow, along with caring support. Her chats with me about the book were as enjoyable as following the fates of our respective Kentucky and Arizona Wildcats.

And my deep appreciation to J.A. Jance who thoughtfully gave her time, advice and support to me for this novel.

Others also gave of their time, support or expertise. A sincere thank you to each: Ronald Binion, LouLou Kneubler, Evan Cutler, Roger Cochran, Rose Sing, Sheryl Glenn, Debbie Belanger, Stephen Burn, Joan Barber, Col. Barbara Jennings, Robert Rutan, Walter Kroon, Jessica Tomlinson-Salazar, Glenda Taylor and Angela Carney.

And most of all, to Ken, my beloved husband and the wind beneath my wings. As is his nature, he patiently supported me every step of the way, both financially and emotionally, always cheering me on and encouraging me in this labor of love. This book would have been impossible without him. He was, and always will be, the angel watching over me.

Last, but not least, to three people who inspired characters in this novel:

Diane Green, another angel with a heart of gold who counseled and healed so many devastated, abused, or rejected people;

David Walker, a man who protected and defended many women and children, often selflessly—a true, noble Sioux warrior; and,

Gerard Butler, who finally succeeded in portraying Erik in all his complex, paradoxical humanity.

To Ken,

the other half of my heart

The world of the future is of our making.

Tomorrow is now.

— Eleanor Roosevelt

1 | REMAINS

January 24, 2040
Paris, France

I scowl at the ragged book on the counter. *That blasted diary! Why did I buy it?* I must have been out of my mind. The antique dealer suspected who my client is and gouged me on the price. What a gamble!

As my panic increases, I glance out my shop window again. Where is Lady Margaret? And why is she so late? Her assistant told me they'd be coming from a funeral in England on one of their private jets and make a stopover to examine the diary. Did something happen? There's been growing furor about Lady Margaret's husband and that strange business of the time-travel technology his company supposedly developed. What if there was a protest at the funeral—or even worse, a bomb? The very thought makes me reach for my antacids.

Frantic, I bark at the wall monitor, "Screen on! Search British news for a funeral any time today."

Within seconds a medieval chapel where a funeral is being held appears on the monitor. A reporter solemnly announces into the camera, "We're here at the funeral for the daughter of renowned barrister Sir Kenneth Ballard."

The camera pans from the reporter over to paparazzi standing near parked limos and protestors waving signs behind a police barricade. As he walks toward the protesters, the reporter says, "Among the many notables attending is Lady Margaret de Renesse who famously avoids publicity. Protestors have taken advantage of this opportunity to demonstrate their opposition to the new time-travel technology controlled by her American husband, Howard Wheaton."

The reporter sticks the microphone in a protester's face and asks his opinion.

"Time travel? Mind bending," the scruffy man replies. "But why should one person be havin' it all to himself?" The reporter nods in agreement, then moves to another protester who expresses similar sentiments.

"Protestors," I huff. I have no idea why they object to Wheaton's control of time travel, but then I don't pay much attention to the news. As long as Lady Margaret pays lavish sums for my antiques, that's all that matters to me.

After interviewing several more protestors, the reporter announces, "The service is over and mourners are leaving." The camera turns back to the chapel, but only focuses on a veiled woman being escorted to a limo by several men, no doubt bodyguards. The woman is identified as Lady Margaret just as a paparazzo rushes within feet of her and aims his camera. In a blink, a large bodyguard pivots and his elbow flies up, deftly sending the camera through the air. As the startled paparazzo scrambles to retrieve it from the mud, the limo speeds away. Good! She got away unharmed—but the funeral was on the midday news report, and it's almost six o'clock. Where is she?

I chew on another antacid. What if Lady Margaret doesn't come at all? What if her interest in the book was just a passing whim—that has passed? But she always asks me to keep my eye out for artifacts from the 1800s, especially from the Paris Opéra or the Commune. She was pleased with the cane I found for her from the Opéra. A unique cane, as I recall, with a handsome ivory lion's head—almost as handsome as the price she paid.

And what if she arrives but doesn't like the diary? I glance around my shop. A pathway has been created through the clutter of antiques so she can sit in the alcove, surrounded by tempting treasures, while she examines the book. I spot the Louis-Philippe armchair and move it into the alcove. Lady Margaret purchased one like it last month, and she must buy *something*. I'm desperate. What if my daughter finds out I bought that diary with the funds put aside for her wedding? She has her heart set on a silk gown despite the outlandish prices now that silk worms are dying off. And my wife, what does she care about the costs? She spends like she's the reincarnation of Marie Antoinette. So what was I to do?

The Pepin of Paris mantle clock strikes six ominous chimes. My stomach churns as I reach for the troublesome diary and thumb through its pages. Quite good condition for a book two hundred years old, and it was written by a woman at the Opéra. My heart skips as a page falls out and lands on the floor. When I pick it up and look for a date, my eyes catch the words "mask" and "cannonballs." Curious, I squint at the tiny script, faded but legible.

20 April 1871

Erik is dead. There can be no doubt. His stark mask rests on the table, its hollow eye staring back at me, like the skeleton that will soon be all that remains.

I can hear cannonballs exploding into the buildings nearby. My hand is shaking so much that holding the pen is difficult, but I must attest to his bitter ending. I know what they say about him. But how could anyone else know what I saw behind his scarred face—what I saw in his soul? How can the spell cast by his genius be described? No challenge withstood his inexorable will. But he is no more.

When Communard rebels came to my room today, they said Erik was executed this morning by their firing squad and demanded I come to identify his body. They forced me to go through the streets even though a bombardment was shelling the city. I feared we would be blown to pieces, but they dragged me to those dreadful chambers beneath the Garnier.

To bid my final farewell I knelt beside his still form, covered in crimson streaks trailing down the black waistcoat. I wept bitterly at the gash on his forehead and blackened bruises on his face, then removed his mask and touched the scarred flesh which has forever been his curse. Their one kindness was to allow me to keep the mask. As the Communards led me out, I heard shovels striking the hard ground. I glanced back and saw them digging a hole to bury him there, alone. In the place he lived so long. Alone.

His life should not have ended this way. Why have men always killed each other over their differences? Why? Once again all

Paris cowers in fear while the government and revolutionaries tear at each other. But the world will go on as it always has. The living will not miss him. I wonder, had they not rejected him, what his life could have meant to the world.

I have written the truth about him in this diary, but I doubt anyone will ever read my words. Would they make any difference? The explosions are getting closer. I must seek a safe place. Now Erik is in God's hands. As are we all.

I shake my head. It's beyond me why Lady Margaret would be interested in that grisly period when the Communards took over Paris. The page turns out to be the last one in the diary. As I'm debating whether or not to throw it away, her Bentley pulls into my shop's courtyard. *Time has run out.* I quickly decide to return the page to its place and rush to the front of my store.

Two bodyguards escort her, but only the large Native American enters. His eyes scan the store like a hawk searching for prey as he walks down the narrow aisles, checking out every hidden nook. At the back of my shop, he goes into the storage room and searches it to confirm that no one else is here. Finally, he returns to the front door and opens it. Lady Margaret sweeps into my shop, dressed in black Chanel and still wearing a veil.

"My condolences, Lady Margaret," I utter solemnly.

She nods politely. "You have the diary of *Adèle Giry*?" Her tone is skeptical.

"Just as I said." I offer her the book. "Feel free to inspect it to your satisfaction."

For a moment she stares at the diary suspended in midair. When she reaches out to take it, her hand trembles. *Good omen? Or bad?* I escort her to the alcove and seat her on the Louis-Philippe armchair. Its cushions are sapphire blue, like her eyes. Perhaps she'll buy it.

Returning to the counter, I busy myself sorting through a crate of books and occasionally steal glances over at the alcove. She has removed the veil, but since she's turned away, I can't see her expression, only the golden hair pulled back into an impeccable chignon.

The clock's loud ticking frays my nerves. Why is she taking so long? Who knows what drives the whimsy of a rich woman? But a woman can do whatever she wants when her husband is reputed to be the world's wealthiest man. Well, some have and some have not. Hopefully, before she leaves, *I'll have.*

As if my troubles weren't nerve-racking enough, her bodyguard stands motionless at the entrance to the alcove. Only his eyes move, following everything I do. A most intimidating man with long, black hair tied behind his neck and broad shoulders nearly filling the alcove doorway. I recognize him as the man who elbowed the paparazzo.

Just as I'm reaching for antacids again, Lady Margaret motions me over. With a catch in her voice, she begins, "This diary ends during a bombardment. By chance do you know what happened to Madame Giry? Did she survive the shelling?"

I swallow hard. *I have no idea.* What will sell the book—that the woman lived or died? I should have thrown away that last page. I decide not to guess and tip the scales the wrong way. "I'm sorry, I don't know." Smiling apologetically, I hold my breath.

She picks up her handbag. *Mon Dieu! Is she leaving?* My heart pounds as I wobble slightly. Then she reaches in and takes out her checkbook. Without so much as a glance in my direction, she fills out the check and hands it to me, her mind elsewhere. *In shock*, I stare at the amount. The figure far exceeds the price I quoted her—more than enough for a silk wedding gown. And the check certainly is good as gold, drawn on one of her husband's banks with her family crest prominently displayed.

I thank her profusely and escort her through the shop. As I'm holding the door, I remember the Louis-Philippe armchair. That would have paid for the wedding champagne! But it's too late—she has already glided past me. Her bodyguards quickly assist her into the Bentley, and she's gone, leaving behind the scent of exotic perfume and my delighted grin.

2 | FATE

April 19, 1871
Paris

Erik Mercier

Explosions pummel Paris, striking ever closer. I race across the abandoned avenue through clouds of smoke rolling between the buildings. Red fingers of fire streak into the late afternoon sky—like devil's talons reaching out of hell. As I race down an alleyway, the rooftop above me explodes, showering down brick and plaster. Before I can pull up my cloak to keep the dust from getting under my mask, a shard grazes my forehead. *Mon Dieu*. The soldiers have turned the cannons! I keep running, hopefully beyond their range.

With each footfall, pain radiates through my head and warm blood trickles down my face. Taking refuge behind a livery shed, I pull out a handkerchief and press it to the gash, all the while disparaging the manhood of the soldier who fired that volley. No doubt my landlady is hiding in the basement of her Auteuil boarding house, also cursing the soldiers and claiming they bomb the finer neighborhoods out of spite. She always says that, and I always agree. After all, she doles out the food and a nod of concession to her ranting is rewarded with a larger scoop from the soup tureen. But why would the soldiers not take advantage of an opportunity to avenge their hatred on the well-to-do? That is the poisoned core in the heart of the City of Light. The reason civil war rages again on the streets—all about the few having so much and the many having so little.

A cannonball explodes into the livery, pelting me with debris. Furious, I flee down the alley again. *Damn the government.* As I run, I keep staunching the blood, cursing them all for their madness. This crazed, patriotic fervor sweeping the city has been a curse on my life since last September when the Prussians laid siege to Paris—and my world ended.

Silence now, except for my boots pounding on cobblestone. The streets are nearly empty as people huddle in their rooms, seeking safety. Another terrifying crash overhead as a cannonball shatters a window. A woman's scream pierces the air. Again I am struck with fear for Christine and Adèle. How have they fared? Surely Raoul left Christine at his family's estate in the countryside before he went off to fight the Prussians. I worry more about Adèle. She had no wealthy nobleman to take care of her, and she moved to Neuilly, which is being heavily shelled. Yet I dare not visit her. She was known to be my friend, so the police may be watching. But after every bombardment, I wonder whether she survived.

Another explosion! How many more will die today? And all for nothing. This is the third rebellion since the Great Revolution a hundred years ago, and no doubt it will end as they all have. After the death and destruction, a few bones of concession may be thrown to the people to placate them. But in the end, the wealthy and powerful will retain their wealth and power, and the people will return to their lives of struggle and misery. Nothing will change. Nothing ever does. I quicken my pace and search the ground for one of the entrances into the tunnels. Crossing Paris above ground has become too perilous.

As I race across a street, a horse bolts out of a livery stable and nearly runs me down. I yell at the rider, but he does not even look back in his panicked flight. Seeking the safety of a café doorway, I stop to catch my breath. To think I came out of hiding two months ago wanting to live again in human society. Even succeeded, passed myself off as a wounded soldier, and no one suspected who I am. But now that I live aboveground, humanity has gone mad, trying to destroy itself and me along with it. And I no longer want to be a part of it—desire only a cottage in the countryside where I can live in solitude. Human companionship is not meant for me. And my hope for love? *Delusion.*

Again I set out, having no choice except to hazard crossing Paris to retrieve the metal box that contains my small fortune. After all, I must deal with my landlady and her greed. My funds on hand have run out, and I need money to secure the relative safety of the boarding house until these fools have tired of killing each other. Then I will leave this City of Suffering and put the past behind me.

A cannonball smashes into the building ahead. *The cannons have turned again*. I dive beneath a wagon and spot the cover of a manhole that leads into the tunnels. Hefting the iron plate aside, I lower myself onto the wooden stairs.

On the first landing I discover the bracket which holds the torch is empty—and I have only a few matches. *Merde!* I will have to travel most of the way without light, but that I can do. Despite being a formidable foe, the cavernous underbelly of Paris has often granted me asylum. Night engulfs me as I descend many stories down the stairwell. At the bottom a faint acrid smell hangs in the cool air. Removing my gloves, I light a match. The small flame illuminates three converging tunnels. I choose the one heading northeast and soon the flame sputters out, leaving me in darkness befitting a tomb.

All my senses become acute to outwit the serpentine passageways. I hold one hand in front to detect overhangs and lowered ceilings. With the fingertips of the other, I read the cryptic code on the wall. Here, the chisel marks feel relatively smooth—surely a gallery tunnel the workmen for the Inspection des Carrières carved out to search for lost quarries.

My hand trailing the wall, I walk blindly through treacherous tunnels. The wall's texture changes, probably a cement buttress constructed to support an abandoned quarry's ceiling and save Paris from being swallowed into gaping holes. Abruptly, the wall ends. I stop and use one of my matches. Its weak, flickering light discloses the large cavern of a quarry. I hurry across, reaching the tunnel on the other side just as the match hisses out and leaves me sightless once again.

Claws grate the ground as rats scurry away from the soft thud of my boots. After some distance the tool marks beneath my fingers change to gouges that feel like dragon scales. These were made by the men who built the soaring cathedrals in the Middle Ages. I always sense their hovering ghosts. Can almost hear the rhythm of their hammers, raping the limestone from mother earth.

At the next conjunction of tunnels, I light my last match and read the Inspection's sign that corresponds to the street above, getting my bearings. The sound of feet shuffling against the stone floor sends a chill down my spine. Those are not rats. Quickly I extinguish the match and listen to determine how many are lurking—at least three from the different timbres of their voices. My hand goes instinctively to my Punjab lasso. I throw my voice, sending a low, rumbling growl reverberating through the limestone tunnels. Frightened voices cry out as they scutter away in panic, and I move on into timeless night.

Lit dimly by lamplight filtering through a street grate high above, a cistern comes into view. The workmen used the cistern's water to make cement for the buttresses. One of their stairways may not be far! I venture back into darkness, clawing at the ragged wall, desperately searching for stairs. Then my hand scrapes against a wood railing. *I am safe!* Relieved, I begin the seemingly endless climb to the surface.

At the top landing, I cautiously lift the cover. The cannonade is far away, and the moonless night sky promises a cloak of protection. After a one-legged Communard hobbles past, I climb out and pull up my hood to conceal my face. Slipping silently through near-empty streets, I stay to the shadows, unseen.

Finally, the majestic Garnier looms ahead. I go to the side of the building and pull off a hidden grate. Stooping low, I make my way down a musty passage until it connects to the lower level's ventilation duct, then crawl through the cramped duct to a secret trapdoor. Smirking, I wonder what Monsieur Garnier would think if he knew how many of these I incorporated into the building.

I drop through the trapdoor into the second cellar. A deserted oil lamp sits precariously at the edge of a workman's bench. I light it and survey my surroundings. So eerily silent now, unlike the noisy activity during construction, when the sounds of hammering and raucous banter assaulted my ears like a discordant symphony. Although the room is unfinished, strewn with wood shavings and piles of lumber, I feel at home. But such sentiments are overshadowed by my disgust for all that has been lost. First the war and siege and now the uprising have halted construction on this grand building. I wonder when, or if, the work will continue.

The wound on my forehead has stopped bleeding, but before I put away the handkerchief, I try to remove the blood embedded in my ring's engravings. When the gold band gleams in the lamplight, bitter memories return. Memories of hope and pain. And faces.

"Curse you," I mutter to the specters. "Curse all of you." Hastily, I pull on my gloves, banishing from my sight the reminder of my follies.

My journey is nearly at an end. At the far end of the room, I discover that the door is locked. Reaching into my waistcoat, I pull out my silver fob and press the ornate engravings until a jagged metal pin appears. With it, I make quick work of the door lock. I grab the lamp and enter a dark corridor, traveling quickly through the maze-like rooms until I reach the stairway, then descend downward into the depths of the Garnier. Finally reaching the fifth cellar, I breathe a sigh of relief. The box I buried with my money and valuables, such as I have, is not far.

Then laughter erupts from around a corner. I snuff out the lamp and slip noiselessly into a room to hide, but a door across the room slams open, and three men in green trousers and blue jackets enter. Communards!

A gangly boy holds high an oil lamp which illuminates a storage room full of kegs. The intrusive light reaches the corner where I have taken refuge, and the boy catches sight of me. Startled, he calls out, "What are you doing here?" The other men aim their rifles.

"Are you a filthy government spy?" an old man demands, his voice shaky. "Or a thief?" He waves his rifle at the wine barrels and stacked bags of flour.

"*Non*. Neither." Calmly, I try to explain, "I worked for Monsieur Garnier and came back for some of my possessions."

The third man, larger, with a nasty scowl, points his rifle at my chest. "Spies are everywhere. I can tell you are one. Hold up your hands."

I set down the lamp and display my empty hands. "I assure you, I am no spy."

"You lie," the man spits.

"Why do you wear a mask?" The old man eyes me. "What are you hiding?"

They approach, rifles aimed. Fear and suspicion have overcome reason. Nothing I say will be believed. Communards accuse anyone who is suspect and shoot them as a spy.

My body coils. Before they can cock their rifles, the Punjab lasso flies from my hand. Snaking through the air, it cinches around the big man's neck. He drops his rifle and clutches the strangling noose. I lurch forward and shove his body against the others. They fall backward onto some barrels, arms and legs flailing wildly.

No time to retrieve the oil lamp. I race into the pitch-black corridor, feral instincts taking over. I run blind, hand scraping the wall. Blood pounds in my ears. How many Communards are in the cellar? Now fate stalks me.

I turn a corner and collide with a soldier, taking us both to the ground. More Communards come streaming through a door. Hands reach down, pulling the man from beneath me. They circle like hyenas, and from every side boots kick viciously. I lash out and kick back. They scream in anger. I use my forearms to deflect the blows, but boot heels drive into my ribs. Pain shoots through my chest. A rifle butt hammers my lower leg, and I feel the agonizing snap of bone. Pain, sickening pain. Then a strike to my forehead and a shock of cold air. My mask—ripped away. I am exposed. Overpowered. I clutch my hands to my chest and roll over to protect them with my body. Then a piercing blow to my head. All goes black.

Swirling, murky darkness surrounds me. I moan. Agony pulls me out of oblivion. I struggle to open my eyes, but they are clotted shut with dried blood. I try to lift my hand but cannot. Ribs are broken. Raising my other hand, I rub away the blood. With effort I look around my makeshift prison. The door is ajar, allowing a strand of light into my shadowy cell.

Voices intrude from the next room. "He is dangerous," someone rasps. "If it is who we suspect, they say he is a crazed murderer."

"What if he struck a deal with the government? The bastard mighta spied on us ta save his own skin."

"But if he is a spy, he might be worth more as a bargaining chip."

"Bargaining chip? You ignorant ass," the voice rumbles, gruffly drowning the others. "We should shoot him right now and be done with it. That devil's lasso nearly strangled Gilbert."

"But it didn't. Gilbert's off duty for the night and stinkin' drunk by now."

"He's better off than us!"

"And what if *Monsieur Masque* is a poor fool like us?" a fretful voice asks.

"Yeah, what if he spoke the truth? What if he only came to get his things? *Sacre bleu.* What if he's not a spy?" The rasping voice rises to an anxious pitch. I hold my breath.

"Enough! It makes no difference." The gruff man ends the quarrel. "When the regiment returns in the morning that bastard will be shot."

I let out a ragged breath. So it is decided. I am to be executed. Desolate, I survey the room for escape routes. *No windows.* My eyes search the floor for grates marking underground tunnels. *None.* I scan the ceiling for an air duct. *Nothing.* The only exit is through the door.

Then I spot it on the floor inside the doorway—my mask. A sliver of light streaks across the black leather. I laugh. So they want me to wear the mask when they execute me. Better that they kill me now and get it over with. I attempt to get up, but pain screams through my splintered leg. I fall back onto the dirt floor, frozen. Sweat pours down my face, stinging my eyes.

The pain makes me acutely conscious of my body. I grimace at the irony that my body will not burden me much longer. In many ways, that is a relief. I have always been at war with my physical self. I take a ragged breath. Even the escape of sleep is beyond my reach. I lie on the cold, hard floor, haunted by memories of things I have done—accomplishments most men could barely imagine. But the many things I have never done also torment me. Human joys that most take for granted have evaded me. A paradox. Ultimately, my life was a paradox.

I send up a futile prayer. *If only I had more time.* But when I pass from this world, who will know or even care? As if in response, a gentle face appears like an apparition. *Adèle.* Will she ever learn what became of me? Or will she wait for years, hoping for my return?

Relentlessly, my hopes and dreams continue to mock me. I cannot escape them any more than I can these cursed Communards. I stare at the ceiling, hovering like the lid of my coffin. My body is too broken to put up another fight. I cannot evade my fate—but I vow that in death my specter will haunt this place forever.

Screams and crashes suddenly erupt in the next room. Wounded cries fill the air as an unseen battle rages. Then the door slams open and three Communards rush in. Cold fear floods through me. Wracked with pain, I prop myself up on my elbow and strike out at my attackers. Hands seize me, pinning me down. One man sprays a mist into my face and the world goes dark.

So this is how it will end.

3 | DEFENSE

Monday, June 4, 2040
Seattle, Washington

COLLIN MCKAY

The elevator opens and I plunge into the crowded corridor. Don't like courthouses. Never have. I prefer university hallways with students chattering amiably or hurrying to appointments. Here, frazzled people stand around looking worried and lost, waiting for their fates to be decided.

The attorneys stand out with their professional garb and matter-of-fact attitudes. One couple frowns as they listen to an old attorney whose jacket bags from sloping, tired shoulders that seem weighted down from dealing with too many people, too many problems. Nearby, two well-groomed businessmen hang on the words of a confident young attorney in a trendy suit.

What with my Scottish tweed jacket, I probably could be mistaken for an attorney, but instead here I am, joining the worried and feeling quite lost. As if my work weren't complicated enough, now I'm dealing with this damned mess. But there's only one person I can think of to take this on—and that we can trust.

I hurry down the corridor, looking for her, but no luck. She must still be in court—room number 44, her legal assistant said. I find it and peer through the door's small glass window. The spectator section is empty, but a hearing is going on. Ah, there she is. I slip in quietly and take a seat at the back. An attorney in an expensive Italian suit stands at the front of the court, addressing the judge. Sporting a suntan that speaks more to hours in the Tuscan sun than overcast Seattle, the attorney hammers his case with all the fervor of a Cesare Borgia.

When the other attorney turns to her client, I catch a glimpse of her face—the large, dark eyes and graceful nose turned up slightly at the tip. It's been three years since I've seen Kathryn. A pang of guilt strikes me. Swallowing hard, I shove the painful memories aside.

Punching the air for emphasis, Cesare accuses Kathryn's client of abandoning her two daughters last Friday and making no attempt to contact her husband or see the children. Despite the dramatics, the judge looks bored. Cesare concludes that the wife is unfit, and since she has no means of support, her request for custody should be denied. The balding husband approvingly smirks at his attorney's attack.

When Kathryn stands to address the judge, I get my first good look. Still wears skirts with matching jackets. Kathryn never did dress informally. Anne always kidded her about that. I lean forward, don't want to miss a word.

"It's true Mrs. Stratton left her home in the middle of the night last Friday," she begins. "It's also true she did not take her children and made no attempt to contact them."

What's she doing? Kathryn just conceded the main points in the husband's case. But then she explains that her client fled in fear of her life through the bathroom window onto the second-floor roof. Then she walked to the highway and flagged down a truck that took her to the nearest emergency room, where doctors treated her for two cracked ribs and numerous bruises and cuts—all from a beating at the hands of her husband.

A snort of denial erupts from the husband. In a hushed voice, Cesare advises him to control himself. Kathryn requests that the medical records be admitted into evidence.

"Objection!" Cesare jumps to his feet. "We don't know that the injuries were at the hands of my client. These could have been sustained in a fall from the roof or even at the hands of some other person. Apparently she hitchhiked. Maybe the injuries were from a tussle with the truck driver."

"Response, Ms. Copeland?" the judge asks Kathryn.

"Mr. Stratton's attorney has conceded my client left the house through a second floor window. Why would she climb onto a roof and risk falling and breaking her leg or worse? Only because she'd already been beaten. She sought refuge in the bathroom but realized the door wouldn't stop her attacker, so she did the only thing she could—escaped onto the roof. The medical records specifically note she was *not* under the influence of alcohol or drugs." Kathryn glances sympathetically at her client and adds, "Neither her husband nor his attorney has alleged my client was in the habit of leaving her family and going off alone at night. All the facts point to her having fled after being beaten by one person—Mr. Stratton."

"Objection overruled," the judge announces. "The exhibits are admitted." The husband glares at Kathryn through narrowed, threatening eyes.

Kathryn continues her factual onslaught, detailing the physical abuse which had increased over the past months as the husband's business lost more money due to the depression plaguing the country. She points out that the wife's fleeing to protect herself and being absent for three days do not constitute abandonment of the children. Methodically, Kathryn describes her client's fears not only for her safety, but also the safety of her daughters. She presents her case with the same persuasiveness and clarity that won every debate at the university against anyone foolish enough to take her on.

The husband grumbles angrily, but Cesare warns him to hold his tongue. After more heated, gut-wrenching debate between the attorneys, the judge grants all the temporary orders. Then he pointedly directs Stratton to remove his personal belongings from the family home under the supervision of a police officer. Everyone stands as the judge leaves the bench. Stratton walks past with his attorney, and I get an earful of foul language. Clearly he's used to getting his way.

Then the young wife breaks down crying. With a reassuring voice, Kathryn patiently answers all her client's questions. When the woman leaves, Kathryn's shoulders relax as she opens her briefcase and puts away her file and old model laptop. I noticed that the other attorney had a Wheaton QRYSTAL quantum computer—and the most expensive model at that. Kathryn evidently doesn't get the pricey fees from her clients. But then, she left the corporate world a few years ago.

Kathryn turns around and spots me. "Collin, what are you doing, lurking there?" She walks toward me, her brilliant smile making me wince. So much like Anne's. "I thought we were meeting at my office."

"Could no' resist seeing you in action." I give her a big hug. "To tell the truth, your hearing was running late, so I came here t' pick you up for dinner."

"Wonderful to see you again. How long have you been here?"

"Snuck in as the other attorney was launching his attack. I enjoyed watching you give him a good drubbin'."

"In his defense, his client probably didn't disclose a lot. I doubt the attorney knew about the beating or the medical reports." She grins. "It helps to have the facts."

"That's all there is to it?"

"What do you mean?"

"Just curious about wha' it takes to win a case."

"Well, getting all the facts isn't as easy as it sounds. The client may not want to admit or disclose everything—may not even be aware of all the facts. So gathering evidence includes digging into any potentially useful information and tracking down and questioning witnesses."

"So *that's* all there is to it, then?" I query.

"No, thoroughly researching all the legal angles is crucial. And having a fair judge or jury plays no small part. Fortunately, the law provides attorneys with a useful tool—we can file a motion to disqualify judges who are biased."

"Tha' doesn't sound like a politically correct thing to do." I've had my own run-ins with the political types at the university.

"No, it's not." She chuckles. "But I don't hesitate to file a motion to remove a judge when needed. So, thorough preparation of the facts and law as well as an impartial judge are usually a successful combination."

"From my understanding, 'usually' is not the correct word when applied to you. Based on wha' I hear, it's more like 'always.' You win just about every case, don't you?"

"How did you come up with that information?" She regards me suspiciously. "And why would it matter to you?"

"T'be honest, I'm in need of a good attorney."

"What did you do? Flunk someone who's got a *lord* in front of his name?"

"Oh, it isn't about me." She's joking, but she's got a point. When I was a professor at Oxford, I didn't go off half-cocked. "However, I do know a person who may be accused o' *things*."

"*Things?* What things?"

"Uh, murder—mostly." I flinch. So much for saving that for later.

She stares at me long and hard before replying. "Murder? Sorry, I don't take criminal defense cases. My practice is mostly civil litigation and cases involving domestic violence and child abuse."

"We can discuss this later." I glance around the room, uneasy. "We have t'be cautious."

"What's this about?" Kathryn takes a step back. "Is that the reason you're here? Why you called to take me out to dinner?"

"Shall we go then?" I punt. "We're going t'be late."

"So you made dinner reservations?"

"O' course. You love French food, right? I got us a table at Le Bouc." I grin and take her briefcase, escorting her into the corridor. It's after five and the swarms of sullen people are gone. As we enter the elevator, I comment offhandedly, "We're going to a meeting first if you don't mind. We'll have dinner after."

"Meeting? What's the meeting for?" She doesn't hide her irritation.

I shrug apologetically. "It's indirectly involved wi' the case I mentioned." When the doors open, I guide her toward the public parking lot. "Shall we take my car?"

Kathryn halts abruptly. "Why can't I follow you in mine? Where are we going?"

There's no way I can tell her here. It's too open. Anybody could be tracking me, listening in. I put on a smile. "Will ya trust me? I thought maybe you could help me out a bit." I don't dare give her any more information. She'd likely bolt right now. "For old time's sake?"

She searches my face for several tense seconds. "I'm not happy about this being sprung on me." Testy, she finally says, "All right."

So far, so good, I'm thinking as we head to my car. When I open the car door for her, she gives me a strange look. *What now?* As I'm driving to the exit of the garage, she seems to be studying the electronic monitors on the dashboard.

"This isn't a hybrid, is it? It's a fully electric car," she says, surprised.

"That it is."

"I've never been in one. Wouldn't have thought this was within the salary of a professor."

"Well, true. This is provided by my employer. All o' his vehicles are electric."

"*Really?* You mean he can afford to pay the extra taxes for using electric cars? Who is this employer? Is he involved somehow with this 'meeting'?"

"Actually, he is."

"So what is his name?"

"You'll know tha' soon enough."

She shakes her head and looks away.

We head toward I-5, but the motorbikes and pedicabs clogging the hazy, grey streets of Seattle slow us down. As we approach an intersection, police sirens begin to blare, so I stop the car. An old van comes speeding down the street, but slams on its brakes at a traffic gridlock. Two men get out and race into the alleyway, followed by a hunter police drone hovering closely overhead. Police cars screech to a halt next to the van. We watch as several policemen give chase while one stays back and uses a crowbar to pry open the van's back doors. When they fly open, a cargo of barrels comes into sight.

"What do you think it is?" Kathryn asks. "Water?"

"Yeah, tha' would be my guess. Probably water runners, wha' with half the country dealing with drought and the other half with water contamination. And here in Seattle we have all this rainwater t' be captured for free and sold for drinking water."

"But how can you blame them? Bootleg water brings high prices in some places. Unfortunately, if they get caught, that's a minimum prison sentence of two years."

"I've noticed the police have been crackin' down on the water runners even more now. Ever since the Powers, T'ang and Bianchetti Corporation cut their backroom deals and got the government to give them exclusive rights to sell and distribute water throughout the country."

She sighs. "Who would ever have thought collecting rain that falls from the sky would be illegal? The PTB Corporation spreads its slimy tentacles everywhere."

"I hear their next move is to make it illegal to grow your own food or sell it without government authorization. And o' course, they'll make sure tha' *only PTB subsidiaries* have authorization."

"No doubt," she says, "they own everything, including the government."

Traffic begins to move again, forming a single file around the tangle of police cars and abandoned van. A tiny black police drone hovers outside my car door, inspecting me, then zooms around to Kathryn's side. She glares back at the drone until it buzzes away.

"Bloody hummingbird drones," I mutter under my breath. "There are more o' them all the time."

"Well, they're large enough to see, so we know when they're around." After a pause she adds, "At least for now."

I don't say anything, but I'm not so sure. Who knows how small they've been able to make the drones? Maybe these are only decoys.

I check my watch. *Damn, we're going to be late.* But there's no rushing through traffic in the clogged Seattle streets. I wind around the pedicabs which slow traffic and squeeze past buses stopped to let out passengers. At a red light we're trapped behind a truck belching out clouds of black exhaust. Kathryn coughs when the noxious fumes reach inside my car. I hate coming into the cities. It would seem that with the gas rationing, the smog would decrease, but a lot of regulations were tossed out because they were considered too expensive to enforce, including the regulations on car exhaust. Maybe paying for surveillance drones drained the coffers.

Finally we enter I-5 and head south. "Where *are* we going?" Kathryn asks warily.

"Olympia. To Land's End, an estate on Puget Sound."

"Any connection to the Land's End on the southwestern tip of England? I was born near there."

"Yeah, that's its namesake," I reply cheerily. She falls silent, studying me. I sense wheels turning in her mind. How am I going to hold her questions at bay for an hour's drive?

"So, why am I going there for a meeting about someone accused of murder?"

"Actually, we'll be discussing tha' matter *after* the meeting."

"Okay, what's this all about?"

"Sorry, I canno' reveal the details yet."

"What's all this secrecy for? Good grief, why are you even involved with someone accused of murder? The only trouble you ever got into was taking a political stand or rocking the boat."

This seems like a handy rabbit trail to take. One by one I revisit the controversial programs at Oxford I participated in. That succeeds in keeping the conversation lively and distracting her for nearly an hour.

Then Kathryn ambushes me. "So, *who* is this person accused of murder?"

"Right now all I'm t' do is take you to the meeting."

"I should have known." The words ooze with underlying meaning.

"Known what?"

"Well, I haven't seen you since Anne's funeral three years ago. I should've known you weren't here just for old time's sake. So, it's business." Her voice is filled with disappointment. "Why, Collin? Anne was my best friend. I wrote and called you, trying to help. But you never replied, not once."

"Sorry. I just couldn't."

"Did I *do* something wrong? *Say* something wrong?"

"No. That's no' your style."

"Then, why?"

"Because you *were* Anne's closest friend. You were practically sisters." *How can I explain?* Anne and she looked so different and yet were so much alike. Anne had the curly red hair of the Irish, and Kathryn, although Irish on her mother's side, has the straight black hair of her father's English heritage. But their eyes, so much alike—brilliant and intense. Wherever they focused their energy, they brought that unique combination of daring and compassion. And their smiles could stop a man dead in his tracks. Anne's surely did that to me.

My Anne. So gentle and loving with me. But she also had that Irish temper. So fiery and fierce when she was angered by the poverty that seems to be everywhere or the wars that always devastate the innocent. That's why she became a photojournalist. She wanted to expose the corruption and greed that causes those tragedies. Whenever she went off on one of her journeys, I was always fearful. Then she was gone. Forever. And I couldn't see Kathryn without seeing Anne. I think that's the reason I froze Kathryn out of my life. Partly from grief, partly out of self-preservation.

"You reminded me o' her. It hurt too much." When I glance over, the pain reflected on her face tells how hurt she was too. "Not calling or explaining wasn't right. Will ya forgive me?"

Her eyes become watery. "Of course. I was a bit hard on you just now. Sorry."

"Friends?" I reach out my hand.

She takes it and gives me a conciliatory smile. "Friends."

A silence falls between us. After a couple minutes Kathryn is studying me again. Maybe music will distract her. "Radio, scan music channels."

"Trying to stall by playing music?"

"Only if it works," I shoot back. She rolls her eyes.

I stop on my favorite channel, unfortunately just as the promo begins: *"PALnet—the Private Advantage Link—your unsurpassed internet connection to the world."*

Kathryn frowns. "Don't you have your own music? I try to avoid the PTB canned programming on PALnet."

"Radio, play my favorites," I quickly order. As my music begins, Kathryn smiles her approval, and we talk once again about our days at Oxford. Thankfully Kathryn doesn't press me for more information. I don't want to scare her off before they can make their pitch for her to take the case. Judging from her reaction, it'll be a hard sell. But we have to try. She's the one we think can do what is needed. More importantly, we feel she has the ability to work with *him*.

Turning onto Cooper Point Road, we drive through Olympia's suburbs, past deserted shopping malls and abandoned restaurants. This unending depression has invaded even these affluent areas. Finally, we're out of Olympia and driving through lush, green countryside with its fresh, clean air. Trees line the road, protectively blocking the view of large homes. We pass the golf course, still neatly manicured for wealthy clientele. Turning down a side road, we drive the last mile through dense forest until we reach the tall brick wall enclosing the estate.

I pull up to the fortress-like gates. Peering into the red eye of the security camera, I declare, "Collin McKay and Kathryn Copeland."

When the gates slide open, two armed security men motion for us to proceed. "Where in hell have you brought me, Collin?" she demands.

I can't look her in the eye. "We're almost there."

We proceed down the long driveway, overshadowed by towering cedar and spruce. After a half-mile the forest ends abruptly. For security reasons, only ground-hugging grass covers the land in this part of the estate.

As she takes in the long line of buildings that trail the cliff above Puget Sound, Kathryn shakes her head. "You called this an estate. It looks more like a military installation. What is this?"

I can't argue with her description. The facades on this side of the buildings are stark and windowless, constructed with monumental blocks of granite that look like they were left over from the pyramids.

"Well, it's no' military for certain. This is a private estate and also somewhat of a business."

"Somewhat? What does that mean?"

"Sorry, I really canno' say anything more just yet."

The road winds through the clearing, between the neat white fence which encloses the pasture with stables on the right and the rambling buildings on the left. I'm relieved when Kathryn turns her attention to the half dozen prize horses grazing in the pasture.

Finally we reach the courtyard outside the one part of the façade which appears inviting. As soon as I park, a waiting security guard opens the door for Kathryn and another takes my keys to repark my car in the underground garage. Kathryn hesitates at the foot of the massive marble stairs leading up to Chinese-style double doors. I give her an encouraging smile and escort her up the steps. As we arrive at the top, one of the doors opens and the elderly twig of a butler appears. With a bow and sweeping gesture of his white-gloved hand, he welcomes us in. Under his appraising gaze, I usher Kathryn over the threshold.

"Good evening, madame and Dr. McKay." The butler draws back his lipless smile.

"Good evening, George." A tad anxious, I add, "I assume everyone's here for the meeting?"

"Indeed. You're late," he sniffs. "Everyone has been in the library for *some time*."

I hope we're not too late. The plan was for Kathryn to hear the last item on the agenda. "We'll hurry right along, then."

As we rush through the mansion, I sense Kathryn's mounting tension. She resents being manipulated, but how could I have told her the truth? Would she have believed it? Will she believe it even now?

4 | CASTLE

KATHRYN COPELAND

I'm stunned by the spacious room we enter. Considering the foreboding stonework on the exterior, I was prepared for something resembling a bunker. Instead, the eccentric butler has welcomed us into what feels more like the lobby of a five-star hotel. Several stories above, enormous skylights flood the room with light. The architecture is starkly modern with white granite walls and highly polished marble floors, but the couches are overstuffed in elegant European style and arranged in conversation groups. European tapestries cover the walls. I suspect they are priceless antiques.

Collin hurries me through this room and into a wide corridor bathed in light by clerestory windows. He's noticeably agitated about being late. Late for *what exactly*? My stomach churns. Nothing seems right about this. Why am I here for a meeting in this bizarre place with the façade of a mausoleum and the interior of an opulent mansion?

Racing to keep up with Collin's long stride, I glance in awe at the museum-quality treasures we're rushing past. Silk-covered couches line the corridor, separated by T'ang Dynasty horses in orange-gold hues atop marble pedestals. Delicate Sung porcelains glow in lighted cases.

We turn down a long, winding corridor. Antique French consoles displaying blue and white Ming porcelains line these walls. Finally, we come to engraved metal doors where an intimidating man stands guard. Without cracking a smile, he opens the door and steps aside. Not knowing what to expect, I hesitate.

But Collin gives me no choice. He ushers me into a room that turns out to be a spacious library with walls covered in mahogany bookshelves, full of leather-covered hardbounds. Unlike the windowless façade that faces the road, this room has magnificent views of Puget Sound, framed by floor-to-ceiling windows. The muted glow of recessed lights reflects off rich wood and plush carpets. Behind us the heavy door closes with a foreboding *thunk*. I feel trapped.

Collin and I settle into chairs by the door, not disturbing the dozen or so people seated on brown leather couches around an immense marble fireplace. Everyone's engrossed in some report. I study their faces. To my increasing discomfort, I recognize a number of well-known public figures, including an heiress to the largest retail corporation in the world and a former secretary of state who tried to bring about Middle East peace treaties without success. A balding man huffs and slams the report closed. He's a controversial member of Parliament and next to him sits the current president of a South American country.

A diminutive Chinese man returns my gaze. His face seems familiar. I look away, trying not to stare. Then I remember seeing his face on the news. He's Dr. Hua, the quantum physicist who made history by developing the theoretical basis of time travel for which he received a Nobel Prize in physics. *Time travel.* The concept utterly confounds me. It's become a hotly debated topic, and I've read a couple articles about Dr. Hua's work. I always take what's reported with healthy skepticism, but it's claimed the technology has now been taken beyond the theoretical stage. Feels surreal to be in the same room with the man who might have accomplished that magical feat.

I try to discern a pattern, some logical connection between these people, but this seems to be a random conglomeration of men and women prominent in business, politics, and science. The only thing I'm certain of right now is my misgivings about why *I'm* here.

"What is this, Collin?" I whisper. "A meeting of the leading members of Who's Who?"

"It's the Executive Committee of the Foundation for Worldwide Action."

The FWA? As I recall, that was created last year to fund ocean and freshwater reclamation projects around the globe. Puzzled, I murmur, "Just what *are* we doing here?"

"Be patient," Collin says under his breath.

I glare at him. His intense, brown eyes turn away as he nervously rubs his beard. He's testing my patience. I study his familiar face—the high brow and pronounced cheekbones of his highland ancestors—trying to figure what's going on in that keen mind. He's always had the straightforward Scottish manner of dealing with people. Why is he so evasive now?

I turn my attention back to the group as one of the men looks up from the report. It's Howard Wheaton! Probably the most famous man on earth. The controversy over his time-travel program, under the direction of Dr. Hua, has been all over the news for the past several months. He's said to be fifty-some years old, but he looks much younger—not a hint of grey in his ash-brown hair and only a few wrinkles in those striking features.

"Now, for the last item on the agenda," Mr. Wheaton states. "The report you just read is to inform you of this situation before it possibly breaks in the news. I'm sure you have questions."

The white-haired former secretary of state speaks up first. "Howard, how exactly did this happen?"

"The man we brought from the past was in far worse physical condition than we anticipated, and the infirmary here at Land's End wasn't adequate."

They brought a person from the past? Really?

"He needed immediate surgery and was taken to the hospital we own in Seattle," Mr. Wheaton continues explaining. "We required everyone who had any contact with him to sign confidentiality agreements, and sizable bonuses were paid for their silence. Despite that, a leak occurred. It was traced to a nurse. We verified that after she pocketed a tidy sum from us, she sold the information to Powers, T'ang and Bianchetti."

The PTB Corporation? I glance over at Collin. What has he gotten into here?

The secretary of state presses, "Tell me that nurse is no longer working for you and you've plugged all the leaks."

"In a manner, yes." Mr. Wheaton hesitates. "The nurse was involved in a fatal hit and run a few hours after our investigator talked to her."

A man with an Aussie accent blurts out, "You don't mean your bloke kil—"

"Of course not. That's not the way I handle things." Mr. Wheaton glares back at the man, and the room goes deathly silent as everyone digests this.

Someone killed that woman to silence her. *A PTB thug? Or is Mr. Wheaton lying? He certainly wouldn't admit to ordering a murder.* My heart starts pounding. I really don't want to be here—feels like I'm standing on crackling thin ice.

"When the PTB media machine gets wind of this, the muck is going to hit the fan," the heiress says cuttingly. "I suspect some of it will land on us. What steps are you taking to keep this from tainting the work of the Foundation or any of us directors?"

"Sir Kenneth has advised us," Mr. Wheaton replies, glancing over at a distinguished man with salt-and-pepper hair, "to release a statement that bringing Mercier from the past has nothing to do with the Foundation. We'll clarify that Wheaton Industries transported him here to test our time-travel technology. To limit any negative publicity, I'll step back from active participation in the Foundation's public affairs until this matter is resolved."

"Each of you can state that you had no involvement with this," Sir Kenneth states, "and that this issue has nothing to do with FWA projects. Make no further comments."

"What in hell possessed you to do this, Howard?" the heiress presses.

"As the report says, it was part of our system's ongoing tests," Mr. Wheaton shoots back. "We knew people from the present could travel into the past, but we didn't know if it worked the other way. We needed to find out and never intended to make public that we had brought Mercier to the future. The plan was to send him back after he recuperated."

"So you claim this was no more than an experiment?" asks a dark-haired man with a thick Russian accent. "Then why didn't you pick some unknown person? Someone innocuous?"

"We selected the person based on specific parameters. It had to be someone about to die from an external cause, so if we were unsuccessful in returning him to the past, he wouldn't be prevented from fulfilling his life's work. That might have a ripple effect."

"Why from an external cause?" A grey-haired woman wearing a brightly colored sari speaks up. I recognize her from a recent article. She's a doctor who is developing new metabolic-nutritional treatments for chronic illness.

"We didn't want to transport someone who was ill. If they died in transit or shortly afterward, how could we determine if it was from time travel or natural causes?"

"What possessed you to choose this particular chap, then?" the member of Parliament scoffs.

"As most of you know," Mr. Wheaton replies, "my wife is interested in nineteenth-century French history. She came across a diary that gave us the information to locate him just before he was to die. The diary also indicated he was wrongly executed."

"If you return him to the past, won't there be ripple effects?" the Russian asks.

"No, there would be no ripple in our time stream that would effect us," Dr. Hua replies.

"What do you mean?" a dignified man in an African agbada asks. I've seen him interviewed about his work in environmental crisis areas. "Wouldn't changing something that occurred in the past create a domino effect on our history?"

"When Mr. Mercier was saved from execution, that created a new time stream. When he is returned to the past, therefore, he will be living on that alternate time stream and will not affect us or the stream we exist on." Dr. Hua smiles patiently as if he's explained this point many times.

The member of Parliament cuts in, "That may all be well and good, Howard, but why choose a chap with his nefarious background? Someone who could possibly bring discredit on your work?"

"Perhaps my wife can best address this." Mr. Wheaton turns to the woman beside him.

Mrs. Wheaton is one of the people I hadn't been able to identify. Her blonde hair is pulled back, highlighting azure eyes. She speaks softly, her precise British accent tinged with French overtones. "Monsieur Mercier was known to be a creative genius, so saving his life had two distinct benefits—rescuing a falsely executed man and allowing a genius to complete his natural life and fully utilize his talents. Wouldn't that be a benefit to humanity?"

"Lady Margaret, I appreciate your good intentions," the secretary of state says deferentially, "but wasn't he also known as a murderer? Maybe even insane?"

"From the information we've gathered," she replies confidently, "it appears Monsieur Mercier has not been portrayed accurately."

"Also, his having a negative impact when he goes back would be unlikely," Dr. Hua interjects. "One person alone would have a statistically insignificant effect on the alternate time stream."

"It still leaves you with the current imbroglio," the Russian argues.

"He's right," the member of Parliament declares angrily. "According to this report, the International Criminal Court of the Americas in Seattle is investigating Mercier for murders he might have committed. How did they get involved?"

Mr. Wheaton bristles under the heated scrutiny. "Powers, T'ang and Bianchetti Corporation has been busy behind the scenes. They informed the French government that Mercier had been brought from the past and pressured them to file criminal charges, since there is no statute of limitations on murder." Smiling grimly, Wheaton continues. "However, Wheaton Industries is in negotiations to purchase and reclaim polluted land outside Paris for a new factory. Judiciously, the French government declined to pursue extradition or file charges. Then Powers, Tang & Bianchetti turned over the information to the Criminal Court of the Americas, which is examining the evidence to see if they have grounds to proceed."

"So the PTB Corporation's game plan is to use the trial to pillory you for bringing Mercier to the present?" the member of Parliament asks.

"Yes," Sir Kenneth says, "this is another one of their maneuvers to get what they want—the time-travel technology."

"And if they get their hands on it," the South American president says, scowling, "they'll find out about the future. That would be disastrous."

The future? What's he referring to? My stomach clenches.

"Why not send Mercier back to the past before charges can be filed?" the Russian asks.

"I can't," Mr. Wheaton chafes. "As the report said, the Criminal Court served me with an injunction that prohibits me from sending him back pending their investigation. At least we negotiated an agreement with the Court to keep this matter confidential. It'll only go public if charges are filed. Although there were rumors that Mercier committed these murders, he was never charged with any of them during his lifetime. The Court may not be able to find sufficient grounds to bring charges."

"Good grief," I whisper to Collin, "who'd they bring? Jack the Ripper?"

"Ach, no," Collin says under his breath. "Well, not exactly."

"Not exactly? Then *who* exactly?"

Collin shakes his head and turns back to the group.

"If Powers, T'ang and Bianchetti is behind this," the member of Parliament scowls, "there is little doubt the court's prosecutors will dig until they find any excuse to file charges."

"Whatever happens regarding this situation," Mr. Wheaton retorts, "the Foundation must keep doing its work. In the meantime, I'll take the heat, and we'll dispute the charges if they're filed. Once acquitted, Mercier will be returned to the past. That'll quell the attacks."

"It damned well better," the Australian growls. "There's too much at stake here."

"I trust you have shrewd attorneys to represent him?" the South American president asks.

"We do," Mr. Wheaton replies confidently.

I blink. He can't be referring to me. I'm not a defense attorney. Why would they want *me* for this case? After hearing what's at stake, I don't want anything to do with this.

"Howard, just pay them whatever they want." The secretary of state wags his finger and chuckles. "You won't miss a million or two."

Mr. Wheaton replies stiffly, "Any further discussion?" When no one speaks up, he announces, "Meeting adjourned. Please join us for dinner in half an hour. Our chef has prepared some specialties for dinner tonight—lobster and oysters, I believe."

"Lobsters? Oysters?" the environmental scientist exclaims. "Those haven't existed outside museum aquariums for years."

"We bought several islands and are developing processes to reclaim their coastal waters." For the first time, Mr. Wheaton breaks into a smile. "We're reestablishing oysters, lobsters, and two types of crab."

Despite the prospect of such delicacies for dinner, the people wear worried faces as they leave. No one seems pleased with the turn of events. I can relate. Neither am I.

Abruptly, Mr. Wheaton addresses us. "Good evening, Ms. Copeland. Collin." *He already knows who I am.* "We're glad you agreed to meet with us."

Agreed? More like *hijacked.* Mrs. Wheaton gives me a welcoming smile, but her haunting eyes make me uneasy. They seem to peer into my mind, as if she can read my thoughts. I feel like Exhibit A. But there's also a wistful, sad quality in her gaze.

"Please join us," Mr. Wheaton adds, "so we can discuss your client, Mr. Mercier."

As Collin and I take seats on a couch opposite the Wheatons, I control my anger. Either Mr. Wheaton is taking a lot for granted, or I've been entirely left out of a rather significant loop. "First, let me clarify, I have *not* accepted Mr. Mercier as my client."

"We apologize for the inconvenience of bringing you here at the end of your long work day." Mrs. Wheaton's voice has none of her husband's demanding overtones. "I know you've had little notice, but we learned about this possible legal action less than a week ago ourselves. Could you please read the report? Perhaps that will help." She nods to Collin, and he hands me one of the portfolios.

I hesitate before opening it. Do I really want to know? Do I want any part of this? Reluctantly, I open it and begin reading. The report goes over the reasons Mr. Mercier was chosen to be brought from the past and says basically what was discussed during the meeting. That is followed by a short biography of Mr. Mercier, which doesn't contain any reference to murders he may have committed.

Then I turn to the last page and find the name by which he is well-known. I look up in shock. "I've heard about this man, but I thought the stories about him were fictional. So, you're saying that Erik Mercier—the person you brought from the past—is that infamous man?"

"Yes," Mrs. Wheaton replies. "However, Gaston Leroux wrote the original book about Mr. Mercier forty years after he died. Leroux pasted together myth and legend which he gleaned from different sources, so not everything in his book is correct. To find out the truth would be part of your job."

"I see. Frankly, this isn't the type of case, or client, I usually represent."

"We're aware of that." She half smiles. "But I feel if you were to hear his story and understand his situation, you'd have a different impression of him. I feel he's innocent, or if he committed any acts he's accused of, surely it was justified. In any case, he deserves the finest defense possible." Her response has an underlying emotional charge, and she's certain he is, *or should be*, innocent? Fairly shaky from a legal perspective.

"Do you have proof to support that?" I ask, feeling like the ice I'm standing on is beginning to fracture.

Before Mrs. Wheaton can respond, Mr. Wheaton interjects, "How about a retainer of a couple million for starters?" That hits me like a plunge into icy water. Mrs. Wheaton talks about a man who's been wronged, but Mr. Wheaton offers money that's nothing less than a bribe. Everything about this feels wrong, twisted. My instincts scream for me to get out of here.

"An interesting proposition. However, respectfully, I must decline." When I stand to leave, Mr. Wheaton stares in disbelief and Mrs. Wheaton gasps. Collin's jaw clenches, but wisely he refrains from saying anything. I no longer trust him. As I walk to the door, Mr. Wheaton calls after me, "Please come back and be seated. We have not finished."

My anger ignites. I turn around and the words explode from me, "Yes! We have!"

I don't wait for his response. Hurrying across the library, I shove open the door and rush down the corridor. I don't get far before my knees give way, and I sink onto the nearest couch. My hand shakes as I take out my phone and call my legal assistant. I want her to send a car for me so I can just get out of here. Now!

But I can't get a signal. I try over and over, with no success. Are they blocking my call? Then I remember what happened to the nurse who didn't go along with the program. Nobody knows where I am. If I disappear, no one would even know where to look.

As I put my phone away and stand up, a dark flash catches my eye. Someone just came around the corner, then stepped back into the shadows. *I'm being watched.* Adrenalin shoots through me and my heart pounds as I race down the endless corridors.

When I finally reach the lobby, the skeletal butler plants himself between me and the exit. I start to make an end-run dash for the doors. Suddenly, strong hands grip my shoulders and stop me—just steps away from escape.

5 | SIEGE

Collin

Her shoulders tense under my hands. "Kathryn, I'm sorry. Will ya give me another chance? *For old time's sake?*"

She shrugs my hands off and turns around to face me. Her eyes flare with anger. "For old time's sake? That's wearing thin, you know. Isn't this really about your own agenda?"

"I'm sorry. Did no' mean for it to turn out this way."

"Just what way did you expect this to go? Keeping me in the dark and bringing me to this—this *gilded fortress*. I can't get a signal to call out. Am I a prisoner?"

"No, o' course not! Kathryn, we need your help. But you can see this is, well, complicated. And confidential. This canno' be discussed outside Land's End. Will ya give me one more chance? If no' for my sake," I hesitate, feeling the heat of her emotions, "will you do it for Anne? She would have at least heard me through."

She gives me a hard stare. "All right, for *Anne*," she says through clenched teeth. "So, what do you want to say?"

"Would you come back t'the library with me so we can talk this out?"

"I'm not going back there," she replies, defiant. "We talk right here. But before we talk about anything, I want to call my office and have them send a car."

Damn. We've really dug ourselves into a deep hole. Lady Margaret is usually good at finessing a situation, but Mr. Wheaton *would* have to jump in with that bribe. He just doesn't understand, but I do. Kathryn's like Anne. She can't be bought—she only does what she believes in. I've got to use that angle to get through to her.

I pull out my palm-sized Qrystal and call security. "Let me have an outside link." I'm told to hold for the head of security.

Tom Cheveyo comes on within seconds. "You've got the link." Then with a chuckle he adds, "Have your hands full?"

"Yeah, thanks." I glance up at the security camera that's hidden in the light above Kathryn's head as I hand my Qrystal to her. "Go ahead and make any arrangements you want."

She calls her legal assistant and tells her where to send a car, then pauses. With a look of distrust, Kathryn asks, "Your security will let the car through the gates to pick me up, right?"

"O' course!" I put on a smile. We've dug a really deep hole.

She finishes the call and hands back the Qrystal, eyeing it with something between awe and curiosity.

"Well, then, let's just sit here and chat while you're waiting." Still steaming, she sits on a side chair near the door, relegating me to an adjacent couch. Casting about for a way to break through the wall she's put up, I start with familiar territory. "Did you know I quit my teaching post at Oxford?"

"No, I didn't. I assumed you were on some special project here for the FWA."

That's good for starters—she's talking to me. "No, Howard Wheaton approached me with his time-travel project and said he needed an expert in European history and languages. Tha' was a challenge I could no' pass up. Been working here at Land's End for almost two years now."

"Surely you'll be returning to Oxford?" she asks in surprise.

"No, I doubt it."

"Sorry to hear that. You were a brilliant professor and your students respected you. And that's where you met Anne."

"I've come to accept the past is the past. There's no bringing it back. We just have to move on." I blink back tears and change the subject. "And I've been able to do wha' most historians only dream about. I've time-traveled back t' some very interesting events."

"Really? You actually went back in time?" She asks with a combination of shock and disbelief. "So where did you go?" Ah! Her skeptical side won out.

"I've witnessed Lincoln giving the Gettysburg Address. Dropped in on Victorian England, then Paris in the 1860s when it was bein' rebuilt—even once during the Commune. In some ways those were totally different worlds from ours, yet in other ways all too familiar."

"It's difficult to get the mind around what you're saying—people traveling into the past."

"But it's true, and many have done it. However, Erik's the only one who's traveled from the past t' the future."

"Why *him*?" she asks incredulously. "Were you out of your collective minds?"

"Is that your legal opinion, then?" I try a small joke.

"Just a common-sense observation." Her eyes search mine as if she's trying to find signs of intelligent life. "Why choose such a notorious man? Good grief, Collin! This man was known as the *Phantom on the Opera*."

"You heard Howard say tha' the person brought from the past had t' fit certain specifications." I shift uneasily in my chair. "Well, he fit them."

"I heard. Someone about to be killed by an extraneous force. And Mrs. Wheaton with her special interest in French history knew of such a person."

"That about sums it up." *I wonder if she'll buy it.*

"Since Mrs. Wheaton knew about his death, surely she'd heard about his *life* as well?" Kathryn presses, "The part about his probably being a murderer?"

"O' course she was aware of that. However, she found a diary written by a woman who knew him personally. Tha' information gives a unique perspective about him."

"A *unique* perspective? Well, that makes all the difference. But aren't there enough books about him to know the kind of man he was?"

"Kathryn, you studied history and know much o' what scholars believed only fifty years ago is now being called into question. History's being rewritten because the best researchers are going back t' original sources and reexamining all the data. Just because something's been written does not mean it's a fact, especially when it's based on second- and third-hand sources, like Leroux's book was. The diary is firsthand information and very credible. You know tha' fact and myth intertwine over time. Wha' if he was wrongly accused?" She gives me a skeptical frown. Maybe she's worried about his being dangerous. "You don't need to feel, uh, nervous about working with him, though."

"Should I be…*nervous*?"

That didn't come out right. "He does have his rough edges, but Dr. Adler—that's the psychiatrist who's been working with him ever since he arrived—she says he's improving."

"Improving?" She glares at me like she's about to go and wait outside for that cab.

I need to extract my foot from my mouth—fast. "Actually, Dr. Adler would be the best one t' discuss that." Giving Kathryn an apologetic grin, I add, "By the way, when you left the meeting, I called and asked her t' join us."

A wall of steely silence goes up between us. I keep glancing down the corridor, hoping Dr. Adler gets here soon. But it's five very long minutes before she arrives.

I make introductions, then try to start the conversation. "Dr. Adler knows Erik better than anyone else and can answer any questions you have."

"Why would I have any questions?" Kathryn replies. "Mr. Mercier is not my client."

"So I understand, Ms. Copeland," Dr. Adler says in her soft German accent. The creases around her eyes deepen as she gives Kathryn a warm smile. "However, you may not be aware that Mr. Mercier has post-traumatic stress. One of the reasons we're asking you to represent him is because of your expertise in handling abuse cases, including those involving PTS."

"How would you know that about me?" Kathryn asks.

"Well, through Collin as well as our own investigations."

"Really?" Giving me a sideways glare, Kathryn's mood shifts to the icy side. Not good.

"May I tell you a little more about Mr. Mercier?" Dr. Adler asks in her gentle way.

Kathryn shrugs indifferently.

Dr. Adler smiles patiently. "I have been working with Mr. Mercier since three days after he arrived here. He had serious injuries and required surgery. When he regained consciousness in the hospital, he was totally disoriented—discovered himself not only in an unknown world, but with invasive medical devices attached to him. He ripped out his IV and oxygen tube, then tore off his EKG monitor leads and tried to get out of bed. He kept demanding that his mask be returned. That had been removed to bandage a laceration on his forehead. It required four men to hold him down while they sedated him. One of the doctors had worked with me to create a post-traumatic stress program for the military. Based on his observations of Mr. Mercier, the doctor felt the behaviors indicated PTS, so he contacted me."

Kathryn remains silent, so Dr. Adler goes on with her monologue.

"I agreed that what Mr. Mercier experienced at the hands of the Communards had probably caused post-traumatic stress. That was compounded by his being brought to the modern world and placed in a hospital with its medical machinery which would clearly appear bizarre from Mr. Mercier's experience. It seemed prudent to ease him into our century. We borrowed nineteenth-century furnishings from the Wheatons' Seattle penthouse and turned his hospital room into a comfortable Victorian bedroom. Based on his reaction to the mask being removed, I directed that it was never to be taken off by *any other* person. He was sedated for several days, but when he regained consciousness in his Victorian surroundings, I was at his bedside. I am fluent in French and answered the many questions he had as sensitively as possible. I was with him every day in the hospital, telling him about the twenty-first century. He is an intelligent and resilient man. He asked perceptive, insightful questions and readily absorbed the answers. I used a QRYSTAL'S hologram to show him the world he found himself in. When he was brought to Land's End, the Wheatons requested I move here to continue helping him adjust."

Although Kathryn still says nothing, I notice that she's now listening with interest.

"During our many conversations, Mr. Mercier has volunteered only a few bits of information about his childhood. I rather expected that he would have suffered abuse in his youth because of his facial deformity, especially since the culture in the mid-1800s was not accepting toward people who were, uh, different. We have found a diary written by a woman who knew him. The diary verifies that when he was a child, he had been put on display in a carnival and his mask forcibly taken off. This would explain his violent aversion to having his mask removed and also indicate he had pre-existing PTS."

Dr. Adler pauses, waiting for any questions from Kathryn, but she says nothing. However, Dr. Adler probably sees the same thing I'm noticing: the stubborn set of Kathryn's jaw has relaxed and her eyes disclose that her curiosity, and her caring, are starting to engage.

"The diary discloses many things about Mr. Mercier's life. It records that he lived a life of rejection—from his parents to almost everyone he encountered. Yet he did more than persevere. He created a life, albeit an unusual one."

That's the understatement of the year, I'm thinking.

"And these murders he is accused of," Dr. Adler states, "he adamantly denies committing. My professional observation is that his behaviors indicate PTS, but I am still assessing him for other psychological, uh, shall we say—issues. However, Mr. Mercier is a very private person and doesn't readily discuss his past. With your background in handling abuse cases, we hope he will open up more to you as his attorney."

"Remember—I haven't accepted," Kathryn interjects.

"I see." Dr. Adler smiles that accepting smile of hers. "In that case, let me give you more information. I've tested his IQ—off the scale—and he has a photographic memory. He's a brilliant composer and a virtuoso on the violin and piano. And there are many other fields he's mastered: architecture, art, history, and philosophy. Despite that, he was never accepted. Now he's been brought to our so-called enlightened society, but are we any different? Will we end up destroying him?"

"I certainly hope not," Kathryn replies—sincerely, I notice.

"Well, then," Dr. Adler says with a persuasive smile, "will you reconsider?"

Kathryn doesn't answer. Still not convinced. I need to give her more food for thought. "As you've heard, the Powers, T'ang and Bianchetti Corporation is probably pulling strings t' get criminal charges filed against Erik. The specialized technology for time travel is no' patented, because Mr. Wheaton keeps it secret and exclusively under his control. No doubt the PTB Corporation will use this trial to inflame public opinion against him. And that's a ploy so Wheaton is forced to turn the technology over to the government which is in thrall to the PTB." I give her a wry grin. "Around here when we refer to Powers, T'ang and Bianchetti as 'the PTB,' we mean '*the powers that be*.' "

"Clever. 'Powers that be' certainly fits Powers, T'ang and Bianchetti," Kathryn says. "It controls the world from the shadows."

I knew Kathryn would feel that way. "Do you want t' know the truth about who killed Anne?" I ask.

Her pained eyes search mine. "You told me at the funeral she was covering a story in Africa. Mercenaries were driving people from their villages, and she was caught in one of the attacks."

"That's wha' I was told. But I could no' let it rest. I kept digging. And I finally uncovered the whole truth. The PTB wanted the mineral rights in tha' part of Africa, so they were paying the mercenaries t' drive the people from their villages or kill them. Anne was there, taking pictures to get the story out, and when the mercenaries attacked, she pushed two children out of the way o' machine guns. They lived—she didn't." *Time to use my trump card.* "You know how Anne was. She always fought against the PTB and their vile takeover of the world. If she were here, she'd go to bat for Erik and want the truth t' be known."

Acute pain crosses Kathryn's face. That hit home. She takes a deep breath. "All right. Against my better judgment, I'll take a look at that diary and whatever information you have. And I'll need to meet Mr. Mercier before giving my final answer."

"Tha' can be arranged." Now I need to mend some fences. "Kathryn, should we go t' dinner now? And would you like to join us, Dr. Adler?"

"No thanks, I've had dinner." With her kind smile, she tells Kathryn, "It was a pleasure meeting you."

As Kathryn watches her leave, she seems to be mulling over what Dr. Adler said.

"Will you let me take you to tha' French restaurant?" I try again, hopeful.

None too happy, Kathryn says, "It's been a long day. I'm tired and hungry. Is it close?"

"Only a fifteen minute drive," I venture, smiling. With a sigh of resignation, she agrees. Now if we can just get over one last hurdle. I look over at the man who's been standing with George by the entrance and give him a nod. He walks over, and I tell Kathryn, "I'd like you to meet Ryan Kirkman."

"Just call me Ryan." He gives Kathryn a disarming smile as they shake hands.

"He'll be your bodyguard," I add casually.

Kathryn blinks. *"My bodyguard?"* She stares up at him.

"Yes, 24/7," I explain, "and he'll need t' take up residence in your guest room."

"But I don't have a guest room, just a small den."

"Does it have a couch?" Ryan asks.

"Yes."

"That'll do."

"But my condo is only approved for water usage for one person."

"Wheaton will pick up the tab for the extra water and penalties," I assure her.

"Why do I need a bodyguard around the clock?" she protests.

"Just to be on the safe side."

Before she can object any further, we hastily shuffle her out to my waiting car. When Ryan opens her door, Kathryn asks him, "Don't you need to bring a change of clothes?"

"My suitcase is already in the trunk," he replies as he gets in the backseat.

"Really?" she says, then fumes silently as I drive through the estate.

Trying to break the ice, I ask, "Have you read any of the books about Mr. Mercier?"

"No. My college roommate read the Leroux book for her French class and told me a little about it."

"Then this is a good place t' start." I pull a small hardbound copy of Leroux's book out of my jacket and hand it to her. "This will give you an idea of the lore tha' surrounded him. Leroux cites an Examining Magistrate's investigation about one death and mentions the inquests of two others. He was never charged with any o' them, but our informants tell us the Court is looking into all three. What with all the legends and myths, you'll need to sift out the truth from the fiction. By the way, there may also be charges alleging Erik was a torturer in Persia."

"Charges as a torturer?" Kathryn blurts out.

That might have been a tad too much information.

"Don't worry, Kathryn. I know you can sort it out." Hoping to defrost the atmosphere a bit, I add, "Now for some great food."

She shoots me a glare like ice picks.

6 | FREEFALL

Tuesday, June 5
Seattle

KATHRYN

The late-afternoon traffic crawls as commuter cars and pedicabs cram the streets. A hummingbird drone buzzes past our car and hovers over the occupant of a weather-beaten pedicab. Ryan watches the drone which seems to be scanning the person much longer than usual. His hands tighten on the steering wheel, expectant. Then the drone moves on down the street, and Ryan relaxes.

I pull Leroux's book out of my briefcase and pick up the text at Chapter Thirteen. The beautiful ingénue soprano, Christine Daaé, is having a heart-to-heart confessional with Raoul, the Viscount de Chagny and finally opening up about her relationship with the Phantom. Abruptly, the book flies out of my hand. Barely catching it, I glare at my newly-minted bodyguard.

"Sorry, Kathryn, not used to the Corvette brakes." He grimaces. "I'll get the hang of it."

I've never let anyone drive my classic Vette before, and its Z06 brakes are touchy. I'm not happy he's learning on my beloved, old car that I inherited from my parents when they moved to Ireland. In a grump, I return to Christine telling the story about the Phantom kidnapping her:

"...something cold and bony enclosed my wrist and would not let it go. I screamed. An arm encircled my waist. I was lifted up. Horrified, I struggled... I thought I would die of fright. I was carried toward the small, red glow, which we entered, and then I saw that I was in the arms of a man wrapped in a large black cloak. A man who had a mask that hid his whole face... I opened my mouth again to scream with fear, but a hand closed over it—a hand that, as it touched my lips, my skin, felt like death. I fainted."

I glance over at Ryan, irritated. He lurked in the courtroom all day and now he's delivering me to my own encounter with the man Leroux described in horrifying terms. Collin shrewdly waited until dessert last night to insist I meet *today* with Mr. Mercier at a secured location. I'm sympathizing with Christine about being drug into the unknown, but I doubt fainting will help.

I return to the book. Christine had given Raoul mixed signals—sometimes invited him into her life, sometimes warned him away. They'd been childhood friends, then he rediscovered her at the Paris Opéra and fell under her spell. Christine proposed that Raoul and she have a *"pretend engagement"*—a strange concept if you ask me, especially since she was wearing a ring from the Phantom. But I've noticed Leroux made numerous references to her occasional disconnect from reality. Naïvely, Christine thought that after their month of make-believe courtship, Raoul would be leaving on a naval expedition and she'd never see him again. Raoul had his own idea. He planned to take her away with him.

Raoul's jealousy of the other man in Christine's life came to a head when her palpable fear made Raoul demand that she tell him the whole truth. To share her dark secrets, Christine led Raoul to the opera house's roof, far away from the Phantom's home in the fifth cellar—and his trapdoors.

But the Phantom followed them, *"flattening itself against the roofs with a movement of its black wings."* The wings were his billowing cloak. Except on the occasion of a masked ball when he wore a crimson and red outfit with a *"death's head,"* the Phantom is always described as wearing formal black attire, and *"his suit was worn by a skeleton."* He appeared to be in his mid to late forties with thinning white hair. He was said to make no noise when he walked, and the accidents around the opera house were blamed on him, but did his skulking in the shadows make him a handy scapegoat?

Declaring *"he's a demon,"* Christine moaned that she was afraid the Phantom would drag her underground to live with him. Raoul proposed that they run away right then, but Christine refused. *"It would be too cruel. Let him hear me sing again tomorrow night for one last time. And then we'll go away."* So they plotted to meet in her dressing room after the performance.

Raoul asked Christine how she became involved with the Phantom. She explained that a man's voice coming from outside her dressing room had proposed to give her vocal lessons. On his deathbed, Christine's father had promised to send her the Guardian Angel of Music. She believed the disembodied voice belonged to that angel, so she *"agreed enthusiastically."* Under the tutelage of the unseen "Voice," her soprano vocalizations and technique improved rapidly over the next three months, and she obeyed the Voice's instructions to wait for the right moment to reveal her abilities. *"And I waited. I lived in a sort of ecstatic dream within which the Voice ruled."* But then Raoul reentered her life, and the Voice became jealous. She swore that Raoul was no more than a brother to her, so her vocal lessons continued *"in divine delirium."*

At the gala performance for the departing directors, the lead soprano didn't show up, but Christine was ready and sang magnificently, winning accolades. Shortly afterward, she informed the Voice she was going to Perros to pay respects at her father's tomb. The Voice said he'd be there to play the "Resurrection of Lazarus" in her father's honor. Christine also wrote to Raoul that she would be at Perros, hoping he would come—and he did. That led to a midnight confrontation in the graveyard between Raoul and the Phantom. Raoul lost. No contest.

Events began to heat up. The grand chandelier fell during a performance, killing a woman in the audience. The same night, Christine was kidnapped by the Phantom and taken mysteriously through her dressing room's mirror, then on a frightening journey through the bowels of the opera house. It seems that Leroux loved to play up the melodrama.

At the fifth cellar, the Phantom rowed her across a lake. Apparently the Phantom lived on the far edge of the lake. There he docked his boat and carried her into his apartment—which happened to overflow with baskets of flowers, no less.

When her kidnapper spoke for the first time, Christine realized the Phantom was also the Voice. She tried to tear off the mask to see his face, but the Phantom stopped her, warning, "*You are in no danger if you do not touch the mask.*"

Christine began to cry, so he told her, "*It's true... I am neither an angel nor a genie, nor a phantom. I am Erik.*"

He promised to show her the way out that first night, yet she chose to stay. Why? That strikes me as odd. The next day, Christine awoke in a lavishly furnished bedroom which even had a bathroom. However, when she bathed, she kept a pair of scissors handy for protection.

After a fine lunch, Erik told her she would be staying for five days—enough time to overcome her fear so that she'd "*come back to see poor Erik from time to time.*" Christine confessed to Raoul, "*His manners, his words—everything about him told me to trust him.*" That's an amazing reversal. She'd just been ready to defend herself with scissors. Leroux wrote that he had seen Christine's letters about Erik. Did she write in those letters that something about Erik had put her at ease? If so, there was more to Erik than was being disclosed in Leroux's book—perhaps even something Christine did not want to admit to herself.

Next, the Phantom took Christine to a room with black wall hangings and a pipe organ. In the center stood an open casket with a red brocade canopy. The Phantom claimed it was his bed. I pause to consider this. Surely the coffin was Leroux's creation, an embellishment he added to create a macabre atmosphere. Besides, Christine's reaction doesn't ring true. She merely turned away and walked over to a music stand that held a score entitled *Don Juan Triumphant*—written in red ink, no less. The Phantom said it was his composition and that he would work on it for days without resting or eating. He declined to play it for her, saying, "*My Don Juan sears.*" Despite all this, Christine remained unruffled and sang a duet with the Phantom. *Really?*

But again the impulse to see the Voice's face won over her better judgment. She told Raoul, "*Instinctively, and with a gesture that I did not control, my quick fingers plucked off the mask.*" Not only did Christine take no responsibility for her action, she had no clue about the trauma it would cause the Phantom—or her own trauma when she saw his uncovered face:

> *"But imagine, if you can, the mask of Death with its four black holes that are its eyes and nose and mouth coming to life to express the sovereign anger of the devil. And no expression coming from its eye sockets for, as I later learned, his fiery eyes can only be seen in the dark…Then he came near me, frightfully gnashing his lipless teeth."*

Did Leroux write that to heighten the horror in the story? Or did Christine write that in her letters? Whatever the case, the man I'm about to meet uses a mask to cover a deformity.

When Christine unmasked the Phantom, he unleashed angry curses—a foreseeable reaction if Christine triggered his post-traumatic stress. She said that after venting his fury, he crawled away *"like a reptile."* I can't imagine him crawling like that—surely the author's hyperbole.

Christine fled to her room, fearful of his threat to never let her go. But when the Phantom began to play *Don Juan Triumphant*, she became overwhelmed by the sounds that seemed to *"mount upward toward heaven as the eagle rises to the sun…sets the world ablaze."* In another about-face, she left her room and swore to him that he was *"the unhappiest and the most sublime of men."* Then Christine burned his mask and stayed with him for fifteen days. She lied to him to gain his trust so he would let her go free. And he did.

After hearing Christine's tale, Raoul pointed out that she had continued to voluntarily visit the Phantom. She claimed her visits were only meant to appease—another example of Christine's naïveté since her ongoing contacts must have given him false hope that she truly cared. Although she swore each visit increased her horror of him, Raoul perceived the contradiction and asked, *"But do you love me? If Erik were handsome, would you love me?"*

Christine's reply revealed her deep conflict, to say nothing of her tendency to waffle. *"Why do you ask me about things that I hide deep in my conscience the way I would hide a sin."*

On the roof of the opera house as Raoul and Christine sealed their engagement with a kiss, *"the surrounding night was so violently ripped apart that they fled as if at the approach of a storm."* They spotted the Phantom perched high above, like a *"night bird that…looked down on them with glazing eyes."* Since they realized the Phantom probably overheard their conversation, why didn't they run away right then? No doubt because of Christine—she vacillated. A lot.

I note that Christine always seemed ambiguous about Erik. Raoul had said to her, *"He must really love you."* Her chilling response was, *"He would commit murder for me."* I pause and gaze out the car window. Could this be true? Was the Phantom a murderer? Does the answer lie in Christine's own words? *"There's nothing to be done against Erik, except flee him."*

It's interesting that the rendezvous between Christine and Raoul occurred in Chapter Thirteen. Leroux used symbolism throughout the book, and that number hints at more than bad luck. It also insinuates betrayal. Thirteen men were at the Last Supper and one betrayed Jesus. On Friday, October 13th, 1307, the Templars were betrayed by the French king who authorized their arrest and seized their wealth. Was Leroux implying that the Phantom was betrayed?

And what have I gotten myself into? I have compassion for a man so badly deformed, but is he also a monster? Did he commit kidnapping and murder? Dr. Adler and Mrs. Wheaton, even Collin, seem to feel there's more to him, to his story, but I don't know what to believe. And, frankly, I no longer know what to expect, but it's too late to back out now—Ryan's turning into the parking garage of the Wheaton Tower. The rush of wind, turbulence, and vertigo overtake me as I freefall down the rabbit hole.

7 | ENCOUNTER

KATHRYN

An armed guard waves us up a ramp, and my Vette enters a space just large enough for a single vehicle. When the doors close behind us, a security scanning light hums as it moves beneath the car. I feel the jerk as the car elevator pushes us upward. When the door lifts, we park in a private garage. The meeting was at four and it's well past that, but court ran late today. I almost expect an oversized white rabbit to appear and remind me of the time.

Riding up the elevator, I glance uneasily at Ryan. His intense hazel eyes say he's all business, but I feel more disturbed than comforted knowing he's got a gun under his suit jacket. The doors open onto a circular foyer crowned by a crystal chandelier. Murals cover the walls and gilded chairs bookend antique consoles with marble tops. Several bodyguards flank the elevator.

A native-American man, solidly built with hair cropped short, military style, steps forward and says, "I'm Tom Cheveyo, head of security." He leads us past gallery walls adorned with French Impressionist paintings, then into a spacious office where two men are seated at a conference table. One has his back to me. I wonder if he's the man Leroux so graphically wrote about, but Tom draws my attention in the other direction. At first all I notice is an enormous desk with legs supported by carved lion's claws. Then, beyond the desk, I catch my first sight of *him*.

He faces away, gazing out panoramic windows at steely skies that seem like an extension of his dark silhouette. Although he stands motionless, there's an aura of intense, restrained power about him.

Noting that his suit is modern, I suppress a nervous laugh. What did I expect? A nineteenth-century evening suit with waistcoat, cravat, and cloak? Actually, I did. But he *is* wearing black leather gloves, and one hand rests on a gentleman's cane.

He turns his head slightly. I can't see his face, just glimpse a corner of his mask—black, just like Leroux described. Tom introduces me to Mr. Mercier's back. Without turning around, the shadowy presence nods his head in acknowledgement.

"An honor to meet you," I volunteer, hoping to put him at ease.

"An honor is it?" His caustic laugh sends chills through me. "A lawyer with wit. How rare." Tom and Ryan exchange knowing looks. Well, I've handled difficult clients before.

Turning to the band of bodyguards, I ask them to leave so I can begin my conference with Mr. Mercier. Tom hesitates, surprised by my request. "We'd prefer to stay," he says firmly.

"The conversation between an attorney and client is confidential and privileged, so I'd appreciate having privacy," I reply pointedly.

"We would keep everything that's said here confidential," he insists.

No, that won't do. I have to gain Mr. Mercier's trust and even getting him to open up to me, his attorney, will be a challenge according to Dr. Adler. Having others present makes that much more difficult.

"Perhaps you need a different attorney, then." I start walking toward the door. From the corner of my eye, I notice Mr. Mercier's head turn sideways as he listens intently.

I have taken several steps when Tom raises his hand, indicating for me to stop. I wait as he thinks over the situation, gazing all the time at the back of the man who stands silently at the window.

"All right," Tom finally says, then points to a console on the conference table. "Just press the button on the right when you're done." Or is he implying *in case of an emergency?*

Looking worried, Ryan glances back at the dark figure as he leaves with the others. Have I already made a mistake sending them out? I walk over to the desk and put my briefcase down. "Mr. Mercier, would you like to sit at the table and talk?"

"No," he responds gruffly. "Is it Mademoiselle or Madame Copeland?"

"Uh, neither, actually. It's Ms. Copeland."

"What does that title signify?"

"It's neutral and doesn't distinguish."

"How uninformative," he growls.

He remains planted, staring out the window, so I can't see his face or the legendary mask. One thing is certain—Leroux was wrong about his age. He's much younger, with ebony hair. And he's not skeletal—in fact, he's quite tall and imposing. But his body language communicates barely contained hostility. Putting him on the spot by asking questions might make him more intractable. I decide to take a different approach. "So, do you have any questions you would like to ask me?" I begin.

"Your actions yesterday bespoke your true feelings. So why are you here?"

Well, that's one I didn't expect. "What do you mean?"

"We were to be introduced following your, shall we say, 'meeting' with the Wheatons. Your hasty departure made that problematic."

"So you're the one I saw in the hallway behind me?"

He freezes, but does not reply.

"I take that as a yes," I say.

"You refused to accept this case," he replies with a challenge in his voice, "yet today you are meeting with me. What changed your mind?"

"Based on a discussion with Dr. Adler, I agreed to this meeting."

"So, they blackmailed you." Abruptly he turns his head to the left. For a moment the black mask comes into view. *I can't see an eye*. Just a dark hole in the leather. Leroux described his face as having "*black holes that are his eyes*." And I don't see a nose.

"You really believe the Wheatons would blackmail me?" I reply, hoping he didn't detect the quaver in my voice.

"You rejected the king's ransom that Wheaton offered you. So was it blackmail or a larger bribe that persuaded you to accept?"

"You don't know me well enough to make such accusations," I spit back, indignant.

"But I *have* dealt with men like Wheaton. Even if you cannot be blackmailed or bribed, you most certainly could be threatened."

"You think Mr. Wheaton would threaten me?"

"Did he not assign a guard to watch you at all times?" He looks in the other direction. Briefly I glimpse his other side. The mask covers his forehead, but not his cheek. I had assumed it covered his entire face as Leroux described.

"So you're implying they've assigned a bodyguard to control me?"

"Just as they do with me every minute since I arrived." Bitterly he adds, "Guards control where I go and what I do."

"They are probably meant to protect you. Our world is unsafe."

"The world has never been safe for me. *My entire life.* The Wheaton cage may be lavish, but it is a cage nonetheless."

"So you don't trust them at all?"

"Do you?"

"I don't know. But let me clarify that I haven't been hired by the Wheatons. I told them I had to see the information they have and meet with you. Be assured that if I accept your case, it will be my choice and not coercion. And if I accept, also be assured I'll make every effort to defend you to the best of my ability and uncover the truth."

"The truth is, I do not belong in this place," he snarls, "or this century."

"Your anger for being placed in this situation is understandable, and it's only right that you—not the Wheatons—have the final decision about your attorney."

"Decision? That is certainly novel. I have not been asked my opinion *at all. Not since I was brought here.*" His voice rumbles through the room, filling it like a lion's roar. It's *the Voice.*

My hands go clammy. "Oh." I clear my throat. "I didn't know." This is a major problem. The situation has been imposed on him, and he resents it. Maybe he needs to vent. "Must have been difficult to travel into the future as you have. I can hardly imagine experiencing that."

"No, you cannot possibly," he hisses.

Good god, how many disorienting shocks has he dealt with adjusting to our world? "It must be a challenge to adjust to so many differences between our cultures. Maybe you were chosen as the first person brought from the past because of your intellect and abilities."

"Perhaps." His voice contains a tinge of civility.

This might be an opening. I decide to test the waters. "They learned about you from a diary written by Madame Giry. Is she a friend?"

"And what difference would that make to you or my defense?" The cutting edge is back. He shifts his weight and leans more heavily on the cane. Strained silence falls between us.

Unless we can talk face to face, this is going to be like using pliers to extract information. Not easy for him or me. Maybe if I can get him to sit at the conference table, that'll put him more at ease and we can talk. I move slowly toward him, hoping he'll acknowledge me. He's so engrossed in his thoughts, he doesn't seem to notice. When I'm a couple feet away, I reach out to touch his shoulder and get his attention, but his hand flies to his mask and he spins around.

Suddenly, I'm overshadowed by a dark presence looming like a black bird of prey. Burning eyes bore into mine, his teeth bared in menace. I gasp. In an instant, I understand Christine.

8 | PARADOX

Erik

My heart pounds wildly.

People jeer at me. Gawk through bars of the cage. I cannot hide my face. My shame.

My throat constricts.

Contempt spews from a nightmarish man. Trapped, I strike back. There on the ground, my mask next to a pool of red.

I cannot breathe. Through the surrounding fog a voice calls to me.

I fight against strong arms holding me down. My face revealed. Their faces, repulsed.

I gasp for air.

Christine, beautiful Christine, screams in horror.

A voice keeps urging me to breathe as oblivion swirls around, trying to engulf me.

"Breathe. Please, just breathe in," the voice says. "Slowly."

With effort, I pull air rasping into my lungs.

That voice, so soothing, bids me, "Now breathe out slowly."

I exhale and fight the smothering fog. When I breathe again, the room begins to coalesce around me.

A woman stands nearby, her eyes fixed on my face. "You are safe," she says, "just breathe slowly, in and out." Her voice is the one that called to me. Disoriented, I stare down at her. "I'm sorry. I didn't mean to startle you." Her words shatter my confusion like glass against a stone floor. The room comes into focus, and I realize my hand is holding my mask in place.

"You tried to remove my mask," I stare down at this woman who audaciously approached me.

"No, I didn't." Her startled eyes stare into mine.

How dare this woman dispute me? *"No one removes my mask."*

"I would never do that," she says, defiant. "I was just trying to ask you to sit and talk."

Is she telling the truth? I search her eyes—large and dark and full of fear, yet she does not avert them to avoid looking upon my face. Only the sound of my heavy breathing breaks the silence as I struggle to calm myself. Then something unexpected happens. The fear in her eyes dissolves. What takes its place confounds me. I turn away and begin pacing, trying to burn off my rage.

"Would you like to end our meeting?" she asks.

That confirms my suspicion—she approached me as a ploy. "So *that* is your game. You tried to anger me just now so I would not want you as my lawyer."

"Of course not."

I peer out at the dismal sky as I pace in front of the windows. I do not want to be here, and the dull pain has returned to my leg. I agree—it is time to end this farce of a meeting. When I turn to inform her, the look on her face brings me to a halt. "Are you repulsed by me?" I demand.

"No. But you're leaning heavily on your cane. Limping a little. I can tell you're still in pain." She shakes her head. "You've suffered a lot."

"There are worse things than physical pain. I do not want your pity." I stop pacing, unable to hide the limp. "You need not concern yourself."

"Is it so difficult for you to believe someone might care?"

"Rarely has anyone concerned themselves with my welfare unless it served their purpose. Why should what happens to me concern you in the least?" I reply with disdain.

She actually hesitates and ponders my challenge. Finally she replies, "I think an English philosopher said it better than I ever could. *'No man is an island, entire of itself…any man's death diminishes me, because I am involved in mankind; and therefore never send to know for whom the bell tolls; it tolls for thee.'* "

"Of course, John Donne," I retort dismissively. Taunting, I turn the tables on her. "But other words of his more accurately characterize mankind: *'Thou are slave to fate, chance, kings, and desperate men.'* "

Instead of the rebuttal I expect, she pauses and becomes reflective. "That's a tragic commentary on humanity, isn't it?"

"Merely what I have always observed." I search her dark eyes. They seem guileless. Does she not understand how the world truly operates? I consider whether or not I want to engage further in this fruitless discourse. Then rage wells up, and I cannot control my words. "Indeed, I have been reading history books about this last century. What do I discover amidst the many 'advanced' sciences and 'improved' living conditions? Two of the bloodiest, most cruel and inhumane wars which have ever been waged, as well as innumerable small ones. Now wars are endless, being fought at any given moment. I know from my own experience, armies may fight for whatever reason, but it is the people who always suffer."

"I agree. But history shows us that if we ignore the plight of others, eventually the same problem, the same tragedy, will come back to haunt us. As Donne said, what happens to others will ultimately affect what happens to each of us." Her long, black tresses float around her face, unbridled by hairpins holding it in restrained coifs as is proper for women in my world. "The law has evolved since the 1800s," she says, her voice turning resolute, "and there are rights and protections available now that didn't exist in your lifetime."

"You actually believe the law can shield a person from the tyranny of rulers and desperate men?" I sneer.

"The law may be imperfect," she persists, "but it's still the best means of protecting the rights of individuals."

"What does that matter to me? Balzac was right. He said that laws are like spider webs. The big flies pass through, only the little ones get caught."

Her eyes take on a glint of determination. "It's true, if you are charged, the prosecution will assert every accusation it can. Even if the allegations are proven to be untrue, it leaves the taint of suspicion. In politics it's called propaganda, and Powers, T'ang and Bianchetti are masters. Are you aware they're probably the ones pulling the political strings to get these charges filed against you?"

"No, I had not been informed. But what you have said proves the world has not changed. Only the names of the players."

"You should know they'll probably unleash a smear campaign on you as well."

"I am accustomed to being vilified if that is what you mean." I add bitterly, "Apparently that continued long after I was dead."

"But you need to prepare yourself for the onslaught. Their tactic is to take any scrap of information, regardless how trivial, and blow it out of proportion to make it damning. By repeating it over and over, they'll try to convince the public it's true."

Her forthrightness is uncommon, almost unsettling. "And how would one know what is the truth?" I lean on the cane to relieve my discomfort. "Do you believe I am guilty of murder?"

"At this point, I don't know all the facts, so I've drawn no conclusions." Well, she certainly does not mince words. We stare at each other until she breaks the silence. "I'm sure you'd like more time to consider who you wish to represent you."

"Yes, I require more time."

"Then this concludes our meeting," she states, unblinking.

I remain by the window as she walks over and pushes the button to summon Tom. When he arrives, she informs him, "If Mr. Mercier decides that *he* wishes for me to represent him, please have Dr. McKay call my office to discuss this matter further."

"I'll pass on your message," Tom says, surprised.

I gloat at the thought. She has declared unequivocally I will choose my lawyer and has given me some small control over my fate. "Pleased to have made your acquaintance, *Ms.* Copeland." I must admit it was a singular experience.

"Pleased?" she says with a half-smile. "You also have a keen sense of wit."

Amused, I watch her leave. As we ride back to Land's End in the Wheaton limousine, I mull over this lawyer who is a woman. In my world only men venture into the courtroom's domain. Yet she has a keen mind and did not hesitate to parry when I verbally sparred with her. And what manner of woman does the work that should be reserved to men? Possesses the courage to defy Wheaton, then withstands my unguarded moments and wrath? Yet that look in her eyes when she perceived my pain was not pity, although I called it such. Pity entails an attitude of superiority, of disdain, but there was none in her. This woman is a paradox—like I have never before encountered.

9 | TRAPS

Kathryn

"How'd the meeting go, Kathryn?" Ryan asks offhandedly as we drive back to my office. I sidestep the question. Actually, *I'm not sure.* Suddenly, he slams on the brakes. *Not again.* Glancing up from the book, I see a boy mere inches from the front bumper. "Damn, that was close," Ryan mutters. "Kids running into the intersection should be illegal."

I roll down the window and hand the boy some money. "But they're desperate," I reply. "Selling things and washing windshields is all they can do to put food in their stomachs when their parents can't find jobs."

At my office, I'm barely through the door when Barb and Eileen ask how it went. I shrug, then ask Ryan to make himself comfortable in my waiting area. Wizened from thirty years of maneuvering in the legal maze, Eileen gives me a probing look. "Didn't go well, did it?" she asks, smoothing a strand of grey hair into her neatly coiled bun. Glancing in Ryan's direction, I shake my head. Barb and Eileen exchange looks—message received.

"Would you mind bringing me an iced tea?" I ask Barb. "I could really use one."

I'm in the middle of a call when Barb brings the tea and some client files. When the call ends, she hands me the files. "Mrs. Patterson called today," she says, shaking her head, "and she asked for an appointment with you tomorrow. Can you fit her in?"

"I don't know how, considering my schedule. Can't she wait until next week?"

"No, not really. Her husband has beaten her again. Broke her arm."

"That's terrible! How many times has she left him? Three—or is this the fourth?"

"The fourth. Good grief, Kathryn, why do women keep going back?"

I sigh and settle back in my chair, exhausted. "As you know from our clients, this happens all too often. Men like this are sociopaths—they have no conscience. But they are often very charismatic, even handsome, and accustomed to getting their way. And that usually includes verbal, emotional or physical abuse. And women can't believe that a person who is supposed to love them would do those things. They also often have the mistaken belief that if they stay and submit to the abuse—that if they are patient and long-suffering—their love will eventually heal the man and the abuse will stop. Usually they don't leave until the abuse reaches a crisis level."

"But Mrs. Patterson's husband is wealthy," Barb interjects, "and every time she leaves, he showers her with flowers and gifts. Then she goes back."

"Yeah, that's part of the pattern. Abusers with money use it to smooth over the past abuse while making promises they will change. Women want to believe that. The monetary benefits, whether gifts or financial support, may make the situation seem better for awhile, but then the abuse begins again. The woman keeps going back until she finally realizes that a man who is capable of doing this in the first place, will not change. Ever. The abuse only increases. Maybe Mrs. Patterson has finally accepted the truth."

"Well, she swears that she's really left for the last time and claims *this* time she'll go through with the divorce."

"Okay, I'll see her tomorrow since she clearly needs protective orders. But that means we'll have to work late again. Are you able to do that?"

"Of course! I've always got your back." She stands to leave. "Just one more thing. Tell me you're not taking this Wheaton case."

"Haven't decided yet." I avoid her eyes, not wanting her to know how conflicted I feel. "I told Mr. Mercier he has the right to choose his attorney, and he hasn't decided either. He doesn't seem to approve of me." I don't mention that he could barely look at me, but was that because of his dislike for *me* or just his mistrust of people in general?

"Then why take this on? You're not a defense attorney."

"I brought that up with Collin. They're also retaining an ex-federal prosecutor—Alexandra Simmons. He feels that'll cover all the bases."

"And just what *base* are *you* covering?"

"Collin was a bit vague. Something about my ability to work with challenging cases."

"Challenging? That doesn't begin to describe this case. You've got a full-time bodyguard now and possibly a client who's the friggin' Phantom of the Opera."

"If you think he's scary, you should meet Howard Wheaton. By the way, what did you find out about him?"

"A lot. Wheaton's wealth is self-made. Of course everyone knows he developed the quantum computing technologies used in all his Qrystal devices. But apparently he's got a genius for business as well. All the scientific breakthroughs developed by his enterprises were spun off into a host of successful businesses, even a couple European banks. And he also owns a number of islands and mansions. Exactly how many isn't known since he keeps their locations confidential."

"That was no mansion. That was a castle—stone walls outside, opulent furnishings inside and completely guarded." Even the thought of it brings back chills. "So what did you find out about his control of time travel?"

"Well, to keep the technology solely under his control, he never filed patents for it. There were dozens of articles attacking him for that, especially by the PTB controlled PALnet News. They argue that the government should have sole possession and control of time travel—"

"And if the government gets its hands on the technology, it will turn that over to the PTB Corporation," I point out.

"You've got that right! But that's not the only bone of contention between them and Wheaton. The Qrystals are based on quantum physics, so they communicate directly and instantaneously with each other and don't connect at all through PALnet which relies on the electrical grid and relay towers. Basically, Wheaton is not only trying to reduce the cost of his Qrystals to make them affordable for the average person, but also to make the PTB-controlled PALnet obsolete so they would lose all their propaganda power. For the past year, Wheaton Industries has also been trying to resurrect Nikola Tesla's theories in hopes of developing free energy. Since the PTB Corporation controls the lion's share of the electrical grids and oil distribution, free energy would undermine their wealth. Wheaton's ultimate goal is to make energy free, so it appears that the PTB is using every dirty trick in the book to discredit him."

I rub my forehead, but that does little to quell my throbbing headache. "Did you find out anything about Mrs. Wheaton?"

"Not much, except that she was born Lady Margaret de Renesse. Both her father and mother were descended from French nobility. She's very good at avoiding publicity, so I'm still working on it." Barb taps a finger on my desk. "What's certain is, they're big-time players. This is dangerous, Kathryn. Is getting roped into their problems a good idea?"

"Frankly, I'm hoping criminal charges aren't filed."

"I second that," Barb shoots back as she leaves my office.

Barb's words, *this is dangerous,* keep echoing in my mind. I can't ignore her misgivings. She's more than a first-rate legal assistant. Her instincts about clients are uncanny, and she has a way of predicting problems that'll arise on a case—as if I don't have enough doubts of my own.

Opening my laptop, I pull up a letter from an attorney that came in today on a new case. But I'm distracted, uneasy. I keep thinking about Barb's warnings. I stare at the laptop—a standard model used by the majority of people who are even able to afford a computer. It connects to PALnet which is supposed to be secure, and I have encryption to protect my legal documents. But is it really safe? For a long time the government has had the ability to get to everyone's emails. Do "the powers that be" also have a backdoor through PALnet that can invade my confidential legal documents? I have worried about this. I wanted to buy a Wheaton QRYSTAL because it communicates directly to other QRYSTALS and has totally secure encoded connections and data storage. The problem is, I would need two, one for me and one for Barb, and I just don't make that kind of money from my practice. Those clients who are well-off pay my full fees, but I use that to support my work for those who can't afford to pay much, or anything at all.

A clicking noise interrupts my concentration. With dismay, I realize my hand's shaking, making the ice clink in my glass of tea. I set it down and look over at the windows. They face the same view of the bay as the Wheaton Tower office. I feel transported there, see his silhouette in front of the window, his back to me. Once again, he turns on me and glares down with those eyes. I shudder.

Nothing in Leroux's book prepared me for what I saw—his teeth bared like the snarl of a lion ready to pounce, and his piercing eyes flared with fury. I don't think I took a breath for the next half-minute, yet he restrained himself and did not unleash his rage. Then he looked through me as if I weren't there. That's when I realized he was encountering apparitions from his past and in the throes of a post-traumatic stress flashback. I used the calming technique I was taught, but by the time he came out of it, we were both in shock—for him, from the fear his mask would be removed—for me, from the brunt of his terrible anger. I know why Christine was afraid of him. How she felt when he vented his rage. His trigger-edged emotions and intensity would be difficult for a young woman to deal with. There's also the fact Christine *had seen* what he hides beneath the mask.

But Christine's being drawn to him is no longer difficult to understand either. Leroux had used poetic license, lots of it. His face isn't a skeletal death's mask. Once his anger dissipated, his presence became nothing less than elegant, even charismatic. Christine would've been fascinated by him and even more attracted because of their mutual love of music.

His face. I was unprepared for his face. The black mask conceals almost all his forehead up to the hairline, cutting across the bridge of his nose in a diagonal slash down to the bottom of his jaw. Surprisingly, the uncovered side is unscarred, his chin and jaw well-formed, and his lips entirely normal. Despite the legend, he does have a nose—long and straight. And his eyes aren't black holes; they're mesmerizing sea green, like crystals. He could even be considered handsome. *Just how bad is the deformity under his mask?*

I give up trying to concentrate and put my laptop in the briefcase. Barb and Eileen have already left for the day, but Ryan meets me at the door. Will I ever get used to being shadowed? On the way home we pick up some food. When we arrive at my condo, he plops his bag of greasy burgers and fries on the bar between my small living room and kitchen, and settles on a barstool. Taking my salad across the room, I curl up in my comfy chair and open the Leroux book.

Christine and Raoul had just fled from the rooftop. They were in her dressing room discussing their plans when Christine discovered she had lost the gold ring the Phantom gave her. She confessed that Erik granted her freedom on the condition she always wore the ring. I look up and gaze out the window at the bay, processing this. Twice Raoul tried to talk Christine into leaving right away. He even expressed his doubts about whether she actually loved him. It seems to me the Phantom's power over Christine went beyond intimidation, or she would have fled right then. But whatever might happen next, I'd put my bet on the Phantom.

Sure enough, the Phantom didn't stand idly by. That night Raoul had a visitor. *"Two eyes, burning like embers, had just glowed at the foot of his bed. They stared horribly at him in the dark."* The next time the eyes appeared, Raoul shot at them, but found no one there—only drops of blood down the drainpipe when the balcony was searched.

Predictably, Christine was kidnapped the next evening while the theater's gaslights went out. When they came on, Christine had vanished from the stage. Since the Phantom was known as the *"trap-door lover,"* it's not difficult to guess how she disappeared.

Raoul went searching for Christine and met up with a mysterious Persian known only by his official title, the Daroga, who had intimate knowledge of the opera house's lower levels. Joining forces, the two men went on an odyssey to find Christine. The Daroga had quite a history with the Phantom, and he warned Raoul to hold his hand at eye level—that it was a matter of life and death. I assume that was a protective maneuver to thwart encircling lassos. After all, the Phantom was known for using a Punjab lasso on his enemies.

With lawyerlike detail, Leroux described the underbelly of the opera house: the prompter's box and trapdoors; the subcellars filled with panels, partitions, staircases, hooks, winches, and counterweights; and even the corridor the Communards used to take their prisoners to the cells in the basement. It occurs to me the man I met today was probably taken down that corridor to await his death.

Leroux clearly went beyond melodrama and into the fantastical to heighten the dangers of this search. Raoul and the Daroga crossed the paths of hellish beings who prowled the underworld the Phantom called his home. When a ghostly shadow in a cloak and felt hat passed by, the two men flattened themselves on the ground to avoid notice. At the approach of the rat killer—a disembodied red face of fire—the men ran but were overcome by scurrying rodents that crawled up their legs. Raoul and the Daroga screamed, trembled, and nearly fainted. Fortunately, the waves of squeaking rats were drawn away by the fiery head.

Surrounding the Phantom's home was a lake inhabited by a mysterious siren whose voice lured people to their watery deaths. To avoid crossing the lake, the Daroga led Raoul to a secret entrance. Unfortunately, it turned out to be a trap that deposited them into a bizarre torture chamber—a six-sided room with walls covered in mirrors and a large, metal tree in one corner. The mirrors reflected onto each other, ingeniously creating an infinite forest, and sunlight poured through a window in the ceiling, bringing the room to boiling temperatures. The mirrored forest and heat caused hallucinations, so a handy noose was provided to allow the victim to hang himself from the tree rather than suffer. Truly the machinations of a sinister mind—or a very creative writer. The Daroga said he believed that was how Buquet, a gossipy stagehand, had died. Could such a chamber have really existed or was this another fanciful myth?

The chamber bordered the Phantom's home, and Raoul could hear Christine's pleas through the wall, so he called out to her. Christine explained that the Phantom had given her an ultimatum. She was to use a key to open one of the ebony boxes on his mantle. One box housed a bronze scorpion and the other, a bronze grasshopper. Turning the scorpion mechanism would signify her acceptance of the Phantom's marriage proposal and turning the grasshopper, her rejection.

Frantically searching for an escape, the men found a trapdoor and climbed down into a lower chamber which was filled with wine kegs. The Daroga referred to the Phantom as a "*lover of fine wine*," but then the bad news hit—the kegs contained only gunpowder. The Daroga quickly put two and two together, and realized if Christine rejected the Phantom and turned the grasshopper, she would detonate the gunpowder. They'd all be sent up to heaven—literally—along with everyone in the opera house. The two men scrambled back into the torture chamber. Raoul quickly overcame his qualms about her marrying the abhorrent Phantom, calling through the wall to Christine and urging her to give the response the Phantom desired.

When Christine turned the scorpion, water poured into the wine cellar and rendered the gunpowder useless. However, the water also rose into the chamber, nearly drowning the two men. Later the Daroga woke up in the Phantom's home, then was carried to his apartment, worse for wear but alive. The Daroga sent for news about Raoul and Christine, only to learn that Raoul's brother, Philippe, Count de Chagny, was dead. When Christine was kidnapped, Philippe had also gone searching below the opera house. His body was found on the shores of the siren's lake. As for Raoul and Christine, they were missing.

Surprisingly, the Phantom showed up at the Daroga's apartment not long afterward. The Phantom protested his innocence in the death of Philippe, calling it an accident, then he proceeded to tell his story. Christine had consented to be his wife if he would save Raoul and the Daroga from drowning. The Phantom agreed, and she kept her promise, allowing him to kiss her. The passage is heartbreaking:

> *"It's so good, daroga, to kiss someone! You can't know....I felt her tears coursing down my forehead....Her tears flowed under my mask. They united with the tears in my own eyes...I tore away my mask so as not to lose a single tear...And she did not run away... She stayed."*

The Phantom professed that he let Raoul and Christine go free because of her kindness and the tears she shed for him. He returned the gold ring that Christine had dropped, giving it as a wedding gift to the couple. Then the Phantom secured her promise that she would come back when she saw his obituary. She was to bury him *"in great secret with the gold ring."* Christine kissed the Phantom's forehead, then quickly left with Raoul, presumably to safer northern climes.

The Phantom told the Daroga that his life was over—now that Christine had left him forever. He asked the Daroga for a favor. Just before dying, the Phantom would send the Daroga some papers Christine had written. When the Daroga received these, he would know Erik was dead. The Daroga was to place an obituary in the newspaper for Christine to see so she could return to bury Erik under the opera house. The book ends simply. *"Three weeks later, the newspaper* L'Epoque *published this obituary: 'Erik is dead.' "*

Leroux added an epilogue that contained some final musings by the "narrator" of the story—supposedly what little information he was able to glean about the Phantom's life. Born in a town near Rouen to a masonry contractor, Erik had run away and displayed himself in a carnival show. *"He must have traversed Europe, going from fair to fair and completing his strange education as a musical performer and magician."* Must have? This appears to be speculation on Leroux's part. Apparently, he didn't really know how Erik developed his abilities.

After a period of Erik's life that Leroux only refers to as "*fairly obscure*," Erik arrived at the great fair of Nizhni Novgorod as a famed singer and ventriloquist. His reputation spread to the sultana of Mazendaran on the northern coast of Iran, then known as Persia. She sent the Daroga to bring Erik to her palace. There Erik "*committed a number of horrors because he seemed not to know the difference between good and evil, and participated in several important political assassinations.*" The Daroga refers to that period as the "*rosy hours of Mazendaran*," which included building torture chambers similar to the mirrored room under the opera house.

I flip back to Chapter 22 of Leroux's book and reread the other passage about the "*rosy hours*." This passage tells about Erik using the Punjab lasso in the arena to kill condemned prisoners. Apparently, the catgut rope had a stone on one end and was thrown like a bola around the victim's neck, then used as a garrote. The thought sickens me. Could the man that I met today have participated in such bloody acts? My god, I was alone with him. And so close.

I turn back to the Epilogue. Erik also designed an ingenious palace for the Shah "*on the principle of a trick box*." It allowed the Shah to go anywhere in the palace without being seen and to disappear "*without anyone's knowing how the trick was done*." The Shah didn't want the secrets of the palace to be known, so he ordered "*Erik's golden eyes to be plucked out*."

Golden eyes? But Christine described Erik's eyes as black holes, and in the first chapter Joseph Buquet described the eyes as "*only two large black holes, as in the skulls of the dead*." Raoul described the eyes at the foot of his bed as like burning embers. So Leroux described Erik's eyes variously as golden, black, or ember red. But *I've* seen them. They're deep, sea green. Leroux researched Erik's life around 1910, forty years after Erik died. Among the facts, Leroux evidently sprinkled myths that had sprung up about the Phantom.

The Epilogue relates that Erik escaped to Constantinople where he designed a similar palace for the sultan. On returning to France, he became a masonry contractor and helped design and build the grand opera house in Paris known as the Garnier. During its construction, he secretly crafted a home for himself within the foundations, surrounded by a lake. The narrator's final appraisal of him is nothing short of astonishing:

> *"Poor, unhappy Erik. Is he to be pitied? Is he to be cursed? He wanted only to be someone, like everyone else. But he was too ugly! And he was required to hide his genius or else play tricks with it. Had he had ordinary features, he would have been one of the noblest members of the human race! He had a heart capacious enough to contain the whole world, but he had, finally, to content himself with a cellar. Certainly, we must pity the Phantom of the Opera!"*

A *capacious heart*? That denotes a heart that is huge, open. Was the Phantom such a paradox, or is this another conflict between reality and myth?

Leroux ended his book by stating that the skeleton disinterred under the Garnier opera house could be identified as the Phantom *"by the gold ring he wore,"* which Christine had returned and placed on his finger.

I puzzle over all this. Clearly Leroux's story is not entirely fiction. The Phantom did exist and through the alchemy of time travel, still does. Incredibly, I've met him. And he was killed and buried under the Garnier opera house—at least before time travel intervened. Dr. Adler confirms he's a genius, musical and otherwise, and he does bear a deformity which he covers with a mask. However, the man I met appears to be in his midthirties. In the book he's depicted as older by ten years or more.

I sigh, exasperated. If Leroux had difficulty getting the facts straight when he wrote his book forty years after the Phantom's death, how much more difficult will it be for me? How do I sift the truth from myth nearly two centuries later? And do I even *want* to know the truth about this man? Or be a part of this case?

Yawning, I close the book. It's midnight and Ryan is asleep on the couch. When I stand, he's instantly awake. "So you're finally calling it a day? Finished the book?" he asks. I just nod, but he presses, "What do you think?"

"Torture chambers, trapdoors, and lassos. Oh my."

Getting up, Ryan stretches. "Feel like you met the Wizard today?"

"Definitely."

10 | PRESSURE

Wednesday, June 6
Land's End

JARROD PEARCE

George nearly runs into me as he's coming out of Erik's suite. "Good morning, Mr. Pearce," the butler splutters. "Monsieur Mercier should be out shortly. I trust you had a pleasant trip."

"As well as could be expected." I don't mention that yesterday we had to rush Mrs. Wheaton out of a conference where she was supposed to make a speech and present a grant for a Foundation for Worldwide Action project. Troublemakers, no doubt in the pay of the PTB Corporation, were picketing and rabble-rousing as usual. But it got out of control. The police were supposed to patrol the street to maintain order, but they sent only a handful of officers. The mob had no problem overturning the police barriers and stormed the front doors. We got Mrs. Wheaton out the back and into her limo just in time. Our tasers dropped a dozen rioters, but a couple got all the way to the limo. Dave and I had to stop them the old-fashioned, hands-on way. I look at my hand and flex it. Still a little sore. But then the Wheatons don't want us to use our guns unless we have no choice.

I grab the newspaper off George's cart and settle on the bench. Feels strange reading a printed paper, but these are still available for those who prefer the old style and can afford it. We have a newspaper delivered for Erik because he's not allowed access to PALnet, but then Howard Wheaton wouldn't allow a regular computer connected to that anywhere near his home. I chuckle. Wheaton never hesitates to express his opinion that everything on PALnet's news channels is propaganda. He always says PALnet is nobody's "pal"—and he's right. But Wheaton also has forbidden Erik to have access to a QRYSTAL. He's concerned about what mischief Erik's curiosity and genius might summon up if he gets his hands on one. Yep, Wheaton is right about that, too.

I skim Erik's newspaper for anything about the incident yesterday. The Foundation doesn't like negative publicity. I find a small article on page three about a "minor" scuffle by protesters at the Foundation's conference. Yeah, so minor we had to escape out the back. The article doesn't mention any reason for the protest. Typical of what passes for journalism these days. I quickly scan the rest of the paper, but find no mention about Wheaton bringing the Phantom of the Opera from the past. *Good.*

Speaking of phantoms, Erik comes out of his suite wearing a black three-piece suit and carrying his cane—the antique ebony one Mrs. Wheaton gave him. It occurs to me his outfit would blend perfectly into the dark corners of an opera house.

I try to start off on a good foot. "*Bonjour*, Erik."

"*Bonjour*, Jarrod." He nods and walks past.

I fall into step beside him. "Have they told you I'm your primary bodyguard now?"

"Yes, I was informed."

"That okay with you?"

"As I said, *I was informed*." He scowls. "I did not know I had a choice."

Looks like we hit a nerve. "So, is it okay?"

"You rescued me from the Communards." He shrugs. "I presume you qualify."

"Good. By the way, nothing about you in the newspaper. No news is good news."

"That is illogical. News could provide important information. Not hearing it may have negative consequences."

"True, but that's not what the saying means."

"Perhaps the saying should be reconsidered," he states flatly.

Explaining English slang to Erik is a helluva challenge. "How'd your meeting with Ms. Copeland go?" Erik doesn't say anything, so I try again. "What did you think about her?"

"She was...uncommon."

"So, she's gonna be your attorney?"

He doesn't reply, just slips past me into the dining room—definitely an evasive maneuver. I grab a plate and follow him down the smorgasbord of food served for the scientists, security personnel, and bodyguards from around the world. I load my plate with Mexican frittatas, ham, and some biscuits and gravy. Erik doesn't eat much, just an omelet, croissant, and cheese. Compared to what he's used to, he says this is a luxury. With all the crop failures happening around the world, it still is. But the Wheatons own over a dozen farms that supply all the food for the estate, so there's never a shortage here. It's one of the perks of working for them.

Collin, Dr. Adler, and Tom are nowhere in sight. Probably having a powwow. Ms. Copeland sure threw them a curveball by telling Erik he's got the right to choose his attorney. He looks around the room and scowls when he notices no empty tables, so we end up sitting with Dave, Josh and three security men.

Cocky and true to form, Josh is bragging about his new assignment, another attorney the Wheatons hired.

"Don't get all worked up, Taylor," one of the guys fires back. "The woman they've assigned you might not have those big, dark eyes like Copeland."

Josh laughs. "Yeah, and the rest of Copeland ain't bad either." Erik gives him a piercing stare. "What's the woman attorney like, anyway?" Josh goads Erik. "You met her personally."

"It was not personal. It was business," Erik replies stiffly, taking it literally.

"She's a lady, Josh, and that's all you need to know," Dave growls. Whoa! Josh even rubbed Dave the wrong way. That's the last thing you want to do with a Sioux whose Indian name is "Matoskah." Nope, Josh, you don't want to rile the "white bear." Josh gets the point and turns back to his food, but then the younger bodyguards all look up to Dave.

"Do you have physical therapy today?" I ask Erik, changing the subject. He nods indifferently. "Good. You'll be back to normal in no time."

"Normal?" Erik mutters under his breath, "My life has never been normal."

I chuckle. I like his dry, caustic wit.

When Erik leaves, I follow. In the exercise room, he only takes off his coat and vest. I watch as Erik works hard at his physical therapy. Even so, he barely breaks a sweat. Must've been in top shape before his run-in with the Communards. He told me he used to climb the flies above the stage.

Following the workout, we head to Erik's private music room. I pull out my QRYSTAL and read some articles that Collin sent me while Erik practices the violin. Actually, I'm not sure why he practices. He doesn't need to. This is like having a front-row seat in a concert hall. I'm not quite sure how to describe his music. Definitely hypnotic, but today the music seems lighter, less intense.

After an hour, Erik goes to the Steinway baby grand. His fingers fly up and down the keyboard as he warms up, then he shifts seamlessly into a Mozart piece I recognize.

He stops at noon, and we head for lunch, but George waylays us. "Dr. McKay requests you join him for lunch," he says, his mouth twitching slightly. Glowering, Erik agrees.

George takes us to the jungle-like solarium crammed with exotic plants Mrs. Wheaton brings back from her travels. Collin is already at the table, talking to his assistant, Harold. I don't like Harold. He's the nervous, jittery type. Thankfully he leaves.

"Glad you could join me for lunch," Collin says with a smile.

"It appears you had little doubt I would." Erik glares down at the three place settings. "As with everything since I arrived." His arrow hits the mark. Collin tenses. This lunch has acid indigestion written all over it.

Collin clears his throat and asks Erik how his new composition is coming. Erik answers tersely, and the conversation falls flat. I ask about Mrs. Wheaton's next trip and help out Collin by discussing the water reclamation projects. With my engineering background, this is up my alley. When the piping hot cobbler with cherries specially grown in the Wheaton orchards arrives, Collin asks offhandedly, "How did your meeting go wi' Ms. Copeland?"

Erik's spoon drops with a thud. "Satisfactory," he hisses and stands up.

"Well," Collin says, taking his last shot, "have you made your decision?"

"Not yet," Erik snarls and storms out. I look pitifully at my cherry cobbler. Cherries are a rarity, even here at Land's End. I cram a big scoop in my mouth. *Damn, it's delicious.* I jump up to follow Erik.

Frustrated, Collin says, "If you find out anything..."

"You'll be the first to know," I mumble through the mouthful and rush out.

When we get to the music room, I take a seat on the couch, but Erik walks straight to the picture window and paces like a caged animal. He told me he's been given no real choices. Finally, Ms. Copeland gave him one. Bet he resents everyone else trying to pressure him into choosing her. Is that what's eating him?

Abruptly, he strides to the piano and starts hammering on the keys, pounding out a dark, intense storm. When it stops, the silence is deafening. He stares at the keyboard, calming down. Then he starts playing again, but this time the music has a distinctive, ethereal quality.

"What's that?" I ask, looking up from the article I'm reading on my QRYSTAL. "It's different."

"Something new. A nocturne. It has been haunting me all day."

"I like it." Now that Erik has settled down, I turn back to the article Collin sent me and lose track of time. When I check my watch, it's three. "Gotta go. We're late for Dr. Adler's appointment."

"Merde," he mumbles, bristling at a schedule not of his own making. When we round a corner, I almost run over George again. After he regains his composure, he formally invites Erik and me to dinner with the Wheatons tonight. Erik accepts but glares at the butler's back as he walks away. Probably thinks this invitation is another attempt to sway his decision. Probably right.

Although we're late, Dr. Adler beams her broad grin. "Would you like some tea?" she asks. I decline, but Erik takes a cup and settles into his chair, unwinding a little. Except when playing his music, Erik doesn't relax much, always on guard, observing everything around him.

"Have you read anything interesting since our last visit?" Dr. Adler starts benignly.

"Indeed," he replies with a perplexed frown. "Two books from the library last evening. Biographies of Eleanor Roosevelt and Margaret Mead." It appears meeting Ms. Copeland tweaked his nineteenth-century male biases. He asks why women want to be equal and do the same things as men. Dr. Adler gives it her best shot, but Erik's not buying.

"Doing men's work *lowers* the status of women," he states. "They are respected and protected in my culture. Why would they want to be involved in such unpleasant matters?"

"Good luck, Erik." I chuckle. "But you'll never figure out what makes women tick."

"Tick?" he repeats, scowling.

"Yeah. That means what makes them think and act the way they do."

But I have to give it to Dr. Adler—she keeps trying. "In your culture, women were considered intellectually inferior, so they weren't allowed into such professions as medicine or law. But women have proven they're capable of working in those fields. Ms. Copeland has a doctorate in law." Grinning slyly, she adds, "And I have two doctorates—in psychiatry and in medicine."

"I see." Erik examines his cane, digesting this.

She takes a sip of tea to hide her grin. "Women were also believed to be physically weak. However, the clothing they wore—the corsets, long skirts, and heavy, restrictive fabric—created strain on their bodies, resulting in many physical illnesses and disabilities."

"Nonetheless, it is obvious that women are not as strong as men. They are patently not physically fit for some jobs," Erik responds smugly.

"True, but our world doesn't require women to have muscles to perform most jobs. Even so, women serve as police officers and in the military."

Erik's eyebrow dips. "So there is essentially no difference between men and women?"

I laugh. "I sure wouldn't put it that way."

He scowls and gives me a dirty look. This continues as the hot topic of debate. In the end, there's no winner, but I'll bet Erik's not gonna get much sleep tonight with all this churning in his head. When we're about to leave, she asks, "How was your meeting with Ms. Copeland?"

Erik freezes. I wait for his stock answer.

"Satisfactory."

"Have you decided if you want Ms. Copeland as your attorney?" Dr. Adler poses the perilous question. He gives a curt shake of his head, and she smiles back. "All in good time."

We go to our rooms to dress for dinner with the Wheatons and that means a tux. Personally, I hate the monkey suits. As I wait for Erik, I tug at the collar. It's already trying to strangle me. But I've noticed that he's as comfortable in a tux as at a grand piano. Soon he comes out of his suite strolling with the grace of a panther, and the black tuxedo adds to that illusion, making him even more intimidating than usual.

George escorts us to the private dining room. When the Wheatons stand to greet us, Erik bows to Mrs. Wheaton and kisses her hand. Makes me feel awkward. I've never seen that done except in the movies. I notice that all Mr. Wheaton gets from Erik is a formal nod, along with a defiant glint.

"Are Dr. Adler and Dr. McKay not joining us tonight?" Erik asks.

When Mrs. Wheaton replies that they are in Seattle on business, Erik's eyes narrow. He probably suspects the business is with Ms. Copeland and that her arm's being twisted too.

Seemingly oblivious to the tension in the air, George intercedes, deftly pouring and serving wine with those white-gloved hands that miraculously never seem to get a smudge or stain. When we're seated at the table, I stare at the array of goblets and silverware at my place. Way too many forks and spoons. This was not the kind of obstacle course the Rangers and Army Corps of Engineers prepared me for. Game plan—eat slowly and follow Erik's lead.

The first serving is oysters. *Damn, I hate oysters*. They're in the shell, floating around in some buttery sauce with green stuff. Erik uses a fork with a center prong shaped like a dagger to spear the slimy critters. He fishes one out and eats it with gusto. Swallowing hard, I go for it. With the help of some bread—and wine to wash them down—I manage to eat them all.

The meal is a succession of courses, each with very little food on the plate. I'm thankful when a chunk of sirloin arrives. The conversation warms up, and I can tell Mrs. Wheaton holds Erik in high regard. When she asks if there's anything he needs, Erik takes a long drink of wine before answering. I imagine he's sifting through a long list beginning with, *get me the hell out of this trial and take me back to my century.*

"I am comfortable, Lady Margaret," he finally replies. I have to admire the effort that no doubt took.

I change the subject to Mrs. Wheaton's upcoming trip for the FWA. She explains that the funds she'll be distributing are for water purification projects in several cities where pollution is causing cancer rates to soar even higher, almost eighty percent now.

"How did the water become so tainted?" Erik asks.

"Most countries have few laws to regulate the disposal of chemicals and manufacturing waste," Wheaton replies. "It's just dumped into the rivers and lakes. The governments of countries that do have some protective laws are paid off to ignore the violations. Now the oceans have also been decimated. Chemical run off from industry and farming along the coasts has destroyed wetlands and coral reefs. Drilling for oil offshore has caused spills that destroyed entire sections of the ocean. Corporations don't care as long as they're making profits."

"Thousands of chemicals are produced now, and they are almost never tested for long-term effects," Mrs. Wheaton says. "In most places water has become so toxic, it isn't safe to drink or even use for irrigation. Still, that water is often used on crops out of ignorance or desperation. The toxic chemicals are absorbed into plants, then farm animals and humans eat them. That causes a wide range of illness, even death."

"And that food can end up anywhere in the world," Wheaton snaps, "on anyone's table. That's why we own farms and fisheries and raise our own food."

"Last January the daughter of a dear friend died from eating contaminated food," Mrs. Wheaton says with a catch in her voice. "She was working with an aid organization in Central America."

"You have my condolences. I experienced cholera outbreaks in London," Erik says, unexpectedly opening up a little.

"We're still dealing with cholera," Wheaton says. "In fact, it's getting worse, breaking out here in the U.S. because the water systems have not been maintained."

"Water systems? So it has been proven that cholera is spread through water? Not through miasmas in the air?" Erik asks.

"Yes, it's a waterborne disease," I reply.

"So, as I suspected." Erik shuts his eyes and grimaces. "It was believed that cholera was spread from miasmas, fumes in the air from waste. But I heard of a doctor who claimed otherwise, that it was spread through contaminated water. In London, the Thames was used to supply water and to dump waste. Paris used the Seine in the same manner. Tens of thousands of people perished during the outbreaks." Then he takes a gulp of wine and adds, "Businessmen and politicians considered it too costly to construct proper water and sewage systems. But the politicians could no longer ignore the problem when they began to feel susceptible to cholera's deadly grasp."

"Nothing's changed, except the modern practice is to manufacture and pollute elsewhere," Wheaton grumbles. "Businessmen keep their own back yards pristine."

"I studied civil engineering at the Sorbonne," I interject. "Aqueducts were finally built to bring lake water into Paris. By the 1860s underground tunnels were completed to hold the water, as well as a new sewer system. Those were so large and impressive, they started giving public tours. If I remember correctly, sightseers rode gondolas through the underground waterways. Boatman stood and pushed them along with poles, isn't that right, Erik?"

Erik puts down his wine glass. "Yes," he almost hisses.

His reaction surprises me. What nerve have I hit this time?

"It's just as urgent to fund water purification projects now." Mrs. Wheaton's voice lowers to a whisper. "If it's not too late..."

Erik gives her a probing look. Does he suspect? They'll have to tell him the rest of their plans sometime. Then dessert arrives—some fancy French chocolate concoction—and I dig in. I'm enjoying the afterglow of a grand meal when it happens.

"How was your meeting with Ms. Copeland yesterday?" Wheaton asks.

Ah, so the time has come. We've talked of many things, so now we get to *the question.*

There's a pause. A long pause. "Satisfactory," Erik replies, icy. Abruptly he says to Mrs. Wheaton, "Dinner was impeccable. Thank you." He gets up, bows, and leaves.

I stay a little longer, trying not to seem impolite, but finally make my escape.

Erik usually spends his evenings in the library, so I track him down there and find him in a secluded corner, reading. I scan the hardbounds on a shelf and settle on a book about the history of Paris. I need to learn a lot more about that. I sink into a leather chair and open the hardbound. Old-fashioned books made of paper have a more substantial feel. I still like to read them from time to time.

All too soon, George shows up with drinks, then asks if there's anything else we'd like. We shake our heads, hoping he'll go away. Unfortunately, George keeps up his patter and asks how our dinner was.

"Good," I respond. Erik says nothing, but his mouth pulls back in a scowl.

"Was your meeting with Ms. Copeland agreeable?" George asks, trying to be polite, but I flinch.

Erik slams his book shut and hisses to me, "It is a pity you neglected to bring my Punjab lasso when you rescued me." Taking his drink and book, Erik strides out of the library.

George's thin lips stretch back in shock. "What, pray tell, is a Punjab lasso?"

"Trust me." I grin darkly at him. "You sure as hell don't want to find out."

11 | DOUBT

Wednesday, June 6
Seattle

KATHRYN

"I hate taking the children away from my wife." The young man sitting in front of my desk rests his elbows on his knees and stares down. "But she was passed out drunk when I got home from work. Food was burning on the stove, almost burned the house down. Our girls are both under three years old and couldn't have gotten out by themselves." With an agonized voice, he says, "She refuses to get treatment. Yes, go ahead. File for immediate custody."

As he gives me the information to file the motion for temporary custody, I also let him vent his anger. Right now he needs someone to listen to his fears and doubts, not just his legal problems. The appointment runs long, but that's normal. I tell him I'll set the hearing for Friday, then escort him to the front office. When he leaves, I breathe a sigh of relief that today has been normal—a hearing, a deposition, and several appointments.

As usual, Barb intercepts me in the hallway and gives me an update on a case she is researching. While we're talking, Eileen comes out of the reception area and jabs her finger toward the waiting room. I turn around. Collin, Dr. Adler, and Ryan have their heads together in whispered conversation. Normal just ended.

Wondering what I'm in for now, I walk over and extend my hand to Dr. Adler who smiles warmly. Turning to Collin, I pointedly don't extend my hand. "What can I do for you?"

"We're hopin' you'll join us for dinner this evening."

Another dinner invitation? He's pushing his luck and my patience. "Sorry, I have work."

"Actually, we'd like t' discuss your representation. The Wheatons' chef is preparing a very fine meal for us at the penthouse."

The sooner I get this over with, the better. "All right. Give me a few minutes."

"We'll meet you at the penthouse," Collin says with a crooked grin, just like when he used to win a hotly contested debate at the university.

As I walk back to the reception area, it galls me that he thinks he's winning. "It's past six," I tell Eileen. "Go on home. Thanks for staying late." Directing a suspicious glance at the three people, she reluctantly gathers her purse and leaves.

Barb follows me to my office and hovers in front of my desk, agitated. "You know they'll pressure you to take the case. Can I give you some advice?"

"Okay, have your say."

"You obviously can't tell me the details. That makes me even more worried about this case—as if a full-time bodyguard isn't bad enough. I've got a real bad feeling about this."

"Truthfully? I feel the same way."

"Well then, get out now, Kathryn. This is dangerous."

Barb leaves, but her words hang in the air. I wish her gut feelings weren't always so dead-on.

During the drive to the Wheaton Tower an uncomfortable silence hangs between Ryan and me. When the elevator opens at the penthouse, there are no bodyguards, just Collin and Dr. Adler waiting to usher us straight into the dining room. Dr. Adler mentions she knows I didn't have lunch. I give Ryan an irritated look. What else has he told her about me?

I'm seated facing a spectacular view of the bay, literally and figuratively with my back to the wall. The dinner is delicious, otherworldly, centered around a course of lobster. Haven't eaten any for years, since before the pollution and oil drilling destroyed the North Atlantic fisheries. I remember even the elites who attended the Wheatons' FWA meeting were surprised that lobster was on the menu.

Collin tries to refill my wine goblet, but I pass—going to need my full wits. The dinner conversation progresses pleasantly. Nothing serious. Nothing about the case or phantoms. I predict that will end with dessert.

When dessert is finally served, I stare down at the large ripe strawberries nestled in rich mounds of whipped cream topping a torte. Since the bees died out, it's rare to see strawberries, and those are usually small and misshapen.

Collin notices my reaction. "Strawberries are unusual, aren't they?" he asks.

I sigh. "I can't remember the last time I ate some like this."

Conversation stops as everyone devours the delicacy. I'm halfway through when Collin says, "I understand you finished reading the Leroux book."

I hadn't told Collin that. I glare at Ryan, but he looks away. *Spy!* I just nod.

"Wha' did you think about it?" Collin asks.

"Interesting. Some clearly comes from Leroux's imagination, like a fiery-headed rat catcher. But as for other parts, you can only speculate where fiction ends and the facts begin."

Dr. Adler chuckles. "Trying to discern what's myth and what's truth about Erik is a challenge. Do you have any concerns? Perhaps I can help."

"You said the charges will probably include the people who died in the opera house. But what about the torture in Persia that Leroux wrote about? Do you think that will be included?"

Collin rubs his chin. "No' sure yet, but I surmise they'll lay whatever they can at Erik's doorstep. The more Erik is vilified, the more they can discredit Mr. Wheaton and claim he misused the time travel technology. A lot's at stake here."

I notice he's always focused on protecting Mr. Wheaton and the technology. "Mrs. Wheaton thinks he's innocent or at least has a valid defense." I turn to Dr. Adler. "You said he denied committing the murders. Do you believe him?"

She sips her wine while considering her answer. "I'm not sure. He's not one to trust people. He's reluctant to discuss anything about those deaths, but there's nothing in Madame Giry's diary that implicates him and it does support Erik's claim that he traveled only in Europe."

"But do you think he was capable of those murders?" I persist.

"I performed the full range of testing, including personality inventories. If you take the case, I'll be glad to go over those in detail with you, but they confirm what we've already discussed. He suffers from post-traumatic stress. However, it is possible that if he were confronted with a serious threat, he may be capable of killing." Her gaze travels from Collin to Ryan. "But then, wouldn't most men be capable of that under those circumstances?" Collin shifts uncomfortably.

"Yes, most men would kill in self-defense," Ryan concedes, "but post-traumatic stress could make a person strike out even from a perceived threat."

"True," Dr. Adler confirms, "that could happen if someone were having a flashback. Under those circumstances, he may not realize what he was doing."

Mr. Mercier's reaction yesterday when I approached him replays in my mind. As it happened, I was focused on helping him, but now I realize the full danger I was in. I push the torte aside, my appetite gone.

"So, during a flashback, Erik would no' be aware of his actions, right?" Collin's eyes glint slyly. "If he didn't know what he was doing, wouldn't tha' qualify as temporary insanity?"

"Even if we allege it occurred during a flashback, that won't be easy to prove, and juries tend to have difficulty understanding how psychological problems can render a person unaware of his actions. Would a jury buy such a defense?"

"We're counting on it." Collin grins shrewdly. "Will ya take the case, then?"

So Collin thinks he's guilty. "After meeting with Mr. Mercier and considering the issues, I've decided I'm not the best attorney to handle this case. Or this client."

"Did something happen when you met with him that's causing concern?" Dr. Adler asks.

Does she suspect he had a post-traumatic stress episode? I decide to keep the incident confidential and reply simply, "No."

Dr. Adler studies me knowingly. I took too long to answer and she suspects something.

"Have you read Madame Giry's diary yet?" Collin smiles, trying his charm.

"No, with my schedule I've only had time to read Leroux's book."

"But Leroux focused on the last several months of Erik's life," Dr. Adler points out. "Adèle Giry knew Erik from the day he arrived at the opera house when he was thirteen. She chronicles the next twenty years of his life with great insight. Perhaps it would give you a deeper understanding if you read that before making your final decision."

"Will you give it another chance?" Collin reaches out and takes my hand. "Just read the diary, and then if you still feel tha' way, I'll back off."

I look down at his hand. He's still wearing his wedding ring. I was with Anne when she picked it out. He's really pulling out all the stops. "Okay, Collin. I'll give you my answer on Friday."

Collin accompanies us to the garage. Opening my car door, he puts his hand on my shoulder as I get in. "Kathryn, you're needed on this case. This goes beyond Erik or you or me. Please remember all that's at stake here."

I doubt he's told me *all*, but I won't play his game. "Has it occurred to you that Mr. Mercier may not want me as his attorney?"

"You're both as stubborn and independent as they come," he shoots back. "You two should get along just fine." I don't reply, just snap the door shut.

It's after nine when I sink into my chair in the living room with a cup of tea. I keep thinking about Collin's parting words. I feel—no, I *know* he's not telling me everything.

Ryan sprawls on the couch, reading. Covertly, I study him over my laptop, still trying to get used to his constant presence. He's truly become my shadow. What was that quote of Queen Elizabeth's? "My care is like my shadow in the sun." Her care was her dedication to her work, to rule England well, and she certainly did that. She spoke those words when she gave up her last chance to marry. I've been married to my work for a long time and have given up on a personal life. Now I even have a shadow following me to confirm it.

So, let's see what Madame Giry has to say about the Phantom. Taking a sip of tea, I insert the quantum chip that Collin had delivered to my office. He called it a "Quip" and said that it can interface with regular computers, but the data is encoded in a format which is impossible to access through PALnet. The Quip opens up the translation of Madam Giry's diary. Each page has been photocopied, so the exact text is displayed on the left side of the page with the corresponding translation of each line on the right side.

The first page displays her maiden name, Adèle Aumont. She says the diary was a gift on her confirmation day in 1837. The first passages are written in the simple sentences of a child. She had just turned seven and was delighted with her white confirmation dress and its fancy, satin-covered buttons and lace trim. In her first entry, Adèle resolved to write only on special occasions so the diary would last her lifetime.

For many years the entries occurred mostly on her birthdays or holidays, particularly Christmas. Her only brother, Andre, was born a year later. She delighted in his golden, curly hair and large blue eyes, so different from her own brown hair and eyes. Clearly she was devoted to him. Over the years, her writing style matured. During her teens, she attended a Catholic girls' school. Several sad entries describe the deaths of friends from cholera. Her eulogies show the tender feelings of a sensitive young woman.

Then tragedy struck during the 1848 rebellion. While riding in their carriage, her mother, father, and brother were caught in the fighting that broke out on Paris streets. Gunshots rang out and the horses bolted, overturning the carriage. All three were killed. Fortunately, Adèle was not with them. She was still residing at the girls' school, awaiting graduation.

Adèle was utterly bereft. It's heartbreaking to read her entries as she tried to comprehend the loss of the three most beloved people in her life. She also had to deal with a new reality. Her privileged life was about to end. Her father was one of several sons of a previously noble family. His home and property were held in life estate, so on his death, all that reverted to the main estate. Adèle's only inheritance was a small investment which her father had put in her name. She received that on graduation, but it yielded only an annual stipend which was not enough to live on.

Abruptly and unexpectedly, she was alone in a Paris of turmoil, of oppressive poverty. One of her uncles helped her find respectable work. He introduced her to the Paris Opéra's manager who deemed her deportment suitably refined to cater to the elite and nobility who attended the Opéra. Because she also possessed an acceptable wardrobe and fluency in English and German, she was hired as the attendant for the private boxes.

So Leroux was correct on that point—she was a box attendant. According to him, she collected blackmail from the theater managers and placed it in Box Five for the Phantom. What will her diary say about that? Adèle doesn't seem the sort of person to participate in illicit activities. Or did her financial situation make her desperate?

After she moved into the opera house, her entries became more frequent, describing the grand operas and their startling ballets—all overwhelming for a young woman educated by Catholic nuns. Her friends from school seemed to fall away. They probably married, and her position would be beneath their social status. Her new friends were her coworkers at the opera house. Hundreds were employed there, and many lived on the premises. Adèle moved into the dormitory with the dancers, called "ballet rats," all young women struggling to survive. They shared everything from their clothes to their most intimate secrets, and Adèle wrote of their plights. Sometimes they lost their jobs because of an injury or something more devastating—a pregnancy.

A year and a half after she arrived at the opera house, Adèle and some ballet rats came upon a carnival when they were returning from a café. The other girls wanted to see the exhibits, and although Adèle was reluctant, she went with them.

Sunday, 26 January 1851

...Inside the carnival, we went from stall to stall, amazed at the human oddities. One man had fur covering his body. Only parts were covered with clothing for modesty. A tall woman sported a beard and responded with bawdy jibes when people laughed at her. We giggled, wondering if the beard was real.

The last exhibit was a cage. In its center, a boy perched atop a stool. He wore filthy pants and a tattered shirt. A frightening red devil's mask covered his face. My heart hurt for him, sitting there, slumped over and staring down at his hands. When a crowd had gathered, a brute of a man unlocked the cage and went inside. He walked up to the boy, who raised his hands in protest. The boy struggled desperately, but he was no match for the brute. The man tore off the mask and held the boy's hands so he could not cover his face. I was shocked to tears.

The crowd howled at the sight of the boy's deformity, a few calling him by abominable names. Throughout this ordeal, the boy kept his head lowered. I broke down crying and fled from that accursed place. I have not been able to sleep tonight. The boy's eyes, so full of pain and shame, keep haunting me.

It's hard to imagine such cruelty to a boy. Leroux wrote Erik had been exhibited in a carnival, but that it was voluntary. What Adèle described was clearly an abusive, forced situation. How long was he subjected to that? It certainly would explain his post-traumatic stress and fear of anyone getting close enough to remove his mask. I remember the mad glare down at me when I approached him—and how his hand instinctively flew up to protect the mask.

Adèle's next entry is only one week later.

Sunday, 2 February 1851

I cannot believe what happened today. What if the director discovers what I have done? I was returning a broom to the storage closet this evening when a shadow of movement caught my attention. I lifted my candle and discovered a boy. He was lying on the floor, curled up behind the large washtub. When I bent over him, he held up his arm to ward me off, pleading for me not to hit him. I could not believe my eyes. It was the boy from the cage. He had wound a torn strip of cloth around the scarred side of his face, like the dressings I have seen on wounded soldiers.

I asked what he was doing here. He said he had snuck in through the alley door a couple days before. He has been stealing food from the kitchen and hiding behind the tub. The back of his shirt was covered with dried blood. He told me that brutish man used a whip on him. Although he had been whipped before, he said this time someone helped him escape.

His face was flushed, so I touched his forehead. It was burning like a heated flatiron. I told him I would bring the physician, but he begged me not to tell anyone. He was terrified about being returned to the carnival. I feared he was right, or that they would leave him on the streets to die.

Mother Mary, help me. I have hidden him here in the opera house. I bade him to be quiet and promised to return and take him somewhere safe. I finally found an empty storage room in the lower levels. I went to the laundry room and took a man's shirt, and a sheet and blanket, then got some tincture of iodine from the ballet rats' medicine cabinet. I snuck into the kitchen and added some bread, cheese, and a small piece of ham to my basket, along with a half-empty bottle of wine.

When I got back to the storage room, he lay there, still as death. I was afraid to touch him, fearing the worst. Then he let out a groan. I woke him gently and helped him stand. Mon Dieu, he was so weak and thin, I had to support him all the way. It was midnight, so the corridors were empty, and we took the backstairs to the room I prepared. He collapsed onto the sheets I had spread on the floor. When I peeled off his shirt to clean the wounds, I was horrified to see his back crisscrossed with scars from previous beatings, as well as new slashes in his flesh. I gently washed the wounds and used the iodine. Even now I shudder, remembering his hisses of pain when my cloth touched the raw gashes, but he never once cried out. While he ate, I remained with him, although we did not speak. Then he lay down to sleep and I left. Just as I closed the door, he said, "Thank you. You are very kind."

Now I am fearful. What if his wounds become infected? What if he dies? What will happen to me if they discover what I have done? Yet in my heart, I know I could neither betray him nor leave him in the storage room to die. Who knows what fate lies ahead for him or me.

"It's midnight." Ryan's voice hauls me back to the present. "Isn't it time to turn in?"

I don't answer, just get up and walk over to the window that faces Seattle's skyline across the bay. I try to relate what I just read to my own life, thinking back on the lobster dinner we ate and comparing it with meager scraps of food. We won't go to bed feverish from gaping wounds caused by a whipping. Won't spend the night on a floor, sleeping on a sheet in the middle of winter. Or live in a cage, bracing for the cruelty of crowds. Yet that actually happened to the man I met—that dignified, commanding man who still carries the scars on his body and horrors in his soul.

"Kathryn?" Ryan's voice is insistent. "Are you okay?"

"I'm not sure. Been thinking about the things we take for granted. Maybe I'll never see them quite the same again."

12 | VENTURE

Thursday, June 7
Manhattan

Lexa Simmons

"Miss Lexa, did you pack bricks?" Frank grumbles over my bulging suitcase, but his kindly eyes crinkle in a grin. As he takes the last suitcase downstairs, it thuds on each step.

Standing in my bedroom doorway, I take a final look around, gazing at all the memories. A clutter of frames hangs above my desk—pictures of friends, high school awards from debate competitions, and my college degrees. A tall bookshelf contains my collection of old-fashioned hardbound books in French and English. And there's the feminine quilts and drapes Mom picked out. She even insisted I have a vanity table and cheval mirror. I wanted a bookcase. She won. I smile through tears, remembering.

"The Wheaton limo will be here in ten minutes," Frank calls up. "I'll get Sylvie."

With a sigh, I close the door. This time, leaving is different. I wonder when I'll return—if ever. The walk down the stairs to the foyer is slow as I look at the family pictures. More memories. When I reach the foyer, Sammie bounds up. Picking up the mop of a dog, I stroke her rusty-gold mane. Restlessly, I stride up and down the long entrance foyer to take in all the family pictures on its two-story walls. Gazing at the portraits of Mom and Dad, I wipe away tears. It's been three years since Mom died of cancer, but sometimes it hurts like it was yesterday. I smile at the pictures of my brothers and me: our college graduations, my brothers' weddings, and recent pictures of Pete's and Samuel's families.

I linger beneath my family gallery. Five generations of Simmons, all watched over by Albert and Alexandra in their ornate, gold-leaf frames. Albert—our clan's founder and the youngest son of an English lord, but not high enough in the pecking order to inherit the family's estates. Dad always said that's why he got away with marrying Alexandra, the daughter of a wealthy Parisian businessman who fled to London right after the Commune. Albert and Alexandra gaze lovingly at each other. Status happily united with money. Just below them hangs the modest daguerreotype of Alexandra's father. His investments in American companies brought the young couple to Manhattan. Albert managed those investments and turned out to have a fine business sense, so the family prospered. He bought this townhouse for Alexandra and it's been in the family ever since, always inherited by the eldest son. And I inherited Alexandra's name. An elegant name, but a bit antiquated. I tell everyone to call me Lexa, and they ignore that at their own peril.

As I peruse the many faces on the wall, I wonder if this is the last time I'll see them.

Still wiping flour-coated hands on her apron, Sylvie rushes from the kitchen. Our sweet-natured tabby cat, Eskimo, trails close behind and rubs my leg as Sylvie gives me a hug.

"When will you be back?" She asks innocently—but then, no one knows except Dad.

"Don't know." I put on a smile. "Maybe you can fly out and visit me."

"The limo just pulled up," Frank announces. He takes the luggage, and I follow him out to the limo. As he closes my door, he says, "Goodbye, Lexa." I draw a sharp breath. He's never said that before. It's always "see you soon" or "hurry home." Did Dad confide in him, or did Frank overhear something? Tearfully, I wave to Frank and Sylvie until my limo turns down Fifth Avenue and they disappear from sight.

As we pass Central Park, I recall tag football games with my brothers. Pete called me a tomboy and always wanted me on his team because I played to win. But children don't play there anymore. It's become a shantytown. Tents of the homeless are pitched everywhere. Only families are allowed to have tents in the Park in an attempt to give some protection to the children. Mothers holding signs describing their family tragedies stand in designated, chained-off areas, but desperately stretch their arms over the barrier at the passing traffic.

The depression that struck five years ago is said to be as bad as the one back in 1932. My father explained that the regulations which were put in place during that depression had kept the economy sound until 1999 when Congress abolished that law and allowed the Wall Street investment banks to again gamble with the money people put in their local banks. The banks nearly failed eight years later, but the government stepped in and funded their rescue. This time the government was too impoverished to do that. Corporations control the government, so the banks just emptied the accounts of everyone to pay off their debts. People lost their jobs, their homes, everything. Thankfully, our family home had no mortgage and my father worked for the government, so we got along.

The history books say America used to have a large, prosperous middle class, but now it seems there are only the few haves and many have-nots. The family you're born into determines your fate. I got lucky. Why do these thoughts, and so many others about what lies ahead, flood my mind now? It feels like the past, present and future are all crashing together as the limo weaves slowly through the Manhattan streets. Bikes, scooters, and minicabs crowd around us, all jockeying for position, and children dash into the street to sell odds and ends. I'm inundated by chaos and noise, but already homesick. Will I ever see this place again?

The Wheatons booked me a private first-class suite on the plane. As soon as we take off and the attendant serves wine, I take out my QRYSTAL. Programming the monitor for confidential mode, I then put on the glasses that allow only me to see the text. I open the Wheaton file and pull up Madame Giry's diary with the English translation. There are inaccuracies in the translation, and we can't have that since the other attorney on the case doesn't speak French.

I still can't believe that I've been hired for this case. That I'll be meeting *the Phantom*. They say his appearance isn't like it's described in the book, except he does wear the mask. I've always been fascinated with his story and read the Leroux novel as an undergrad. The book depicts the Phantom as probably guilty of three murders, as well as committing torture in Persia. If charges are filed, I'm praying he's not guilty or that there are some *really good* extenuating circumstances. But as Collin said, whether he's guilty or not isn't all that's at stake. More than his fate depends on the outcome of this trial.

As I read Adèle's diary, I can't help comparing her with Alexandra, my grandmother six generations back. I wonder if Alexandra ever went to the Paris Opéra? Did Adèle Giry seat her? Maybe their paths crossed, one as the privileged, the other as the servant. If so, the thought saddens me. After reading the diary, I feel Adèle possessed innate nobility.

When the plane touches down with a jerk, my life begins irrevocably on a new course. Walking through the airport, I feel both excited and unsettled by what lies ahead.

Collin is waiting at the luggage carrousel. "Alexandra," he says as he shakes my hand, "pleased t' meet you."

With a sharp edge in my voice, I correct him, "That's *Lexa*."

"Well, then, *Lexa*"—his grin says he won't make that mistake again—"we're glad you're joining our venture."

Collin turns to the man standing next to him—a rangy, muscular man whose sandy hair is cut high and tight. "Josh Taylor is your bodyguard," Collin says.

"Pleased to meet you, ma'am," he drawls.

"You'll be havin' a bodyguard with you around the clock."

"Why?" I give Josh a double take.

Josh smiles broadly, but mischievous eyes check me out from head to foot.

"Just a precaution," Collin replies offhandedly. "Just in case."

"In case of what?" I demand.

"Oh, you never know. This'll be a high-profile trial, and we don't want to take any chances." Shifting nervously, Collin adds, "And Lady Margaret insisted on this."

"*Really?*" Mrs. Wheaton didn't say anything about this when I had dinner at their Manhattan penthouse. As we're leaving the airport, I search my memory of that meeting. She said she'd just seen my father in Paris, then asked me about my studies at the Sorbonne and my work as a prosecutor. Disclosing the situation surrounding Mercier, she told me indictments would likely be served. When she revealed what was at stake and made me the offer, I was overwhelmed. She suggested I think it over and handed me a letter from Dad. I didn't sleep much that night. And when I met with her the next day we only discussed the work I'd be doing. I'm *positive* she never said anything about a 24/7 bodyguard.

"We're going to the Wheaton penthouse for dinner," Collin informs me as we settle in the limo. He rubs his beard. "Sorry you had t' come aboard on such short notice, but the indictment could be served any minute. Did tha' cause you problems at the prosecutor's office when you resigned?"

"It burned some bridges with the higher-ups." I shrug my shoulders. "But I haven't taken any time off for almost a year, so I used accrued vacation as my notice. Worked nonstop this last week getting my cases in order and turning them over."

Collin hands me the key for my condo in the Wheaton Tower. "It's go' a great view of the bay." He adds nonchalantly, "By the way, Mr. Taylor will stay in the second bedroom."

"Oh really?" I didn't know that *either*. "Does Ms. Copeland have a bodyguard living with her?" I glare at Collin, but he nods and evasively looks out the window. "I see." But I wish I didn't.

When we arrive at the penthouse, I feel at home—like I'm back in Paris. The Wheaton penthouse in New York is ultra-modern, but here I pass Impressionist paintings and enter a living room filled with gilt chairs and velvet settees, slightly at odds with the sweeping panoramas of the bay. I'm admiring the view when a silver-grey haired woman walks up and introduces herself as Dr. Adler. She's really short, but has a killer smile.

The wine is served right away and everyone settles into chairs around a coffee table covered with drool-worthy appetizers.

"I understand you're very familiar with Paris," Dr. Adler says.

"Yes," I reply, munching on sourdough bread topped with salmon. Love salmon. It's a rare delicacy and my family only serves it at Christmas. "My father was an attaché at the embassy for five years when I was in grade school. Ten years ago, he was reassigned there, so I got my undergraduate degree at the Sorbonne."

"Did you enjoy living in Paris?" she asks.

"It's my second home. In fact, one of my great-grandmothers was born and raised there."

The conversation turns to innocuous subjects like the charms of Seattle and Puget Sound, but I sense an undercurrent of tension that's almost palpable. "So when do I meet *him*?" I bring the conversation back to business.

"Tomorrow we'll drive you to Land's End to meet Mr. Mercier," Dr. Adler replies. "But first, we plan to take you to meet Ms. Copeland, the other attorney who we hope will be your co-counsel."

"I've been told about her. I think our different areas of expertise will complement each other well. But I thought she already accepted the case."

"No, not yet." Collin shrugs. "When we met with Ms. Copeland, she did no' accept the case as we had expected. She met Erik on Tuesday and has been going over the documents."

I don't like the sound of this. "That's two days ago. She still hasn't decided?"

"No, and she told Erik *he* has the right t' decide whether he wants her as his attorney. Tha' threw in a monkey wrench." He sounds worried. "He's still thinking it over."

"So, you don't have confirmation from *either* of them?"

"No, actually, we don't." Collin's brow creases deeply. *Yep. Way worried.*

I don't know what I can say in front of the others. "Could I talk to you in private, Collin?"

His expression goes south, but he leads me to a small office. My first question spills out, "Does Ms. Copeland know about the Wheatons' project?"

"No."

"Will she ever be told?"

"Only if we feel it's necessary."

Then it dawns on me. "Does Mercier know about it yet?"

Sheepish, Collin shakes his head.

"Well, you'll have to tell *him* sooner or later," I point out.

"When the time is right. Sorry about this. I hoped tha' he would have agreed to Ms. Copeland before you arrived. Tha' way he would've chosen his primary attorney, and we could introduce you as her co-counsel. It would get around the sticky issue of us no' asking his approval for hiring you."

"So you haven't told him yet that *I've* been retained?"

"That about sums it up."

"Oh hell!"

Collin studies me acutely. "Are you still with us, then?"

"Of course. I've signed on to the venture. How could I back out now?"

13 | GAUNTLET

Friday, June 8
Seattle

KATHRYN

"Objection, leading the witness," I state for the fifth time. The judge sustains my objection and tells the attorney to refrain from asking his client leading questions. The attorney sputters an apology. He's fallen into that trap because of his client's irrational ramblings. He skims his notes, stalling as he decides on a strategy.

The young woman on the witness stand squirms. She keeps giving contradictory testimony about what happened the day she passed out at home, leaving the stove on and endangering her two toddlers. She doesn't want to admit she was drunk, but she keeps slurring her words, not even able to stay sober for court.

Impatiently, the judge recesses for lunch.

As his wife leaves with her attorney, my client groans, "I just want this over."

"I understand," I say. "But everything you're doing is to protect your children." Still, having to listen to one's life laid bare is nothing less than traumatic. His shoulders slump. "Get some fresh air and have a decent lunch," I tell him.

I walk to the back of the courtroom with my client. When he leaves, I turn to Ryan who is lurking there. He shows me a message on his QRYSTAL from Collin:

It's happening. Erik to be arraigned at 1PM. We're taking Lexa to court. She meets Erik there and will represent him today.

I decide to take my own advice. "We need some fresh air and lunch."

It's a sunny day—feels good to be out of the courthouse. As we're walking, I pull out my phone and check my messages. One from Barb says that the Wheaton story has hit the news. We hurry to McMurty's Grill and take a small table in the bar near the large wall monitor.

The midday PALnet News is just completing a "pundit" analysis of the current presidential campaign—typical attention focused on polls, typical avoidance of the issues that matter to the people. The PALnet logo and promo follow. *"PALnet—the Private Advantage Link—your unsurpassed internet connection to the world."*

"Unsurpassed? Bull!" Ryan huffs. "Since the PTB Corporation bought up all the cable, satellite and internet companies, it's the *only* access to the internet any more."

The next report covers the latest business fraud scandal, another favorite topic of the news. Despite how much was lost, I notice that no one is ever prosecuted. As usual, the corporation paid fines and the executives involved remain in their positions. Fines have just become part of the cost of doing business in this scam economy. Actually, it occurs to me that's no longer "news." The next report is about the drought in the Midwest and crop failures. Still no mention of the arraignment.

I pull out my phone and scan the news. Finally, I come across the headline: WHEATON MISUSES TIME-TRAVEL TECHNOLOGY. The article states that Mr. Wheaton's Research and Development Lab used time-travel technology to bring Erik Mercier, the "Phantom of the Opera," from the nineteenth century. Mercier is to be arraigned today and charged with a number of murders he allegedly committed, as well as crimes against humanity for committing torture. The article clarifies there's no statute of limitations for those crimes. Staying just this side of legal by inserting "alleged" in all the right places, the clear implication is he's dangerous and possibly insane. For transporting him to the present, Mr. Wheaton is labeled as irresponsible.

As the waitress returns with our lunch, the monitor over the bar flashes a bulletin. Standing at the entrance of Seattle's International Criminal Court of the Americas, a reporter tells about the case that is about to begin there.

"I haven't heard much about that court before," Ryan says.

"Most people haven't. It opened only two years ago and serves the Americas. Most of the cases are low-key, involving drug and water traffickers, smuggling and money laundering."

The reporter's expression and voice are dramatically ominous. "It's expected that both Howard Wheaton and the man known as the "Phantom of the Opera" will be here momentarily. Alexandra Simmons, an ex-federal prosecutor, has just arrived. It's believed she's the attorney for the Phantom. We go now to our reporter in the courthouse."

The camera pans a lobby crammed with loud, clamoring people more befitting Mardi Gras than a courthouse. A reporter sticks his microphone in the face of a tall, blonde woman exiting the security station. "Are you Alexandra Simmons?"

"Yes." She gives him an irritated look and a perfunctory smile.

"Can you confirm you're representing the Phantom?"

She doesn't reply, just vigorously elbows her way across the lobby. The camera doesn't catch anything except her receding back. Her bodyguards hold back the reporters as she darts behind closing elevator doors.

"Good job. Couldn't intercept her." Ryan grins. "She'd make a great halfback."

The scene switches to the courthouse's rear entrance as two limos enter the underground garage. The reporter explains, "No doubt Howard Wheaton and the man notoriously known as the Phantom of the Opera are inside the limos. The media will not be allowed to film in the garage or the courtroom, and the Phantom isn't being taken through the lobby, so this is as close as we'll get to the action." I notice that the reporters never use Mr. Mercier's name, but only refer to him as "the Phantom."

Several people at the bar loudly add their own commentaries. "Wheaton's just trying to protect a murderer to pull his own irons out of the fire."

"Oh, he's got plenty of money to buy his way out of this," a woman chimes in.

"This is what happens when they mess with the natural order of things," a white-haired man blurts out. "This time-travel stunt will be the downfall of mankind."

Ryan and I exchange glances. The propaganda is already working. But the media circus isn't the only thing bothering me. I told Collin I'd give him my decision today. If I take the case, will I also have to fight through crowds to get to court? Will my life ever be the same?

"I wonder what he looks like under the mask," a woman at the next table says.

"Yeah. And when he came through time travel, I'll bet he showed up in the buff," her friend replies. They both laugh. I glance at Ryan, sickened. He just shakes his head.

Now pictures of famous actors who played the Phantom of the Opera flash across the screen. Several faces are grotesque. "He'sh a freak." A drunk man calls out. "Lock 'im up."

I can't stand any more of this. I throw cash on the table and rush out of McMurty's. As I hurry down the street, Adèle's words come back to me—how she was shocked to tears when his mask was ripped off and he was exposed to the crowd's derision. Then when he took refuge in the opera house she helped him, and risked everything. She could have gone to prison because she stole clothing and food for him. But most of all, she gave him care and compassion. She didn't consider him a freak; she considered him a human being. And I'm acutely aware he is a living, breathing, *feeling* human being. I saw an inscription on a sixteenth-century church in Italy: *It is the divine right of man to appear human.* But I also believe it is each man's divine right to be treated humanely. He deserves no less.

But what if Leroux was correct? What if he killed those people or even committed torture? I've skimmed through the diary, and nothing in it indicates he went to Persia or implicates him in the three deaths. But Adèle had a close relationship with him. Would she have been careful not to write anything incriminating?

I'm halfway down the block when Ryan grabs my arm and jolts me to a stop. "Damn it," he says with grit teeth. "Don't run off like that. *Ever.*"

I pull my arm from his grasp. "I couldn't listen to that for another minute."

"Well, you'll have to develop a thick skin. You'll be hearing a lot more."

"That depends on whether I take this case."

Neither of us speaks the rest of the way. As the courthouse looms ahead, I check the time. It's one. The arraignment's beginning. I keep thinking about him. He never met his attorney before today. How did he feel about that? How will he feel when he has to stand and listen to the charges? Especially if he's innocent? *And he may be innocent*. I can't forget the horror Adèle felt when she saw him trapped in that nightmarish cage, trying to defend himself. No one stepped forward to defend him then. Hasn't he been traumatized enough? The feeling that I'm in the wrong place overwhelms me.

"Ryan, can you get Collin for me?"

He places the call and hands me his QRYSTAL. "Collin McKay. Leave your message."

"It's Kathryn. I've decided."

14 | FURY

Land's End

Erik

Incessantly, my mind keeps going over everything that happened at the courthouse. Once again, I was put on display. The gawking people in the hallway. The smirking prosecutors and that judge, condescending as he peered down at me. When the charges were read, I had to stand and deny them like a common criminal.

As our limousine enters the underground garage at Land's End, I rebuff Collin's attempt to speak with me. When we enter the elevator, he says, "Erik, we've gotta talk."

Barely able to contain my rage, I ignore him and charge out of the elevator. George—the fool—is standing in my way, and I nearly knock him down. I stop and help him right himself, then turn on my heel and escape to my music room. Going straight to the piano, I place my fingers on the keys. My hands seem detached, as if they do not belong to me. But they do. All that they have done, for good or ill, belongs to me. Of their own volition, they begin to play a composition of mine—a dark one, written during a time of despair, when Christine was slipping away.

They lied to me. They told me I had the right to choose my lawyer. How dare they call me just before I left Land's End and inform me that someone had been retained without my knowledge. I met the woman mere moments before going to court. Her only words were instructions to deny all the charges and say nothing further. I was no more than a pawn. Told what to do. Directed where to go. *Powerless.* Forced to listen while everyone around me discussed my fate.

My fingers crash on the piano keys, sending up agonized chords. Where was *Ms.* Copeland? Why was she not there? Has my vacillation caused her to reject the case? Or does she not want to affiliate herself with a monster such as I?

I twist the music, turning it dissonant, darker. How much money did Wheaton pay *this* lawyer? When I met with her after the court hearing, she averted her eyes and gave me no opportunity to ask questions. I hammer a raging crescendo. How *dare* Collin impose her on me!

"Trying to break the piano, Erik?"

So, Jarrod has arrived. Why am I not surprised? I sneer at him but lighten my touch on the keys and flow into a reverie, losing myself in the music.

As expected, Collin and Dr. Adler also arrive, no doubt to foist that lawyer on me—a confrontation I welcome.

"I know you're upset," Dr. Adler begins. "Let's talk. We only want to help."

"Help?" I grab my cane and walk to the windows as my anger boils over. "Dragging me to court to be accused of evil crimes and imposing on me a lawyer I have not approved or even met before. Do you consider that to be *helping*?"

She inhales sharply. "We're sorry. Ms. Simmons only arrived late yesterday afternoon. We were bringing her to Land's End today to meet you. Unfortunately, the arraignment occurred first. This wasn't the way we intended it to happen. *Truly.*"

I gaze out at the Sound. *So, they have been busy behind my back.*

"We've been telling you, Erik, tha' we did not know when you would be charged," Collin says, launching his attack. "It's why we've been pushin' to retain an attorney for you."

"Ultimately, you did just that," I fire back angrily. "Without my knowledge."

"We did wha' we were able to on short notice. The papers were served this morning, and you had t' appear immediately for the arraignment. Mr. Wheaton did everything he could. He prevented your being taken away in handcuffs."

"Handcuffs? Do you mean manacles?"

"Yes. The usual procedure is t' be arrested and taken to the arraignment."

I puzzle over this. "But why is *that lawyer* representing me?"

"Ms. Simmons was a federal prosecutor," Dr. Adler replies. "She graduated from the Sorbonne and is fluent in French with extensive knowledge of French history and culture. Imminently qualified to represent you as your second counsel."

"My *second* counsel?" I scoff.

"Ms. Simmons wasn't intended to serve as your main attorney." Collin's voice turns acid. "Ms. Copeland was."

"So, she has declined." *Just as I suspected.*

"Not exactly," he says with an irritating smirk. "She left a message while we were in court. I returned her call as soon as your arraignment was over, but she was in a hearing herself. She called me back just a few minutes ago." He pauses, taking satisfaction in keeping me on tenterhooks. "She agrees t' represent you. *If* that's wha' you want."

"Indeed?" This is unexpected news. I am uncertain what to make of it. I have been convinced ever since receiving the call from Dr. Adler about the new lawyer that Mademoiselle Copeland had made up her mind not to represent me.

"Regarding Ms. Copeland," Dr. Adler says, "did anything happen during your meeting with her to make you feel uncomfortable about her as your attorney?"

"Not as far as I am concerned. Did she express such reservation about me?"

"No, when we had dinner with her, she said nothing at all," Dr. Adler replies. "She's quite tight-lipped, you know." Her veiled comment is no doubt meant to reassure me that Mademoiselle Copeland keeps everything confidential.

"Erik, time's a wastin'," Collin presses. "You're going to need two attorneys and you need to make your decision damn soon." A loud whack resounds on the piano behind me.

I spin around. Collin has thrown down a newspaper. I go over and pick it up. A large, black headline announces the trial. Beginning with a rancorous attack on Wheaton, the article ends with a litany of my alleged pernicious acts. Blood pounds in my veins as I read the venomous words. "So again I am considered to be an inhuman creature."

Heedless, Collin replies, "They're already beginnin' the smear campaign. Ms. Copeland told me what she overheard at lunch. People are already believing some outlandish things. She was clearly upset."

This confounds me. Despite the defamatory statements troubling her, she nonetheless decided to serve as my lawyer? Most people would distance themselves from someone accused of such heinous acts and feel fully justified not to get involved.

Collin folds his arms. "Frankly, I don't think you will find anyone who'll be more competent or more committed t' your case."

"Committed? What do you mean?"

"Well, she knows the risks, and she's prepared to take them on."

This assertion is mystifying. If she is aware of dangers, why would she knowingly accept them? Silence descends over the room as I stride restlessly back and forth, pondering this conundrum. If I accept Mademoiselle Copeland, then I am acceding to their wishes. Still, she was the first to give me a choice. And I cannot fathom why, despite everything, she wishes to take on my misfortunes. She is truly paradox on paradox.

Finally, I stop pacing. Expectant faces stare at me as I announce, "I accept Mademoiselle Copeland."

15 | WOUNDS

Saturday, June 9
Seattle

RYAN KIRKMAN

"Hey, Ryan, got a minute?" Tom Cheveyo calls out from Kathryn's bedroom.

"Coming," I reply. Kathryn glares at me over her laptop. When I get to her room, Tom is bending over a tiny, electronic box beneath the window. "What's up?"

"Just want to show you where the jammers are." Tom grunts as he gets up. The whine of a saw comes from Kathryn's closet. "We're also installing a wall safe."

I wander over to the closet where Sanjiv, a technician from Land's End, is installing the safe. Kathryn's perfume hangs in the air. I survey the shoes and clothing, all neatly organized—like everything in Kathryn's condo and probably in her life until we showed up. "Leave it neat."

"Yeah," he snorts, glancing around. "I get what you mean."

Back in the living room, I sit at the bar and finish my breakfast, then chat with Sanjiv as he installs the front door's biometric lock. Every now and then, Kathryn glances up. She didn't know this was part of the deal when she accepted the case. Hell, she's still trying to accept getting stuck with me.

Tom interrupts her, asking for a minute to explain the equipment. Kathryn puts aside her work and gives him grudging attention. He settles on the couch and puts his bulging briefcase on the floor next to him. "Now all your rooms have jammers," he begins. "Those interfere with TLEs—technical listening equipment. We also checked for bugs. You'll be happy to know, we didn't find any."

"Yes, quite relieved," Kathryn replies with a hint of sarcasm.

"As you can see, Sanjiv is switching out your wall monitor here in the living room and installing one from Wheaton Industries which blocks eavesdropping. We installed a wall safe in your closet and a lock on your front door. Both are biometric. We also need to go to your office and install a biometric door lock and office safe. We'll check for bugs and put jammers and motion detectors on the doors and windows. Everything will be monitored from the Wheaton Tower's security center a block away."

"All right," she sighs with resignation. "I'll call Barb. She's working at the office this morning and will let you in."

Tom opens his briefcase, takes out a notepad-sized QRYSTAL and hands it to Kathryn. "I have two more of these for your office staff. Use them exclusively for Erik's case. They've been encrypted to communicate only with each other."

Then he takes out a palm-sized QRYSTAL. "I also have one of these for each of your staff," he says as he gives it to her. "They should take the place of any other phones you may have at the office or at home so all your communications are secure. I will send one of my team on Monday to show you how to operate them."

"Is there anything else?" Kathryn asks.

"No, that covers it. Just be sure that every night the QRYSTALS, documents or anything else related to Erik's case are locked in the safes."

Kathryn receives all of this with a slightly overwhelmed expression.

"Don't worry," Tom says, "it's our job to monitor everything."

As she stares down at the QRYSTALS, I can tell she's not all that reassured. After Kathryn and I imprint our retinal patterns on the biometric locks, they leave.

I browse the hardbounds filling the shelves that cover one wall of Kathryn's tiny living room. Quite a collection, unusual in this day and age. I choose a novel and stretch out on the couch. These are becoming our usual spots. Me on the couch and Kathryn in the chair, her feet propped up on the footstool. Each of us involved in our separate work, rarely talking. But now she's wearing a major frown. Is she having second thoughts about taking this case?

Maybe I can up the ante. *"Radio on. Scan talk channels."* The fifth channel hits pay dirt. *"Stop scan."*

A grating voice blares out its typical rant: "Well, folks, just when you think you've heard it all, something like this comes along. Yep, the most advanced technology known to humankind has been used to bring us a good old-fashioned, nineteenth-century carnival freak show."

Kathryn stops working as the harangue goes on. "Can you picture that, folks? Actually, we don't have any pictures of this monster because he's being kept under wraps—and I certainly hope it's a straightjacket—at the Wheaton enclave south of Seattle."

"He's a jackass!" I spit.

"A *highly-paid* one." She glares at the radio.

The attack goes on. "We have information confirming he's so grotesque, he has to wear a mask." The blood drains from Kathryn's face, but the jerk is only warming up. "What's the world coming to? One of the wealthiest men on the planet owns the technology for time travel, and what does he use it for? To bring a deformed freak who may have committed murders and possibly torture to the present. Is that the best Howard Wheaton could do with his trillions?"

"Radio, off," Kathryn orders, fuming. "How can he get away with that?"

"Happens all the time." Looks like my plan worked. "Erik doesn't deserve it, does he?"

"No. He doesn't." She rubs her temple. "Do you know Mr. Mercier very well?"

"As well as anyone. I was his bodyguard until being reassigned to you. I was also on the rescue team that brought him from the past."

"You were? How did you manage to get him out?"

"It wasn't easy, and we only had the information in Madame Giry's diary to go on. The rescue team went back the day before his execution to do reconnaissance."

"Who else was on the team?" She's switched into attorney mode now.

"Jarrod and Dave. Both served in military special forces. Jarrod's also a civil engineer, so he obtained a current blueprint of the lower levels, and we scouted the area where the Communards set up operations. Dave's a superb tracker and kept us out of the Communard's way. We tracked several to find out where the prisoners were held and verified that Erik hadn't been captured yet."

"So, why were you on the team?"

"We knew Erik would need a doctor."

Her dark eyes widen. *"You're a doctor?"*

"Yes. Specialized in emergency and trauma medicine. I've been in charge of Erik's medical care since he got here." I can see the gears turning and more questions lining up.

"How did you get him out with all the Communards around?"

"It was the middle of the night. We overheard the soldiers talking about the melee Erik had caused and that he was being held separately, next to the guardroom." I stop and consider how much detail she can handle. "We located the guardroom and moved in. Jarrod is fluent in French, so he did all the talking. Told the guards we were sent to get the prisoner. We were dressed as Communards, but they didn't recognize us, so we had a fight on our hands and had to use our tasers. One guy was tough and kept coming at us. Dave had to stun him manually. You know, with his fist."

She doesn't even crack a smile. "Were any of them killed?"

"No, our orders were not to kill anyone if we could avoid it."

"So what happened when you found him?"

"Erik had been dumped on the floor and hadn't been given any medical care. They probably figured if he died, it saved them the trouble of shooting him." She inhales sharply. *Damn, too much detail.* "He was in a lot worse condition than we expected. But you've got to give it to the guy, he still tried to sit up and fight us off. I used a spray anesthesia to knock him out."

She shudders. "How'd you transport him with a broken leg?"

"Oh, I was prepared. I had a nineteenth century-style satchel crammed with modern medical supplies. I bandaged the wounds and used a flex splint on his leg. Even started an IV. We're able to transport two people at a time, so he transported out just as he lay, and I went with him. He'd lost a lot of blood and needed surgery because his leg had a compound fracture."

"Collin gave me his medical records. Those indicate a number of wounds."

"Yeah, he was in bad shape. He had a broken rib and some cracked ones. Lots of contusions and lacerations on his forehead, shoulders and arms. Strangely, his hands came through with only minor bruises. But Erik told me he was on the ground when they used their rifles butts on his leg, so I'm guessing he must've curled up to protect his hands."

"He uses his hands to play music." Kathryn stares thoughtfully at her hands. "He'd protect them at all costs. But the records also indicate he suffered from malnutrition."

"Yeah. He's a tall man, almost six foot five, but when we brought him back, he only weighed one hundred seventy pounds. Lots of people were malnourished or starving because of all the chaos in Paris during the Prussian siege and then the Commune."

"And there were scars on his back?" she presses.

"Yeah, his back is crisscrossed with scars from beatings. The wounds went deep enough to cut to the bone, which is why the scars are still so noticeable."

"That confirms what Madame Giry wrote." She clears her throat. "Ironically, it also gives her information more validity. It appears a number of tests were performed concerning his facial, uh, condition. He was tested for Sturge-Weber syndrome, but that was ruled out."

"Right. Because Erik was underweight we also tested for porphyria. Leroux described Erik as always gravitating to dark environments. People with porphyria tend to be thin and extremely sensitive to light. Those tests were negative too."

"You know," she hesitates, "when I first saw his mask from the side, his eye was in shadow, so I couldn't see it. And he didn't turn enough for me to see his profile. It actually did look like he had no eyes or nose."

"Well, think about it. He prowled the opera house at night, in dark corridors where the only lighting was gaslights or candles. If you saw him only from the side and in dim light, that's the impression you'd get, especially with that black mask."

"So Leroux relied on hearsay and embellished that with creative exaggeration."

"I think you could come to that conclusion just by seeing Erik in person."

"And so will the jury. The uncovered part of his face makes it clear the skeletal description of him isn't accurate. That helps cast doubt on other previously accepted 'facts.'"

"Good point."

"The report says that a hemangioma was also ruled out as the cause of his facial deformity. The final diagnosis was hamartomas with a number of benign growths on one cheek and across the forehead." With a halting voice, she adds, "But what does it mean 'exacerbated by surgery'?"

"The scars were caused by more than hamartomas. To a modern surgeon, it looks like botched surgery. Modern practice is to *not* operate on hamartomas since they may decrease on their own and surgery could cause worse deformity." I consider whether to continue, but she's going to be working with him. She needs to understand the level of trauma he's experienced. "Anesthetics weren't used until 1846. Before then, there was only opium or alcohol, and those caused numerous difficulties, so surgeons operated fast. Precise, meticulous surgery as we know it today simply didn't exist. Erik confirmed that he had numerous large growths on his face. Surgery was decided on when he was five years old—that was in 1842—so he was given alcohol. He was unconscious during surgery, but the surgeon cut deeply, trying to get all the growth. There was so much bleeding, the incisions were cauterized. When he woke up, he was in tremendous pain. The scars healed... badly." Kathryn's face goes ashen.

The medical description I wrote in Erik's records was "profoundly, irreversibly scarred." Most people would call it grotesque. His skin is ravaged and twisted in some places, and so paper-thin in others that his veins and bones can be seen. I keep that to myself.

"Thanks for your help," she says softly, then returns to her work. I catch her brushing away a tear, yet I know she's tough. I've seen her deal head-on with difficult situations in court, and Tom and I were monitoring her meeting with Erik from the hallway. She stood her ground when he had his post-traumatic stress episode. She's got guts. Later, when Dr. Adler asked her if anything happened, she protected Erik and kept it confidential. I think Kathryn did that because of her high sense of honor, but does she fully understand that others might not operate on that level? As Dad used to say, a person's greatest strength can also be their greatest weakness. Her courage and compassion make her the right attorney for Erik, but I'm thinking she needs someone to watch her back.

"Ryan?" She interrupts my thoughts. "I understand why you were Erik's bodyguard. He needed your medical expertise, but why were you assigned to guard me? I'm in perfect health."

"Erik doesn't need a doctor any more, and Collin said you needed someone to keep the reporters from harassing you." Although she nods, she's doesn't buy it and stares out the window, puzzling.

No longer in the mood to read, I turn on the sports channel, but my thoughts keep wandering back to Kathryn's last question. She isn't in any significant danger—Erik's the most likely target. All they told me was Mrs. Wheaton ordered it. I watch Kathryn out the corner of my eye. I've known her for less than a week, but one thing is certain—I don't want anything to happen to her.

16 | CHARGES

Monday, June 11
Seattle

Lexa

"Hi, I'm Kathryn." A friendly voice startles me out of my concentration on Madame Giry's diary. Standing in the doorway, Kathryn takes in my already-cluttered desk. Humor sparks in her large, coffee-brown eyes. "Looks like you've settled in," she says with a smile. "I hope this office is working out for you."

"It's fine. Sorry to be taking over Barb's space."

"Barb's a trooper," she says. "But we've got to hit the ground running on this case. Why don't we grab our lunches and work in my office while we're eating?"

As I walk around the desk, I note that she's quite a bit shorter than me, but her handshake is strong. I like her energy. She's self-assured, but also sincere.

In the break room, Barb's working at her new make-shift desk. When I pop my burger and fries into the microwave, she looks up. "Sorry," I say, wincing, "gotta be distracting, working here."

"I suspect it's going to get worse," she deadpans, then turns to Kathryn. "You've got appointments from two to four this afternoon with several attorneys who applied for the position."

"Do they know the job is only for a few months?"

"Yeah, but jobs are scarce. I set appointments with the three who've done the most trial work. I'm especially impressed with Jake Foster. He worked for the DA and has several years of trial experience—probably the most qualified to step in and help with your caseload. And I've hired the new legal assistant. He starts work tomorrow. The office next door will be ready to move into by then. The rented furnishings arrive today."

"Thanks, Barb," Kathryn says, as she gathers up her salad and iced tea.

Juggling my books, QRYSTAL, food, and coffee, I follow Kathryn to her office, and we settle in at the conference table. I'm starved and dig into the fries as I'm opening the QRYSTAL.

"So how did court go last Friday?" Kathryn asks, wasting no time.

"Where'd you like me to start?" I mumble between bites. "The charges or our client?"

"The charges."

I notice Kathryn puts off discussing our client. "He's charged with the murders of Joseph Buquet, Madame DuPellier, and Philippe, the Count de Chagny. Also with crimes against humanity for torture, which is the ground that the court used to claim jurisdiction. The prosecution obtained the inquest records for Buquet and Madame DuPellier, and the reports of the Examining Magistrate who investigated the count's death. The deaths occurred in August and September of 1870. They also uncovered historical documentation of torture chambers in Persia similar to the one described in Leroux's book. The torturer there wore a mask."

"Leroux's book said the Persian known as the Daroga gave a deposition implicating the Phantom," Kathryn says, munching on her salad. "But weren't his statements disregarded?"

"Yeah. In his report, the Examining Magistrate indicated he'd heard about a man '*living in the shadows of the opera house*' who was purportedly blackmailing the directors, but he didn't think it was worth his attention. He dismissed what the Daroga said. Even referred to him as being '*touched in the head*.' The Magistrate thought Count Philippe's death might have been caused by a fight between the count and Raoul over Christine Daaé. No one was ever charged."

"And Madame DuPellier and Joseph Buquet—was anyone charged with their deaths at that time?" she asks.

"My preliminary research indicates that no charges were ever brought against anyone."

"Then why is our client being charged with them now?"

"Good question. Buquet's body was found in a basement of the opera house. He'd been hanged, but strangely the rope was never found. The inquest concluded that it was a suicide."

"Never found? How could he hang himself and *then* get rid of the rope?"

"Well, the prosecution isn't overlooking that rather significant point either."

"So how does that implicate our client?" She frowns.

"Because Buquet's throat was severed. Hanging doesn't do that. Severing is typical of a garrote, like a Punjab lasso. The prosecution dug up the Communard records about our client's execution. He used a Punjab lasso on a soldier when they captured him."

Kathryn stops eating and pushes her salad aside. "Was the soldier killed?"

"No, but the records confirm our client had a Punjab lasso—not a common weapon."

She winces. "What about Madame DuPellier?"

"Death by chandelier during a performance. Just like in the book."

"Leroux implied the Phantom killed her because she was hired to replace Madame Giry."

"Yeah, the prosecution also claims that was our client's motivation," I reply with a mouthful of burger. "Madame Giry is alleged to be his accomplice since she collected the blackmail from the opera's directors—and he wouldn't want to lose a good accomplice."

"Was there any mention in the inquest about Madame DuPellier being hired as a box attendant? Or was she just a regular audience member?"

"Don't know, but I'll find out. As for Count Philippe, his body was discovered in the underground waterway. He died the same night Christine got kidnapped. An investigation was held because the count had a head injury—looked like he'd been struck, then drowned while he was unconscious."

"So how is our client connected with Count Philippe's death?"

"The count was seen going to the lower levels of the opera house after Christine was kidnapped. Probably trying to find her and Raoul. According to the allegations, our client killed the count when their paths crossed later that night. Buquet was killed the same night. The prosecution alleges Buquet also got in our client's way."

"Buquet? The same night?" Kathryn asks, surprised. "But Leroux wrote that Buquet died some time before Christine's kidnapping."

"I read Buquet's inquest documents. According to those, he died the same night."

Kathryn sips some tea, puzzling. "Why do you think Leroux didn't get the date right?"

"Remember, Leroux researched Erik's life four decades after Erik died. Supposedly, Leroux patched together information from people who'd worked at the Opéra and from Christine's letters, as well as the memoirs of Moncharmin, the Opéra's director. Maybe Leroux only heard about the inquest and never saw the actual report. If so, he just used a little creative license and wrote that Buquet was hanged in the first chapter. Starts the book off with a bang, doesn't it?"

"Definitely." Kathryn's brow crinkles. "But Moncharmin said in his memoirs that Buquet died during the departing directors' farewell party, *not* the night Christine was kidnapped. Moncharmin could've gotten the timing wrong if he wrote his memoirs many years later. Check on that, Lexa. If Moncharmin is wrong on this point, that calls into question other statements he made about the Phantom. And go over the inquest records and the Magistrate's investigation. Follow up any leads or discrepancies. So, what other evidence do they have?"

"Christine's letters may have turned up."

"Really? Do her letters support the charges?"

"Christine wrote that she felt the Phantom committed two of the murders in cold blood."

"What?" She looks up from her notes, startled. "Was that in the allegations?"

"No, the prosecution is still trying to authenticate her letters, so they're not part of the evidence. Yet. But that was on PALnet News today. I suspect someone on the prosecution team leaked it to the press." I fish out another fry. They're really good, seasoned with garlic salt.

"Still, Christine's letters are only hearsay."

"Yes," I agree, "but all of the evidence leads to the same person—our client."

"However, most of it's circumstantial," Kathryn replies, exasperated. "Unless, of course, Christine actually witnessed any of the murders."

"I certainly hope not. Have you been able to get any information out of our client yet?"

"No, our meeting was several days before he was arraigned. Just to introduce us. And I assume you didn't discuss the case with him at the arraignment."

"That's right. I only had enough time to advise him to say nothing. Just deny the charges." I cough to clear the catch in my throat. "I don't think he liked it. At all. He wasn't happy about anything."

"What did he do?"

"He barely spoke to me." I laugh nervously. "You know, it felt like a page out of the book. His eyes bored into me. I couldn't look him in the face. And when he stood to hear the charges, I could feel his anger seething. He hated being in the spotlight, but at least he followed my instructions. By the time the arraignment was over, I was totally rattled."

Kathryn stands and grabs her briefcase. "I've got to go. Got a settlement conference at one. But I'll be back in time for those interviews and the appointment with Mr. Mercier."

I nearly choke on my burger. "*He's* coming here today?"

"Yep. My first conference with him is this afternoon."

I watch as she rushes out the door. I'm sure glad she's the one who'll be interfacing with him. And I wish her luck. She'll need it.

17 | GUARD

Land's End

JARROD

I search the solarium, then head to the Japanese garden. Mrs. Wheaton doesn't allow security cameras in the garden, and if he got anywhere near the fences, the sensors would have picked him up. Don't find him at the koi pond, so I go up the path to the gazebo. Ah! There he is. On the bench and bent over a sketch pad. His back is to me, but without looking up, he asks, "Is it time, Jarrod?"

"Yep. We've gotta leave for the attorney's office." I peer over his shoulder at his drawing. He's sketching eyes—large, dark, and definitely female. When I try to get a better look, he closes the pad and glowers at me. "So, who're you drawing?" I grin, needling him.

"No one," he says, shrugging. "Merely keeping my hand practiced." Irritated, he takes off down the path. At the elevator, George hands Erik his black, kid-leather gloves and the antique cane. During the limo ride Erik keeps fidgeting with the cane's handle. Those eyes he was drawing—I keep wondering if they belong to the legendary Christine.

When we arrive, Lexa Simmons comes out of her office to greet Erik. I notice they both avoid eye contact. After a few awkward moments, another woman comes down the hallway. She gives Erik a welcoming smile. Her dark eyes spark with warmth and humor. For a second, Erik seems disarmed. Then it dawns on me—*the eyes on Erik's sketch pad.*

"Good day, Ms. Copeland," he says formally, "may I introduce Mr. Jarrod Pearce."

I shake her hand. "Erik's bodyguard. Just call me Jarrod." I'd heard the talk among the bodyguards about Copeland's looks. They're right. Then she gives me a smile that would waylay an army. *Hell,* she can call me any name she wants.

"My receptionist has gone for the day," she tells me, "and there are no more appointments, as agreed. My legal assistant, Barb, will return from court soon. Is that a problem?"

"No, but I'll need to lock your deadbolt so I can monitor who's entering."

"That's fine." She smiles up at Erik. "Shall we get started?" Her cool-headedness seems to put him at ease. I can see the relief on Ms. Simmons's face when she returns to her office. *Amazing*—the difference in Erik's attitude toward the two women.

I snap the deadbolt into place and join Ryan and Josh in the sitting area. Ryan pulls out his QRYSTAL and brings up the hologram of Ms. Copeland's office. "What are you doing?" I ask.

"Tom's security team installed a hidden camera in Kathryn's office. She wants her conferences to be confidential. I respect that, so I won't listen in. But I'll be watching."

"So she doesn't know about the camera?"

"Nope." Ryan sets the QRYSTAL on the table between us. The hologram shows Erik standing at the window, staring out. Ms. Copeland's at her desk looking a bit perturbed.

"How's life treating you, Taylor?" I grin over at Josh.

"Could be better. Lexa's into tennis, so we played a few sets Sunday. She beat my butt."

I laugh. "Just 'cause she's a woman and you're a bull rider, doesn't mean she can't whoop you."

"Good to see you taken down a notch or two." Ryan grins, leaning back and stretching.

"But five out of five?" Josh grouches. "That downright sucks. Maybe she's a ringer."

"Don't worry," I chuckle. "Keep playing tennis with her, you'll improve. Might even win a set." Josh snorts and shakes his head. It's a kick to watch him squirm. He's got that Texas bravado in his blood. But anyone who rode Brahma bulls and came out with no more than a couple nasty scars has a lot of guts and dumb luck. Then he joined the Marines. Not much he's afraid of except losing to a woman. I lean back and relax a little. Not much down time around Erik, so it's a luxury to shoot the breeze. "Any exciting stories about your weekend, Ryan?"

"Nope. I went with Kathryn to her Quaker meetinghouse Sunday morning."

"Quaker?" Josh asks. "Like the guy on the oatmeal box? What do they do in church?"

"Mostly meditate," Ryan replies. "Sometimes a person says a prayer or shares a thought."

"You're kidding," Josh snorts. "I'm Baptist. We like music, gotta raise the rafters."

"They may be quiet in church, but they're movers and shakers outside," Ryan replies. "I did some research and found out that Quakers are not only pacifists, they started the antislavery movement and lots of other social movements over the last several hundred years."

"No kidding." Josh lets out a low whistle. "Impressive."

"Yeah," I agree, watching the hologram. Erik's still at the window, and Ms. Copeland's patiently talking to his back. Maybe Dr. Adler and Collin knew what they were doing when they chose her.

Ryan shoots me a knowing look. "How was your weekend with Erik?"

"He was real moody. Still getting over the court appearance. Pulled his disappearing act again on Saturday. Couldn't find him anywhere for hours, then he saunters into dinner like nothing happened. All day yesterday he pounded the hell out of the piano."

"So what else is new?" Josh chortles. "Did you catch the game yesterday, Ryan?" As they start to dissect the game, someone buzzes at the door. Ryan puts the Qrystal in his pocket, and I go unlock the deadbolt and check the woman's ID. It's Barb, and she huffs off to her office, none too happy. I rejoin the guys just as Josh is gloating over a bet he won. But then, Josh is always betting.

Ryan turns the hologram back on. So far Erik hasn't stomped out, and Ms. Copeland hasn't called for help. That's promising. Maybe she'll work some magic and shed some light—not only on the facts of this case, but also those dark places where phantoms hide out. But I'm not placing my bets just yet.

18 | SHADOW

Kathryn

His black, intimidating presence hovers in front of the windows. I stare at his back, wondering if that's all I'll see of him today. "Please make yourself comfortable, Mr. Mercier. Feel free to sit on the couch."

"I prefer to stand." His voice—*the Voice*—fills the room. I was afraid he'd say that. I notice he's still using the cane and shifting his weight. Is his leg hurting, or is he just uncomfortable being here?

"I'd like to clarify something first. Was it *your* decision for me to be your attorney?"

"Yes, it was."

"Was your decision free of coercion?" I press.

"Yes." He faces me, his eyes flaring a deep emerald. "Was *yours*?"

My breath catches. Will I ever get accustomed to his piercing eyes and that mask cutting across his face like a dark lightning bolt? "It was."

"I am edified to hear that," he replies. Do I detect a tinge of approval in his voice?

Then he turns back toward the window. I resign myself to talking to his back. "Do you have any questions about the arraignment?"

"No, what happened is abundantly clear." Then he adds bitterly, "Wheaton posted an ungodly amount of money and will now make certain I go to trial."

"But Mr. Wheaton is also on trial in the public's opinion. As I said before, the Powers, T'ang & Bianchetti Corporation is doing everything it can to discredit him."

"But it is *my head* in the guillotine, *not his*," he snarls.

Appalled, I ask, "Hasn't anyone discussed with you what the sentence might be?"

"No. After the arraignment, the lawyer did not speak with me."

"I'm sorry." *My god, this must have been tormenting him.* "Let me explain. The death sentence is prohibited by international law. It's considered cruel and unusual punishment. Most countries have adopted that standard, and the Criminal Court of the Americas complies."

"How long might the *imprisonment* be then?"

"As little as five years, but possibly more. Possibly a life sentence."

"So," he hisses, "is it not cruel and inhumane to confine a person to a cage? To allow the body to live, but deprive a man of what feeds his soul?" He begins to pace restlessly, like a trapped panther seeking escape. Of all people, he knows what it's like to be caged. In prison, there'd be no piano, no violin, no way to play his music. Now I realize, for him, that would be worse than death. The burden for taking this case just got heavier.

"We'll all work hard to make sure that doesn't happen."

"And if it did, why would you care?" Then he sneers, "Why do you do this work at all?"

"Law is a tool that can help people. I'll do everything I can to help you be acquitted."

"In that venture, I wish you good fortune. I daresay you will need it."

Is that a confession of his guilt? Or a fatalistic attitude? "Do you have any other questions about the arraignment?"

"You mean the charges? No, they are quite clear. What are your plans to refute them?"

"Regarding the allegation of torture in Persia and Turkey, we need to prove you were never there. When you weren't living in Paris, you were only in England or Zurich, correct?"

"Indeed. But how do you prove it?"

"One important piece of evidence is Madame Giry's diary. May I refer to her as Adèle?" He tips his head in approval. "Do you feel the diary is accurate?"

"To the degree Adèle saw or knew what was happening."

Just what is he implying with that highly conditional endorsement? "She personally witnessed you in Paris during 1851 and all the years from the end of 1858 through 1870. It'll be strong proof of your whereabouts during those years. But her diary isn't enough proof for the years you were living in London or Zurich."

"Why would they accept some parts of Adèle's diary as proof and not others?"

"Because when she writes about seeing you in Paris, it's considered to be direct eye witness evidence. Did Adèle ever visit you in London or Zurich?"

"No, of course not."

"Then her diary entries would be based only on her belief about where you were during those years. That's considered hearsay and not generally acceptable as evidence."

"But I wrote letters to her."

"Unfortunately, we don't have those."

"So, how do you propose to prove I was in London and Zurich?"

"I need to know whatever you can tell me about those years—where you lived and worked, and the names of people you knew. We'll use that to track down any tangible evidence that might verify you were there."

He stops and glowers at me. "In other words, you wish to pry into my private life?"

"I don't want to pry. But any fact you share, however insignificant it may seem, could possibly lead us to useful evidence to prove what you did or did *not* do."

"You want evidence to prove I *did not* do something?" he smirks.

"Proving a negative is difficult, but it's exactly the position we're in."

"What of the three murders? Adèle does not say in her diary I committed those."

"That's right, she doesn't. But we need more proof than that. I'll need to go over your relationships with those three people."

"I did not even know the count or the woman in the audience. I never met them."

"There are allegations you had motives for wanting them out of the way. They connect you to Count Philippe because of your relationship with Christine Daaé and Raoul de Chagny. And to the lady in the audience because of Adèle. But Joseph Buquet—did you know him?"

"Indeed, I knew *him* very well," he replies with scathing intensity.

My stomach sinks. At the very least, there was bad blood between the two men. "May I ask some questions about the years when you weren't living in the opera house?"

"That depends on the questions," he huffs.

I decide not to ask him yet about the carnival where he was put on display and beaten. That's too sensitive. I'll have to build trust and a comfort level first. Cautiously, I wade into the questioning. "Was Adèle's account of how you met accurate?"

"Yes."

"Is there anything more you would like to tell me about that?"

"No."

A different tack is clearly needed. "How long did you live in the opera house the first time?"

"From February 1851 until August that year."

"The Paris Opéra at that time was not located in the Garnier, was it?"

"No, the Garnier opera house was still being constructed when I last, uh, *ventured* into it in 1871. For the previous fifty years the Paris Opéra had been located in the Salle Le Peletier. *That* is the opera house which"—he pauses, considering his words—"*I frequented.*"

"Did anyone other than Adèle know you were living there?"

"Of course not. I was in hiding the entire time."

I can envision a frightened boy roaming the dark corners. "Why did you leave?"

"They caught me one night. Luckily they didn't discover I was living there or Adèle's involvement. Because of that incident I felt compelled to leave as soon as possible."

"So you went to London to live with your uncle?"

"Julien Mercier was not my uncle. He was the brother of my guardian."

"Guardian?" The Leroux novel said he was raised by his parents. And Collin told me the father was a count. "So, you weren't raised by your natural parents?"

"No." He seems surprised at my question. "Did you not know?"

"No, I didn't. Who was your guardian?"

"Charles Mercier. He and his wife took me in soon after I was born. My real parents wanted nothing to do with me." He spits out the last words like venom. *So, his being outcast by society mirrored his rejection by his own parents.* "Charles was an architect and masonry contractor in Rouen, but he had died just before I was *indentured* to the carnival. His brother, Julien—also an architect—had moved to London to oversee the construction of St. Mark's Cathedral. I corresponded with Julien, and he offered me a job."

"You traveled alone from Paris to London?"

"Yes," he replies curtly.

"Wouldn't that be a dangerous trip for such a young boy?"

After a pause he almost snarls, "Move on with your questions, mademoiselle."

Mademoiselle? Evidently, I've hit a nerve. As his words appear on my QRYSTAL screen, I highlight his reply and type in my note: *sensitive issue, what happened on that trip?*

"What did you do at St. Mark's?" I ask.

"I was skilled at carving ornamental details in stone pediments, so that was my work."

"Skilled? When did you learn how to carve?"

"When I lived with Charles Mercier. He taught me many things—how to play the piano and violin, and how to carve in stone. He had a workshop in his home where I learned carving. Charles said I had natural talent. Julien knew this and hired me."

That gives me an idea. My client's obviously well read and very articulate. Maybe he had a formal education. There might be school records. "Did you attend school anywhere?"

"*Non*. What school would ever have accepted me?" His voice thunders through the room. "Or do you imagine I had private tutors as if I were the *acknowledged* son of a count?"

I'm speechless. That's exactly what he was—the son of a wealthy family, in fact of the nobility. But that was not how he lived. They discarded him. In frozen silence we stare at each other across the room. His turning on me at our first meeting flashes to mind. What will he do next? "I didn't mean to offend you, Mr. Mercier."

Breathing deeply, he struggles with his emotions but doesn't reply. I'll have to be more cautious with my questions. His wounds are deep and still painful when touched.

We're still in a standoff when Barb sweeps in. She comes to an abrupt halt and quickly assesses the situation—his dark glower and my wariness. "Sorry to interrupt," she says, placing several files on my desk, "but you need to sign these. They've got to be mailed today." As I sign the papers, she asks my client, "Could I bring you a cup of coffee?"

I blink at Barb. She *never* offers to bring coffee to clients. That reminds her of working as a waitress to support herself and her children while she attended college. She hated it. At most she brings me iced tea on occasion. What's she up to?

"Yes," he finally replies. *Score one for Barb.*

"And you, Kathryn?" she asks with an innocent tone. "An iced tea?"

"Yes, thank you." I finish signing the papers and hand them back. Barb's smug expression tells me she might just be managing a coup. I'm going to hear about this.

While Barb's gone, an uneasy truce descends. He begins pacing again. I keep glancing at the clock. It seems to have stopped. Finally, Barb returns, balancing a tray with our drinks and an assortment of paraphernalia. After dropping off my tea, she goes over to the table in front of the couch and deposits the coffee, sugar packets, a bowl of creamers, and napkin with a spoon. She smiles at my pacing client. "Your coffee is ready."

He nods but doesn't move from the window. Apparently, he's not going to sit down until she's gone. I'm learning he requires lots of personal space. Barb takes the hint but flashes me a look of victory. Yep. I'm definitely going to hear about this. When she leaves, he scrutinizes the coffee, and after considering the logistics, yields and sits down. I suppress a *hallelujah.* Barb's a genius. Not only did she get him to sit, he's actually facing me.

He picks up a sugar packet. "Using paper to contain sugar is wasteful." His voice drips with disapproval. "I have observed that about your culture. In mine, sugar is made into cubes and placed in a bowl. Perfectly efficient," he lectures as he tears a neat, straight line across the top of the packet. "Too many things are thrown away, like handkerchiefs. Why make them of paper?"

Leaning back, he takes a sip. I'm relieved he doesn't use the cream. It's in disposable containers. We drink our respective beverages, bracing for the ongoing duel of words. When he sets the cup down, he picks up his ebony cane. His fingers trace its elegant handle, the carved ivory head of a jungle cat with prominently exposed fangs. The cat's eyes are small gemstones of vibrant green—just like its master's.

As I drink my tea, I notice he's wearing a gold band. Leroux mentioned a gold ring on the finger of the skeleton dug up in the Garnier's basement. Could this be the ring? Christine was supposed to return *after* the

Phantom died to place it on his finger and bury him. But he was wearing it when he was executed. And Adèle said in her diary that it was the Communards who buried him. This raises more questions. Many more.

I push the images of graves and skeletons from my mind and begin, "So, you lived with Julien Mercier in London. Did he have a family?"

"He was married and had five children."

"That must have been a very busy household."

"Indeed. But I had the attic room and stayed out of the way."

"Weren't you considered part of the family?"

His thumb rubs across the animal's menacing fangs. "I was *never* part of the family. Julien believed his brother took on the responsibility to raise me. When Charles died, Julien felt he should fulfill that obligation, so he hired me, and I paid him room and board."

His tone is indifferent, as if he's accustomed to relationships based on impersonal circumstances rather than affection. I take a different tack, asking about his work. He relates that he was assigned to carve ornamentation on the pediments. "How long did you work at St. Mark's?"

"Almost a year. Then my work shed was relocated to Julien's backyard."

Relocating the shed seems odd. "Didn't others also carve the pediments?"

"No. That was my job alone." Holding the cane like a rapier, he stabs at the coffee table's leg. Something about moving the shed bothers him.

"Why was the shed moved?"

"Julien felt..." After a long pause, he says, "He felt it would be more convenient."

As those words appear on my screen, I flag them but change the subject. "Are there any documents, payroll records or anything else to prove you were employed at St. Mark's?"

"Workers were paid in cash." A smile quirks at his mouth. "But I did leave my mark. I carved my name and the date on the top edge of a pediment."

"Wouldn't that be covered up when it was installed?"

"No, I carved it on a protruding edge and laid the stone myself one night."

"Could you draw a diagram and show where it was placed?" I walk over and hand him a paper tablet. He draws with quick, deft strokes, marking where the signed piece was set into the church. Definitely a key piece of evidence. "Did you carve your name anywhere else?"

"Yes, on two statues. I carved my initials on their bases." That's probably not enough to connect him to the carvings, but I ask for details anyway. Then he adds, "I also earned money by selling sketches of churches."

This is promising. "Do you recall the name of anyone who purchased your drawings?"

After a pause, he replies, "Most people purchased the pictures without discussion. But I recall two—an old deacon named Peter Thornsby and a well-dressed woman named Eleanor Sewell."

"Good. We'll try to find their descendants. They might have inherited the sketches."

"That would be very unlikely, would it not?"

"We have to follow any lead—the sketches would be antiques that might have been kept."

"Antiques?" The uncovered eyebrow dips low. "I drew those less than twenty years ago."

"It's not easy living in our time, is it?" He begins to say something, but looks away, disconcerted. I quickly ask the next question. "Did you do any drawings other than churches?"

"A portrait of Julien and his wife. It was an anniversary gift." His voice flattens. "They took it with them when they moved to Wye."

"So, Julien moved his family to Wye?"

"No, only the children." He frowns darkly. "Julien and his wife had died of cholera."

Another tragic turn in his life. "I'm sorry. That must've been horrible."

With a deadened voice, he replies, "Indeed."

I shift uneasily. "When did that happen?"

"August 1853, during one of the cholera epidemics in London. Their children sold the family house and bought a farm in Wye. I was told to find other accommodations."

"I see." Only too well. Another abandonment by the Mercier family. His body language tells me he's tensely wound and trying to hide his agitation from dredging up these memories. I clear my throat. "Would you like to call it a day?"

"Yes." Without hesitation, he grabs his gloves, stands and strides to the door. I have to hurry to escort him out. I'm startled when our hands touch as we reach for the doorknob simultaneously. I pull mine back.

"In your world, do gentlemen not open doors for ladies?" he asks darkly.

"Perhaps our world *has* lost the concept of ladies and gentlemen," I respond, flustered.

"Indeed." He opens the door and steps aside. When we get to the waiting room, his bodyguard walks over. Like Ryan, Jarrod has a military bearing, but he studies us with acute curiosity, trying to figure out how the meeting went.

"We'll resume our conference tomorrow," I say, extending my hand. He hesitates. I wonder if he feels as awkward shaking hands with me as I feel having someone open my door. When his hand takes mine, I realize he's not wearing gloves. His fingers are long and thin, but strong. A musician's hands. Then with a formal tip of his head, he's gone.

Back in my office, I glance uneasily at the window where he stood. Did I think that he'd leave some spectral residue? I need to get a grip. Suddenly, near the window a shadow glides over the carpet and climbs the wall. A shiver runs up my spine.

19 | HAUNTED

Land's End

Erik

"How did it go, Erik?"

"Pardon?" I stare down at the golden-crusted crème brûlée.

"How was your meeting today with Ms. Copeland?" Dr. Adler repeats.

I do not respond, feel almost detached as I attempt to eat. The caramelized crust tastes like grit, reminding me of that custard I dug out of the garbage at the opera house. A wave of nausea floods through me. I had brushed the dirt from the surface and devoured it, ignoring the bits of embedded grit. I did not care—had not eaten since escaping from the carnival.

I finish off my wine. It is my third glass but not enough—I still remember. *Does Ms. Copeland have any idea the horrors she has unleashed?* The room begins to feel confining, suffocating. I excuse myself and rush to get out, to get air, but the corridors close in on me like the serpentine tunnels beneath Paris.

At the door to the terrace, a servant asks, "Can I bring you anything?"

"Cognac," I snarl. "A full decanter." I cross the terrace and quickly descend the stairs that trail down the cliff. I seek a secluded place on the lower deck with no prying eyes, although Jarrod will no doubt plague me with his presence. In the farthest corner, I throw myself onto a chair and glare out at the Sound through the wall of windows that form part of this castle's bulwark. The windows have special glass, which even bullets cannot penetrate according to Jarrod. Speaking of the devil, he arrives and pretends to ignore me. And I ignore him.

Distractedly, I watch a sailboat, its virginal sail and hull glistening immaculately as it accepts each oncoming wave. Everything in the Wheatons' world seems clean. But this is not the world I came from. I slept in filth and rat droppings on a closet floor for two days before Adèle found me, shaking with fever. For warmth, I had covered myself in dirty rags, but I was just as filthy, infested with lice. I had not had a proper bath since being indentured to the carnival by my guardian's shrew of a widow. If cleanliness is next to godliness, surely I was in hell during the seemingly endless six months I was displayed in that cage.

The clatter of glasses is disturbing as the servant places a tray on the table between Jarrod and me. As he pours my cognac, I notice the table's intricate mosaic tiles of wildly colored butterflies. *Mon Dieu,* the pattern is gaudy enough to adorn a vanity in Diva Carlotta's dressing room. I snort at the thought and down the glass of cognac, then reach for more.

"You've been hitting that mighty hard all evening. Haven't you had enough?" Jarrod intrudes.

"I am just getting started."

He gives me an appraising look. "Trying to get wasted, huh? Was your meeting with your attorney that awful?"

"No more unpleasant than a tooth gone bad."

"Hit some nerves extracting information, did she?" He chuckles.

"Most painful." She began by prying into how I first came to the opera house. But she doesn't need to know everything—like my stealing food out of the kitchen's garbage pail, just like the rats. Would she want to know the rats trotted over me at night on the way to the kitchen?

The cognac burns down my throat. By the second night I was so delirious with fever, I could not even scavenge for food. I was lying there, awaiting death when Adèle's gentle face hovered above me, her hair braided like a halo around her head. I thought an angel had come for me. She said she would return to help me. Then she vanished, and I felt she was only a creation of my fevered mind. In the next moment, I would be terrified that if she were real, she would betray me and have me put out on the streets. By the time she came back, I was half in this world and half in the next. She supported me the excruciating distance to a cold, musty storage room, to a bed she had made with sheets on the floor. When she helped remove my shirt, my skin felt like it was peeling off because the material had embedded in the bloody gashes on my back. And that iodine she used burned like acid.

Wordlessly, Jarrod and I sip our drinks. The cognac spreads warmth, like the wine Adèle brought me that first night. She steadfastly continued to bring food, dress my wounds, and cool my forehead with a damp cloth. She even tended my baser needs, taking away the chamber pot. But for her care I would have died in the broom closet. As I pour more cognac, I reflect that my body would only have been discovered when someone decided to use the washtub. I laugh darkly.

"What's eating you?" Jarrod asks.

"That woman. She understood nothing."

"Yeah? Like what?"

"Did she think I could saunter about the opera house like a Sunday stroll on the boulevard? I was always in hiding, always in fear of being found out."

"Yeah, but I'll bet that didn't stop you from getting around the opera house, did it?" Jarrod goads. "How old were you?"

"Thirteen," I huff. "What difference does that make?"

"I'll bet you explored every nook and cranny." Then he grins slyly. "Maybe even spied on the dancers?"

"Never!" I snap. *Well, perhaps a little.* "You are quite right though. When I got my strength back, I began to venture out, lurking in the shadows. I learned to be invisible." I wince, recalling how small and frightened I was—more like a mouse than a phantom.

I remember timidly exploring my new world, sneaking from room to room and stumbling upon the workshop. Amazed by the array of tools, I studied each to learn its secrets and divine its use. One night, I made myself a papier-mâché mask like my guardian had taught me, replacing the rag that had been covering the scarred side of my face.

"So what did you find?" Jarrod's voice pulls me back.

"What do you care?" I ask, suspicious.

"Just curious about what a boy gets into in an opera house."

I take another swallow of the golden liquid, thinking back. "Well, I came across a cavernous storage room with rows upon rows of costumes—outlandish styles and exquisite fabrics beyond anything I had ever seen. Half of the room was filled with huge flats covered in exotic scenes. There were piles of swords, helmets, and all manner of theatrical trappings. A veritable treasure trove." With a slightly inebriated chuckle, I confess, "I felt like a pirate venturing into foreign lands. Found a scimitar and fought imaginary battles with ghostly soldiers beneath Roman pillars. Even climbed atop an elephant, a magnificent beast made of wood."

"Was that when you came across the trapdoors?" he asks.

"Ah, yes, I discovered the trapdoors beneath the stage and all the clever passageways throughout the building." *They were wondrous*, but I refrain from admitting that they became my pirate's caves, and that I learned the secrets of every hidden space.

"So maybe you have some good memories of your time in the opera house."

I sigh, recognizing the truth of it. "Yes, the best of my childhood. Then I kept hearing siren-like voices. They lured me out of the darkness. One night before a performance, I slipped into a private box and watched the performance from my hiding place." *Mon Dieu,* I will never forget the voices, how they soared above the orchestra and echoed off the domed ceiling. And the gaslights made the dancers luminous, like apparitions. I can still picture the ballet rats whirling across the stage, their skirts floating above long, beguiling legs.

"Sneaking in to watch the opera was pretty risky, wasn't it?" Jarrod asks, scrutinizing me.

"Oh, I became quite skillful." Indeed, I rarely missed a performance. Each was a living spectacle with dance as its heart and glorious singing its soul. That was when the power of music bewitched me, became a passion, a need as strong as that for food and sleep.

"So why'd you leave all that?"

"A guard discovered me one night and threw me out. He thought I had snuck in from the streets." I laugh wryly. "I limped for a week from the force of his boot on my backside. But that was a warning. If they had discovered I was living there and connected me with Adèle, we would both have been thrown out into the streets. So I wrote to Julien, my guardian's brother who lived in London. He offered me a job and a room. The problem was, train and boat fares required funds, and I had none. Adèle offered to loan me money, but I refused, so we argued on the roof of the opera house. She may be gentle-natured, but she has the determination of a diva. She gave me the money." I do not mention that she also handed me a package that contained shirts, trousers, and shoes, so that I would be decently attired in public. I was overcome, speechless.

I swish the cognac in my glass, recalling the last memories of the Paris Opéra. Those I will share with no one—how the night before I left, I snuck in to see Meyerbeer's *Robert le Diable*. Hidden behind the drapes of Box Five, I watched as Bertram, the devil himself, tempted his own son, Duke Robert. Succumbing to Bertram's temptations, Robert failed to win the hand of Isabella, his love. But Robert had a human angel helping him, his foster-sister, Alice. During Alice's aria, I spotted Adèle tending patrons across the theatre. Torn by the mercurial emotions of a boy on the brink of manhood, I realized I would be leaving her, and I did not want to.

I remember getting caught up in Robert's desire to unite with Isabella. I watched breathless as nuns who had broken their vows emerged from graves to seduce Robert. They cast off their habits and skimmed across the stage, their legs exposed under gauzy skirts. Despite their allures, Robert resisted and went to Isabella's chamber. When she begged him not to kidnap her, Robert gave in to her pleas and left without her. I felt incensed that his love for her was denied. I take a gulp of cognac. Was that a premonition of my own fate?

But Robert's story was not yet over. When midnight arrived, the devil returned to the netherworld, having lost his battle for Robert's soul. In a final crescendo of music, the cathedral doors opened and Isabella stood radiant in her bridal gown, waiting for Robert. I was spellbound. Then the curtain closed, and I went numb with dread. I was leaving the Opéra and Adèle, not knowing if I would ever return.

Jarrod interrupts my reflections. "Traveling to London had to be an adventure."

"Indeed." *Ms.* Copeland called it a dangerous trip. She was right. Had I known what lay ahead, would I have gone? Yet, the paradox is unavoidable. Had I never left the opera house, I would not have found the opportunities to master my art. "At Calais, I boarded a steamer to England. The boat tossed like a top on the Channel, so I spent the entire trip at the railing, emptying the contents of my stomach. When I disembarked at Dover, I pitched side to side like a drunken sailor all the way to the boat I boarded for London."

Jarrod laughs. "So…London. What was it like?"

"Overwhelming. Coming up the Thames, everything seemed bigger than Paris—the city, the bridges, and the sailing ships." I swallow hard. "And more frightening." I had spotted children dressed in no more than rags, wading in the muck at the river's edge. An old man told me they were mudlarks who scavenged for discarded items deposited by the currents. I had watched the mudlarks, fearing that their fate would become my own if Julien did not accept me. I pull myself back and realize Jarrod is staring at me.

"Did Julien meet you at the dock?"

"No, he had sent directions to his home. I hurried through the docks and got to the city as fast as my legs could carry me." The buildings were grand, and the carriages and horse teams impressive, but poverty was everywhere. Ragpickers pushed carts with every manner of discarded rags, and pure-finders gathered dog feces to sell to tanners.

I gaze across the Sound. In the twilight, the trees are turning into shadows, engulfing houses in darkness. Only pinpricks of light betray human habitation. It was also nightfall that first day on my long trek through London, and the buildings towered menacingly around me like hulking monsters. "I had not eaten all day," I explain, "and there were lights coming from a corner pub, so I went in." It occurs to me I was probably seeking refuge as much as food. I had to show the barmaid my coins before she brought me some watery soup with beans and limp vegetables. At least the bread was fresh and hot. "Since the pub served only beer, I had my first pint—choked it down, wishing it were wine and that I were back in France."

Ms. Copeland and her damn prying. The memories keep escaping from that prison where I keep them safely locked away. When I took my coins out to pay, I noticed a man at the bar watching me, his face tanned like leather. I was accustomed to people staring, but he sneered at me, fueling an urgency to seek the safety of Julien's home. Then he followed me out. Panicked, I ran down the street, stealing glances over my shoulder. He kept following.

My boots pound on the sidewalk as I slip into an alleyway, trying to disappear into the shadows. My hands shake, fumbling at the knot cinching my knapsack. The knife...where's the knife? My hand searches frantically. There! I slip it into my belt, then seize the Punjab lasso from my coat. My heart pumps in terror as the man turns into the alleyway. I stay frozen in the deep shadows and hold my breath. He almost passes by, but his squinting eyes spot me. He flails out and his hand knocks off my mask. "You little devil," he snarls when he sees my face, then he lunges at me. The lasso flies from my fingers and deftly snakes around his throat.

The world goes blank. Then I find myself kneeling beside his crumpled, motionless body. My mask lies on the ground. My hand picks it up. Numbly, dirt is shaken off and the mask returned to my face. I snatch a glance in all directions. The alleyway is empty. Run! Into the shroud of night. Then a streetlamp casts faint light on my hands. They drip with red. I stop at a public fountain and scrub away the crimson gore. My heart still pounds in my ears. I flee, always looking back, always terrified of what may be following.

"Erik?"

I grab for my mask and strike out at the voice.

"Whoa, are you all right?" *Jarrod's voice.* "You just called out."

"It was nothing," I state as his face begins to materialize.

Jarrod stands in front of me, peering down. "You were somewhere, but I don't think it was here. You want to talk about it?"

"*Non. Talking* is not what I need." I swig more of the fiery liquid, but it does not squelch the memories. I ran for an hour, hearing footsteps behind me, seeing shadows, fearing it was the police, or even more horrifying, the man's specter seeking revenge. Ms. Copeland said she wanted to know the truth about me. I have never told anyone about my encounter in that loathsome alley. Would she want to know *that* truth?

When I arrived at Julien's home, he greeted me formally and his wife asked if my journey had been pleasant. All the while their children gawked at me. I told them what they wanted to hear—that all went well. But one person suspected I committed some vile deed. Julien's eldest daughter, Yvette, showed me to my room in the loft. When I put down my knapsack, she gasped. In the darkness, I had not seen the crimson splatter on my bag. I made up a story about helping a dog that was hit by a carriage. Yvette's eyes told me she did not believe me. Thereafter she never trusted me, and because of her, the other children always shunned me.

I opened my bag that night and found the Punjab lasso lying on top, coiled like a sleeping serpent, but I could not recall putting it there. I hid it under my mattress, then fell on the bed, entirely spent. Staring at the ceiling, I tried to recollect what happened, but those moments are a black abyss. I have never been able to remember.

I reach again for my goblet. Flickering light from a nearby lantern reflects off the table's butterflies, shifting their colors. "Shouldn't you take it easy?" Jarrod asks.

He is beginning to annoy me. "*Easy* is not my way," I retort.

"So I've noticed," he says with a wry grin. "You were telling about moving to London. How long were you there?"

"Five years."

"Is that when you learned English?"

"Indeed," I reply, relieved to talk of mundane recollections. "Julien was a Freemason and had a large collection of books. I spent my days working at St. Mark's and nights reading Balzac, Hugo, Donne, Locke, even Newton, in my loft room. And I devoured the writings of Shakespeare. That's how I taught myself English. *Ms.* Copeland thought I had a formal education." I shake my head in disgust. "*Absurd.* Who would have paid for such a luxury? Half my earnings went to Julien for room and board and the other half was saved to repay Adèle." But nature intervened. Although Julien's wife was not the tidiest of housekeepers, she excelled at cooking. Her rich soups, roasted meats, and breads resulted in my body growing in every direction. By November, my savings had to be spent on clothing and shoes. I remember going to the East End, to a shop where immigrants sewed ready-made clothing for the working class. The shirts and trousers were ill fitting but inexpensive, and I purchased a threadbare coat and gloves to keep my hands warm when I carved.

But I felt guilty about spending the money set aside to repay Adèle, especially when I received a birthday card from her in mid-November. She even sent a cross-shaped bookmark crocheted by her own hands and a letter filled with gossip about the Opéra. I had not written her since arriving in London, yet she had sent me gifts for my birthday. Overcome, I held them in reverence. On that day, Adèle became my family.

"Didn't you start drawing too?" Jarrod asks. "That's mentioned in the diary."

"Yes. I wished to send Adèle a gift for Christmas but had few funds. So, I purchased some linen paper and chalks. I taught myself the techniques of foreshortening and shading, then drew Adèle's portrait and sent it to her." She put it in a garishly carved wooden frame and always displays it on her dresser.

And Adèle's letters aroused an old longing in me. I had food, clothing, and a roof over my head, but the things I craved most were missing—the excitement of the Opéra, the splendor of drama and dance, and most of all, music. My craving for those gnawed at me. I was desperate to find a way to bring music back into my life, and I came up with a plan.

"Drawing Adèle's portrait gave me an idea," I admit, feeling strangely gregarious. "That winter, I sketched each house in the neighborhood, developing my technique. On the first Sunday of spring, I set out for St. John's Wood and found a stately church. I was a curious sight—a boy wearing a mask and drawing a church. An elderly deacon sat down beside me and watched as I sketched. Then he purchased my drawing, exactly as I had intended." Each Sunday I sat in front of a church, never failing to sell my handiwork and adding more money to my coffer.

But the undertow was always there, waiting to pull me down. Taking another gulp of cognac, I remember when Julien introduced me at St. Mark's, how the other workers stared at my mask. One man demanded to know what it covered. Julien told him it was none of his business, and if I tended to mine, nothing else mattered. Then he assigned me to work alone in the carving shed. As for the workmen, they kept their distance, at least for a time.

Why did Ms. Copeland have to ask about the shed—why it was moved from St. Mark's? *That nightmare returns, engulfs me. The sun is beating down from a cloudless sky. The workmen grumble and want to go home early. I leave the carving shed to get a drink. No one speaks as I fill my cup at the water barrel. When I turn around, I walk straight into a man standing behind me and spill water all over him.*

Big and barrel-chested, he sneers, "A mite clumsy, aren't ya, lad?"

"I am sorry, monsieur." His clothing is filthy, reeking of sweat. The thought occurs to me some water might do him good, but I merely reply, "I did not know you were there."

He pokes my shoulder with his thick, grimy thumb. "I was standin' right behind and ya can't see me? Are ya blind?"

"No, monsieur. I said I was sorry."

"Maybe ya could see better if ya didn't wear that ugly thing on yer face."

Instantly, I know his intention and dodge around him, running furiously back to my shed. There is no lock on the door, so I brace my body against it. I dig in my heels, but the battering shoves against the door knock me down. They rush in and pin me to the ground.

The man I supposedly offended stands over me. "Let's get rid of this thing on yer face." A spray of saliva hits me along with his words. "So ya don't go around, bumpin' into us."

I scream for him not to do it. The men laugh as he tears off my mask, but their laughter stops abruptly. Releasing me as if my flesh had turned into burning sulfur, they gawk at my naked face. Horrified, they back out of the shed. I lie on the ground, not crying. Once again I cram my feelings down and bury them in that dark cavern somewhere in my soul, along with the horror of that man in the nightmarish alley and the humiliation of being displayed like an animal in a cage.

I blink and gaze around. Jarrod quickly looks away, caught in the act of spying. When I pick up my glass, the garish mosaic butterflies flutter slightly. I lied to Ms. Copeland. The shed was not moved for convenience. Julien was furious about the incident and blamed me as much as the other men. He did not want it to happen again, so he had the shed moved to his yard. Perhaps it was not a complete lie. The shed was moved for convenience—Julien's convenience. For me, it was miserable. There were no shade trees, and the tin roof radiated the heat of the sun like an oven. I began work at daybreak and finished by mid-afternoon, spending as much time as possible in my loft room where the skylight let in cool breezes.

Jarrod coughs, breaking into my thoughts. "You were talking about sketching churches," he says. "How did that work out?"

"I gained a certain notoriety, so more buyers came to bid on my artwork, driving up the price." I try to appease Jarrod's curiosity without disclosing too much. Actually, I was quite successful. By fall, I was able to send a bill of exchange to Adèle and repay her. That year for my fifteenth birthday, Adèle sent me a book of poetry. For Christmas, I sent her the sketch of a church, and she wrote back that she hoped someday I would send a self-portrait.

"By the next spring, I required new clothing. For the first time, I went to a tailor shop and purchased a linen shirt, stock, and proper jacket. That proved most profitable. My finer attire attracted more affluent clients and higher fees."

"Is that when you started wearing black clothes?" Jarrod asks, overly curious.

"No," I reply bluntly. "That was Herr Wagner's idea."

"Wagner, *the composer Wagner*, gave you advice on what to wear?" Jarrod asks.

"Indeed." I recall well what he said—that wearing all black would be intimidating and keep at bay people's questions about my mask. He was right, but that kept the people distant as well. I turn away from Jarrod, have had quite enough of his invasive questions—his and *Ms.*

Copeland's. So much happened that year, so much more than a change of attire. Things that can come back to haunt. In April, St. Mark's nave was consecrated. My work there ended, so Julien put me to work carving the statue of an angel for a Catholic church.

That angel. I pour more cognac, spilling some on those annoying butterflies. Ms. Copeland said the deaths of Julien and his wife must have been horrible. *Horrible* does not begin to describe dying of cholera. That day comes back to me as if it were yesterday. The sun was beating down on my shed's tin roof, raising the temperature to miserable levels. I was chiseling the wings on the angel statue. White dust would cake my forehead and mix with sweat, working its way under my mask. I was tired and hungry and waiting to be called for lunch.

That's when I heard Bobby's cries. The little boy stood at the shed's door and yelled that something was wrong with their mother. I raced into the house and found her on the kitchen floor, vomiting and violently ill. Yvette and I carried her upstairs to her bedroom. The poor woman had copious bouts of diarrhea and was thirsty, but when we gave her water, she could not keep it down. Then Julien was brought home, so ill that his workmen had to carry him. When I realized he had the same symptoms, my blood ran cold. We had heard of a cholera outbreak. Yvette was frantic, so I instructed the men to carry Julien up to my room to tend him myself.

When the doctor finally arrived, he confirmed our worst fears—cholera. He administered opium and ordered us to stop giving them water. I will never forget how Julien's skin began to turn cold, almost bluish. I was appalled when the doctor took out castor oil. The gypsy woman at the carnival would give castor oil as a purgative, so I challenged the doctor. He assured me that was prescribed for cholera and administered it over my objections. I took care of Julien while the castor oil painfully flushed additional fluids from his body and his condition worsened.

Shortly after nightfall, Madame Mercier sighed her last, shallow breath. The children's wailing filled the house, while hour after hour Yvette and I tended Julien. His eyes remained aware throughout the ordeal, conscious of his wife's death and that he would soon join her. *His eyes haunt me still.* By the time the clock chimed midnight, his lips had turned ghastly blue. I sat next to him, holding his hand. Without any final words, Julien closed his eyes. Moments later, his pulse stopped. Gently, I placed his hand back on his chest. I wanted to cry, but I was beyond tears. Despite our exhaustion, none of us could eat or sleep.

Throughout the night, we scrubbed the beds and floors, then washed the linens and our soiled clothing.

The next morning, we dressed Julien and his wife in their Sunday attire, then Yvette went to the undertaker to order two caskets. The deliveryman deposited them on the front stoop. Everyone believed that cholera spread through miasmas in the air, so no one wanted to get too close to the house of death. After we placed Julien and his wife in the black velvet-lined caskets, side by side in the parlor, the children would not stop crying. I held the two youngest while Yvette comforted the older ones. By evening, flowers and baskets of food were left on our doorstep by the neighbors. I set out soup and bread for the children, but the sight of food sickened me, and I could not eat. When I went to my room that night, the stench of dying hung in the air. I threw open my windows and looked out at the night sky. As ever, the stars looked down dispassionately.

The next day, the undertaker and his assistant bravely entered our parlor and helped carry the caskets to the hearse. We jostled in the suffocating carriage to the graveyard where the minister from St. Mark's waited beside the newly dug graves. As the caskets were lowered, it occurred to me the couple was being laid to rest in foreign soil instead of their native France. The children sobbed, but for me, no tears came. I committed everything I had been through those two horrific days to that deep, bottomless pit.

Numbly, I look at the night sky over the Sound. The stars still look down on me with indifference.

I had been carving an angel when Bobby came to get me. In my room the night of the funeral, I wondered whether the angel would watch over the children and me, perhaps sparing us. Or was it an omen that even the angels would yet abandon us to the unrelenting, merciless disease?

20 | ANGELS

ERIK

"I wonder if angels really exist?" The words pour out before my mind filters them.

"What?" Jarrod jerks his head around and gives me a quizzical look. "Did you just ask *me* about *angels?* If they exist?"

"Apparently, I was foolish enough to pose such a question."

He chuckles. "Well, people have been asking that for a long time. No one's proved it one way or the other. Guess I'd weigh in on the side of belief and say, yeah, there are angels."

"Belief?" I scoff. *"That* I can accept. In fact, right now, I *believe* I will have more cognac." As I refill my glass, Jarrod studies me, his curiosity not well masked.

Maybe I *should* believe in angels. Were they watching over us when Julien and his wife died? We passed the next days in terror that we harbored the disease and it would strike again. Miraculously, it did not.

A week after the funeral, a worker from St. Mark's came to offer his condolences. He twisted a hat in his hands as he recalled seeing Julien and his wife at a wedding the day before they came down with cholera. I asked if anyone else at the wedding had contracted the disease. Five people, he said, and three had died. The groom survived, but his bride had not. The groom was one of those who held me down when my mask was torn off. The man's fearful eyes kept darting toward me as he spoke with Yvette, then he took his hasty leave.

So there it was. The ceremony was south of the Thames, where cholera was the worst. Julien's children had not gone to the wedding. Perhaps angels were watching over them after all.

Baskets of food kept appearing on our doorstep, and I tried to help by giving Yvette my fee from carving the angel. One evening I came in to dinner after an exhausting day of carving. While I washed in the kitchen basin, I could feel Yvette glaring at my back. As I dried my hands, I turned to face her. She said nothing, but her eyes coldly condemned me as the devil who damned their family.

Then more bad news overtook us. Yvette was informed that Julien's savings would not be sufficient. She decided to sell the house and purchase a small farm outside London that could support them. By October, Yvette and the children had departed in hired carts, piled haphazardly with the residue of their lives. Never heard from any of them again.

My goblet is empty, yet I am still conscious, still remembering. I resolve to try harder. As I reach for the decanter, I notice those aggravating butterflies are now flitting about.

Then, Tom arrives—also uninvited. "What's up?" he asks. "What're you drinking?"

"Cognac for Erik and orange juice for me," Jarrod replies. "A real high-class party."

"Gotta fix that." Tom pulls out that irritating device and makes a call. "Send down some beer. Throw in some chips and salsa." He makes another call. "Hank, cover us from the upper terrace."

The server arrives with beer. He also deposits a bowl of reddish sauce and a basket with what must be chips. Disturbingly, they are dark blue. Tom uses one to scoop up the sauce.

"Try some," he says with a challenging grin.

With misgivings, I immerse a blue-black chip into the lumpy sauce. When I bite down, it crunches. I bolt forward in the chair. My mouth burns like I just bit a hot coal. Gulping some cognac, I try to put out the fire. "*Merde,* are you trying to poison me?"

"Nah, that's the way it's supposed to be." Jarrod chuckles. "Salsa has chilies."

"Chilly? That is the hottest thing I ever tasted."

Tom laughs. "Chili is a hot pepper. You're right, it gives the salsa a kick."

"Kick? That was a wallop." I drink more cognac, but that further inflames my torched mouth. My eyes begin to water. I wipe my uncovered eye but cannot reach the one beneath the mask.

"Take your mask off if you need to," Jarrod says. "We don't care."

I glance at him, shocked by his suggestion. "That will not be necessary," I snap.

"Do you always wear it?" Tom asks offhandedly.

"Not at night."

"Looks like it would irritate your skin." Jarrod squints at me, examining my mask.

I shift uncomfortably. I have never discussed my mask before. "A little," I reply.

"Have you always had to deal with it irritating your face?" Tom asks.

"No, when I was young, the masks were papier-mâché. Those did not bother me."

"Why'd you stop using papier-mâché, then?" Jarrod presses.

"It was not durable." The cognac has definitely loosened my tongue.

"Were your masks always black?" Tom asks.

I shake my head.

"So why did you start wearing black ones?"

"Herr Wagner recommended it."

"*The* Wagner?" Tom asks.

"Yes." Why does everyone use *the* in front of Wagner's name?

Jarrod examines me quizzically. "I'll bet women notice that black mask."

I glare at him and do not reply, so Jarrod and Tom change the subject from masks to mademoiselles. They argue about the male endowments which entice women. I scoff. If one wears a mask, women are not interested. *Ever.*

Unbidden, her face floats in front of me—the landlady's daughter in Zurich. The cognac must have conjured her. Long, blonde curls frame her delicate face. Her graceful body and engaging smile mesmerized me. She seemed to notice me as well. But on that day, that cursed day, I was in bed with a head cold. My mask lay on the table. She entered my room to bring clean linens and saw my face. *She screamed.* Her mother was blunt. Told me not to go near her daughter and to leave. I swore never again to expose myself to ridicule or rejection. But I was wrong. My gaze falls on the gold ring. There *was* Christine.

I smash one of the darting butterflies with my goblet. Placing my feet squarely under me, I stand, taking care not to wobble.

"You're leaving already?" Tom asks, too loudly.

"Yesh." Must get to my room. On my own volition. *"Messhieurs, bonne nuit."*

My legs must not betray my condition. Stairs seem endless. Steadily—must walk steadily across upper terrace—past servant at the door. Beneath my feet, floors ripple in waves. Finally reach my sanctuary. Lock door. Throw off jacket. Fall onto bed.

Rolling onto my back, I pull off the mask and study it. The vacant eye socket peers back, jeering. With all my might, throw it against the mirror. It cracks. I grimace.

Through the skylight, blackness of night peers down at me. Dots of light move in dizzying circles. Then I see her large, dark eyes. So deep. *They pierce my soul. "Ses yeux, ses beaux yeux."* Blessed oblivion descends as the words slip out—*"Mademoiselle Copeland."*

21 | SPECTER

Tuesday, June 12
Seattle

KATHRYN

Barb accosts me in the hallway outside the lunchroom to give me papers. She's in a grump. I can relate. When I go in my office, I glance at the window, where *he* stood yesterday.

"Checking for ghosts, Kathryn?" Lexa grins, but as I join her at the conference table, the grin dissolves. "Speaking of our client, how'd the meeting go?"

"Slow. I have to extract everything a piece at a time. It's like playing chess."

"Bet he's a master at chess too. So, you think he's withholding information?"

"Definitely. He keeps his answers brief. Once he avoided my question, but his reaction told me something happened. Something traumatic."

"Why can't we use time travel and go back to the 1800s?" Her tone is hopeful. "We could just film his life. Show that to the jury."

"Great idea. But filmmakers can create any historical setting or any effect. Since the Wheatons have the wealth to afford that, anything we film would be challenged as suspect and excluded as evidence. There's no way to verify such a film is authentic. So we have to rely on old-fashioned legal methods and find tangible evidence to prove where he lived and what he did."

After we finish going over my notes from the meeting, Lexa asks, "Didn't you discuss Christine with him?"

"No, I didn't bring her up at all. I'll need to establish trust first. It takes time to wade into subjects that are emotionally charged."

"Yeah," she says, "good idea."

"But speaking of Christine, there is something I noticed yesterday that's been bothering me. Do you remember the gold ring mentioned in the book?"

"Sure. Leroux said the Phantom gave a gold ring to Christine."

"It's mentioned again on the last page." I open the book to the passage. "This is where the narrator says he recognized the skeleton buried under the Garnier as Erik's: *'I recognized him...by the gold ring he wore. No doubt Christine Daaé had come down and slipped the ring on his finger before burying him, as she had promised to do.'*" Closing the book, I look over at the window where he stood. "Our client is wearing a gold ring on his right hand."

"In France the engagement ring is traditionally worn on the right hand."

"So, you think he's wearing an engagement ring. Maybe her engagement ring?"

"It's a distinct possibility."

"But he was wearing it when the Communards executed him, so Christine didn't have the ring in her possession and didn't go back to put it on his body. And we know from the diary she didn't bury him. Now I'm wondering if he ever gave it to her."

"Or did he give it to her and she'd already returned it?" Lexa counters.

"There's also an interesting discrepancy between the two passages about the body. The one at the beginning of the book doesn't mention a ring being found on the remains, but the ending passage does. And something else bothers me. Why was the ring still on the body? When Adèle identified him, why didn't she notice it?"

"For that matter, why didn't the Communards steal it before they buried him?" Lexa's mouth puckers up, perplexed. "You know, from what I can tell by the references to the performers and operas, it appears Leroux set *his* story around 1880 or 1881. That's almost ten years after the Commune, so Leroux couldn't write that Mercier was a victim of the Communards. Leroux had to devise other ways for the body to be buried with the ring."

"Having Christine return to put the ring on the body certainly ended the book with a poignant twist. I have a feeling that whatever the truth is, there's an intriguing story behind that gold ring."

"That's not the only one. The book is a mixed bag of references and dates." Lexa lets out a sigh of frustration. "Leroux was an international reporter for *Le Matin* from 1894 to 1906 and traveled throughout Europe and Asia. Some elements of the story could have come from what he learned on his travels. He wrote that Erik used a Punjab lasso. A sect of assassins in India called the Thugees used such methods, but that cult was put out of business by the British in the 1830s."

"But the Communard report said Erik used a Punjab lasso, so that wasn't Leroux's imagination."

"True enough, but other references in the book are a lot more tenuous. Leroux said Erik was in Persia during a war between Afghanistan and Persia, but that would have been in 1856, and Madame Giry's diary indicates he was in Zurich then. And supposedly, Erik learned some of his techniques from Vietnamese pirates. But Vietnam was a French colony after 1888, and most likely Leroux got his ideas about the pirates when he traveled there."

"Leroux mentioned a fair at Nizhny Novgorod. Did you check that?" I ask.

"Yep, that was the trade center of Russia and famous for its annual fair throughout the 1800s. Leroux also traveled in Russia and was there for the 1905 revolution. It seems to me that he drew on his experiences as a reporter to spice up the story. For example, the book says Raoul was supposed to be going on a military expedition to the poles, but those mostly happened decades later. Leroux famously got an exclusive interview with the captain returning from an Antarctic expedition in 1904. So, the historical dates and references are all over the place, some way before the 1881 setting for the story, and others a decade or more later. Leroux even referenced some operas in his story which did not exist until many years later."

"Well, those discrepancies support our position that the book does not accurately represent Erik's life." I check the time. "I have to be in court in half an hour. Could you go over my notes from the meeting and check for discrepancies? Check whether the dates he said he worked on St. Mark's correspond with the dates of its construction. And find out anything you can about Julien Mercier. Then contact St. Mark's and see if they can verify whether our client's name is carved on that pediment."

"I'll also try to track down the drawings," Lexa replies, "but not the statues. He only carved initials on them, so they wouldn't be adequate evidence."

Grabbing my briefcase, I hurry to court with my shadow in tow. Again Ryan drives, and I grudgingly admit his chauffeuring gives me extra time to work on my cases. The extra security may be prudent, but there are always raised eyebrows and whispered comments when we walk down the courthouse hallways. At least when the trial's over, Ryan will move on, and I'll get my life back.

The judge recesses the hearing just before noon. I'm looking forward to a relaxing lunch, but when I walk back to Ryan, he says, "Check your messages. We need to go to your office."

As we're going down to the garage, I check Collin's message first: "Will meet at your office at noon. Hell just broke loose." Lexa's message says a motion was delivered from the prosecutor's office, and it's a major curve ball. She attached the motion, so I'll read it while we're driving. Barb informs me Collin has arrived. *So much for a relaxing lunch.*

When we pull out of the parking lot, we're surrounded on all sides by reporters. "What do you think about bringing witnesses from the past to testify?" one calls out. Another yells, "Is the Phantom worried about what they'll say on the witness stand?"

Can't believe what I'm hearing. I pull out my Qrystal and read the motion. "Incredible! Ryan, they're seeking a court order for Mr. Wheaton to use time travel to bring Christine Daaé and three others to testify."

"Oh, I can believe it. The PTB will do anything to win this case." He speeds up, deftly weaving around crazy mid-day traffic.

Lexa and Collin are already waiting in my office. Collin is sitting on the couch, smoking his pipe and puffing out a cloud that settles over the room.

"Have you seen the motion?" he growls.

"Yes, I've read it. Is that possible? Can the witnesses be brought safely to the present?"

"Been discussing tha' with Howard and the scientists at the lab. Erik's transport went without any hitches, so technically it's doable. But we don't *want* to do it."

"What are the objections?" I ask, but I've got a pretty good idea.

"First, when they're brought here, they'll see the future. As we know from Erik's reaction, that's a culture shock and takes some adjusting. Secondly, returnin' is also a problem. They'll remember the present and blabber about it. We canno' have that."

"But even if they told someone, who'd believe them?"

Lexa shifts uncomfortably, and Collin avoids my gaze. "Trust me. There'd be a problem," he states flatly. "You're t' oppose the motion."

Trust him? The more he talks, the *less* I'm able to. Where's the man Anne and I used to know—the prankster with a contagious love of life? It's like his body's been kidnapped and someone devious has taken over.

"All right. Lexa, would you please gather all the information about the problems and draft the response with our objections." I give Collin a curt smile. "If you'll excuse me, I have to get back to court."

Ryan barely gets me to court in time. The testimony and oral arguments take longer than anticipated. By the time the case has been submitted to the judge and court adjourns, it's almost four.

Although Ryan pushes the speed limit, I'm ten minutes late for my appointment with Mr. Mercier. Eileen has already left for the day, and Barb is at the courthouse. Lexa comes out of her office to flag some additional information she wants me to cover.

Then Jarrod walks over from the waiting area. "I need to give you a little heads up. Erik heard about the witnesses being brought from the past. He's been in a black mood ever since."

I've been psyching myself up all day for this meeting. Now his bodyguard says that my client with the black clothing and mask has an attitude to match. I hate Collin. And I've decided to never forgive him for bringing me into this. "Thanks for the warning. I'll tread lightly."

"Good luck," he tosses back.

At the door of my office, I take a deep breath, bracing myself. When I enter, I gaze over toward the window. He's not there. I glance at the couch—empty. I look around the office, but he's not here. Are they playing some prank? I go back to the front office. "Jarrod, I thought you brought Mr. Mercier for an appointment."

"I did. He's in your office."

"No, he's not." The men are a blur as they sprint past me. Hearing the ruckus, Lexa comes out into the hallway. Together, we rush to my office and watch as Ryan and Josh search in vain to find how he escaped. I shudder. Has he actually vanished?

Jarrod checks his Qrystal. "He's still in the building." His words are clipped and fast. "On this floor, sixty feet northeast of us." Then he touches the screen. "Two other people within ten feet of him." Grimly he adds, "Could be a hostage situation."

The men race past Lexa and me. We stand frozen, staring at each other.

22 | SNARED

ERIK

The door slams hard, ricocheting against the wall. Men explode into the room, pointing their guns in every direction. Their arrival ends my brief taste of freedom. When Jarrod's eyes adjust to the dim light, he spies me in the darkened corner. Guardedly, he walks toward me while the others search the room. I glance at my watch and smirk. "I was gone nineteen minutes. What took *you* so long?" Jarrod is not amused. I did not expect he would be.

"There's another door back here. It's not locked," Ryan calls out. "Want me to find out what's on the other side?"

"Yes," Jarrod says, keeping his eyes riveted on me. "Josh, back Ryan up. They may be outside." *They? He knows about the others?* I give no hint I know what he means, but Jarrod scrutinizes me warily and shoves me behind a tall shelf, sending a sharp pain through my throbbing head—the revenge of the cognac. When the door is opened, bright light blazes into the room. No one is there. Of course not. They would have disappeared by now, like apparitions into the ether. But I know they existed. Unfortunately, so does Jarrod.

Ryan and Josh step into the corridor and search in both directions. Finding no one, they return and lock the door. Jarrod calls Tom on the annoying device, then informs me, "Tom's on his way." I assume a pretense of indifference. Then he snaps, "Let's get back to the office. By the way, Erik, our chasing you left both your attorneys unprotected. Let's hope no one visited *them* while we were here."

I wince. The women being endangered had not occurred to me. Josh scowls and Ryan casts an acidic glance my way as they hurry me along. Each man keeps his hand on his gun, ready at the least provocation. Jarrod cautiously opens the office door, and I hear startled gasps as he enters with his gun drawn. After he inspects the office, we enter. Ms. Simmons stares at me with apprehension, but I find Ms. Copeland's expression most disturbing. Her dark eyes probe me with questions, but I also detect deep sadness, even sympathy, devoid of anger or judgment.

Jarrod takes me to Ms. Copeland's office. I walk over to the window and gaze out at the city, at this strange, foreign land. I am powerless and can only await my dishonorable return to the prison of the Wheaton mansion. I listen for the door to open, anticipating that Ms. Copeland may come in, but she does not. Jarrod sullenly occupies the couch, his eyes boring into my back.

"Is Ms. Copeland not joining us?" My voice cuts through the cold, awkward silence. I had hoped for a reprieve—today is too soon to dredge up more ghosts from my past.

"No, she's staying in the front office until you leave. Then Ryan will take her home. Don't worry," he says caustically, "you won't have to meet with her."

I will not have to meet with her? So will she now refuse to represent me? Unease spreads through me. I begin to perceive how they regard my actions. I wanted to escape their constraints, if only for a brief time. But this world has contrived its own clever devices. I am beginning to perceive how difficult it is to hide anywhere—or anything.

My leg throbs, reinjured in the escape attempt, but I disregard it and begin pacing. I anticipated they would consider my escape a misdeed. But they discovered that others met with me, so this has escalated into a serious offense. After today, will they consider sending me back—perhaps even to that Communard cell? My situation has turned perilous, like the currents of a whirlpool, threatening to pull me down into the undertow.

I survey the city which reflects gilt rays of late afternoon sun. This country, this new world, was always fabled to be the land of cities of gold. It sometimes *seems* that way. Glorious things exist now that could not have been imagined in my time. But today, I came into contact with the shadows lurking in this gilded world's dark underbelly. The same unseen tentacles that snaked through my world are still here, still operating in the recesses of this deceptively advanced one.

I catch sight of one of those strange flying machines circling over the adjacent building. Jarrod calls them drones. Apparently, they keep watch from the sky. Perhaps the specters no longer hide in the subterranean realms.

When Tom arrives, he stands next to me and gazes out the window. "I hear you tried to take a holiday."

"I desired a change of scenery."

"When I heard about your stunt, I was damned angry. But driving here gave me some time to think about your little adventure. I grew up in a Hopi village on a high mesa. It seemed like the land stretched on forever, and I was free to walk and explore it. My world was boundless, and I'm thinking your world in the opera house meant the same to you."

I regard Tom with new respect.

He folds his arms over his chest. "I think I'd feel like you and want to escape from being watched all day and night. Maybe it's time for Collin to tell you more about what's at stake."

So, perhaps now I will find out why *I* was chosen to be brought into the future. I have always felt they were withholding information—that they have a secret agenda. Yes, it is time they are forthright with me.

As Jarrod and Tom escort me through the front office, Ms. Copeland watches from a distance. Will this be the last time I ever see her? I take one last look into her dark eyes. She smiles back faintly, and I nod a regretful farewell.

23 | PHANTASM

Land's End

COLLIN

The waters of the Sound have gone murky grey in the twilight by the time I pull into the underground garage. George corners me as I leave the elevator. His eyebrow lifting in butlerly disapproval, he says, "You're *late* again."

"Late? Good grief, man, I've been drivin' at breakneck speed t' get here." But then, George does fancy himself the Keeper of the Gate. "I hear the meeting is being held in the library." He nods and leads the way. My eyes adjust to the dim lighting as I cross the spacious room. Bookshelves line the walls, containing one of the finest private collections of hardbounds in the world. I glance wistfully at the high-backed chairs in the corner. I'd rather be there, engrossed in a real book instead of dealing with the latest crisis our unpredictable Phantom has caused.

Everyone is gathered in front of the Sienna marble fireplace that dates from the Renaissance. Tom and Dr. Adler occupy one of the leather couches, and Howard and Lady Margaret, the other. I take the chair next to Jarrod. As George is handing me a scotch, Howard growls at Jarrod, "So, how the hell did he get out of the office?"

"We don't know yet," Jarrod says defensively. "The windows in Ms. Copeland's office don't open. The only door goes to the reception area, and offices don't have trapdoors like an opera house. But it was exactly nineteen minutes from the time I left him in her office until we found him in a storage room."

Tom looks perplexed. "I thought his meetings with Ms. Copeland were being monitored."

"Yes, Ryan's been monitoring them without Kathryn's knowledge, so he doesn't pull up the hologram until after Kathryn goes into her office." Jarrod shifts uneasily and adds, "Before Kathryn goes in, Erik is alone. So what's there to watch?"

"His disappearing act?" Howard fumes.

"Erik is believed to have supernatural powers," Lady Margaret says thoughtfully. That takes me by surprise, but when I glance around, it appears everyone's actually mulling it over.

"He's also said to be a magician," Dr. Adler adds. "Perhaps his escape has more to do with that talent. His reputation at the opera house was based on his ability to disappear."

Jarrod leans forward. "I'd like to agree with Dr. Adler that there's a rational explanation, but there's no way he walked past us. His disappearance sure felt spooky."

"It certainly did." Kathryn's voice startles me. I look around and find her standing in the doorway. Behind her, Ryan points subtly at his ear. So, she's heard everything we've said, including the bit about eavesdropping on her conferences with Erik. The set of her jaw tells me we're in for it. "When I heard there was a meeting this evening," Kathryn says, arching an eyebrow coolly, "I thought I should be here in case you had any questions I could shed light on."

Lady Margaret smiles and motions for her to join us. "Any insight you can provide is appreciated."

Howard signals me to take over the meeting, so I ask Jarrod, "How do you know other people were with Erik?"

"We hid a tracking sensor in his boot." Kathryn gives me an accusatory glare as Jarrod continues. "I switched to thermal imaging and there were two people close to him."

"Could they have been outside the storage room you found him in?" I ask.

"No, I doubt it," Jarrod states. "They were standing only a couple feet from him."

"Did he admit there were others?" Jarrod frowns and shakes his head, so I turn to Tom and ask, "Did you talk t' Erik about these two people, then?"

"I've asked him, but he sidestepped the question. I didn't get anything else out of him."

Howard clears his throat. "Could Erik be conspiring with the PTB?" An uneasy silence falls over the group.

"I don't think so," Jarrod replies. "If Erik was doing that, he's smart enough to keep it a secret. The more I think about this, the more I feel he was just trying to test the boundaries. Erik doesn't know about the tracking sensor in his boot or thermal-imaging technology. Maybe he thought he could actually pull it off."

I play devil's advocate. "Maybe he did plot an escape on his own, but wha' do we make o' those two people? Might he have had connections we do not know about?"

"That's not likely," Jarrod says. "He doesn't have access to a QRYSTAL or PALnet."

Rankled, Howard says, "Yet he apparently walks right through walls...."

I try to catch Kathryn's eye, but she looks away. She's steaming over the surveillance—and biding her time.

"So," I summarize, "all we know for certain is he disappeared out o' Kathryn's office. We don't know how he got out, and he may or may no' have planned to meet with two unidentified people."

"In other words, we don't know a damn thing," Howard growls. "But he refuses to explain himself and that makes it hard for us to trust him. What do you think, Dr. Adler?"

Dr. Adler smooths her skirt, thinking. "Perhaps we should look at this from his viewpoint. Perhaps we should consider whether he feels he can trust us."

The room goes still again as her words sink in. I gulp some scotch, then point out, "We've tried to gain Erik's trust. But he's never been forthcoming. Tha' aside, if Erik is entirely innocent in regard t' those two people, why won't he even admit they were there?"

"Maybe he feels we would consider him complicit with them," Dr. Adler responds. "Perhaps he fears we'd send him back, possibly even to the very time and situation he was rescued from. Wouldn't we be worried about that if we were in his shoes?"

"But we'd never do such a thing to him," Lady Margaret states emphatically.

"Perhaps not, but he doesn't know that," Kathryn points out, somewhat testy. "And he doesn't like facing a public trial that delves into his private life and could end in a prison sentence."

Dr. Adler takes a sip of wine. "Last night, after Erik's meeting with Ms. Copeland, he acted strangely at dinner." She looks at Kathryn. "Without your disclosing confidential information, what part of Erik's life did you discuss?"

"We only covered the period from his first time at the opera house through his early years in England."

"Did you sense anything distressed him?" Dr. Adler asks.

"Yes, at one point he even told me to move on to the next question."

Howard breaks in. "What were you talking about?"

"I'm sorry," Kathryn states firmly, "I can't disclose any of his specific comments. That violates attorney-client confidentiality."

"But something upset him so much, I hear he got drunk. What's *your* point, Dr. Adler?" I ask.

"I was wondering," she replies, turning to Kathryn again, "did you discuss Christine?"

"We didn't get into that at all."

"Did you intend to discuss Christine today?"

"No, and I didn't tell him that. It's a sensitive subject, so I don't want to rush into it."

"Perhaps Erik thought you might," Dr. Adler says, "so he may have sabotaged the meeting to avoid the subject."

"What's your assessment?" Howard asks Kathryn. "Do you think he could be in collusion with the PTB?"

"I do think he's holding back information, but he's a very private man. If he doesn't admit he saw two people in the storage room, it doesn't necessarily imply anything conspiratorial." Kathryn looks over at Jarrod. "If you can track him, can't others do that?"

"It's possible."

"Even the PTB?" she presses.

Jarrod flinches. "They could."

"So, what if they knew he left my office before you discovered it?" Kathryn asks. "From what I *overheard*, you weren't using your surveillance system until our conference began, right?"

Jarrod realizes the cat's out of the bag. Apologetically, he says. "Yeah, that's correct."

"What if the PTB has also been keeping close tabs on him," Kathryn asks, "and they got to him first?"

"It's an interesting theory," I counter, "but we won't know the truth so long as Erik's close-mouthed. Wha' do you think, Tom, about having another talk with him?"

"I'll try it again, right after the meeting."

"That will not be necessary." The words resonate throughout the room, uttered by a deep voice from the dark corner of the library. All eyes turn toward the sound. As my vision adjusts, I begin to make out a shadow in the haze. Dressed all in black, a phantasm emerges slowly from the library's dusky recesses and moves toward us. Instinctively, I cross myself.

24 | CONSPIRATORS

KATHRYN

A ghostly silhouette glides out of inky mist at the room's edge as if coalescing from the ethers. Cold sweat breaks out on my palms as my mind struggles to discern what's preternatural and what's real. Eerie silence falls over the room—not even the sound of footsteps can be heard.

"Just how in the *hell* did you get in here?" Mr. Wheaton breaks the hypnotic spell.

"Did your *devices* not inform you of my presence?" His voice is chillingly calm but entirely human. Too sonorous for a ghost. His mouth curls up at the corners, not quite a smile. Mr. Mercier comes to a stop next to a high-backed chair and rests one hand casually on it, towering over us. He's dressed all in black, even a black shirt and tie.

"This is our home," Mr. Wheaton retorts, "and we don't have security cameras or sensors in the hallways and living areas. So I repeat—how did you get into this room?"

The dark figure smirks. "There are those who say I may have supernatural powers." He glances at Mrs. Wheaton. "And others who think I am a magician." His gaze shifts to Dr. Adler, then back to Mr. Wheaton. "But that is for you to conjecture."

"I can see the door from here," Mr. Wheaton growls, "and you did *not* come through it." He glares heatedly up at Mr. Mercier who remains standing, unruffled and in command. I look from one man to the other. The battle of wills is on.

"Erik, wha' are you doing here, then?" Collin's tone does nothing to defuse the tension.

"I heard there was a meeting this evening," he replies. "I thought I should be here in case you had any questions I could shed light on." I'm stunned. He quoted my words verbatim, but his tone is not mocking. When he glances at me, I catch my breath at the intensity in his eyes.

Collin scowls. "All right, since you want to help out, can you explain how you got out o' Ms. Copeland's office or no'?"

"No."

Annoyed, Collin tries another tack. "Why did you leave Ms. Copeland's office, then?"

"That has already been discussed quite thoroughly tonight. I can provide nothing more."

Like the first Queen Elizabeth, my client seems to be adept at giving an "answer, answerless."

"Well, as you no doubt *heard*, we don't know wha' to make of this meeting you had with those people. That's mighty suspect. We need you t' tell us who they were," Collin demands.

"I do not know. Their conduct did not include such courtesies as exchanging names."

"You had no' seen them before?"

"No."

"How did you happen to meet them?"

"It would be more accurate to say they met me."

"Can you explain that a bit?"

"I was proceeding down the hallway when they approached me. They displayed their guns and ordered me into the storage room. Since I had no weapon with which to defend myself," he snarls the words and gives Jarrod an accusatory glare, "I was in no position to object."

"Did they say wha' they wanted?" Collin asks.

"Yes. They were abundantly clear. It serves their purpose for this trial to proceed." His jaw clenches. "Indeed, they laughed. They said it would be inopportune for me to miss the trial by escaping"—he glances over at Jarrod and Tom—"my bodyguards."

"You're thinking *jailers*, right?" Collin snaps back.

"Under the circumstances, why would I *not* feel that way?" His words stab at Collin.

"I don't deny you've been held in close quarters since you arrived," Collin concedes. "But, man, you were badly injured and needed t' mend.

We've just been guarding you to keep you safe. You know tha' our intention is to return you to your time when you've recovered…."

"Return me when I recovered from my injuries?" Mr. Mercier cuts Collin off sharply. "Is that truly *all* you intended?"

I've wondered about that too. A twitch plays at the corner of Collin's mouth. He *is* holding something back. However well-intentioned they may claim to be, the Wheatons have an agenda and Collin is part of the inner circle. I survey the faces around me. How many of them know the *real* reason for bringing him to the present? One thing is clear to me now—Mr. Mercier and I are both pawns in their schemes.

"We've only wanted to do wha' was right. Remember, we're the ones who rescued you from execution," Collin replies, trying hard to finesse him. "It was never intended tha' your presence here would be known. Things got out o' hand when the criminal charges were filed, and we've all been forced into a situation *none of us* wants."

Angry, Mr. Wheaton slams his drink down. "I'm also in a difficult position. I posted bond, and as a condition, I'm under an order which requires me to bring you to trial. Isn't that right, Ms. Copeland?"

"Yes." I look up at Mr. Mercier and add, "Mr. Wheaton has placed himself in jeopardy of sanctions if anything happens to you."

"We regret wha' you're facing, Erik," Collin says. "It's no' something we anticipated."

"Nonetheless, because of *your* intrigues"—he scowls—"*I* am the one who must stand trial."

Impatiently, Mr. Wheaton interjects, "The bottom line is, can we work together?"

"What I overheard tonight satisfies me sufficiently so that I am willing to continue working with you," Mr. Mercier replies with a steady gaze.

"But why should we trust you?" Collin challenges.

"If I were in league with your enemy, I would not have revealed myself tonight."

"How do we know," Mr. Wheaton presses, "you won't change sides when it suits you?"

"Although their ultimate goal is to discredit you and confiscate your technology," Mr. Mercier almost snarls, "they have no qualms about destroying me in the process. I have met men like these before, men of the same inhuman nature. I would gain nothing by serving them. For the duration of the trial, it serves both our interests to work together."

Collin rubs his beard. "Do you give your word you will no' try to escape?"

"I may be able to walk through walls"—he smirks—"but it is clear you can *see* through them. Even if you do not catch me, *they* are waiting nearby to make certain I do not get away."

"One last thing we need to address." Collin glances nervously in my direction. "Do you want Ms. Copeland to remain your attorney?"

The question takes me by surprise, but maybe that was a factor in the disappearing act.

"I consent to Ms. Copeland serving as my lawyer," Mr. Mercier replies. "Indeed, I have found her to be the only person who is trustworthy." His eyes glimmer with challenge as he adds, "The question remains whether *she* will continue to represent me."

He just handed me the opportunity to withdraw. I realize this is my last chance. I still know so little about him—not even if he's guilty of murder. I only know he's a unique man with extraordinary abilities. Then I remember the passage from Madame Giry's diary: *If the world had not rejected this man, what could his life have meant to it?* I take a deep breath. "Yes, I'll continue as your attorney." My client responds with a subtle bow of his head.

"However, I do have a condition," I state, glaring at Collin. He winces. "You need to give me your word that there will be no monitoring *of any kind* of the conferences with my client, and that is *not* negotiable." I notice Mr. Mercier is riveted by my demand.

"All right, Kathryn," Collin says with a reluctant nod, "agreed."

"Then my business is complete," my client says abruptly. "Good evening."

As he starts for the door, Mrs. Wheaton calls after him, "Monsieur Mercier, just one more thing." He stops and turns slowly, as if apprehensive she may say something to upset the precarious truce. "I am sorry," she states simply. Is she apologizing for his having to endure the trial? Or all that he's suffered at the hands of unthinking humanity? He also appears mystified at her meaning and stares at her for a moment, then leaves without responding.

"Damn." Mr. Wheaton pushes the call button. "I could use another drink."

"You know," Tom says, "I don't blame him for trying to escape."

"Yeah, I'd go stir crazy being under scrutiny like he's been," Jarrod agrees.

Tom rubs the back of his neck. "He comes from a different world. I understand how he feels. I felt the same way when I left the reservation and went into the military."

As George replenishes the drinks, I ask to speak privately with Mr. and Mrs. Wheaton about the case. They agree but request that Collin and Dr. Adler remain.

Tom glances at Ryan and Jarrod. "I think we've got a few things to discuss too." As they leave, Ryan informs me that he'll be waiting at the elevator.

Turning to Mr. Wheaton, I get directly to the point, "Collin told me you were opposed to bringing witnesses from the past."

"Absolutely!"

"The scientists at the time-travel lab told me tha' since there was no problem transporting Erik, it can be done," Collin says. "But, Howard, the other thing to consider is if we oppose this, the media will say you're trying to obstruct justice and prevent the witnesses from telling wha' happened. You'll be painted as trying to cover up the truth."

"If we oppose this motion, what are our chances of winning?" Mrs. Wheaton asks.

"The prosecution has the right to call witnesses, but no one has ever asked for time travel to be used. We can oppose their motion, and the issue will go to a hearing. There's no predicting which way the judge will rule since this is unprecedented."

"I don't care. Oppose it!" Mr. Wheaton scowls. "We'll take our chances in court. I will not have the technology subject to the whim of others."

Considering that the final word, I take my leave and hurry down the long corridors. I pass a large doorway that opens into an enormous, elegant room on two levels. To my surprise, Mr. Mercier is sitting at a grand piano on the lower level, but he's not playing, just sitting with his arms folded and gazing up toward the doorway. He catches my eye, almost intentionally. Is it my imagination, or do I detect a conspiratorial glint?

25 | VOWS

Saturday, June 16
Interstate 5

KATHRYN

"Kathryn!"

"What?" Startled, I look up. *Are we crashing?*

Ryan throttles down the Vette and passes an old bus. "You just agreed that the sky is falling in."

"No, I didn't," I snap, irritated that he interrupted my concentration. "Why would I say that?"

"You've been glued to that QRYSTAL and no matter what I say, you just agree." I sputter in denial and he flashes a devious grin. "Better be careful what you agree to."

"Good advice, but way too late. Apparently I agree to things that get me into trouble, even when I'm careful."

He chuckles. "So you don't usually represent masked men from the nineteenth century who're accused of murder?" I laugh and go back to my reading, but he persists. "Can't you ever take a minute for yourself?"

"Someday, maybe. But Collin and Tom won't allow a certain masked man to come to my office anymore. The weekend is the only time I have to go to Land's End, so right now, I've got to review my notes for today's appointment."

Ryan shrugs in concession, and I return to Adèle's diary. Lexa has highlighted the passages I need to focus on. Adèle's closest friend among the ballet rats was Lorraine whose brother, Jules Giry, often dropped by the opera house. Adèle described him as tall and thin, with blue eyes and curly golden hair, just like her brother's had been. Jules also took notice of Adèle. It was not long before he was bringing her flowers and taking her on walks through the Bois de Boulogne. Although Jules worked as a Paris policeman, he was studying math at the Sorbonne and dreamed of teaching. She wrote that he rowed them around the lake, that he held her hand on their walks, that he'd steal a kiss. Clearly, they were falling in love, and four months after they met, they became engaged. Mr. Mercier reentered Adèle's life a month later.

Monday, 20 August 1855

Today, Jules and I met Erik at Gare St. Lazare. I had not laid eyes on him since I put him on the train four years ago. He was a mere boy then and now he's a full-grown man, nearly eighteen years of age. When I asked in my last letter how I would recognize him, he wrote back that it would not be difficult, that he would be the man towering over everyone, the one wearing a black mask. I laughed at his self-deprecating humor. He was that way even as a boy. I was excited but anxious about our meeting. He has become an accomplished musician and is moving to Zurich to further his career. Considering the importance of his connections, I worried that he would look down on me, a mere box attendant. When the train pulled into the station, I searched the crowd for him, and truly he did tower above everyone. There he stood, a raven-haired man with a black mask, wearing a dark suit. People seemed to keep their distance from him as he waited with a trunk and violin case, surveying the crowd. Although he bore little resemblance to the boy I remembered, I was certain that dignified, striking man was Erik.

When he spied me, there was instant recognition and something more—sincere warmth. We stood there speechless, staring at each other. Tears came to my eyes, and he turned away, motioning for a porter to carry his trunk. When he faced me again, we had composed ourselves. I introduced him to Jules and the two men shook hands with cordial ease. After his trunk was settled into his room, we went to a café. What a gay reunion we had. Erik told many stories of London, and I shared mine about the Opéra. I drank a bit more than usual, and the years apart seemed to melt away.

The entries over the next nine days are filled with Adèle's excited preparations for her wedding, and Erik attended the opera every night.

Thursday, 30 August 1855

Erik takes great pleasure watching all the performances from the boxes. We reminisced about how, as a boy, he watched from behind the velvet curtains. The performance tonight was Meyerbeer's Le prophète, one of Erik's favorites. He said perhaps this opera was a favorable omen and prophetic of good things to come. I can still see Erik's smile when he said the dark days may be over for us. The thought fills me with happiness and hope.

Little did Adèle know what was to come for her or Erik. Perhaps it's a blessing in all our lives we don't know what lies ahead. Adèle and Jules were married two days later in a civil ceremony. That night, she wrote about the church wedding to take place the following day.

Friday, 31 August 1855

I am now Madame Giry and can hardly believe it, since I am still residing in the dormitory. Jules and I agreed we will not begin our honeymoon until after our church wedding tomorrow. But late this afternoon, Erik and Lorraine accompanied us to the magistrate's office to witness our civil marriage. Afterward, Erik took us to a restaurant to celebrate.

During the dinner he lavished on us, Erik asked me why I was melancholy. He notices everything, whether the smallest detail of architecture, the proper rendition of an aria, or the least nuance in the behavior of the people around him. Once again, I shared with him the feelings that have been haunting me all week, the ghosts of my beloved family. Erik patted my hand and said that all will be well.

Still, I am so nervous about our wedding. I chose Église Saint-Sulpice, which I attended with my family, although I had not gone there since their deaths. Father Lucien remembered my parents and kindly agreed for Jules and me to wed in the renowned cathedral, even though we are poor. But my heart aches that my father will not escort me down the aisle, nor will my dear maman be there to shed tears of joy. And my dear little brother, I miss him so.

I skim over the passages describing her white satin gown trimmed with lace and buttons from her confirmation dress. Her bridal bouquet of white roses was a gift from Erik. Adèle's account of her wedding was written two days later, after Jules and she left for their honeymoon.

Sunday, 2 September 1855

Erik did not disclose what he planned, even as he escorted me from the opera house and supported me up the cathedral's stone steps. His strong arm steadied me the long distance down the nave and around the altar to the Chapelle de la Madone. At the Chapelle, he placed a gentle kiss on my forehead and said not to worry, then he left. Trembling, I lit candles for my family and prayed for the strength to walk the aisle by myself. When I returned to the entrance, my friends from the Opéra were waiting. They said my face was as white as my wedding gown. The ballet rats fluttered their fans at me like desperate butterflies, but nothing helped my nerves.

Then I heard it. Thundering sounds filled the cathedral with unearthly music from the grand pipe organ in the balcony. Magnificent chords and cascading notes left me breathless. An ecstatic crescendo swept me forward, casting away all worries. I found myself walking joyously down the aisle, looking into the face of my beloved Jules. The music enfolded us and expressed our love, like God's blessing on our marriage. We stood before the priest, but no one spoke until the music ended. When it did, we felt the sacred ceremony had already occurred. Still, we went through the ritual and spoke the vows that united our souls. When Jules kissed me, music again filled the air like a chorus from Heaven. Jules and I walked up the aisle embraced by transcendent harmonies. Never before had I heard such music, but I felt surely it must be Erik's own creation.

Interesting. My client's music seems to have a profound effect on everyone. I skim through Adèle's description of her wedding reception at a small café—a lively celebration with friends from the opera house, Jules's family and Mr. Mercier.

Erik handed me a small, red velvet box, saying it was something I had asked him for. Inside was a gold chain with a locket made of intricately carved ivory. When I opened the locket, I was stunned to find portraits in oil of Jules and Erik, the two people dearest to me in the world. I cried, unable to speak. I have seen many such miniatures with flat, unnatural faces, but these portraits are so lifelike. They remind me of those I saw at the Louvre by Rembrandt who drew with such realism, he would add shadows to the faces. The portraits of Erik and Jules have the same quality, both seeming to be lit from an unseen lamp off to one side. The light falls across the uncovered side of Erik's face, leaving his black mask in shadow. I will wear this every day of my life. Next to my wedding ring, my most cherished possession.

Lexa highlighted that passage, but I doubt it will have much significance to the case. That evening was the last time Adèle saw Mr. Mercier for several years. She left on her honeymoon, and he departed for Zurich. A number of diary entries mention letters from him. That's evidence our client was in Zurich during those years, but it's not definitive.

I skip the next couple years that cover Adèle and Jules's short time together. Tragically, when Jules was killed on duty, she wrote nothing in the diary for six months, as if no words could express her grief. The next entry was Meg's birth, clearly bittersweet for Adèle. Although joyous over her healthy little girl, she had cried, realizing Jules would never share in his daughter's life.

The directors of the Paris Opéra allowed Adèle to work as a costume seamstress when her pregnancy began to show. But since she was popular with the patrons, after Meg was born, Adèle was allowed to resume her job as box attendant and even given a small room. It's clear from her entries that tending a baby by herself and working long evenings began to take a toll on her health. She reported losing weight and had a cough that got progressively worse.

Tuesday, 13 October 1858

Erik's train was late. When he approached, my breath caught. He seemed like a black shadow, his face and demeanor darker, and his eyes filled with deep sorrow. He wrapped his arm around my shoulders and held me, not speaking a word. Then he asked to see little Meg, and I moved the blanket aside. With a look of desolation, he gazed at her and said he was sorry about Jules, that he had been a good man.

Then he noticed my clothes were soaked through from the cold rain. He reproached me gently and hired a carriage to convey us to the opera house. I still have a cough, so he insisted on carrying little Meg up to my room. I changed the baby into dry clothes, and Erik took her back into his arms and rocked her. As I changed my dress behind the screen, he began to sing in a deep, infinitely soft voice, beautiful and soothing. I had never heard him sing before, and his voice filled the room, wrapping us in tranquility. Meg was soon asleep.

I went to the opera house's kitchen and fetched a warm meal. As we ate, I sensed that his sadness for my loss is only part of the dark mood that has settled over him. Something dreadful must have happened in Zurich. When he finished eating, he returned to the rocking chair and stared into the fire, brooding. I made a decision then never to pry into his private affairs. He is a man who feels deeply and does not speak of his wounds. I will not tear them open by probing into them. I resolve to be his friend and help him as I can.

The mantle clock chimed and brought him out of his reverie. He walked over to the baby's crib and for some time gazed at her with genuine affection. I will never forget his next words. Without lifting his eyes from the sleeping baby, he said, "You need not fear. I will always watch over you and Meg." I can hardly believe he made such a vow, yet I know he meant it. He is not a man to take oaths lightly. For the first time since Jules died, I do not dread the future or what it will hold for Meg and me. I feel now that we will survive.

Mr. Mercier's promise to watch over them clearly meant the difference between life and death to Adèle. My heart sinks, realizing what it meant to *his* future. I mull over Adèle's words—*"He is a man who feels deeply and does not speak of his wounds."* I'm discovering all too well how deep his emotions run and that he doesn't easily share information about himself. Adèle said she wouldn't reopen his scars by asking about them, and that's just what I've been doing. But I have no choice. Ironically, for his sake, I'll have to navigate those turbulent waters. And try not to get pulled into the whirlpool.

26 | TRUCE

Land's End

Erik

Standing on my balcony, I stare out at the Sound, dreading the imminent conference with Ms. Copeland. Restless, I go inside. My violin calls to me, so I open the case and stare down at it. One of my memories, long forgotten and buried along with so many others, comes back. It was a Sunday, and I was walking home after sketching a church and selling it for an unusually high fee. Fate must have guided me past the house with the estate sale. A violin in the parlor window caught my eye. I rushed in, barely daring to hope. It turned out to be a fine instrument, but costly. Perhaps it was my youth and earnestness, or that I turned my pockets out to show the man I was giving him all my money. He finally accepted my offer and told me to leave before he changed his mind. I paid hastily and ran.

I take the violin out of its case and begin playing. The soothing melody eases my frayed nerves as it always has. I remember that day long ago, how I lifted the precious instrument from its case and held it in my hands, regarded it with awe, as though it were my very soul. And perhaps it was. For the first time in over two years, I drew a bow across the strings of a violin, awkward and hesitant. But soon it began to sing for me. I vowed never to be separated from music again and practiced until my fingertips bled and calloused over. Still that was not enough. I needed lessons to advance my technique.

It comes back to me now as I play, gazing out at the Sound—how I screwed up my courage and went to the home of the famed music teacher, William Markham. When he saw my mask, he politely refrained from asking questions. I could afford only two lessons a month, and we agreed to begin the following Saturday. That week I practiced every spare moment. When I arrived for my first lesson, Monsieur Markham handed me several scores, each of increasing complexity. When I finished, I awaited the verdict. Would he deem me unfit to be his pupil? After an agonizing moment, he regarded me intently and said, "Most surprising." I stopped breathing, fearing his next words. "You have a unique style, very promising." Then he offered me weekly lessons for the same fee and extended his hand. Astounded, I reached out and took it, sealing the bargain. No one had ever offered their hand to me before. I felt honored, almost human.

The buzzer goes off and George's bony countenance hovers on the monitor like a disembodied skull. "Monsieur Mercier, it is time for your conference." Resigned, I place the violin in its case and grab my cane. George awaits to lead me solemnly down the corridor. It feels like a walk to the gallows, this being forced to dredge up the events of my life once again. If this were the opera house, I would slip into the shadows and disappear, but considering the repercussions from my previous attempt at delay, it seems wise not to push my luck any further.

George stops at Lady Margaret's office and stares into a mechanism. My silver fob is useless on such contrivances, but happily, not all doors in the mansion have them. When George opens the door, I step into the room and survey its seating arrangements. Two chairs sit side-by-side in front of a large Louis Philippe desk. *No, too close.* Across the room a pair of settees face each other with a large trunk located between. *That will do.* In this delicate dance of probe and parry, I must take the lead today without appearing to do so.

I choose the settee facing the window, but the view of the Sound does not distract me from my dread. I reach into my vest and take out my fob. My hand manipulates the rare device, deftly shifting it from one shape to another. *You see, Henri? I have mastered it. You would be proud. You always said I was your finest student.* In my mind's eye, I conjure Henri's face, lit by the stage footlights that cast sinister shadows on his features as he performed his ingenious feats of illusion. Countless times I have used the tricks and ploys he taught me to gain entrance and move about undetected. *And how did you fare? Did you survive the madness of Paris? Did you survive the war and the Commune, my friend?*

The sound of George at the door with Ms. Copeland! In a flash, the fob is back in my vest, and I stand to greet Ms. Copeland as she enters.

When I indicate the other settee, she thanks me and takes her place. As she opens her briefcase, a soft, frustrated sigh escapes. I suppress a smile at the inadvertent disclosure of her feelings.

"Would *you* like a cup of coffee?" I ask as a truce offering.

"No, thank you. I don't drink coffee."

"I remember. You drink a cold beverage, do you not? Iced tea?" She nods, so I push the console button, and George is fussing over us in seconds. "Would you please bring tea? Hot Earl Grey for me and iced tea for Ms. Copeland."

George arches an eyebrow at her. "What type of tea?"

"Peach, please." As George scuttles off, she turns to me. "Are you ready to begin?"

"Do I have a choice?" I parry. She winces, so I say, "I apologize. That was ungentlemanly. Please proceed."

"We left off with Julien's children moving to Wye. So, where did you move to?"

"Into the home of William Markham, my music teacher."

"You had a music teacher?" she asks, surprised.

"Indeed. How could I achieve a level of mastery without one?"

"You said your original guardian had taught you to play the violin and piano. You must have missed playing."

"Truly." She has an innate ability to see into people. Does she also have second-sight? *That* could present problems. "I had not played either since being sold to the carnival." The look I saw at our first meeting comes back to her eyes, making me uneasy. Attempting to avoid any discussion of the carnival or that cage, I hasten to add, "I decided to take lessons and found an elderly maestro who lived nearby in Marylebone."

"But given your, uh, circumstances, how did you manage that?"

"By sketching churches, I saved enough to purchase a violin. I began with violin lessons each Saturday, but by the following January I was also taking piano lessons on Sundays."

She regards me thoughtfully, suspecting there is more to the story. There is, but I will never tell her. And I will never forget what happened that Christmas. Yvette, who always suspected the dreadful act I had committed on the night I arrived, came to my room and interrupted my practicing to fetch me for dinner. As she stood in my doorway, her condemning eyes stared at my violin.

"Don't think you fool me with your façade of music and learning," she said almost as a threat. "I know what you *really* are."

Because of that incident I sought to be away from the Mercier house whenever possible and dredged up the courage to ask Monsieur Markham for permission to practice on his piano. I decide to oblige Ms. Copeland's curiosity with some innocuous details. "I would arrive at Monsieur Markham's home at noon on Sundays. We would invade his pantry and make a meal while he shared stories of performances throughout Europe, even in America. Then he would tutor me all afternoon on the piano. He was a demanding teacher, but patient." *Those magical afternoons.* Sometimes I felt as if I were the music or that the music was me. "The piano lessons ended in the spring when I had to resume drawing churches to replenish my funds."

"Was that the year Julien and his wife died?"

"Yes, late that summer. When Monsieur Markham learned what happened, he insisted I move into his home. He was a widower, and his two children had moved north of London. I suspect he was lonely. He had a large home with a garden shed where I worked on another angel I had been commissioned to carve. Even though I returned to sketching churches on Sundays, the rest of my time was consumed with music lessons and practice." I pause for a moment, reflecting. "Strange, is it not, how mundane life goes on even after tragedy has intervened? Almost as if it never happened."

She regards me with sadness.

I feel uncomfortable and change the subject. "Then that fall, an unexpected opportunity arose—strangely, the very day of my sixteenth birthday. A church offered Monsieur Markham the position of organist. He declined but told them I should be hired instead."

My freely offering information takes her by surprise. She asks with the quirk of a smile, "So you also knew how to play the organ?"

"No, I did not, but when I protested because of my lack of training, Monsieur Markham dismissed my concerns. He accompanied me to the interview and assured the deacons I would be ready the following spring when their organist retired. They hired me, conditional upon my performance." Also conditional upon my using the back stairwell to the organ loft so as not to cause "undue distress" because of my mask.

"My understanding is that the organ is very challenging to master."

"Truly, but Monsieur Markham was a determined man and taught me the complex techniques. He even paid the wages of the men who worked the bellows of the church organ, so I could practice on its three consoles—those are the keyboards." And I practiced tirelessly—reveled in sublime sounds from myriad stops and sent majestic chords blasting out towering pipes. Sounds reverberated off stone walls, filling me with a sense of unbounded power. "The next spring, after my first service, the deacons confirmed my hiring." But they never did invite me to social gatherings at the church. No doubt to avoid undue distress.

"Would there be any record of your salary from the church? Did you possibly perform at any concerts where there would be printed programs with your name?"

"No, no concerts or printed programs, and my church salary was paid in cash from the weekly offerings. Commissions from weddings and funerals were also paid in cash. Because of those, I no longer needed the income from sketching and carving."

But the privacy I reaped from carving *was* needed, so when the angel was carted away, I became depressed at losing the seclusion to indulge my secret passion—singing the glorious songs I had heard at the Opéra. Monsieur Markham noticed my black mood and pried the truth from me, then included voice lessons to his brilliant tutelage. He taught me tirelessly—told me he believed I would leave a mark on the world. He was correct. He just did not foresee the manner of mark it would be. At the thought, a dark laugh escapes, and Ms. Copeland looks at me, startled. I try to cover my lapse. "You have more questions?"

"Am I correct in understanding from Adèle's diary"—her voice is tinged with awe—"that you studied with *the Richard Wagner*?"

With irritation I reply, "Yes, *the* Richard Wagner." I am relieved that George returns with his tray. As he fastidiously serves tea and pastries in his white-gloved manner, I reflect on how Monsieur Markham plotted to bring me to Wagner's attention. The London Philharmonic Society had engaged Herr Wagner as conductor for the 1855 season. We attended his second concert late in March, and I gloried in Wagner's unique renditions of a Mendelssohn violin concerto and Beethoven's Ninth.

At the reception afterward, Monsieur Markham introduced me to Wagner and regaled him about my talents. I was apoplectic, but my aged mentor had nerves of steel and wore down Wagner who consented to hear me play. With a group of his select friends, we retired to a private parlor.

Someone gave me a violin and bow. I stared at them in my hands as the room swirled around me, but I gathered my wits, determined not to make a complete fool of myself. I performed pieces from Beethoven and from Wagner's *Der fliegende Holländer*. As always, I lost myself in the music and forgot everything but the hypnotic sounds. When I lowered the violin from my shoulder, I was relieved to hear applause.

Monsieur Markham then pointed out I was also a gifted pianist, so Wagner asked me to perform on the pianoforte. Again, I played a Beethoven piece, as well as one of my own compositions. When I finished, Wagner asked me to take a seat next to him. His eyes often focused on my mask, but he refrained from any inquiries about it and instead asked probing questions about my training. Then he asked me to play for the guests at another party to be given in his honor. Stunned, I accepted. Over the next week I prepared endlessly.

At the next reception, I played both violin and piano, closing my eyes and soaring with the music. Afterward, Wagner offered to tutor me in composition if I moved to Zurich where he resided. I was speechless, but Monsieur Markham accepted for me, offering to fund my expenses. During the carriage ride home, I looked up at the stars. For once, they were not laughing at me, taunting. Indeed, that night they seemed to dance for me.

The door thuds as it closes behind George, bringing me back to myself. I realize Ms. Copeland is studying me over her glass. "You were telling about Wagner," she prompts.

"Monsieur Markham was invited to a private reception in Wagner's honor and insisted I accompany him. He also insisted I wear the superfine black wool suit with brocade waistcoat and silk cravat he had purchased for me in appreciation for saving his life when he got cholera—"

"Mr. Markham got cholera?" she interrupts. "How did you save his life?"

The room begins to lose its sharp edges as if a fog is descending. The fear returns. I pick up my cane and brace myself against it. The terrifying news came like smoke on the wind, warning of fire close behind—the news that cholera had broken out at Broad Street, not far away.

"One evening, Monsieur Markham began to feel weak and dizzy," I reply, feeling almost disconnected from my body, "and I supported him to his room just as horrible illness was overtaking him." Must not shock her with the details of what it was like to tend the vomiting and diarrhea of this dear old man and our growing terror that it was cholera. He sent me to fetch a homeopathic doctor who lived nearby. As I ran to get him, it felt like the angel of death was snapping at my heels. I was terrified for him—and for me. Was my fate also sealed?

Numbly, I continue explaining, "His homeopathic doctor confirmed it was cholera. He poured something from a vial into a glass of water. I held the old man and administered the concoction." I remember bracing myself for the nightlong horror ahead, for the vigil by his bed while tending his needs and witnessing his agonizing death.

"Miraculously, he went into a deep, peaceful sleep. There were no further bouts, and he survived. I plied the homeopath with questions. He said that with homeopathic care, the death rate from cholera was ten percent, but over half died under the care of medical doctors." The ghosts of Julien and his wife seemed to hover around me, haunting me. What if they had received that treatment?

"Although it was believed that cholera was caused by miasmas in the air, a tenacious doctor named John Snow claimed that the outbreak came from a public water pump at Broad Street. He had the handle removed to prevent that water from being used again, and the epidemic stopped. Many still disputed Dr. Snow and simply disregarded his belief that cholera was spread in water. But our housekeeper said that while visiting her family, she got water from that pump for Monsieur Markham. I also came to believe that water was the source of the contagion. Although Monsieur Markham survived, hundreds died by drinking from the Broad Street pump, including some of the housekeeper's family." I cannot help but reflect that angels seem to be fickle in distributing their blessings.

I pull myself back from that other world, just want to leave it behind. "But you were asking about Herr Wagner, were you not?"

"Yes, and you were telling me about going to a reception for Wagner."

"Well, that evening, Monsieur Markham importuned Wagner to hear me play. I performed both the violin and piano, even some of my own compositions."

"You were also composing?" she asks, amazed.

Her penchant for displaying genuine emotions charms me. This time, I do not suppress my smile.

27 | TRIGGER

Kathryn

"Indeed," this man with the black mask replies matter-of-factly, "I had been composing for over a year. Herr Wagner was pleased with my work and said he would mentor me in Zurich. I accepted, of course."

"Of course," I repeat, dumbfounded. I stare at this enigma who is preoccupied with the bejeweled lion's head on his cane, seemingly nonchalant about what he just said. His life ranges from horrific to extraordinary. I clear my throat. "Adèle wrote that on your way to Zurich you stopped to attend her wedding. Did you visit with anyone else there?"

"No, I had no other friends."

"The diary says you were in Paris for two weeks before Adèle's wedding. Was it during that time you painted Jules's portrait in the locket?"

He tips his head to me in confirmation.

"From Adèle's description, it was exquisite. She said she'd wear it every day."

"And she did, at least until I last saw her. The diary ends the day I was…shot. Do you know what became of her?" His voice goes flat. "Did she die in the bombardment?"

"I'm sorry, I don't know." He avoids my gaze and tries to hide his emotions. I feel frustrated that I can't help him, can't even provide him with this information. "Well then, how long were you in Zurich? Did you have any jobs there?"

"For three years. I performed at receptions and gave private music lessons. Having Herr Wagner as my mentor opened those doors."

"Were there printed programs or any kind of documentation for those performances?"

"No, I never performed in concert halls."

"When did you return to Paris?"

"In October of 1858. I remained there until my *unanticipated excursion* to the future."

"Did Wagner teach you composition as he'd promised?"

"Indeed, he would review my compositions and critique them prodigiously."

"So you became friends?"

"I would not say *that*. I only met with him weekly or saw him occasionally when I performed at some function. My relationship with him was that of student and mentor. He was a busy man, occupied with his own affairs." A corner of his mouth curls up. "Both music and otherwise. When I left Zurich, we had a falling out."

Well, that's a rather terse summary of a significant relationship. There's got to be more, but my client maneuvers the conversation to the wealthy patrons who retained him to give recitals or tutor their children. He spins colorful anecdotes, describing their personalities and proclivities, like the son of a wealthy merchant who was a fervent student but had a tin ear. His recitation goes on for nearly an hour. Clearly, he took every opportunity to immerse himself in music and perform whenever possible. But it's also clear that the innate fear people held for what lay beneath the mask relegated him to a separate existence on the perimeter of society.

"Where did you reside in Zurich?" I ask.

"In a mansion converted into a boarding house by a widow." He turns wistful. "I occupied a top floor room with a splendid view of the lake."

"It must have been difficult to leave when you returned to Paris."

His expression freezes. Abruptly, he pushes himself out of the settee and strides to the window, beginning to pace. "It was time to leave," he replies evasively.

Ah. I've hit a nerve. What happened? "Had your lessons with Wagner ended?"

"It was time. That is all." He turns his back to me. "When Adèle wrote me about Jules's death and her illness, I went to Paris to see how she fared." Unexpectedly, he hisses, "So, now you want to delve into my life in Paris?"

"Um, let's discuss that in our next meeting. Would that be agreeable?" The dark glare he gives me communicates that he is satisfied with the reprieve but discussing that part of his life will never be *agreeable*. At least we have accounted for the years away from the opera house. No torture chambers. No Punjab lassos. Just work, study, carving, drawing, pianos, organs, and violins. *And Wagner.*

In the corridor, Ryan and Jarrod scrutinize me as if trying to figure out whether the lion tamer has emerged with or without claw marks. Just as I extend my hand and say goodbye to Mr. Mercier, George unexpectedly materializes.

"Dr. Adler invites you and Dr. Kirkman to dine with Mr. Mercier and her," he says with a bow.

I'd planned an evening at home working on client cases, but Ryan gives me an encouraging nod. I put on a smile. "Yes, thank you." My client's expression becomes unreadable.

George says he will escort us to the "grand piano room" where we can visit until dinner. It turns out to be the spectacular, oval-shaped room I saw in passing the other night. The upper level has oversized chairs around game tables and black leather couches that contrast sharply with white marble floors. Paintings by renowned modern artists dominate stark white walls. Broad stairs curve down to the lower level, where richly upholstered chairs and couches are arranged in a semicircle around the room's focal point, a Steinway grand piano. Behind the piano, massive windows highlight a panorama of the Sound.

Ryan and Jarrod take seats on the upper level, and George leads Mr. Mercier and me down the steps. We choose adjacent chairs, keeping a comfortable distance. Absentmindedly, he taps out a cadence on the arm of the chair. The sound of Jarrod and Ryan's laughter makes the silence between us even more uncomfortable. I can't think of anything to say, so I look out the expanse of windows at the Sound. A hawk is soaring effortlessly above the water, then with a startling dive, it descends on some unseen prey.

I begin, "Did you see the hawk…?"

"Would you like…?" He says at the same time.

Awkwardly, we gape at each other.

"You were saying, Ms. Copeland?"

It dawns on me we've never gotten past using last names. Maybe it's time. "Please, call me Kathryn." I smile.

He peers at me, his eyebrow dipping tentatively. "And you may call me Erik."

Feels like a small door just opened. "Well, Erik, did you see the hawk swoop down?"

"No." He hesitates. "I was just wondering..." Has our conversation already stalled? Clearing his voice, he continues. "If you would like me to play one of my compositions."

He's offering to play for me? I never imagined that. "I'd love it," I manage to say.

He goes to the Steinway and settles on the piano bench. His shoulders relax, and his hands hover above the keyboard for a moment. Then he begins to play a soft nocturne, his fingers gliding effortlessly over the keys. The notes meld into dark sounds and unusual rhythms. Hypnotic chords merge with a sensuous countermelody. The music enfolds me, takes my breath away. *Never before had I heard such music,* Adèle wrote. Now I understand what she meant. Closing my eyes, I feel the music flow through me, taking me to some otherworldly realm.

Suddenly a gong clangs from the doorway above, shattering the spell. Abruptly the music stops. My eyes pop open. It's the omnipresent butler, announcing dinner.

George leads us to a private dining room where Dr. Adler greets us with her beaming smile. "I overheard your new composition. It is beautiful. Have you named it?" she asks Erik.

"No," he replies curtly. So, Dr. Adler gets the same terse responses I do. Yet he talked at length about his life in Zurich. Did he open up because he enjoyed those years, or is he getting somewhat comfortable with me? Or was it a distraction, a subterfuge?

The dinner is another luxury of rare foods. The salad is topped with cucumber and succulent avocado. I had forgotten how they taste. The main course of salmon has a luscious curry compote with apples, pears and almonds—all from the Wheaton farms since they are rarely available in grocery stores. I especially savor the apple, recalling the childhood pleasure of an apple pie made by my Irish grandmother's loving hands. I begin to relax, enjoying the delicacies.

Dr. Adler asks for more of the Côte Rôtie. The young server seems nervous as she pours Erik's wine, and the bottle grazes his glass, knocking it over. Scarlet wine pours out on the white damask tablecloth, diffusing outward like a spreading flush. Flustered, the young woman picks up the goblet and hurries away to get a cloth to clean it up.

Erik stares with horror, transfixed by the spilled wine. His eyes stay focused on the red stain as he rises slowly to his feet, then he rushes from the dining room.

"What do you make of that?" I ask Dr. Adler.

"Apparently the wine triggered a post-traumatic stress reaction." She scrutinizes the stain. "Something about spilled wine brought back a traumatic memory."

I study the spreading edge of the stain as it moves toward the base of my wineglass. "That red, what does it remind you of, Dr. Adler?"

She looks at me with sudden realization. "Blood."

28 | CRIMSON

ERIK

Red wine flowing across white. *Red. Harbinger of death. Violent death. Nightmare images of oozing, crimson blood.*

Horror consumes me. Must escape. Must get out. I flee, run across the terrace and descend the steps to the deck. At the far end, I sink into a chair. My eyes attempt to focus on the Sound, but I see only red as my vision clouds over.

A ghostly hand reaches out and touches my shoulder. I recoil at the hazy figure hovering above me. "Erik. I'm here," it says. *Who is this specter? I am entrapped in the dark alley! That vile man is reaching out to grab me.* I strike out. My fist meets with flesh and bone. I blink, trying to make out my foe.

"Erik, it's me. Jarrod." The specter starts to recede. "I'll get Dr. Adler."

I gasp for air. A ringing begins in my ears, like a hollow, distant echo. I cradle my forehead, suspended between this world and the encroaching void. Footsteps pound, getting closer. They stop, but I cannot look up. Cold sweat pours out as I attempt to pull air into my lungs. Murky fog threatens to engulf me. I dare not pass out, dare not show weakness.

Someone kneels in front of me, and a voice reaches through the fog. "Erik, you are safe," it says. "We're here to help." Still I cannot breathe, cannot speak.

The voice directs, "Erik, breathe slowly in, through your nose. Remember what you've learned. Hold the breath, count to five. Then breathe out slowly through your mouth. Relax, relax. Just keep breathing." I do as I am bid. The ringing recedes. As my breath begins to flow, I lean back and rest my head against the cushion.

"Keep your eyes closed," the voice says. "Just rest and relax."

I comply, not yet ready to face whoever is present. I focus on breathing, on calming the pounding blood in my veins.

Strong fingers wrap my hand around a glass. Something is placed in my other hand. "Take this pill, Erik," a deeper voice commands. I manage to swallow it, then the glass is removed. Near me, I hear shuffling of feet and chairs squeaking. Who is here? Whom must I face? For several minutes, I gather myself. Enough time to push down and lock away what has resurfaced. I will myself not to think of *that* now.

Reluctantly, I open my eyes. Dr. Adler sits next to me, and Ryan stands just in front. Not far away, Ms. Copeland—no, she said I could call her Kathryn—occupies a bench. Jarrod is just behind her. All witnessed my vulnerability. I am mortified.

"How are you doing?" Ryan breaks the uneasy stillness.

Although my throat is still constricted, I manage, "I require no further assistance."

"Are you certain?" Dr. Adler asks.

"Quite certain."

"If we can be of help, let us know," she says as she rises.

Kathryn stands and turns to go, but she gazes back at me with those beautiful, questioning eyes. I do not want her to leave, but only manage to say, "Good evening, *mademoiselle*."

"Good evening, *Mr. Mercier*," she replies softly.

When they have gone, I rest my feet on the cushioned ottoman and reflect on their expressions. No glares of disapproval, no irritation fraying their voices. In my world, condemnation would have been bestowed without a façade of civility. Only Jarrod remains, sitting at a distance, mindful of my need for privacy.

Twilight reflects a rainbow of colors on the clouds. Pristine white gulls with wings like waistcoats of formal grey sit atop a piece of driftwood. In unison, they take to the air, soaring effortlessly over the water. I rub my temple, trying to ease the pulsating ache behind my eyes. How can this world contain such beauty and yet such ugliness? I have always sought to render its beauty in my music and art, even in my architecture. But the ugliness of the world always seems to intrude. Always seeks to destroy me.

Still, I am not the only one to have suffered. The love between Adèle and Jules was a thing of beauty, and the insanity of this world destroyed that as well. I remember their tender kiss at the altar. They complemented each other perfectly. Adèle's caring and somber nature was balanced by Jules's protective and jovial temperament, both open-minded and openhearted.

But the world intruded. Father Lucien told me that Jules tried to protect a woman from her brutal husband. The woman's screams could be heard on the street below. Jules was on police duty that night. Being a good man, he intervened, although the law allowed the husband to do with his wife what he would. The crazed bastard pulled out his derringer and shot Jules point blank. Ugliness won out that day and destroyed something precious. Something beautiful.

The Sound begins to fade into a dream-like cloud, and the hammering in my head eases. Ryan's drug must be working. My eyelids feel heavy. As sleep overtakes me, the face of Jules appears—so young, so hopeful about his future, so joyous about sharing it with Adèle.

But fate stepped in. Someone cut short Jules's life, someone evil. Again, red flashes before my eyes. The blood, everywhere. So what does that make me?

29 | ENIGMA

Dr. Diane Adler

"Are you all right?" Ryan asks me when I reach the upper terrace.

"Climbing three flights of stairs is challenging for an old bird like me," I reply, chuckling. While I catch my breath, I look down on the lower deck to see how Erik is doing.

"He'll be okay," Ryan says, reading my mind. "What I gave him should knock him out."

A row of poplars rims the edge of the terrace, like dramatic exclamation points in their round Italian urns. Ms. Copeland stands in the shadow of a poplar, so deep in thought she doesn't look up when we walk over. We all gaze down at the dark-clad figure. As a psychiatrist, I find it telling that, except for white shirts, Erik's clothing is exclusively black. Is his choice of color a manifestation of how he feels about the world or about himself? Or is it his manner of protection—creating a dark, foreboding presence which keeps people at a safe distance? If that's his intention, it certainly seems to work.

"I can't imagine what he's lived through," Ms. Copeland murmurs, "or suffered."

"I agree. What he's accomplished is a testament to his singular intellect and abilities."

"Something in his soul too, don't you think? Something indomitable." After a pause she adds, "There's another quality I haven't been able to identify yet. But I sense it."

"There's much about him we haven't figured out," I reply. "He's an enigma."

"Wonder what triggered his PTS this time," Ryan says, worried.

"The wine looked like blood, but he's never discussed such an event with me. Did he say anything to you that would relate in some way?" I ask Ryan. He shakes his head.

"He hasn't said anything to me that fits, either." Ms. Copeland leans against the balustrade, studying Erik. "But he's said things that make me wonder what he's withholding."

"Could you stay a little longer, Ms. Copeland?" I ask. "Since I'll be the psychiatric expert at the trial, maybe this is a good time for us to begin discussing the case."

"Sure, but please call me Kathryn."

"And call me Diane." I glance down at Erik who has fallen asleep. The drug Ryan gave him is working. *Gut gemacht.* He needs to rest. Since this trial came up, he's been under too much stress and his behavior is becoming more erratic. As we walk to the library, George says he'll bring drinks. Diplomatically, Ryan goes to the other side of the library and selects a hardbound to read. Even though he's a doctor, he doesn't let his ego get in the way. Serving as a bodyguard these past couple months couldn't have been easy for him, yet he's done it with grace. Even gained Erik's acceptance. I overheard conversations between the two men that indicated a respectful relationship had taken root. Then, out of the blue, Ryan was reassigned as Kathryn's bodyguard. I've wondered about that.

We sink into leather chairs facing both the fireplace and windows. Brilliant oranges, yellows and pinks refract off clouds as the sun sets above the Sound and deep green forest.

Kathryn takes in the books lining the walls. "I'll bet this is an amazing collection. I'd love to spend time here, just browsing."

"Lady Margaret has superb taste. She brought many volumes from her family's French estate."

"My legal assistant did some research and found articles about her philanthropic work, but there wasn't much about her personal life. Just that she's forty-two, married Howard Wheaton ten years ago, and they have no children. She appears to guard her privacy."

"Closely. You may not know she was an Olympic equestrian. That's why there are horses here at Land's End. She loves to ride." Then it occurs to me that I don't know much about Kathryn's private life. "What hobbies do you enjoy?"

"Music. Hardbounds. And I love driving my Vette. I save up my gas ration coupons so that I can drive to the ocean once a month."

"The weather's nice this weekend. Perhaps you can go for a drive."

"Is that your professional advice?" she asks with a half smile.

"Sorry. I didn't mean it that way." I take off my glasses and rub the bridge of my nose. "With the stress of the case, perhaps we all need time off to relax."

Staring out the window, she says, "You're not the only one who's said that to me."

When George serves our drinks and departs, I take a sip of Chablis and begin. "What were you discussing when you felt Erik was withholding information?"

"The first time, he was mentioning his trip from Paris to London. I said it seemed dangerous for a boy of thirteen to travel that far by himself. He said to ask the next question."

"Did he seem upset or angry?"

"A bit of both, I think." Then she adds, "But when it happened today, it was more subtle. He was discussing his time in Zurich and seemed to be opening up. When I asked why he left Zurich, he got up and began pacing."

"He told me that he left to help Madame Giry," I interject, "but I think that only contributed partly to his decision."

"Just bringing it up caused him to become so upset, I ended our conference." Kathryn frowns. "So far, we've only gotten to his return to Paris. Discussing his life there will be challenging. I hope he doesn't do his disappearing act again." She looks at the corner where Erik had appeared seemingly out of nothingness. "Have you been able to discuss those years with him?"

"No, he's very tightlipped about that. Never has mentioned Christine. But how can you blame him? Although she didn't physically harm him, if Leroux is correct and she removed his mask, that would have triggered memories of past unmaskings that *were* very traumatic. When that happens, someone with post-traumatic stress may strike out at the person who triggered the memories, causing her to fear him." I get to the point. "But today his PTS was different. It was not related to anyone threatening to unmask him. The spilled wine evoked a memory of something else."

A pained look in her eyes, Kathryn asks, "What can be done to help him?"

"I'm teaching him breathing techniques to use when the physical reactions begin. But there are other therapies available. One is to have an anchor, such as a beloved person or even a place that gives comfort.

I would also like to use direct exposure therapy, but that requires the person to talk about the trauma, and Erik's very reticent to discuss his past. That technique needs to be done carefully, with a professional, so the person doesn't go into a PTS reaction. Repeating the process gradually diffuses the emotions caused by the trauma and helps the person develop coping mechanisms."

"I wonder if Erik will ever open up and talk about what really happened."

I put my glasses back on and ponder this. Erik said that Kathryn is the only person he trusts here. Perhaps she could be successful in reaching Erik on that level. I notice that she's now using *Erik* instead of *Mr. Mercier*, so they are becoming comfortable with one another.

"Do you think the wine reminded him of blood from a wound?" she asks, changing the subject. "Maybe a fatal one?"

"You're wondering if it could have been at his hands?"

"Yes, possibly someone he's accused of murdering," she says tentatively.

"Perhaps, or even a situation we know nothing about."

"It's my understanding that when a person has post-traumatic stress, he may not even remember the situation that caused it."

"That's true. Sometimes the memory of a traumatic event has been suppressed because the person cannot deal with it. If that has occurred, a triggering event may or may not cause a flashback, but still the emotions associated with the trauma could be experienced, such as panic or fear or anger."

"So a person with PTS may have an emotional reaction without knowing why."

"Certainly, and the reaction can be as severe as if there were a full-blown flashback. You see, the subconscious mind remembers, and even the body can experience shock or other reactions, such as difficulty breathing."

"In that case Erik may not admit he committed a murder," she says, her brows arching, "because he doesn't remember it himself."

"Yes, or he may have witnessed someone else commit a murder and blocked that out."

"That makes my job a lot harder." Kathryn sighs.

"Your job of defending Erik or finding the truth?"

With troubled eyes, Kathryn murmurs, "Both."

30 | CHIMES

ERIK

The wind blows Adèle's curls around her face and her gentle eyes welcome me. So long since I have seen her. She makes her way through the milling crowd. Our hands touch as tears well in her eyes. Barely able to control my emotions, I turn away. When I look back, a young man with blonde hair and intense blue eyes stands beside her. Jules. He extends his hand, his manner forthright. I like this man.

Jules and I are walking in the Bois de Boulogne with Adèle between us. The day is hot, my jacket slung over my shoulder. We find a sheltering tree and Adèle spreads a blanket in the shade, sharing the delicacies from her basket. After we feast, I lean back on the tree and observe them. Jules reaches out, tenderly brushing a wisp of brown hair from her face. He has a kind, generous nature, and they talk easily with one another. I feel happy for them.

The opera house. Familiar corridors loom ahead, dimly lit by gas sconces. From the shadows above the entrance foyer, I watch finely dressed men remove their cloaks as elegant women preen, bejeweled with priceless baubles. Adèle appears, attired in a modest burgundy dress. She takes me to a vacant box as the curtain rises. Amid the mystical glow of footlights, the music and grandeur begin to cast their spell. Panicked, Adèle rushes in. The man who rented the box is coming! The drunken barrister staggers into me just outside the box and apologizes. My heart pounds as we race through dark passageways to safety. Gasping for breath, Adèle crosses herself, and we double over in laughter.

Adèle, sobbing in her room. I take her to a small café. The waiter smiles slyly, believing us to be lovers seeking privacy. Shadows of palm leaves play on Adèle's face as she weeps. She dreads the walk down the aisle without her father's supporting arm. Darkness engulfs me. I go from door to door trying to find something.

The doors of Église Saint-Sulpice open and its towering nave looms before me. A priest emerges from dark shadows. His brown hair radiates from a balding pate like wires on a chimney sweep's brush. His vestments are rumpled and askew. He makes no mention of my unusual appearance, and I make none of his. I ask for permission to play the organ for Adèle's wedding. With a conspiratorial grin, he agrees and guides me up to the organ loft. I sit in wonder before five banks of keys and myriad stops. Reverently, I touch the keys played for the wedding of Victor Hugo. My hands shake. So little time to learn the secrets of its nature.

Adèle appears, beautiful in her wedding gown. While she prays, I slip away and climb to the organ loft, my heart hammering. My music must carry her down that long nave. The banks of keys loom before me. I dare not fail. I set my fingers free and coax every note to sublime expression. When the last chords fill the air, I gaze down at the altar where Adèle stands next to Jules. She is radiant. My heart soars as I watch them kiss tenderly. Husband and wife. I send rapturous music throughout the grand cathedral.

The lights in the café glow on Adèle's joyous face. When she picks up my small gift, I tense, my fingers digging into my palms. As she lifts the necklace from the box, she gasps. Her eyes gaze at me, filled with tears as she puts it on. Lovingly, Jules fastens the clasp, and the world seems beautiful. Surely whatever sin I have committed has been expiated. The Fates will smile on us all. The café fades and disappears into the mists. Non, do not go!

Breezes blow the curtains back from my windows, exposing storm clouds over Zurich. I wring out a washcloth. So cool against my bare face, so soothing on my feverish forehead. I am sleeping fretfully when a woman's scream pierces the air and my soul. My eyes shoot open, horrified to see her at the foot of my bed. She stares at my face, then her blonde hair streams wildly in her desperate haste to flee. The angry face of the landlady hovers, spewing her venom, ordering me to leave and never again see her daughter.

Impending doom hides in every corner. Nightmarish faces surround me. I must escape. Running, forever running. At the end of a long tunnel, a door appears. When it opens, a letter is thrust into my hand. Such jagged writing, so foreign from Adèle's usual, delicate script. Full of pained words. I collapse into a chair. Jules dead, Adèle alone—and there is a child.

The train pulls into the station. Blustering winds blow cold rain mercilessly. Adèle's face, white and drawn with circles of illness darkening her eyes. I peer down at Meg, so tiny, with her father's golden hair and bright eyes. Stabbing pain slices at my heart. Jules. He will never see his beautiful daughter, and she will never know him. I gather them into the carriage and take them home. There, on Adèle's dresser, Jules's picture draped with black ribbon. I look at it as I hold Meg in my arms and rock her gently while singing a lullaby. Adèle's rasping cough comes from behind the screen. My feelings in turmoil. What will become of Adèle and the child? As I stare at the flames in the fireplace, terrifying images ravage my mind. A wailing cry shatters the air.

I wrest myself awake. With the back of my hand, I wipe the sweat from my face and glance furtively over at Jarrod. He is engrossed in reading. The cloudless night sky, filled with stars, is indifferent to me. But the nightmare will not leave. The sound of crying remains starkly vivid. I was barely twenty-one, and my fate hung in the balance as I held Meg and rocked her while contemplating my path. Whatever I decided, there would be no going back. My mind spun out each conflicting possibility, weaving all the interlocking threads of my life like a spider spinning an intricate web.

In the end, I became caught in the web. It happened when little Meg awoke and cried out. Adèle rushed to her, then covered her shoulder with a towel and nursed the baby beneath it, modestly facing away. Emotions raged through me as I observed the simple ritual of love between mother and child. And it broke my heart. I had not received such devotion from my own mother.

When Adèle put Meg in the cradle, I turned my gaze back to the fire so she would not know I had been watching. The orange-hot flames licked at the two small logs in the fireplace until they broke into pieces and were consumed. Clearly Adèle was very ill. What if she were turned out onto the streets? What horrible existence awaited her? Perhaps even violence at the hands of dangerous men. Jules would not be there to protect them. Fate would consume Adèle and her child with uncaring, fiery indifference.

For me, opportunities beckoned in London and Zurich. Monsieur Markham wrote he had arranged an audition with a symphony orchestra and invited me to reside with him again. He felt certain I would rise to the level of a renowned soloist. The church also wanted me to resume as organist. Or I could return to Zurich and resume my studies with Herr Wagner. I was assured of earning a comfortable living there, and the connections I had already established would open doors for me when I was ready for my compositions to be performed. Wagner had fumed at me when I explained my intent to leave. He declared that connections were critical to the success of a musician or composer—that if I left, I would be throwing away everything I had accomplished.

But there was Adèle and Meg. I could not take them to live with me in London or Zurich because Adèle and I were not married, nor was she formally related to me. Living together would compromise her reputation forever, and there was still the chance she could meet someone and marry again. But that prospect would be ruined if she had been living with a man, unmarried. No one would believe that our relationship was platonic, but it was never that of lovers. And Adèle was so heartbroken over the loss of Jules, I knew it would take a long time for her to heal before she could let another in. Ultimately, she never found anyone who could take his place. But for me, remaining in Paris meant starting all over again, a musician in a city with too many people and too few jobs. Would I be accepted into the opera houses without contacts as an entrée? And my mask—would that undermine my chances?

I can still hear the clock striking nine. I did not realize then that the chimes marked more than time. They divided my life into two distinct parts. I made my decision to stay in Paris so I could watch over and protect Adèle and her child. Impersonally, each stroke of the hammer severed my past from my future. I did not know what was in store for us, but I knew I could not abandon this woman who had so unselfishly stood by me and saved my life. Nor could I let her daughter —and Jules's—perish.

I remember walking over to the cradle and gazing down at little Meg. When I told Adèle my decision, her eyes could not hide her astonishment or her relief. Neither of us knew then, certainly not until many years later, the decision made that night—the pact we entered into tacitly—would lead down the path which separated me from all my hopes and dreams. And set me on the road to ultimately becoming a haunted, hunted man. A phantom.

31 | WINGS

Sunday, June 17
Washington coast

Kathryn

Just outside Olympia, a straight stretch of highway opens up. No cars in sight. With music blasting, I throttle up my Vette.

"*Kathryn!*" Ryan glares at me. "You're going 120."

"Giving my car and me some wings."

"Just make sure they're not angel wings," he fires back. I ease up, just a little. "Great, 110. That makes all the difference."

I grin. The powerful engine sends us flying. Time seems suspended. I'm free! When I spot an oncoming car, I ease back to the speed limit.

"You always drive like that?" he asks.

"Only when there aren't other cars on the road."

"I guess I'll pray for steady traffic. I'm supposed to deliver you back in one piece."

"Sorry. This is how I relax."

He gives me a sideways grin. "Yeah? Well, I've got to admit, you sure can handle this car."

At my favorite spot on the beach, I pull off the road and park. As Ryan gets the cooler out of the trunk, I grab my Qrystal. "What's that all about?" he says, frowning.

Heading for the beach, I toss back, "Got work to do."

"Hasn't anyone ever told you, when you go to the beach, work isn't on the list?"

I halt and he nearly plows into me. "You thought I was just going to gaze at the ocean?"

"Well, it's my opinion *as a doctor* that some time off is healthy."

"Look, Ryan, my schedule next week is crammed. I've hired a new attorney and will be spending a lot of time getting him up to speed about my other clients. I've got to finish rereading Madame Giry's diary because Lexa has made important notations throughout the text. This might be one of the few chances I have to study these before meeting with Erik next Saturday. I know you brought a picnic, so I'll take *time off* to eat. Okay?"

"You better! George had the Wheatons' chef send over our picnic lunch from the penthouse, so you know it'll be something special."

We trek down the beach, and I climb onto a large boulder whose edge juts over the water. Below, the waves gently lap against the rock and strands of seaweed catch listlessly in the crags. The seagulls' calls blend with the hypnotic rumble of waves. Lulled, I close my eyes to absorb the sounds of the ocean and the sun's warm rays. The acrid tang of seaweed hangs in the air, mixing with the smell of salt water. In this perfect place, I meditate. When I open my eyes and gaze toward the horizon, I realize I needed to come here today.

I pull out my QRYSTAL and pick up where I left off in the diary. Lexa highlighted most of the next section, so clearly Erik became important in Adèle's life. He rented an apartment on the Left Bank and told her that he enjoyed looking out his attic room at the skyline of Paris and watching the stars. Each evening, Erik took care of Meg while Adèle worked, and he frequently took the baby for walks so Adèle could rest.

Christmas 1858

This morning Erik arrived, laden with gifts. For Meg, he brought a stuffed animal and for me, a wool coat in the latest fashion. I could not help but cry. Ever since my parents died, all my coats have been secondhand, quite worn and threadbare. In my excitement,

I kissed him on the cheek. He drew back, startled, and turned his attention to the basket he brought. It contained a feast: oysters, brioche, cheese, and a fine wine. He was pleased with the socks and scarf I knitted to keep him warm on the long walks from his apartment. Afterward, I asked him to accompany me to mass at Église Saint-Sulpice. The cathedral is magnificent at Christmas, and I wanted to light some candles. I persisted, and Erik finally gave in, but he insisted on hiring a carriage out of concern for my illness.

The cathedral was filled with banks of flickering candles. I prayed at the Chapelle de la Madone while Erik held little Meg. As I lit candles for Jules, Papa, Maman, and my little brother, their faces appeared before me, reducing me to sobs. Erik said we should not stay for mass, but I wanted to hear the grand organ, so we sat in the back pew. He held me while I wept softly on his shoulder, and Meg snuggled on his other shoulder and slept.

I took comfort from the organ music, although it did not rise to the soaring beauty of Erik's. His expression revealed he was of the same mind. After mass, Erik sought out Father Dupres, the senior priest, and I waited while Erik explained his background and asked to be considered for the position of assistant organist. But Father Dupres said the organ of Saint-Sulpice was grander and could not be compared with those in other churches. Dismissively, he told Erik no position was open, but I saw how his gaze kept straying to the mask. Erik also noticed.

During the ride home, Erik peered out the coach window, fuming. He carried Meg up to my room, then left. The pain in his eyes haunts me. Dupres's rejection cut deeply. What if other people are like the priest and Erik cannot find work? What will he do?

Erik continued to come daily to care for little Meg, and Adèle's health slowly improved. From a homeopathic doctor, he purchased a remedy that cured her cough. To save money, he no longer hired carriages and walked everywhere. He applied for any position suiting his musical abilities, but somehow they were always filled. Adèle wrote about his increasing bitterness. He felt that the jobs were not available *only to him*. Then, an opportunity presented itself when a violinist at the Opéra injured his hand.

15 March 1859

Before Erik's audition began, I snuck into a box on the first tier. When he arrived, he swept off his cloak and looked so fine in his black suit. But the conductor, Monsieur Duclos, told Erik that he must remove the mask for his audition. I was shocked and could tell Erik's anger was boiling under the surface. Still, he controlled himself and replied that he needed to wear the mask so as not to offend anyone's sensibilities. But Erik's words did not quell the conductor's objections. Monsieur Duclos became more indignant and stated either Erik's face was presentable in public without the mask, or he was simply not presentable at all.

I was terrified, watching Erik loom over Monsieur Duclos, a mouse of a man whose mustache twitched nervously like whiskers. I prayed Erik would not strike him, as much as Duclos deserved it. Finally, Erik said in a voice so cold it gave me chills, "You will regret this, monsieur." Then he grabbed his cloak and violin case and was gone. I still cannot believe the conductor never heard Erik play a single note.

I ran from the box as fast as my legs could carry me, trying to catch up with Erik. At the rear door, the stagehand said Erik had left mere seconds before. I raced into the alley and searched both directions but could not find him. How could he have disappeared so quickly?

It is midnight, and Meg sleeps peacefully. Erik did not come tonight. I am exhausted but cannot sleep, cannot get Erik out of my thoughts. I fear for him.

Her diary entries became frantic when she didn't see Erik for over a week. Then he appeared one evening as if nothing had happened. He came to care for Meg, just as before, but his appearance upset Adèle. He had circles under his eyes and had lost weight. They settled into their old pattern, but Erik was more sullen and withdrawn. His continuing weight loss alarmed her. Incredibly, the gentle-tempered Adèle ordered Erik to come earlier every evening to eat with her. From that time on, it became their habit to share dinner together.

3 April 1859

Erik's brooding usually makes our dinners sullen. Happily tonight he was in good spirits. Perhaps because today is Meg's first birthday. Again, he brought her a dress and toys, but he also brought something new—a parcel containing ivory parchment and pastels. He has decided to support himself once again by selling drawings. When I asked if he would be drawing churches, he said he had a different idea. He has been visiting the Louvre and studying the masters. He plans to draw the dancers. That explains why I have seen him watching the rehearsals from Box Five recently.

By the time I returned from my work, he had drawn one of the ballet rats in mid-leap. She appeared lifelike, suspended above the ground in effortless flight, her skirt billowing like clouds. But she also had a mystical quality, like a sprite who had crossed over from the other world. I told Erik he would have no trouble selling his work. He was not so certain and said his drawing was not the formal style currently in fashion.

23 June 1859

To earn more money, Erik has taken up painting with oils. Today, he painted pirouetting ballerinas with light glowing from below. It had an ethereal quality, and the vivid colors and bold *brushstrokes perfectly captured the dancers' movements. Surely this will bring more money.*

Lexa notes that Erik's style sounds similar to that of Degas, famous for portraying the dancers at the Paris Opéra a decade later. The similarity was so compelling, she wondered if Degas had seen one of Erik's paintings and was influenced by his style.

1 August 1859

When Erik hung up his waistcoat, I noticed something was amiss. I told him that his laundryman was not pressing his shirts properly, and he should complain. He said he would have to complain to himself. That is when I learned he can no longer afford his attic apartment. Instead, he has let a small room, just large enough to hold a bed, dresser, and chair.

And he can no longer pay for his laundry. He now carries a bucket of water to his room and hand washes his clothing. A clothesline hangs in front of the window. He made a jest that the drying shirts have the added advantage of serving as curtains. I was heartbroken to hear this, but he said the room is not so bad. It has a Franklin stove in the fireplace to heat his iron and the water for his tea, and will keep him warm in winter. He assured me he would master the art of ironing, but admitted he would miss gazing at the stars through the skylight.

That September, Richard Wagner moved to Paris to live with his estranged wife. Although Adèle encouraged Erik to pay a social call on his former mentor, he always refused. Adèle suspected they hadn't parted on good terms but didn't press Erik for an explanation.

Erik's new landlord prohibited music being played in the apartments. But the opera house's residential area was vacant during the evening performances, so he began to play his violin in Adèle's room as he lulled Meg to sleep.

Christmas 1859

Again, I cried when I lit the candles for my family at the cathedral. Again, we sat in the last row. When the organ began thundering, Meg awoke with a start. Erik rocked her gently and shushed her but to no avail. When the music swelled, Meg let out a wail to rival a banshee of the dark north. Erik chuckled, but I was mortified as we hurried from the cathedral. Once outside, he could not contain his laughter. I chastised him for committing sacrilege, but confess I giggled when he responded by patting Meg on the back and complimenting her "impeccable taste in music."

In January and February of 1860, Wagner conducted one of his works at the Italian Theater in Paris. Although Erik attended all the performances, he never made his presence known to Wagner. Adèle's concerns about him deepened. He spent most of his time between his room and hers, only venturing out to sell his paintings or walk occasionally with them through the park where she noted he was frequently subjected to offensive stares. I can discern from Adèle's descriptions of Erik's behavior, that by the age of twenty-two, he was already living the life of a recluse, turning in on himself.

That April, Meg turned two, and it became apparent their small room was too confining, so Adèle began taking her to ballet rehearsals. Meg loved to watch the dancers and mimicked their movements to the delight of the ballet rats. That fall, Adèle shared startling news with Erik. She had overheard the Mistress of Ballet announce that the Paris Opéra would perform Wagner's *Tannhäuser*. Everyone was shocked since that opera didn't contain a ballet piece. Erik could hardly believe this turn of events.

Lexa's annotation explains that the Paris Opéra's ballet tradition rose to the level of sacred cow. A ballet was always strategically located in the opera's second act for the benefit of the young male aristocrats. That allowed them to arrive late from dinner to ogle the young ballerinas from whom they often chose their mistresses. Usually those men left after the ballet performance ended, skipping the operatic parts. Obligingly, Wagner modified *Tannhäuser* for its Paris debut and included a ballet.

Adèle pestered Erik, insisting that Wagner would surely hire him. Reluctantly, Erik agreed to approach the maestro and seek a position as violinist.

"Kathryn, ready to eat?" Ryan's voice intrudes. "I'm hungry. Isn't there some law against starving the hired help?"

"Don't know. That's not my area of law."

"Well, then, can I point out that the sunset's going to be beautiful?" He grins cajolingly.

"You're incorrigible." I grin back. "Okay, I yield."

He grabs the cooler and joins me on the rock. As he opens the bottle of wine, I take out glass containers with the delicacies prepared by the Wheaton chef—fruit salad with apples, strawberries and even rare bananas, curried rice and salmon, and asparagus covered in a cream sauce. We start by digging into an assortment of hors d'oeuvres and fresh sourdough bread. "Don't forget to leave room for dessert," Ryan says with a contented grin. "It's chocolate cheesecake."

As we eat, a gentle breeze flows off the ocean. I love these hours when the sun moves toward the edge of the world, when its magical rays paint the sky with a tapestry of ever-changing colors.

We settle into a comfortable chat, so I decide to bring up the issue that's been bothering me. "Can I ask you something about Erik? He wears a gold ring. Was he wearing it when you brought him from the past?"

"Yeah, we found it when we prepped him for surgery. Why?"

"Lexa and I wondered why the Communards didn't steal it before they buried him. Or why Madame Giry didn't remove it when she identified his body."

Ryan gazes out at the sunset, thinking. "I remember. He was wearing leather gloves, so you couldn't tell he had a ring on. They probably just didn't notice it."

"Thanks, that helps." So Erik was wearing the ring when he was executed. But Leroux wrote that Christine returned and placed it on the Phantom's hand and buried him. Was that Leroux's creative storytelling? Or did he get that from Christine's letters? *Christine's letters.* If they are authenticated and admitted at trial, will they provide some clues to navigate this maze—or turn out to be a minefield?

32 | BISHOP

Wednesday, June 20
London, England

LEXA

London traffic is crowded this morning and painstakingly slow. I call Mr. Preston on my QRYSTAL, but he doesn't answer. After I leave a message that traffic is slowing us down, I mumble under my breath, "At this rate, we'll be late for our appointment."

Josh glances at me from the driver's seat. "Let's see what we can do about that." He pulls the car into the small opening in the next lane, causing the driver behind to honk in protest. But that's only his warm-up. He starts weaving between cars, pedicabs and motorcycles like a race car driver.

"Are you crazy?" I ask him after a near miss.

"Don't want you stressin' over being late."

"Well, it's working. Now I'm just worried about getting there alive."

As he swerves wildly from one lane to the next, I grab the dashboard to steady myself. Then he makes a turn—into the wrong lane—and misses a pedicab by inches.

"Left, Josh. We're in London. You don't turn into the right-hand lane."

As Josh weaves back into the correct lane, the man in the pedicab yells out a cockney-accented epithet. I'm not sure whether to scream or laugh. When he flips us off, that tips the scales. I laugh.

"Concentrate on the road, will you?" Blake says from the back seat. "And if you turn into the wrong lane again, I'm driving."

"I may not be sure which side to drive on, but I'm your man if we need to make a fast getaway."

"Good grief!" I sputter. "We're only going to a church, why would we need a fast getaway?"

"To make sure you and whatever you retrieve today gets back safely," Blake interjects.

"We're only picking up a piece of stone and a picture. Why on earth would we need a fast getaway? I've been to London dozens of times—never had a problem. I've always been just fine taking care of myself, after all I hold a black belt in karate."

"Good." Josh snorts. "Makes our job a lot easier. If anyone gives us trouble, we'll sic you on 'em."

Mumbling a few choice words under my breath, I watch the traffic, *closely.* Then I spot the sign to Regents Park and the London Zoo. "We're almost there." I point to the sign. "Did you know St. Mark's is next to the London Zoo?"

"That's handy," Josh says. "Don't have to go far for camels and donkeys at Christmas."

I roll my eyes. "In a way, you're not too far off. St. Mark's was nicknamed the Zoo Church. They hosted tea parties in the church garden for visitors to the zoo before it was hit by bombs during the Battle of Britain."

"What's the Battle of Britain?" Josh asks.

"In 1940, Germany ran bombing raids day and night," Blake jumps in and answers. "It went on for months to break the morale of the Brits in preparation for a German invasion. But it didn't work and the invasion never happened."

"You're a history buff?" I peer around at Blake.

"I was stationed in London," he replies. "It has *some* history."

I point out St. Mark's spire just ahead, and Josh pulls into a parking space. As we walk to the church, I take in its austere Gothic exterior. The stone façade is a patchwork of grey limestone. At the front corner a tall spire creates a bleak silhouette against overcast skies. "Hard to believe Erik helped build this church nearly two hundred years ago," I murmur.

"Most things about Erik are hard to believe," Josh quips.

"But the original church he worked on was destroyed, wasn't it?" Blake asks.

"Yeah, I heard all about it when I spoke to the groundskeeper, Mr. Preston. He's got this great, raspy voice and told me one story after another. He grew up near St. Mark's, and his grandfather told him about terrifying nights in the shelters, hearing the explosions above and feeling the earth tremble. The church was hit with an incendiary, then a few nights later was bombed into rubble. It was rebuilt after the war."

"So how did this piece of stone we're picking up survive?" Blake asks.

"Mr. Preston said that some of the broken pieces were saved as mementos. He remembered one in particular because it had letters engraved on it. He found the stone and called me back. It turned out the stone fragment has the letters *i k* and *m e r*. When I explained to Mr. Preston those letters were part of a name, he was excited that the engraving had finally been deciphered. He got the bishop's permission for us to borrow the stone as evidence for the trial and even agreed to testify as to its authenticity."

The main entrance is unlocked, so we enter and look around for Mr. Preston, but he's nowhere in sight. I'm looking forward to meeting this genial man with a penchant for storytelling. While we wait, I take in the beautiful church, with its white columns flanking the nave and classic rose stained-glass window. Behind the altar stands a jaw-dropping reredos panel gilded in gold and painted with jewel-colored Byzantine figures.

"Lexa! Taylor!" Blake yells out. "Over here!"

I spin around. Blake's kneeling next to a crumpled blue heap. Someone must've passed out. I rush over, but Josh gets there first and drawls out, "Daaamn."

I come to an abrupt halt near an elderly man dressed in work clothes. Blood oozes down the front of his coveralls and pools on the floor. A scream reverberates through the church. Then I realize it was me. "Is he…is he…?"

After feeling for the pulse on the man's neck, Josh says, "Yep, as a doornail."

My heart pounds as I whisper, "Let's get out of here."

"No," Blake snaps.

"Why not?" The adrenaline begins to surge. "We can't be implicated in a murder."

"We can't run." Blake grabs my shoulder. "London has more security cameras than any other place on the planet. They could identify and track us. If we run now, we look guilty."

"He's right," Josh says. "I saw a security camera in front of the church."

"Why don't we go out the back door? Would they have a camera there?"

"There may not be, but we've certainly been recorded entering. If we leave out the back, it'll look suspicious. Taylor, call Tom," Blake orders. "I've got something to do."

In a stupor, I watch Blake jog toward the front of the church. Nausea hits me. I struggle to keep my breakfast down. Vaguely, I'm aware that Josh is talking on his QRYSTAL. After a short conversation, he tells me, "The Marines are on the way."

Blake returns moments later, tensely coiled. "What were you doing?" I ask. "Don't tell me you had a gun."

"Then don't ask." His expression is unreadable. "Is that Preston?"

"I can't say for certain." My stomach begins to churn in earnest, and I deliberately avoid looking at the man on the floor sprawled in his own blood. "I only know that based on his stories he would have been elderly and that he was the groundskeeper. Sort of like this man. Should we check the body to see if the stone is there?"

"No!" Blake's abruptness makes me jump. "We don't want to leave fingerprints or tamper with anything that could physically connect us with the body."

"That stone's long gone," Josh says. "It's a sure bet whoever killed this old gent took it."

"Shouldn't we call the police or someone?" I mumble.

"Yeah..." Josh is interrupted by a woman entering the front door. She sees us and walks in our direction. The staccato click of her heels on stone competes with the pounding of my heart. Then she spots the body and the blood. She shrieks and runs out of the church in panic.

Josh gives me a wry glance. "Well, that takes care of calling the police."

My stomach gurgles, and my knees are dissolving into mush. I walk over and collapse onto a chair. Surely that's Mr. Preston. He was so full of laughter and stories when I spoke with him two days ago. Now he's dead. I turn away and gaze toward the front of the church, at the beautiful gold panels above the altar. Saints and apostles gaze serenely back, making what lies on the floor even more surreal.

We don't have to wait long. Within minutes, the doors slam open, and the police come barging in. Josh and Blake hold up their hands. "We're unarmed," Blake yells out.

I don't say anything, just keep my forehead resting in my palms and my jaws clamped shut. The policemen shout something, and then I hear more shoes pounding on the stone floor. While the police check the body, Josh and Blake continue to stand protectively in front of me. I hear footsteps approaching, then a voice announces, "I'm Inspector Kincaide, and this is Sergeant Collin. We're from the Yard."

I look up just as a policeman kneeling next to Mr. Preston shakes his head, verifying he's dead. The inspector cites his legal authority and informs us that we'll be checked for weapons. While policemen search Josh and Blake, a policewoman politely but firmly asks me to stand. While she pats me down, she has me turn around. Once more the lifeless body comes into view, and I feel dizzy. When the policewoman is done, I sit down again.

"Do you require medical attention?" Inspector Kincaide asks, slightly irritated.

I look up through my haze of wooziness at the middle-aged man with thinning hair and a pudgy face. He peers at me with beady eyes.

"No, I'm okay."

The much younger Sergeant Collin pulls out a paper notepad and begins writing as the inspector asks us—in a distinctly accusatory tone—why we're here.

"We were picking up a stone from the groundskeeper for a legal case." I swallow hard. "Is that man on the floor the groundskeeper?"

"Indeed he is. Did you get the stone from him?"

"No, we didn't."

"When did you make those arrangements?"

"Two days ago. We flew in from Seattle today to pick it up." Then I remember our other appointment today. "We're also planning to pick up a painting. It's related to the same legal matter. And it just occurred to me the woman we're to meet could also be in danger. Can you send a police officer to her home?"

"What's her name," he asks with calm detachment, "and when was your meeting?"

"Her name is Madeline Sewell. We have an appointment at twelve thirty at her home." I give them her number and address, and the inspector directs the female officer to contact her.

We're interrupted by another police officer who asks to speak privately with the inspector. The two men walk some distance away to talk. Kincaide stares down at his shoes as he listens intently. Blake and Josh remain on alert, watching everything around us. Uneasily, I realize we're at the mercy of the police in a foreign country where I don't know the laws or our rights. I can't believe this has happened. Now I realize why the Wheatons have retained so many bodyguards, and for the first time, I'm glad.

When the inspector returns, he scrutinizes us, stony-faced. "Where was the groundskeeper when you arrived?"

"On the floor right where you see him," Blake answers. "He was already dead."

"Did you see anyone else inside the church?"

"Just a woman. She came in right after we found the body, but she ran out and we assume she called the police."

"What door did you enter?" The inspector keeps digging.

"The front," Blake replies.

"Did you leave the church at any time?"

"No, none of us did." Blake frowns. I'm also worried about where this is going.

"We'd appreciate your coming with us to the Yard for further questioning." The inspector's gaze sweeps ominously over us as he advises of our rights, British style.

"Are we being arrested?" I ask.

"No, you're not being arrested or formally charged *at this time*. We're merely asking for your cooperation in this murder investigation."

The policemen direct Josh and Blake toward the door, but they refuse to budge without me. "Well, can you get up now?" the inspector asks me icily. As I stand, my stomach clenches and makes its decision. My breakfast spews up. All over the inspector's neat tweed jacket.

33 | COUNTERCHECK

Seattle

Ryan

"Yeah, Tom. We'll be right there." I put down the Qrystal. *Damn, it's 0300.* I jerk on my jeans. As I'm pulling on my t-shirt, I head for Kathryn's room. She's gonna hate me waking her up since she worked until midnight. And I stayed up with her, reading that French history book Collin gave me. "Kathryn, gotta talk to you." I knock on her door and wait.

When she opens it, she's barely awake. "What?" she mutters, groggy.

"Tom just called. Something's happened in London with Lexa and her bodyguards."

"What!"

"The man they were meeting at the church was murdered."

"Mr. Preston? Oh my god." Her dark eyes spring wide open. "Are Lexa and the men all right?"

"They're okay, but they've been taken to Scotland Yard for questioning."

"Questioning? As suspects or witnesses?"

"Not sure yet. Tom wants us to meet him at your office ASAP. He's going to take everything on Erik's case to Land's End. They'll set up an office for you there."

She runs her hand through her tousled hair. "I'll just be a minute."

It's more than a minute, of course. I wait impatiently at the door, then rush us to the car. As I push the speed limit getting to the office, my mind's in full gear. It's gotta be the PTB behind this, but how did they find out about the stone fragment? Only QRYSTALS are being used for this case, and they're secure and not connected to PALnet. All materials for the case are locked up every night. We monitor the office from our security cameras, and the jammers stop electronic eavesdropping. The QRYSTALS given to Kathryn, Lexa and her staff have interference signals which prevent eavesdropping even when they are calling phones connected through PALnet. Don't know how the PTB found out, but we sure as hell can't let it happen again.

At the office, I latch the deadbolt and tell Kathryn not to open the safe until Tom and his men get here. After a thorough search to make sure nothing's been disturbed, we wait in her office. Restless, I walk over to the window and look out. Kathryn comes and stands beside me. "I wonder what's happening in London," she muses, worried. "Do you think they're being framed for the murder?"

"I certainly hope not, but this might be the PTB's doing." I feel a low burn of anger starting. "If it is, they just had an innocent man killed for a piece of stone, so they could do anything." I don't share all my concerns with her—that the PTB could turn this into a smear campaign if one of the attorneys is implicated in a murder. That could have serious fallout for the case—and for Kathryn.

As we wait, we look out the windows. Lights randomly punctuate the office buildings, and moonlight glistens off the bay's waters. So calm out there. So much turmoil in here.

My QRYSTAL goes off. It's Tom saying they're in the building. Kathryn follows me to the front office and is startled when I pull out my gun. I release the deadbolt but expect Tom to use his override code on the keypad to open the door. When he enters, the three men with him remain outside, guarding the hallway to make sure we aren't bothered.

"Sorry to get you up in the middle of the night," he says to Kathryn, "but we need to secure the case files right away."

"I understand," she replies grimly as we go to the storage room. While Kathryn packs the QRYSTALS, documents and books Lexa is researching, she asks Tom, "Did Lexa get the stone or Erik's drawing?"

"Don't know," he replies, frowning. "We haven't been able to talk with Lexa yet, and I've had only a brief conversation with Taylor. I contacted the Wheatons in France and all I know is that they sent an attorney. Can you come to Land's End later today? We'll have more information by then." Kathryn agrees and hands the box over to Tom.

We all go down to the parking garage together, guns drawn. As I drive out of the garage, I glance at my watch. "It's almost noon in London."

"I wonder how Lexa's doing?" Kathryn rubs her forehead. "Radio on, scan news."

On the fourth station, a male voice drones, "...at St. Mark's Church in London. The two murder victims, both elderly men, were shot..."

"Stop scan." Kathryn inhales sharply. "Two murders?"

"Oh hell," I mutter under my breath.

"...Alexandra Simmons and two male companions have been taken to Scotland Yard for questioning. Ms. Simmons is one of the attorneys defending Erik Mercier, charged in the Criminal Court of the Americas with various murders and crimes against humanity. Mr. Mercier, famously known as the Phantom of the Opera, was brought from the nineteenth century as part of Howard Wheaton's time-travel program. Mr. Wheaton's monopoly of that technology is currently under congressional investigation for alleged abuses."

"Well, the PTB didn't waste any time, did they?" My anger heats up.

"They're already implicating Lexa in the murders. And what do they mean about investigating Mr. Wheaton for alleged abuses?"

"I don't know. Hadn't heard anything about it." I shift gears and speed the Corvette over deserted nighttime streets. I've got a feeling this is only going to get worse.

34 | KNIGHT

London

LEXA SIMMONS

"How're you feeling?" Jane peers around the door. "Would you like a cuppa?"

"Just water, please," I reply, still queasy. I like Jane. When I barfed all over the inspector, I stood there like a tree stump, but she was cool-headed. Almost amused. I haven't figured out if she just took it in stride as a hazard of the job or doesn't like the inspector. She returns and hands me a cup of water, no ice. They don't do ice much in England. I give her a smile, and she leaves me to stew in this bleak room furnished with only a metal table and hard chairs. I hate being here alone. Not that Josh didn't give it his best shot and try to stay with me, arguing that he's my bodyguard. But they insisted on questioning us separately.

The door opens again and a tall man in a grey suit that matches his salt-and-pepper hair walks over and extends his hand. Sea blue eyes spark with intelligence and humor, putting me at ease. "Good day, Ms. Simmons. I'm Kenneth Ballard, your solicitor."

I shake his hand, relieved. "Call me Lexa."

"Lady Margaret contacted me. I understand you found yourself in the vicinity of a murder."

"Yeah, I'm really glad you're here." I smile grimly. "It's like the cavalry has arrived."

"Well, in England the tradition is that a knight rescues the fair lady." Despite his smile, his eyes take on a serious glint. I catch his unspoken meaning—we have some challenges ahead. He sets his briefcase down but remains standing. "Two solicitors from my firm are meeting with Mr. Taylor and Mr. Reynolds." He scrutinizes me and pauses. My stomach goes queasy again. "I was listening to the news as I drove over. They're reporting what happened at St. Mark's. Apparently there were *two* murders."

"Two? There was another?" My stomach clenches. "Who? When? Where?"

"I can tell you're a solicitor," he says with a half smile. "Apparently, a derelict was sleeping off his ale in the courtyard behind the church. He was also shot. I surmise that whoever killed Mr. Preston escaped through the courtyard, and the other poor bloke was in the wrong place at the wrong time."

"I can definitely relate. They won't stop at anything, will they?"

"No, they won't," he replies bitterly. Surprised, I look up. Pain—or is it anger—flares in his eyes. "And if they can incriminate you in the bargain, so much the better."

Before I can respond, Inspector Kincaide enters. He gives my solicitor a curt, "Good day, Sir Kenneth." *Sir* Kenneth? He wasn't kidding about a knight coming to my rescue.

The inspector eases his body, heavy with middle-aged spread, into the chair across the table. He states everything will be recorded and begins. The first questions are perfunctory, covering the same information already discussed in the church. Then his attitude markedly changes. "Ms. Simmons, did you know there was a second murder at the church?"

"No, I didn't know."

Kincaide's eyebrows shoot up in mock surprise. "You mean Sir Kenneth hasn't informed you that a second murder occurred?"

"As a matter of fact, Sir Kenneth told me a second murder was reported on PALnet News, but I can't necessarily rely on that can I?" I return the inspector's gaze and state, "And I certainly don't have any personal knowledge about a second murder."

The Inspector's eyes narrow. "Did you go into the courtyard?"

"No. We entered the front of the church and remained inside."

"Did you hear anything, such as a gunshot?"

"I did not."

"Did you observe anyone entering or leaving the church?"

"Blake already told you that a woman came in and saw us. Aren't there cameras on every street in London? Didn't one of those record someone going out the back?"

"No, the courtyard behind the church is well below street level. The cameras are aimed at the street above, not down into the courtyard." Kincaide adds with a snide edge, "And it's for me to ask the questions. Other than the woman, did you hear a door closing or footsteps?"

"No."

"A gun was found in the church. What do you know about it?"

The queasiness returns. "A gun?" I ask, taking just a beat too long.

"Yes, and we're doing tests to see if it's the murder weapon." He becomes more intense. "I repeat, do you know anything about it?"

"No." My heart pounds faster. I'm glad Blake never said whether he had one. *Exactly.*

He eyes me suspiciously. "If you know anything about this gun you need to speak up."

"And *I repeat*, I don't *know* anything about it."

"What about your bodyguards? Does it belong to one of them?"

"We flew into Heathrow at six this morning and went through their security. They found no guns."

He stares at me. "Did either of your bodyguards meet with anyone since you arrived?"

He's like a bulldog—really got his teeth in this. "No. After leaving the airport we went straight to the church."

"How long were you in the church before the police got there?"

"About twenty minutes, as we've said."

"That would have been long enough to hide a weapon, wouldn't it?"

I glare at him. "I wouldn't know."

He frowns. "You said you had an appointment with Madeline Sewell and felt she may be in danger because she has a drawing that you were also obtaining for evidence, correct?"

"Yes, and I'd like to know if she's all right."

"She's quite safe. Why did you think she wouldn't be?" His tone is condescending.

"Well, it seemed possible that whoever murdered Mr. Preston to obtain the stone may also kill to obtain the drawing that she has. It's evidence in the same case."

"We contacted Miss Sewell and sent police officers to her flat. The flat hadn't been broken into, and the picture was still hanging on the wall. That raises a very interesting question. Why would someone kill to obtain one piece of evidence," the inspector says with a sneer, "but leave the other one untouched?"

"I don't know," I reply.

"Inspector, have you personally gone to Miss Sewell's flat?" Sir Kenneth interjects.

"No." The inspector glares back.

"So, you haven't seen the painting yourself?" Sir Kenneth presses. The inspector shakes his head. "How do you know it's the one Ms. Simmons was purchasing?"

"Because Miss Sewell told the officer it was, and the officer saw it."

"Does your officer have personal knowledge about the picture so that he can identify it as the one Ms. Simmons was obtaining for evidence?"

"Of course not." Kincaide's getting testy. I'm getting intrigued.

"We don't actually know that it's the same one, do we?" Sir Kenneth asks pointedly.

"What are you getting at?" The inspector scowls.

"Don't you think we should go there to check out the picture in person? That painting may be relevant to two criminal cases." Sir Kenneth presses. "What is there to lose?"

For several long moments, Kincaide seems deep in thought. Then with a sigh of resignation, he states for the record that the interview is over. He pushes out of his chair and excuses himself.

We wait, watching the clock and wondering what Kincaide is up to. After forty-five minutes Sergeant Collin comes in. "Miss Sewell says she can meet us at her flat in an hour. Is that satisfactory, Sir Kenneth?"

"Most satisfactory," my solicitor replies. As Sergeant Collin takes us through busy hallways, I catch no sight of Josh or Blake. The inspector joins us, and we go to his car, a luxury model with deep, leather seats. Makes me wonder just how well inspectors are paid—or does this one have other sources of income? During the drive, I puzzle over the drawing. It's good news for Erik's case if his drawing is intact but bad news for ours, undermining my theory that Mr. Preston was murdered to keep evidence out of our hands. And we're the only people who were at the scene of the crime, which Kincaide seems predisposed to drop at our doorstep.

We pull up to a building that appears to have been converted into flats. The inspector leads us down a stairwell, and Sergeant Collin knocks on a door tucked below street level. A woman answers right away and awkwardly motions us to enter. Miss Sewell appears to be in her late fifties, her brown hair streaked with grey, and a permanent wrinkle of uncertainty and sadness separates thin eyebrows.

The small flat seems frozen in time—about two centuries ago. The couch and chairs are slipcovered in threadbare chintz, and a Victorian cabinet matches the faded wallpaper. "Was anything amiss when you met the police officer today?" the inspector begins.

"No, the doors and windows were locked, and the picture was right where it has been hanging." She points to the wall above the couch. Sure enough, there's the picture—a detailed rendering of a Gothic style church, exactly like the sketch Erik drew for us.

Sir Kenneth and I walk over to examine it more closely. "Do you notice anything unusual about the drawing?" he asks me. I examine it closer. Then I see it—or rather what *isn't* there.

"Inspector, have you noticed the drawing doesn't have a signature?" I point out.

The inspector scrutinizes it. His jowls seem to pull his mouth into a frown. "So this is worthless to you. We don't need to take up any more of Miss Sewell's time."

"Don't you think the church's placement is skewed?" I ask the inspector. "Notice how there's almost no space below the church? The lower foreground is missing."

"That's where the signature should be," Sir Kenneth adds.

Agitated, the inspector thrusts his hands into his pockets. "Obviously it wasn't signed."

I turn to Miss Sewell. "When I talked to you on the phone, you said it was drawn by Erik Mercier. How did you know that since it has no signature?"

She fidgets with her blouse's collar while she searches for an answer. "Uh, I inherited it from my grandmother. She told me he drew it," she replies nervously.

"When did she tell you that?" Sir Kenneth asks offhandedly.

"When?" She seems confused.

"Yes, how many years ago?"

"Well, she died twenty years ago. It would have been before then," she answers feebly.

"You remembered his name after all this time?" Sir Kenneth asks.

"Yes," she mumbles, looking away.

"Are you implying," the inspector interrupts, "that the picture wasn't stolen because it's worthless as evidence without the signature?"

"That would be my deduction," I reply.

"You have an overactive imagination." The inspector starts toward the door. "I think it's time to go."

"And I think the drawing bears closer examination," Sir Kenneth states, not budging an inch. "Don't you think we need to remove it from the wall and have a closer look?"

For several tense moments the inspector hesitates, then with an exasperated shrug, he takes disposable gloves from his pocket and puts them on. Carefully, he lifts the picture off the wall and places it on a table.

"Turn it over so we can see the reverse side," Sir Kenneth directs.

Grudgingly, the inspector complies. Everyone peers at the plain brown paper that seals the backside. "No signature or date there, either," the inspector snaps. "As I've said, this is meaningless."

"Perhaps the bottom of the picture was folded to make it fit the frame," Sir Kenneth suggests. "Let's lift off the backing paper and have a look."

The Inspector slips the blade of a penknife between the paper and frame. It comes apart easily, exposing the back of the drawing. I let out a sigh of disappointment. The paper was cut to fit the frame, and there's still no signature.

Smug, the inspector says, "You see? Nothing."

He's right, but something else catches my attention. I glance over to see if Sir Kenneth noticed too. He shakes his head subtly. I take that to mean I shouldn't let on. "Has the drawing always been in this frame, or have you had it reframed?" I ask Miss Sewell.

"No." Her eyes dart from me to the inspector. "No, I haven't touched it."

"I think that concludes our business here," the inspector growls.

"We'd still like to buy the painting," I say to her. "I have a check made out in the amount we agreed. Could I take it now?" Her face turns pallid.

"No, I don't think so," the inspector says, abruptly picking up the picture. "This should be taken to the Yard for forensic tests," he tells Miss Sewell.

"Yes, yes of course," she stammers.

On the drive back to the Yard, no one talks. I keep going over in my mind what I saw on the drawing that Sir Kenneth didn't want me to disclose. I wonder if that's why we waited so long before they said we could go to Miss Sewell's home. They needed time. And they think we didn't notice, which is best for Miss Sewell's sake.

When we get back to the Yard, we're ushered into the same interrogation room where I make a final statement to the inspector. "There was clearly another reason for Mr. Preston to be killed."

"What would that be?" The inspector asks condescendingly.

"Even if we didn't have the stone fragment, Mr. Preston could still have testified to its existence and the evidence on it. So, he might have been killed to prevent his testimony."

When the inspector leaves, we settle in for a wait. "My *deduction*?" Sir Kenneth chuckles. "Good show, Watson. But now the inspector will be working on your bodyguards. He'll set a few traps to see if he can snare them."

"No doubt," I reply. Two tedious hours pass before Kincaide returns. Disgruntled, he announces we're free to go but orders us to remain in England while they investigate. Blake, Josh, and their solicitors are allowed to join us, and Sir Kenneth proposes that we stay in his townhouse. We accept.

A police officer escorts us through the maze of hallways. When I spot the exit ahead, I sigh with relief—just want this nightmare over. But as we step out the door, we're engulfed by reporters shouting questions about the murders. About the phantom's case. And about Howard Wheaton's involvement. Sir Kenneth handles the reporters, saying we were nothing more than unfortunate victims ourselves.

Within moments a car pulls up to the curb, and the driver opens the rear door for us. Blake dives in first, then Josh pushes me in and slides in next, slamming the door. Sir Kenneth jumps into the front seat, and the driver speeds away. I fold my arms over my stomach, but thankfully there's nothing left in it.

35 | SCARS

Seattle

KATHRYN

Yawning, I punch the button and send the elevator to the courthouse's garage. My hearing went well, but I'm exhausted. Couldn't sleep last night thinking about Lexa and poor Mr. Preston. When the elevator opens, I'm startled to see two Wheaton bodyguards. They have orders to drive us to the mansion, but Ryan calls Tom to verify this unexpected change. His expression turns grim. Inside the limo, I confront him. "Okay, what did Tom say?"

"Security's tightening up some more. I'm being assigned one of the converted vehicles."

I stare at him. "*Converted* vehicle?"

"It's lined in bulletproof steel, and the windows are made of two-inch thick bulletproof material. Even the tires are a special design. Tom doesn't want to take any chances." He clears his throat. "Your Corvette will be stored at Land's End to keep it safe. You won't be driving it until the trial's over."

"You've got to be kidding."

"Nope." He says regretfully. "Sorry, but those are the orders."

Anger clashes with confusion. Could I be in such danger they need to take these measures? And my Vette. *I can't drive it?* I'm beginning to feel like a prisoner. *Like Erik.*

"Why don't you get some sleep?" Ryan coaxes as the limo speeds down I-5.

I ignore him and stare out the window at the grey sky. It's gloomy, just like my mood. I can't sleep. My mind keeps churning about all the ways my world has been turned upside down ever since Collin showed up.

When we arrive, Tom and George are waiting at the elevator. I give Tom a sharp look, but he doesn't blink. George steps forward like a diplomat with a peace offering. "Good evening, Ms. Copeland. Monsieur Mercier and Dr. Adler invite you to dine with them."

"Give them my thanks, but I have to work tonight. Perhaps another evening."

"In that case, may I bring supper for you and Dr. Kirkman?" he persists. It occurs to me George is more than a butler. He's the Mother Superior of this compound.

"That will be fine," I concede.

After he takes our dinner requests, George seems satisfied and disappears around a corner.

Tom grins. "You'll get used to it."

"Do I have a choice?" I ask, testy.

Tom ignores my question and leads us down a corridor I haven't been in before, finally stopping at a rustic wood door. He directs me to stand in front of the retinal scanner, and when it's programmed, we enter my new office—impressive and furnished in elegant Wheaton style. Two antique settees face each other by windows that frame the ubiquitous Puget Sound views. Potted ferns and botanical artwork soften the room's formality. My desk has two leather chairs in front and a credenza nearby which is dominated by a crystal vase with long-stemmed yellow roses.

As I sit at my desk and encode my thumbprint on the credenza's keypad, Tom and Ryan settle in the chairs. "I know you're upset about the car," Tom says. "Lexa will have the same restrictions. Sorry, but we're tightening security."

"So, what's next? Moving me into Land's End full-time? Trust me—that will *not* happen," I state emphatically. "I have other cases and clients. And a life."

"A bodyguard and secured vehicle should take care of it," Tom replies. "Are you aware *two* people were murdered in London?"

"Yes. Who was the second one?"

"Some guy was sleeping on the ground behind the church. The killer had no qualms about getting rid of a witness. And, of course, the stone fragment is gone."

"Horrible." I rub my forehead, try to ease the throbbing. "How are Lexa and the men?"

"Glad to be out of the Yard. They're staying with their attorney, a friend of Mrs. Wheaton's. Lexa feels the inspector might be in the pocket of the PTB. He seemed to be trying to implicate them, and they're ordered to stay in England during the investigation."

"And Erik's drawing. What happened to it?"

"Interesting story. It wasn't stolen, but the part of the picture with the signature had been cut off."

"Miss Sewell never told us that," I blurt out. "Was she conning us?"

"Don't know exactly what went down. Lexa couldn't say anything more."

"Aren't the QRYSTALS secure?"

"Yes, but someone could be eavesdropping where she's staying, and we're not taking any chances. Land's End is the only place we can totally secure. All eavesdropping devices are blocked inside the boundaries of the estate. Security cameras and sensors focus on every inch, except the enclosed gardens and inside living areas—after all, this is the Wheaton residence—so you are to work on Erik's case only here."

"What about Barb, my legal assistant? Can she work here?"

"No, she has children who could be kidnapped or threatened. She could be blackmailed."

I swallow hard. So *that's* why Lexa and I qualify to work on this case. We have no children, no husbands. We can only be threatened personally, which explains the bodyguards. "Can Barb and Eileen prepare the legal documents filed with the court? Those aren't confidential, and their expertise is important."

"That will be alright."

"If you're so worried about blackmail, what about all the bodyguards? How do you know they can't be coerced?" I give Ryan an apologetic smile. "Present company excepted."

"None of the bodyguards are married or have children." Tom's voice takes on an edge. "Each was recommended by one of the elite Wheaton bodyguards, and most have special forces or CIA training. They're put through extensive psychiatric evaluations, *and* they all have something in their backgrounds that gives them a personal motivation, a stake in what the Wheatons are trying to accomplish."

I frown. "Like what Anne's death meant to Collin and me, for instance?"

"Like that, for instance." Tom unflinchingly returns my gaze.

"Sounds thorough, but I've read that the PTB has taken mind manipulation and reprogramming to sophisticated levels. How do you know someone hasn't slipped through and is a Manchurian candidate?"

"Because of Mrs. Wheaton." When I stare at him, puzzled, he says, "The last qualifying test is a personal interview with her. She has certain gifts and can tell if a person has been programmed or is untrustworthy. Or lying."

I remember the first time I saw Mrs. Wheaton at the FWA meeting. It felt like she was looking right into me. "In other words," I clarify, "she has strong intuitive, or possibly psychic abilities?"

"Perhaps," Tom answers evasively. "So, when will you start working here?"

"Not until my Saturday appointment with Erik. I just hired another attorney, and I'm familiarizing him with the cases he's taking over. My schedule this week is totally booked."

The buzzer goes off, and I check the monitor. *George with dinner.* I press the button to let him in.

"Do whatever it takes," Tom says, standing to leave. "The Wheatons will cover any expenses."

With efficient formality, George serves our dinners. As he gathers up his trays, he glances over at the yellow roses. "Lady Margaret had me bring those for you."

"I see. Well, they are lovely. Thank you."

He gives me a lipless smile and slips out the door.

I gaze at the roses. Flowers don't make this fortress any less unnerving. I feel trapped in every direction. Tom's words keep replaying—that the bodyguards don't have wives or children, and that they have some experience which makes them personally invested. I study Ryan, over on the settee eating his dinner. I wonder what it was for him. It seems the more I learn about this situation, the less I know. And things just keep getting *"curiouser and curiouser."*

Frustrated, I spear some salad with my fork and eat as I get back to work, picking up where I left off in the diary. Wagner was rehearsing *Tannhäuser* at the Paris Opéra. Under considerable prodding from Adèle, Erik had agreed to approach Wagner about a position as violinist. She was certain Erik would finally gain entrée into the Opéra, his talents would be revealed, and his career launched.

But timing is everything. Despite Wagner receiving Erik warmly and wanting to hire him, Monsieur Duclos, the Opéra's conductor, intervened. Duclos, described as a mouse of a man, apparently had the memory of an elephant. He recalled Erik's attempt to audition for him almost two years before as well as their heated argument over Erik's mask. Again, Duclos vehemently opposed Erik's being hired, and sadly, the directors backed him. Wagner apologized, explaining his hands were tied.

Adèle was devastated for Erik. His hopes of ever performing at the Opéra were quashed. Once again, Erik stayed away for a week. When he returned to resume care of Meg, Adèle noticed his moods had turned darker.

Lexa made detailed notations throughout this section. Princess Pauline de Metternich, the wife of the Austrian ambassador to Paris, pulled the strings for Wagner's opera to be performed. The famous, fashionable princess was the Princess Diana of her day and a close friend to France's Empress Eugénie. During a party in the Tuileries, Princess Metternich told the emperor she had heard Wagner's *Tannhäuser* in Germany and said it would be a departure for the Paris Opéra from its usual fare. The emperor, Napoléon III, had been raised and educated in Germany, so he was amenable to a German opera being presented. At his behest, the Paris Opéra agreed.

Lexa's notes about the *Tannhäuser* rehearsals are fascinating. No opulence was spared, befitting the prestige of an opera being produced at the emperor's bidding. Wagner rehearsed the opera an unprecedented one hundred sixty-four times. Stealing into Box Five, Erik watched each rehearsal and became engrossed in every facet of the production. For months, Erik regaled Adèle with stories about how Wagner paid attention to every detail, from music to staging.

As rehearsals for *Tannhäuser* continued into 1861, Erik's moods became mercurial. When the rehearsals went well, he was transfixed.

But sometimes his mood turned dark, and he'd vent angrily that he could play the score better than the musicians who were hired. The unspoken truth hung heavily in the air: Erik would never be given the opportunity. On the night of the grand premiere, Adèle smuggled Erik into a second-tier box.

13 March 1861

Tannhäuser was heralded as a glorious event, and I have never seen so many tiaras and jewels. With great ceremony, the Emperor and Empress were seated in the Imperial Box by the directors, who also escorted Princess Metternich to Box Five. The princess was resplendent, every bit the grand lady all Paris has been talking about.

Then the evening went terribly wrong. The men of the Jockey Club arrived just before the second act. As always, they expected to see the ballet, but it was already over. They began to tap their canes loudly on the floor and chant, "Le Bal-let, Le Bal-let," calling for their favorite ballerinas. To my horror, then they raised their white-gloved hands and blew whistles. Their behavior was abominable and ruined the performance for everyone. When the rowdy men jeered at Princess Metternich, the audience turned and stared at her. Disgraceful. After the second act, I rushed to her box to see if I could be of assistance, but the princess and her entourage swept past me on their way out. She had tears in her eyes. I was mortified.

Lexa confirms what Adèle described. Wagner bent over backward to accommodate Parisian tastes. He had the opera translated from German into French and even included a ballet piece, but he placed it in the first act. Lexa notes that Wagner probably put it there in his ambition to create original forms. But, adding insult to injury, his ballet was avant-garde.

At the second performance of *Tannhäuser* Adèle was equally horrified by what happened. The emperor and empress attended, but Princess Metternich stayed away. Again, the Jockey Club employed whistles and catcalls, drowning out the music and causing another fiasco.

24 March 1861

For the third time, Tannhäuser was performed. What a debacle. Thankfully, the Emperor and Empress did not attend, nor did Princess Metternich, nor even Monsieur Wagner. But the aristocratic ruffians were there, so disruptive that fights broke out during the first act. The performance had to be suspended for fifteen minutes on both occasions. Some of the patrons I was attending tried to applaud the opera, but the jeering only got louder. When the performers attempted to sing, they were hissed and hooted.

I met with Erik afterward. I was shaking from distress and told him that never in my twelve years as a box attendant had I witnessed such atrocious behavior. He told me rumors had been circulating even before the opera opened that such disruptions might occur. Erik tried to explain these political intrigues to me, but I could not grasp what it all meant.

Lexa connected the political dots for me. These three performances of *Tannhäuser* became the most infamous debacle in the annals of opera during the nineteenth century. Her notes relate the historical context—that the Jockey Club had much more at stake than a prurient interest in watching ballerinas. They definitely had a political agenda. The Jockey Club was an elite group of rich men and the nobility, who were conservative rightists that wanted to reestablish the Bourbon kings as well as regain their own power and privilege. They were zealously opposed to Emperor Louis Napoléon who had popular support and leanings. The emperor had even granted French workers the right to strike, a policy that was aggressively opposed by the wealthy businessmen, many of whom were Jockey Club members. Since the *Tannhäuser* opera was performed at the dictate of the emperor, they seized this opportunity to embarrass him.

According to Lexa, the Jockey Club demonstrations also represented a clash of cultures between the French and the Germans that would result in three wars between those countries over the following hundred years. Prophetically, all the political undercurrents coursing just beneath the surface in 1861 during *Tannhäuser* were violently played out ten years later when war broke out between France and the Prussians who laid siege to Paris.

Wagner withdrew *Tannhäuser* after the third disastrous performance. Princess Metternich came to his aid, so the opera's debts were paid, but Wagner left Paris and never returned.

And Erik descended into a deeper depression than ever. The diary records his withdrawal into himself as he kept running into society's walls. So many times in my own work, I have seen how desperation and isolation can turn into dark and dangerous emotions. Adèle observed that in Erik and badgered him until he agreed to accompany her to Easter mass at San Sulpice.

31 March 1861, Easter

Erik kept his promise and carried little Meg on our walk to church and held her during mass. We sat in the last pew in case Meg started crying when the organ music began. She did. Erik chided me with a look of irritation when we got up to leave. Surprisingly, Father Lucien stopped us at the doors. We hadn't seen him for several years, but his smile is unchanged and beams pure joy. Although Meg was still bellowing, he bid us follow him.

Father Lucien took us to his small office and invited us to be seated while he walked over to a bookshelf and took out a hidden tin box. He opened the lid and showed Meg rows of dark chocolates, then told her if she stopped crying, she could have one of the delicacies. Her eyes got large, and she forgot to cry as she chose a chocolate. Father Lucien offered a piece to Erik and me, and I took one, but Erik declined. The Father smiled kindly at Erik and said he also deserved a piece. Erik was so taken aback, he actually ate one.

Father Lucien seated himself behind his desk and looked at us inquisitively. He asked how I was faring, taking care of a child by myself, clearly trying to find out if Erik and I had married. I explained my situation and that Erik was like a brother, always helping with Meg.

The priest could not help but notice how thin and pale Erik has become and asked about his health. Erik bristled and responded that he was fine. Father Lucien said he remembered the magnificent organ music Erik played for my wedding and queried whether he was employed as an organist. Erik replied that he had been unable to obtain any work as a musician, so he had taken up painting to support himself. As Erik spoke, I could tell that Father Lucien was taking stock of Erik's once fine clothing. Although neat and pressed, his black wool suit is showing signs of wear, becoming threadbare at the elbows and knees.

To our surprise, Father Lucien informed us that Église Saint-Sulpice needed an assistant organist and asked if Erik would be interested. With bitterness, Erik admitted he had approached Father Dupres and been turned down. Bluntly, Erik expressed his opinion that his appearance had disqualified him for the job. Father Lucien shook his head, saying that once Father Dupres made up his mind, it was "devilishly" hard to change it. He gave Erik a look of regret, and my hope melted away like snow under the spring sun.

Finally, we heard muffled sounds announcing the end of mass. Father Lucien escorted us back to the doors, but as we turned to leave, I was astonished to see Princess Metternich talking with Father Dupres in the atrium. Only three weeks ago, I had seen her at that disastrous performance of Tannhäuser. When the princess spotted Erik, she whispered to a lady-in-waiting. I watched, transfixed, as the woman approached us and introduced herself. Her manner was formal and unsmiling, which made me even more uncomfortable, but Erik took the matter with calm composure. The lady-in-waiting asked him to speak with the princess. He agreed and held out his arm to escort me. When he asked Father Lucien to accompany us, the Father said he would not miss the opportunity even for a new robe.

Our little group followed the lady-in-waiting across the atrium. When we arrived, the princess silenced Father Dupres' s rambling discourse. The grand lady turned and gave us her full attention as introductions were made. Erik bowed gracefully, and I curtsied as best I could with wobbling knees. Even Meg tried to curtsy, which caused the princess to break into a melodious laugh. The princess gazed acutely at Erik with her dark brown eyes. I remember her exact words because they startled me so. "You are the one who defended me when I left the Opéra during Tannhäuser, are you not?"

Erik confirmed that he was. I knew nothing about this incident. All I knew was that the princess left in tears after being ruthlessly heckled. Then the princess smiled and thanked him for what he had done. She said he had been most kind and brave. Erik replied simply that it was his honor.

Unexpectedly, the princess continued the conversation and asked Erik what he thought about Wagner's music. With commanding confidence, Erik informed her he had studied composition under Wagner's tutelage in Zurich. The princess received this with great interest and questioned Erik about his music training. Clearly, she was impressed by his mastery of the violin, piano, and organ.

What followed is still a wonder to me. Father Lucien spoke up and told the princess he had heard Erik play Église Saint-Sulpice's organ. He said the music made him feel like angels were present. The princess said she would love to hear Erik play. Father Lucien, bless his soul, spoke up once again and informed her not only was an assistant organist being sought, but Erik was interested. Then the dazzling princess turned to Father Dupres and said she hoped he would entice Erik to take the position since she would love to hear this music fit for angels.

All eyes were on Father Dupres. I had witnessed the Father's dislike of Erik's mask, but clearly he was considering the princess and her patronage. After a few moments, he bowed and offered Erik the position. Erik grinned wickedly as he accepted. What Erik had not been able to do in two and a half years since returning to Paris, the princess accomplished in minutes. Stunned, I was barely able to curtsy as she departed like a radiant moon, surrounded by her cloud of courtiers.

Although agitated, Father Dupres addressed Erik civilly, not wanting anything untoward to reach the ears of the princess. He asked Erik how soon he could be ready to play for mass. Erik replied that if he were allowed to practice every night, he would be ready in three weeks. After ordering Father Lucien to make all the arrangements, Father Dupres departed.

Erik was stunned, Father Lucien beamed, and I felt faint. Thanking the dear father profusely, we left. Erik did not stay for dinner, but I overheard him arrange to begin practicing this evening. Surely he is there at this moment. As for me, my heart overflows with joy for him.

21 April 1861

Today Erik played the organ at Saint-Sulpice for the first time. I sat in the back pew, ready to take Meg out if she cried at the organ music, but I was determined to hear Erik's music if only for a few moments. I prayed all would go well, and the princess would be pleased.

Erik played gloriously. Such majestic sounds—sometimes so soft I stopped breathing, and at other times so powerful I was transfixed.

Then I realized Meg was listening happily. Something special infuses Erik's music, an ethereal quality which cannot be described.

After mass, I hid in the shadows and overheard Princess Metternich ask Father Dupres to bring Erik to meet with her. I watched the princess and Erik converse while Father Lucien stood nearby. The princess praised Erik's music, and he actually smiled. Father Dupres seemed unusually sullen, but all of Father Lucien's teeth showed, his grin was so broad.

When the princess left, I hurried over to congratulate Erik. Upon hearing Meg had enjoyed his music, he smirked and said that was an even higher compliment than that of the princess. We accompanied Erik and Father Lucien to a café for the happiest of celebrations.

Lexa noted that she was aware of Princess Metternich from her studies in French history, but she did some additional research and attached a bio page about her:

"Princess Pauline Metternich, born 1836 in Vienna, Austria, died 1921, was the only granddaughter of the famous Austrian chancellor Prince Klemens von Metternich. In 1856, she married Prince Richard von Metternich who became the Ambassador to the French court of Emperor Napoléon III from 1859 to 1870.

"Although her clothes set style trends, the princess was also avant-garde in her attitudes and famously smoked cigars. A patroness of the arts, she helped promote the careers of Richard Wagner, Camille Saint-Saens, and Franz Liszt, and befriended famous writers of the day, such as Alexandre Dumas and Prosper Merimee. She was musically talented herself and participated as a vocalist or director in amateur operas in her home. Later in her life, she sponsored a famous annual ball to raise funds for charitable causes.

"She had three children, all daughters. The first was born in May 1857, and the second in April 1862, a year after the Wagner debacle. The third daughter was born in June 1870, in Paris, barely three months before the Franco-Prussian War began. Two of her daughters had tragic lives. The middle daughter was murdered by her alcoholic husband, and the youngest was mauled by a dog when she was a child. Her face was so badly scarred, she never married."

What? I drop my fork. Princess Metternich was clearly one of the most wealthy and influential women of the nineteenth century. She had a privileged life with connections to the highest social and political circles throughout Europe. Yet one of her daughters never married, presumably because of the scars on her face. Scars that set her apart and most likely resulted in society rejecting her. *Just like Erik.*

I push aside my plate as my mind reels over this tragic coincidence. I can't help but wonder if the paths of Erik and Princess Metternich continued to cross. They had so much in common. Did a friendship develop? But there's nothing more in the diary about the princess.

22 April 1861

Meg finally stopped crying and is sleeping quietly. I cannot stop shaking, perhaps more from distress than cold. Erik is gone, and I fear he will never return. After the joy of his playing for the first time at Saint-Sulpice yesterday, I could not have foreseen such a calamity.

Tonight, we were having a joyous dinner, talking about Princess Metternich and that his position as assistant organist is assured. We were so happy, reliving yesterday's events. Erik had often held Meg in his arms, carried her or rocked her to sleep. When she crawled onto his lap, it was not unusual. But we were preoccupied with our conversation and laughter.

That is when it happened. Meg reached up and yanked off Erik's mask. For one horrible moment, all of us froze. Then bedlam broke out. Meg let out a scream of terror. I had not seen his uncovered face since that day so many years ago in the carnival tent. His ravaged face! I had pushed the sight from my mind. May the Blessed Virgin forgive me, I gasped from shock.

Erik set Meg on the floor, his face contorted with despair at her screams. I picked her up, trying to comfort her. Then Meg dropped his mask. Horrified, he swooped down and picked it up, putting it back in a flash of movement. Before I could quell Meg's outburst, Erik grabbed his cloak and was gone. I did not even have time to beg his forgiveness. I am haunted by the anguish on his face, his devastation. Could anything I say take away his pain?

Adèle didn't realize that meal would be the last she would ever share with Erik. I know from my previous reading of the diary that after that night, he hovered in their lives like a ghost. He always seemed to know when they needed something—medicine when they were ill or new ballet outfits for Meg as she grew. Warm cloaks and new shoes would be left in their room on Christmas. When needed, money appeared in a red envelope next to Jules's picture. On occasion, Adèle encountered Erik in the opera house's dark corridors and they would talk, but he would share only sketchy fragments of his life. The incident with Meg tearing off his mask seemed to push Erik into isolation. After that, he descended into the underground world, into the darkness of night and his music.

The buzzer again. I struggle to pull myself up, out of the dark recesses of Erik's world. I check the door monitor. It's Diane, so I push the button, letting her in. I invite her to take a seat in front of my desk, but she remains standing and studies me with concern.

"It's too bad you couldn't join Erik and me for dinner," she says.

"Sorry, but I'm preparing for Erik's next conference." I rub the back of my neck.

"Have a headache?"

"Yes. It's been a long day, and I didn't get much sleep last night."

"I can imagine. Perhaps a walk in the Japanese garden would do you some good."

"There's a Japanese garden here?"

"Yes, didn't you know? Lady Margaret loves gardening, so Land's End has a number of hothouses where vegetables and flowers are grown for the estate. But the Japanese garden is like a sanctuary. I'd love to show it to you."

"You know, I could use a little fresh air, and there's something I would like to discuss with you."

Ryan looks up from the couch and says, "I'll stay here and catch a nap to get ready for the drive back."

"You mean you'll let me out of your sight?"

A grin quirks at his mouth. "The gardens are totally secure."

Diane leads me through the maze of hallways. "This goes on forever," I murmur in awe.

"It does feel that way, so many interlocking buildings on the cliff's edge. The design allows almost every room to have a view of the Sound. But did you know that all those picture windows have steel doors which can close over them in a moment's notice?" With a Cheshire cat grin, she adds, "These buildings are tsunami- and earthquake-safe. Quite extraordinary."

Finally, we enter a spacious solarium. Nothing of technical engineering here. Only earth-inspired, luxurious rattan chairs snuggle beneath exotic trees in terra-cotta pots. Going out French doors, we pass through a redwood arbor. Almost magically, I find myself in a Japanese garden so large the far edges fade into the evening haze. Native pines and spruce tower over Japanese maples and gnarled bonsai. A stream meanders through the garden and flows into a tranquil pond. The stone path leads us to a moon bridge which arches over the stream. There we pause and watch the gold and silver streaks of koi darting through the water. As wondrous nature enfolds me, I yield to the peace and calm of this sanctuary.

36 | PAWNS

ERIK

Most days I visit the pond in the upper garden to feed the koi. Not today. I take the serpentine path that trails down the hill. Pine needles littering the pathway crunch under my boots, releasing a pungent odor. The garden is hushed, almost mournful. Reflects my mood.

At the lower garden, I go to the arbor. I need to be alone, and *they* permit it since it is safe here. Like a diva, the estate is gilded, but that is only a façade. In truth, it is a bulwark against the world. Wisteria winds around the pillars of the arbor and onto the tiled oriental roof with its upturned corners. Supposedly that protects against evil spirits, like the gargoyles on medieval churches. Perhaps it will ward off the ones that always haunt me.

I collapse onto a stone bench. As I gaze around the grotto, I notice a bonsai tree with contorted branches. Cynically, it occurs to me that even it has been twisted by the hands of man into unnatural shapes. Again, my anger flares over the murders. But to those in power, the two men were merely pawns. Just like me.

"This is so peaceful."

Kathryn's voice! It's coming from the upper garden.

"If I were Mrs. Wheaton, I'd never want to leave here," she says.

"Lady Margaret feels the same way."

So Dr. Adler is with her.

"I can see why. But she's gone a lot, isn't she?"

"Yes, she's very involved with the Foundation. She uses her family's status and connections to open doors in many countries. Lady

Margaret has a unique talent for picking much-needed projects, then overseeing them to make sure they succeed."

"Such as choosing Erik to be brought to the present?" Kathryn presses.

"Yes, she takes a particular interest in any matter affecting him. She has deep respect for Erik."

I have also wondered about Lady Margaret's notable interest in me.

"So, Kathryn, what is it you wish to discuss? Is it about Erik or the case?"

"Both. Lexa has annotated the diary, so I'm rereading it. Her notes have been invaluable, especially about Princess Metternich."

They intend to talk about me? What should I do? If I return to the mansion, they will see me, know I have been listening. My best course is to remain here until they leave. Undeniably I will be eavesdropping, but that has always been necessary for my survival.

"After Meg's incident with the mask," Kathryn says, "Erik distanced himself from Adèle and didn't share his personal life with her. The diary doesn't mention the princess again, but is it possible there was a continuing relationship between Erik and her? After all, Princess Metternich was known for associating with musicians and intellectuals."

I inhale sharply. *Just how deeply do their conjectures probe into my life?*

"Considering her position in society, the princess had the ability to seek out Erik and befriend him," Dr. Adler says matter-of-factly. "What makes you suspect she did?"

"Because Erik was one of the architects for the Garnier opera house, and Emperor Louis Napoléon commissioned its construction. Maybe the princess brought Erik's designs to the attention of the emperor, who then recommended them to Garnier. Just a hunch, of course."

"Perhaps you're right about that," Dr. Adler replies.

But unnerving. Kathryn seems to connect random facts and deftly weave them into tapestries. What other threads of my life will she crisscross and connect?

"The princess wrote two memoirs that were published after her death in 1921. Lexa's trying to obtain copies. Maybe they'll contain reference to Erik."

Her memoirs? Did she reveal our relationship? Surely the Princess would have taken care not to mention that. I glare up the hill, unsettled.

"If the princess continued as his friend, that would fit a pattern I've noticed."

"What pattern?" Kathryn asks.

Why do they keep dwelling on the princess? I cock my head to catch every word.

"There always seemed to be one person in Erik's life who cared about him. He was not accepted in society, so his foster father privately educated him, even taught him to play the piano and violin. Then Adèle nursed him back to health and befriended him."

"But his uncle and the children never treated him as one of the family," Kathryn says.

"Even so, he was provided with books to satisfy his intellect, and we know he ate well. It was during those years he grew so tall." Dr. Adler's laugh tumbles down the hillside. "However, I agree he didn't receive affection, but when Mr. Markham entered his life, he became more than a music teacher. He was like a grandfather. After that, Erik was mentored by Wagner. Then Adèle and Meg became his family. When that ended, he had no personal connections, unless…"

"Unless Princess Metternich was there," Kathryn concludes.

"Yes. She may have fulfilled an important role in his life, preventing his disassociation from humanity. Erik has been rejected by society in one form or another all his life. Even subjected to abuse and beaten. Had that been unrelenting, he could have become sociopathic or developed a fractured or multiple personality, but I observe none of those syndromes in him."

"So his contact with the princess may have prevented a deterioration of his emotional condition?"

"Adèle's description of Erik just before he met the princess indicated depression to the point of losing weight. The princess's intercession came at a critical juncture. Being hired for the position of organist probably stabilized him before it was too late."

"What do you mean *too late*?"

"He was possibly suicidal," Dr. Adler replies.

I was desperate. I propel myself from the bench and stride to the balustrade, staring up the hill in disbelief. *How is it these women can discern my private life and feelings so acutely?*

"Then his commission as an architect for the Garnier," Dr. Adler says, "connected him with other people. So Erik always had someone who served as his lifeline. Sometimes as a mentor or role model. Sometimes as a friend such as Adèle. And possibly even, Princess Metternich. I think these relationships were touchstones that saved Erik from developing more serious psychological disorders."

Is that pattern truly embedded in my life? I had never considered that.

"Even my initial contact with Erik was as a mentor to him. At first, he came by my office almost daily to discuss our world, but he no longer does. He rarely comes for his counseling sessions, either, and seems to be withdrawing back into himself. I'm noticing behaviors that indicate he may be slipping into depression. And alienation."

"If he disconnects from us, that could create serious problems," Kathryn replies. "Adèle noted that Erik's moods got darker after he withdrew from her. He seemed to become more obsessive and demanding, like that situation with the money. Apparently the directors considered the payments he demanded to be blackmail, but Adèle said it was Erik's salary. She also mentioned a number of other incidents, like a trapdoor accidentally opening under the conductor, Mr. Duclos. Then the chandelier killed the woman in the audience. She said the gossip around the opera house was that the Phantom was behind those. If that was true, the pattern of behavior exhibited by Erik, that is, by the *Phantom*," Kathryn hesitates before adding, "was dangerous."

"But we don't know that he did any those things, do we?"

"No, but when Christine was kidnapped, Adèle felt only Erik could pull that off. By the way, don't you find it strange Adèle doesn't mention anything about Count Philippe's death?"

"Yes," Dr. Adler says, "that is unusual since she always wrote about noteworthy events."

"Adèle did write, however, that Meg was hysterical when she returned to their room that night. But Meg would never say why."

Sacre bleu. Why did she bring that up of all things? Images of that night are unleashed. I grip the railing and stare down at my hands. *They seem detached, as if belonging to someone else. Yet, I know they are mine—hands which create music and things of beauty. Hands which have sundered flesh.* Breathing deeply, I struggle to ward off the ghosts.

"He denies ever leaving Europe, so he couldn't have committed the murders in Persia."

This is agonizing. I do not want to hear any more of this, but I am trapped.

"But Count Philippe or Buquet? Or the woman? Do you think he could he have killed any of them?"

"Yes, it's possible," Dr. Adler replies. "He had a number of motives, including vengeance."

Kathryn responds, but her voice recedes as they walk away, so I cannot make out her words. *They concede that the reality of my life is complex, but how could they possibly understand the paradoxes of my existence. And how much dare I reveal…to Kathryn?*

37 | STEALTH

Thursday, June 2
London

LEXA

"Good morning, Ms. Simmons." The clipped British accent of the housekeeper drags me from my sleep. "I regret to wake you, but Sir Kenneth called and said he'd like to meet with you downstairs in the library in an hour. Would that be satisfactory?"

"Thanks, Mrs. Whitcomb, I'll be there." I groan. Just want to go back to sleep. Jet lag is bad enough, but I spent a good part of yesterday feeling like a squashed amoeba under Kincaide's microscope. Still groggy, I will myself out of bed and head to the shower.

When I return, a pot of hot tea—Earl Grey no doubt—is waiting for me. And hot scones. I passed on supper last night and went straight to bed. Surely my stomach has settled enough by now. Tentatively I take a bite. Sure wish blueberries were still around. Loved blueberry scones when I was a child. But these are flaky and I'm hungry, so I devour every one.

As I'm leaving, I check myself in the cheval mirror and push my hair behind my ears. It's at an awkward length, but Collin said I can't cut it. The mirror's carved-oak frame features a unicorn spying on a maiden. I look around the room and make note of its floral chintz and vanity table. There's a woman in Sir Kenneth's life, but who is she?

As I'm going down the grand staircase, I notice the large formal portraits covering the walls. No doubt Sir Kenneth's ancestors. A pang of homesickness comes over me. When I enter the library, I spot an elegant silver tea service between several high-backed chairs. Mrs. Whitcomb really gets around. And evidently has an abundant supply of teapots.

But I bypass the tea. The hardbounds lining the walls are calling to me. The ancient oak bookshelves give off the faint smell of embedded wood smoke. Walking past the rows of books, I run my fingers over the smooth surface of aged leather and embossed script.

Many of the titles are written in florid old English, like "Travels into Several Remote Nations of the World, in Four Parts. By Lemuel Gulliver, First a Surgeon, and then a Captain of several Ships." Now we simply call it *Gulliver's Travels.* I chuckle. That definitely loses something in the translation. When I open the book, Jonathan Swift gazes back, and I discover it's a first edition published in 1726. How many generations have held this very book in their hands? How many were changed in some way by its whimsical tales?

On adjacent shelves are novels by Dickens and a full set of Sherlock Holmes. I pick up a volume of Holmes's stories and discover it's another first edition.

A sharp cough behind me makes me jump. I spin around, still holding the book. Sir Kenneth is watching me with a quizzical grin. "Oh!" I clear my throat. "I hope you don't mind me browsing through your books."

"Of course, not," he says, smiling. "I notice you've found one of my favorites."

"You're a mystery buff?"

"Yes, Holmes in particular."

"I'm not surprised. You didn't miss anything yesterday." As I put the book back, I add, "I'd like to hear your theories about—"

"I'm *very* interested in hearing your thoughts as well." A distinctive woman's voice—throaty with an elegant British accent and slight tang of French—interrupts me. I turn and find Mrs. Wheaton has just entered the library. "Thanks for taking time to meet with me this morning," she says to Sir Kenneth as they exchange the hug of longtime friends. With a warm smile, she says to me, "Your father sends his love. He'll be flying in from Paris to see you."

"Thanks." I'm glad Dad's coming, but very curious why Mrs. Wheaton is delivering a personal message herself. Sir Kenneth invites us to sit in the chairs surrounding the tea service.

"How are you doing, Lexa?" she asks.

"I've had better visits to London."

"I'd like to hear what happened yesterday from the time you arrived at the church," she says as she takes a paper notepad and pen out of her purse and hurriedly writes something. I wonder what *this* all about? She holds the notepad up for us to read: *Is room protected from eavesdropping with jammers?* Sir Kenneth shakes his head, and she jots another note: *Write anything sensitive about the case.*

My stomach starts clenching again. Could we actually be spied on in Sir Kenneth's home? Aren't we safe, even here? I definitely won't be mentioning Blake's brief disappearance or my suspicion he disposed of a gun. Whatever I say aloud must be limited to what the police know. I begin by telling her about Mr. Preston. "When I spoke with him on the phone, he was so funny, so willing to help us. Then, when I saw his body…it was horrible."

"What an unbelievable tragedy," she says. With a look of sympathy, she leans forward and picks up the silver teapot, filling three antique china cups. She serves the tea as if we had a little tête-à-tête every day. "I'm so sorry for what you've been through."

As I relate what happened next, she sets her cup down, picks up the pad and writes: *Erik said he always signed his drawings. Sure it's his?*

I need to write my response, so I create a diversionary tactic. "That's great tea. May I have more?" Mrs. Wheaton takes my cup, rattling it audibly as she refills it. I pick up the notepad and jot: *Certain. Looked just like sketch Erik drew.*

She hands me the tea and takes the pad. I'm explaining about the inspector and his questioning, as she scribbles: *What about signature? Painted over?*

No, the bottom cut off, Sir Kenneth scrawls.

She jots back: *How could you tell?*

Sir Kenneth busily writes while I confess to throwing up all over the inspector. Mrs. Wheaton's eyes sparkle with humor at my description of the inspector's face. "I'm sorry, that must have been very upsetting for you." The corner of her mouth quirks slightly with a smile. "And I suspect not terribly pleasant for the inspector."

"Not much," I chuckle.

Sir Kenneth holds up his reply: *Drawing not centered. Section below church too small in proportion to church and sky. Examined picture. Cut to fit frame.*

I start my recitation about the gunpowder test and my fingerprints being taken. To give them more time, I toss in a couple anecdotes about the procedures.

Mrs. Wheaton shows her next question: *PTB involved?* Sir Kenneth nods firmly. She gives him a searching look, then jots: *Why do you think that?*

I'm going on about the inspector's interrogation, making it clear for any prying ears I didn't know about the second murder until Sir Kenneth and the inspector informed me. I tell everything in detail, stalling for time since Sir Kenneth is writing a lengthy explanation. Finally, he passes it back to us: *The cut edges. Only one side AND bottom were cut. Paper is thick linen. Uncut edges discolored from age. Two cut edges distinctly white, indicate recent cuts.*

With a questioning look, Mrs. Wheaton writes: *Why does that indicate PTB involved? What if Sewell cut picture to fit frame?*

I'm now relating what happened at Miss Sewell's flat. Placing my hand on Mrs. Wheaton's arm, I draw her attention back to what I'm saying. "Miss Sewell assured us the painting hadn't been tampered with." I lower my eyebrows skeptically and add, "She said her grandmother gave her the painting over twenty years ago, and that it's been that way for *some time*."

She gets the point and scribbles: *So Sewell lied?*

Sir Kenneth nods with conviction and responds in his sprawling handwriting: *She was VERY nervous. We spotted newly cut edges but said nothing, INTENTIONALLY.*

As I'm speaking, Mrs. Wheaton reads the new note Sir Kenneth passes her. *Another clue, wallpaper faded—previously hung picture was larger.* Impressive. I flash Sir Kenneth an admiring grin. I'd missed that. Then he writes: *Didn't want it known we were on to them. Likely Sewell was bribed, blackmailed, or threatened.*

I take the pad and write: *Could put her in jeopardy. Don't want another murder.*

She sighs with agreement and says aloud, "So, it appears we're at a dead end. The painting has no signature and is useless to us?"

Sir Kenneth jots: *Inspector took it. Supposedly for further examination. Doubt we'll get to inspect or see it again.*

Nodding, Mrs. Wheaton adds, "Luckily we didn't pay for the painting before we knew this. Poor woman. If she'd told us when we contacted her that the painting didn't have the signature, we could've saved everyone the trouble. Apparently, she really needed the money." She takes a sip of tea, thinking. "So, Kenneth, how long before Lexa will be allowed to return to Seattle?"

"Whenever the inspector feels he can't justify keeping them. Probably a week or two."

"You should use this time to rest and recuperate," she says to me. "What will you do with your free time here?" I oblige and chatter on about wanting to attend plays. They put their heads together and write furiously back and forth, developing a game plan.

Sir Kenneth scrawls: *Everyone in your organization is compromised. Cannot send anyone to England without being spied on or followed.*

Frowning in frustration, Mrs. Wheaton writes: *Still need someone to search for evidence. Must prove Erik resided in England.* As I keep up my monologue, they stare at each other, communicating wordlessly. Then Sir Kenneth prints in large letters: *ME!*

She tilts her head in thought and takes the notepad: *You'd be perfect, but in serious danger. You know what they're capable of.*

A fleeting look of pain crosses his features, then he scribbles furiously: *Know what I'm getting into. Who else can you trust? My investigator can follow leads while pursuing other investigations. No one would know real objective.*

Rubbing her temple, Mrs. Wheaton leans back in her chair. I'm not sure if she's thinking or trying to ease a headache. I SOS that I'm running out of talking points.

She writes: *Nothing outside our estates or Wheaton Industries can be secured. Must encode communication. Begin sending personal messages to Lexa, pretend relationship. When uncover information make no reference to it. Ask Lexa to come for visit. She'll fly over, pick it up personally.*

Then she seamlessly takes up the conversation with me and recommends restaurants.

Taking the clandestine notes from her hand, Sir Kenneth walks over to an antique cuspidor. He gets a lighter from the fireplace and holds the flame to the corner of the pages. As they are consumed by the fire, he gives us a devious wink and drops them into the cuspidor.

38 | POWERS

Saturday, June 23
Interstate 5

RYAN

The traffic on I-5 slows down as road barriers funnel the cars into one lane. What now? An accident or problems with the road? They're not maintained much anymore but repairs are never done on weekends. Could be traffic is being rerouted around some road hazard.

When the cars ahead slow down to a crawl, I check my watch. Kathryn's conference with Erik is at 1300 hours. We'll never make it at this rate. I call Tom and let him know we'll be late.

Irritated, Kathryn looks up from her QRYSTAL. "What's the problem?"

"Don't know," I grumble. She's been edgy all day. *But hell*, she can't get a break. Her workload is unending, and now she'll be spending Saturdays on these meetings with Erik. *Maybe I can do something to distract her*. I scan the radio, but every talk channel is discussing the murders in London or the other hot topic—Wheaton's control of the time-travel technology. The drumbeat of attacks against Wheaton is getting more intense, like the drumroll before an execution. Congressmen known to be in the PTB's pockets—and that's most of them—are calling for an investigation. As I switch to a music channel, Kathryn pulls out a hardbound.

"Whatcha reading?" I ask. *Maybe this will work.*

"A history book Lexa gave me about the siege and Commune." She adds pensively, "It's incredible that Erik lived during those chaotic times. What he must have witnessed."

"Yeah, I agree. Collin gave me a French history book, and I've been reading about that."

Her eyes flash suspiciously. "Why is he having you read French history?"

Well, I blew that. Gotta cover my slip. "Helps me understand Erik better."

"I see." Her voice goes flat. "So you may be reassigned to Erik?"

"Possibly. After the trial's over."

"But isn't Collin sending Erik back right away if he's acquitted?"

"Maybe he'll stay a little longer," I lie. "Collin wants me to watch over him." At least that part's true. She gives me a dubious stare like she's on her guard and doesn't trust any of us. But why should she? We haven't told her all the truth. That bothers me. On orders from Collin and Wheaton, I can't even tell her I'm going back with Erik. But they're wrong. Kathryn should be told a lot more. To derail her train of questions, I maneuver the subject back to history. "What really struck me was that the French had *four* revolutions by Erik's lifetime. We only had one revolution and still have the same government—despite some bumps along the way."

"Bumps?" Her voice registers disgust. "What's even left of our constitutional rights? Ever since the NDAA was passed back in 2012, the military has the right to detain *indefinitely* anyone suspected of being connected to terrorism. What if the person is innocent? There is no right to an attorney or trial until the end of hostilities. And conveniently, terrorism never ends."

"And there's always a war, somewhere," I mutter.

"Exactly, and due process has gone out the window." She folds her arms over her waist, almost protectively. "A college friend of mine became a reporter. He's always nervous about who he interviews or what he reports for fear of being accused of aiding or abetting something connected to terrorism. So much for freedom of speech and the press. And what do you call our government forcibly putting down protests against water contamination or rationing? Now protestors are arrested based on local, restrictive laws and strip-searched, then they face trial and possibly prison—so much for peaceful assembly and redress of grievances under the constitution."

"Still, like I said, there hasn't been a revolution." I veer around a stalled bus. "Yet."

"But don't the corporations like Powers, T'ang and Bianchetti own the politicians? The presidential election this year is merely a competition of who has the most campaign money. Few people even bother to vote anymore since both candidates are wholly-owned subsidiaries of the corporations. Even the Supreme Court ignores the Constitution to serve corporate interests. Can the case really be made that we have the 'same' government?"

"I'll have to be more careful what I say,"—I shake my head—"I'm talking to a lawyer."

"Sorry, but I deal with this every day. People are getting desperate. Since Seattle still has drinkable water, people are flooding into this area, but they can't find jobs and the government doesn't pay unemployment anymore. So many escape into drugs and alcohol and that leads to violence. Families take the brunt. Things just keep getting worse."

And they'll be getting a lot worse, but I'm not allowed to tell her about that, either. "Getting back to my original point, France had its Great Revolution in 1789, the same year the US Constitution went into effect. Over the next hundred years, France had three more revolutions, two monarchies, three republics, and two empires under two different Napoléons. Our countries went down totally different paths after their revolutions. I think it was because of the generals—Washington and Napoléon."

"Really? Why?"

Good, no more questions about Collin and me. "Both were in positions to take total power. Washington didn't, but Napoléon did. When the French rewrote their constitution in 1799, they set aside the previous Declaration of Rights and vested power in three consuls. One of them was Napoléon, and he maneuvered himself into the position of First Consul and then five years later got rid of the republic by declaring himself emperor."

"Why do you think the French gave up their republic and accepted Napoléon as emperor?"

"He did some popular things, like the new law code that ended a system which had favored the ruling classes."

"Ah yes." She nods. "You mean the Ancien Régime. Lexa's notes said that was the political system in France since the Middle Ages. All the power and privileges were held by the king, the Catholic Church, and the aristocracy. The people were left out in the cold. Literally. As could be expected, that imbalance in power created extreme imbalance in wealth. Most of the people lived in grinding poverty, so that's why they famously took up their pitchforks and rebelled in 1789 with their Great Revolution."

"That's also why Napoléon's new laws were so popular. They limited that abuse of power by the nobility and established a jury system."

"But did you know the guillotine was used in France until 1978?" In a pained voice, she adds, "In fact, Erik thought that if he were found guilty, he would be executed by guillotine."

"I had no idea. That had to be eating at him."

"Yes, different cultures, different assumptions."

Our line of cars comes to a full stop. We exchange uneasy glances as flashing lights ahead indicate some kind of police cordon and several hunter drones whir overhead. *What the hell's going on?*

After a long, uneasy silence, I try to strike up the conversation again. "Napoléon was a real mixed bag for the French people. Although he limited the power of the nobility, he also didn't hesitate to use force or even spies to ferret out any opposition to himself. Then he banned freedom of the press by closing or censoring newspapers."

"Sounds familiar. Our security agencies can eavesdrop on us through PALnet without subpoenas and do body searches without probable cause," she says. "And the PTB gets around our freedom of press by owning and controlling the media so they can manipulate the information through PALnet News."

"Napoléon manipulated public opinion too, and he was good at using propaganda to get the people's support. He appealed to their ideals and played on their fear of losing their freedoms. Made them worry that the exiled French nobility would return or that other countries would invade France. Then he used that fear to justify his military campaigns and ended up taking over parts of seven or eight countries. Made an empire for himself."

"And created many enemies for France in the process."

"Definitely. He won the battle of Austerlitz against Russia and Austria, then defeated a larger Prussian army the next year and even marched into Berlin."

"So you think those defeats motivated the Prussians to lay siege to Paris in 1870?"

"Absolutely. People have long memories and don't forget attacks on their country. They bide their time and wait until they can get payback. The Prussians did, three generations later."

"And they took revenge in full measure," Kathryn states.

"Yep, and Napoléon overreached when he invaded Russia in 1814, leading to his downfall. The Russians burned their crops as they withdrew, then fought a bloody battle at Borodino, one of the deadliest in history. Napoléon led a huge army of 600,000 into Russia and only 27,000 men came out. The Russians paid a hellish toll as well—over a half million soldiers and civilians were killed."

"Horrible. Erik said that no matter what the fighting is about, the people always suffer."

"He's right, but soldiers suffer too. Always. Even if they aren't wounded, they come back with psychological scars." I clench my teeth, thinking about my own nightmares of battles and death. "You know, post-traumatic stress wasn't recognized by psychologists until the Viet Nam vets were being counseled. But it always existed. In the First and Second World Wars they called it 'shell shock.' Even the French soldiers who fought for Napoléon had the symptoms."

"Ryan. I'm so sorry..."

I glance over at her. Those dark, compassionate eyes read right through me. I swallow hard and look away. As we inch forward in the crawling line of vehicles, I get a glimpse of police cars with flashing lights and several army trucks blocking the road fifty yards ahead. I hit the brakes when a rickety truck piled high with furniture and belongings pulls in line ahead of us. It sways precariously under its top-heavy load, so I keep my distance.

"Another displaced family," Kathryn says with a sigh. "But you mentioned Washington in comparison to Napoléon. What were you getting at?"

"Both generals became leaders of their new countries, but they took their countries in totally different directions," I reply, glad for a change of topic. "Washington could've seized power, just like Napoléon, but he didn't. After the Revolutionary War, one of his officers wrote to him and said that the army would back him as king. Washington wouldn't even consider it. And as president, he rejected European titles. Even though he'd been a general, he didn't create a standing army. When the Whiskey Rebellion occurred, he just called up the militias. Because France had helped America win its war of independence, Napoléon asked us to join the French in their war against Britain. Washington refused, kept our country out of war. Then in his farewell speech, he warned America to steer clear of foreign entanglements and focus on *internal* matters. Good advice."

"Advice long ignored. I always found it interesting that Washington never joined a political party," Kathryn says. "He warned that political parties would create polarization and lead to deadlocks in government. Boy, was he ever right."

"He even refused a third term—just handed over the reigns of power and walked away."

"Can you imagine any of our politicians doing that now?" Kathryn asks.

"No, and Napoléon didn't do that for France. He led his country into endless wars and left it bankrupt instead. And an entire generation of men, devastated. When Napoléon was overthrown, the nobility and kings came back, so the people were oppressed and impoverished all over again. Those were the years Victor Hugo wrote about in *Les Misérables*—the France that Erik was born into, with all the cruelties he suffered."

"But evidently the fallout from Napoléon's rule didn't end there." Kathryn's voice takes on an intense undertone. "His wars created enmity between France and other countries. That led to the Franco-Prussian War during Erik's life and then two world wars. When I think back on how egos and the thirst for power led France and Europe down such a disastrous path—well, I wonder. Would it have been possible to change the currents of history if other choices had been made?"

Her words jolt me. *Why did she bring that up?* But all I can say is, "Interesting idea."

Suddenly, police and army soldiers descend on the ramshackle truck ahead of our car. They throw open the doors on both sides, yelling at the people and ordering them to get out. A man, his wife and three children pour out. The police begin grilling the man as his wife watches in fear, the children clinging to her. Then the police take the keys and pull the truck over to the roadside where the soldiers go through all the furniture, clothing and even children's toys, dumping everything into a ditch.

"My god, what did they do?" Kathryn says, anguished. "Not have the right papers?" She reaches for her door handle, but I hit the lock.

She turns on me, angry. "Unlock that door!"

"No, I can't let you get involved. This could get out of hand real fast. I don't want you in the middle of gunfire." I keep watching as the man is thrown on the ground and kicked. "Need to get us the hell out of here."

An army corporal walks up to our car and lowers his head, peering through the window.

"What's up, anyway?" I ask.

"We've had a report of terrorists moving some bomb materials and guns," he says, all tense and wound-up.

"Foreign terrorists?"

"Nope. Home-grown," he replies. "I need to see your IDs."

"I'm a retired army doctor." I give him a friendly smile as I hand him my ID.

The corporal reads my ID with a scanner, then gives me a keen look to verify the photo. "Major Kirkman, this checks out, but it says you're licensed to carry weapons. Armed now?"

"Yes, I am. I'm the bodyguard for Ms. Copeland here."

"Then get out of the car and keep your hands above your head. You, too, ma'am, get out and keep your hands up." He orders another soldier to go around the car and cover Kathryn. She turns to me, her eyes large and frightened.

"Just do what they say and don't argue the point," I tell her.

"But we haven't done anything wrong."

"Hopefully, that'll be enough to keep us out of trouble." I get out slowly, keeping my hands high.

I'm told to lean against the car, then the corporal pats me down, finding my gun in the shoulder holster. He takes it and tells the other soldier to search Kathryn.

"She doesn't have any weapons," I call out, trying to waylay the search.

"At this level of alert, we can check anyone and anything," the corporal snaps back and orders the soldier to proceed. Kathryn is told to place her hands on the car. As the solider thoroughly pats down her body, she keeps her eyes shut tightly. I watch, outraged, wanting to stop this, but I can't. Gotta keep my own temper under control. I grit my teeth. Any wrong move, any suspicious comment could land us in deep water.

When the soldier finishes, he calls out, "Nothing!"

"What are you doing on this road today?" the corporal asks me.

"Ms. Copeland is an attorney, and I'm taking her to a meeting with a client in Olympia."

"Where in Olympia?"

"The Wheaton estate, Land's End."

"We'll make a call and check that out." The other soldier takes us to the roadside while dogs are brought over and our car thoroughly searched. Kathryn watches, silent, but I can tell she's shaking. From fear or anger? I put my hand on her shoulder, trying to reassure her.

When they finish, the corporal walks over and states with military precision, "I spoke with head of security at Land's End. He confirmed your statement. You can go, but your gun is being confiscated." Then with an apologetic grimace, he gives me a quick salute and adds, "Sorry for the inconvenience, Major." He escorts us to our car, then motions to the police to let us through the cordon. When we're a quarter mile down the road, I hit the gas, just wanting to put distance between us and the flashing lights.

I look over at Kathryn. Her anger is palpable. "And that is what's left of our constitutional rights," she says scathingly.

"At least we can still bear arms," I shoot back as I put my thumb over a small biometric light on the dashboard and punch in the code. The interior roof slides back, exposing four guns. I reach up and take one, slipping it into my shoulder holster.

Kathryn stares at me, stunned. "What if they had found those?"

"They can't. The gun compartment is lined with metals that block any scanning devices." I glance over and grin. "Remember, this is an armored car. Has some interesting features."

I call Tom and tell him what's happened. For the rest of the trip Kathryn reads her book in silence, icy silence.

When we turn off Cooper Point Road into the forest, a white-tailed doe and two fawns are crossing the road. I stop the car. The glen beside the road is covered with lush ferns. Moss and ivy cling to spindly pines between the draping cedars. It's so tranquil.

Kathryn puts away her book and watches the deer. "They're not afraid of us at all," she breathes out. "Beautiful aren't they?"

I look over at Kathryn. "Oh, yes." When the deer have crossed, sadly, I drive on.

Outside the gates of Land's End we encounter a gauntlet of news vans and parked cars. Cameras track us as I slowly maneuver through them. Several reporters jog alongside the car, shouting questions at Kathryn.

"Will it never end?" she groans.

"No. Not until the trial's over."

39 | BREACH

Land's End

ERIK

"May I bring you anything, Monsieur Mercier?" George asks as I enter the grand piano room.

"No," I reply brusquely, and hurry down the steps to the lower level. All morning I have anticipated the opportunity to compose on the exquisite Steinway while I await today's conference. I put my papers and pen on the music rack and open the fall, resting my fingers on the sensitive keys which respond perfectly to my touch. The rich sounds are beyond anything I am accustomed to in the pianofortes of my century. I replay the passage, each time devising new variations of counterpoint, but the subtleties are proving elusive. The passage begins to resolve, almost effortlessly, and I float with the music.

Voices intrude from the corridor. *Curse George.* He left the doors open on the upper level, and I need silence to hear the music, to feel it. Closing my eyes, I block out the world, allowing the music to coalesce in my soul and flow out my fingers.

When footsteps pound down the marble stairs behind me, I turn around on the piano bench, glowering. Jarrod stops abruptly on the bottom step and says, "Sorry to interrupt. Ryan called and said they got caught up in a police cordon on the highway, and they'll be late. So, keep right on doing…what you're doing."

He interrupts, then tells me to continue what he interrupted! Exasperated, I turn back to the piano. Jarrod settles on the couch and takes out his annoying device.

The only shadow that used to follow me was my own, and it was as silent as a windless cavern. Now I yearn for the solitude which once seemed a curse. But even if returned to the nineteenth century, apparently I will not be alone. Collin has finally been forthcoming about the Wheatons' plan to send a group of their people with me. He confided their agenda, but I doubt he told me the whole truth. As for my part, I confirmed what he wanted to hear—that I would go along with their scheme. For now, my life has become an oarless boat. Fate, along with these intruding people, controls the rudder. I have no choice but to cooperate with them and hope to find myself deposited back in 1871 Paris. Then I can escape into the tunnels and disappear in the darkness. At that, I am quite skillful.

Focusing on the nocturne, I try new combinations. Irritatingly, Tom's voice breaks through my concentration. "Jarrod, the Wheatons are returning this afternoon, so the reporters are like locusts outside the gate. Ryan's arriving soon with Kathryn. I'm sending an extra security team to the entrance, and I want you in charge. Make sure everyone gets through without a problem."

"I'll get right on it," Jarrod says as he bounds up the stairs.

As Tom leaves, he nods at me. "Sorry to interrupt, Erik."

But Tom's words leave me disturbed, and I can no longer concentrate. I abandon my music and race up to the corridor. "Tom," I call out, "is Ms. Copeland in danger?"

He stops and awaits me. "We're just taking precautions," he replies with his probing gaze. "Don't worry, her vehicle is armored."

"Why is it armored?" This does nothing to put me at ease.

"She'll be okay," he says. "We'll see to it."

He hurries off, preventing me from asking any further question. Focusing on music is no longer possible. I walk to the elevator and stare uneasily at the closed doors.

"Cognac?" George's high, nasal voice intrudes.

"Yes," I growl. When George returns, he strategically places the decanter on the table beside a couch. Reluctantly, I sit down and take a gulp of cognac. Why am I feeling so conflicted? Working on my composition today—or at least trying to—was my attempt to distract myself from the questions Kathryn will inevitably ask. But the possibility she is in danger is also unsettling. Time passes like the slow drone of a bagpipe. Several glasses of cognac later, the elevator lights blink.

I stand when the doors open and bow my head curtly, not knowing what to say. Kathryn is startled to see me. She seems anxious, almost distracted, as we exchange greetings and proceed to her office. Going directly to her desk, she takes out a stack of papers and opens that contraption which contains her notations. Feeling restless, I walk to the windows and look out at the Sound through a cognac-softened haze.

While she reads, I puzzle at the volume of information they have already compiled about me. In my world, if a person has a birth certificate or a baptismal record or marriage license, it is likely to be the only written evidence he exists. Before arriving here, I did not possess even those. But the Wheatons are thorough. They had already found my birth certificate and baptismal record. Those documents attest to a hasty baptism only three days after my birth—no formal ceremony in a cathedral to announce the birth of a count's son and heir. Perhaps they did not expect me to live. Perhaps I disappointed my parents by not dying and ridding them of their deformed child.

My foster father took me aside on my tenth birthday and told me that someone—he never said who—had placed me in his care when I was only three days old. That would have been the same day as my baptism. Then he placed a gold medallion in my hand and told me that its embossed crest belonged to my family. He made me solemnly swear to keep it always but tell no one. He said the medallion would eventually lead me to the truth of my birth. And it did.

When Kathryn looks up, I observe that her face is pale and drawn, but it would not be appropriate to pry into her personal affairs. "After you returned to Paris," she begins, "did you ever visit Zurich or London again?"

"No." A pang of regret stabs me. I never saw Monsieur Markham again. He died two years later. His last letter arrived a week after his death.

"Is the diary accurate about, uh, your work over the next several years?"

"About my being turned down for any position I applied for? The diary is correct. No one would employ me, so I resumed selling paintings."

"Do you know the names of anyone who purchased those?"

"No, my paintings were all sold to art dealers."

"Could you tell me their names?"

"That would not be helpful. When the siege was over, I went to their shops to collect monies they owed me, but like so many of the wealthy businessmen, they had fled Paris, and I do not know how they disposed of my paintings."

"I see. How long were you an organist at Saint-Sulpice. Did you work there regularly?"

"I worked there for nine years, until 1870. At first I performed for several masses a month. Then other endeavors demanded my time, so I performed only on occasion. I do not believe there was any record of it. Father Dupres always paid me in cash."

"Would there be any record of"—she hesitates—"where you lived those years in Paris?"

"I doubt it. Rent was paid in cash. My landlady's only concern was to be paid timely and in full, or she would put the tenant out on the streets without hesitation, without conscience. That was why I ventured out that last day. My funds on hand had run out. It was the *greed* of my landlady that forced me to travel across Paris during a bombardment to retrieve my savings. That was when the Communards captured me."

"I didn't know," she murmurs. There again, that expression in her eyes.

"Did you know," I sneer, "that the greed of the landlords was one of the reasons the Communards rebelled? During the siege, payment of rent was waived. Then after the war ended, the newly elected government in Versailles passed a bill requiring all back rent to be paid within two days. It became one of the sparks that ignited the uprising."

"But Leroux said you lived, uh, underground," she says, confused.

"After the siege, I moved into a boarding house. But it is true that I had been living underground since the incident with little Meg—the one concerning my mask." Without warning, the vision of the child's terrified screaming and Adèle's shocked face loom before my eyes. Taking slow, deep breaths, I try to ward off the emotions and keep them from engulfing me. When I pull myself back, my hands are shaking. I turn away to give myself time to regain control.

"Are you all right?" Kathryn's soft voice comes from behind me.

For many moments, I do not answer, steeling myself to do what must be done—to disclose what I have never shared with anyone.

Finally, I exhale and face her. "After what happened with Meg, I came across three rooms beneath the city that had been carved out, probably for storage. Each room had a ventilation shaft to the surface that also provided light during the day."

"So, were the rooms beneath the Garnier?"

"No, my rooms were located between the old opera house, the Salle Le Peletier, and Garnier's new one. The two buildings were but a short distance apart, and there is a tunnel in that part of the city which passed by both of them. My rooms were in a connecting tunnel between the two opera houses. They were also close to the underground waterway. Those rooms were my home for almost ten years...until the siege ended."

"Lexa wrote in her notations that the waterway was part of Emperor Louis-Napoléon's projects to rebuild and modernize Paris."

"Indeed. New aqueducts were constructed to bring clean water to Paris. Underground waterways were built that had brick-lined barrel ceilings so tall one could stand in a boat and use a pole to push it through the water. During the Paris Exposition in 1867, that become a popular attraction." I took Christine to Saint-Sulpice in those boats, but that I will not mention. "At night, I sometimes used the tunnels and boats to move about Paris."

"In the book, the home of the Phan..., uh, your home, was surrounded by a lake."

"You neglected to mention the siren in the lake," I add wickedly, no doubt prompted by the cognac.

A slight flush spreads across her cheeks. "I assumed that was the author's imagination."

"You are correct. No lake siren. Not even a lake beneath the Garnier." She looks surprised, so I explain, "When they dug down to create the basements, the excavation flooded because of the underground water table. I assisted with that challenge. First, the water was pumped out, then a retaining wall of cement was constructed to contain the water. The water beneath the opera house flows through a man-made channel."

"I assume you furnished the rooms?"

"Of course. Simply at first. But as my income rose, I purchased fine carpets and tapestries. My home was furnished most comfortably. I even had a collection of books."

"Any larger furniture?"

So she wants to know if Leroux was correct about certain unusual furnishings. "I had larger pieces like settees and bookcases delivered to the opera house," I answer evasively. "I took them apart and carted them to my rooms. I even installed Franklin stoves in each room."

"And maybe even an organ?" She gives me a quizzical stare.

"Yes, even a large pipe organ, which I dismantled to transport. It required several months to repair and refinish, but was quite worthwhile."

"You said your home had three rooms. One was a sitting room and one a bedroom?"

"Indeed. And the third served as my music room."

Her eyebrows arch. She wants to know if what Leroux wrote was true—whether a coffin draped in red brocade occupied the center of the room. After a sufficient amount of time to heighten her suspense, I volunteer, "There was only an organ." The unspoken question hangs in the air. Taking distinct pleasure in her dark eyes sparking with curiosity, I delay as long as possible. Finally I say, "No coffin graced my rooms."

A smile plays at her mouth. "Has anyone ever said that you're a very difficult man?"

"Not to my face," I retort, admiring her audacity.

She chuckles, then proceeds, undeterred. "You said you obtained a contract with Garnier. Considering the problems with, uh"—she hesitates again—"obtaining employment, how were you able to submit your architectural plan to him?"

I overheard Kathryn's conjecture that my friendship with the princess continued. No doubt she will be gratified by my response. "Through Princess Metternich."

"The diary didn't mention anything more about Princess Metternich after your meetings with her at Saint-Sulpice." Her eyes twinkle with vindication as she asks, "So, those weren't your only contacts with her?"

"They were not."

"May I ask what happened when you first met her at the *Tannhäuser* premiere?"

"Yes, you may *ask*." With my abruptness I try to shut the door on any further discussion of the matter. I take her off guard. Her dark eyes widen, guileless. Unexpectedly, some intrinsic barrier inside me yields. Nothing occurs so sharp or painful as a rending. It is more like an opening which allows a sliver of light to pierce the darkness. I walk over to the settee and sit down, taking a deep breath. "At the premiere, the members of the Jockey Club maliciously disrupted the performance. They even turned in their seats and aimed catcalls at the princess. During the next intermission, she left. I was concerned that further outrages may be directed at her, so I raced down to the lobby. Three dandies were tapping their canes and making obscene noises as the princess and her entourage were about to pass. So I used my cane to disarm them."

"Disarm them? With a cane?"

"Yes, with wushu techniques, a cane can serve as an efficient weapon."

"What is wushu?"

"An ancient form of martial art that utilizes wooden staffs. The Chinese acrobats in the carnival were masters. I studied their movements and have practiced them ever since. Wushu also has the advantage of not exposing one's hands to undue injury."

"Did the Chinese acrobats teach you about the Punjab lasso?"

"No, a man from India taught me that skill. He was the knife-thrower at the carnival." I also learned about knives from him. He disclosed their secrets, how to find the balance and nature of each knife, and how to throw them with deadly accuracy. She does not need to know that I also mastered that skill.

She stares at my hands. "So you disarmed all three?"

"One must move quickly, of course," I explain smugly, recalling the startled yelps of the three fops. "Knocking the canes out of their hands rendered them quite disarmed, both physically and socially. They were embarrassed and left without further incident. I apologized to the princess for their rudeness and escorted her to the carriage."

"That certainly explains why the princess remembered you." She chuckles again. "How long did you know her?"

"About nine years, until she left Paris when the war with Prussia began in 1870. Not long after, she gave birth to her third child." A wave of sorrow swamps me. "I never saw her again." The words slip out. A laxness no doubt induced by too much cognac. Looking up, I find Kathryn's eyes pensively studying me.

"You said she submitted your architectural plans to Garnier. How did that come about?"

"A year after I began playing at Église Saint-Sulpice, a new organ was installed—a magnificent one with seven thousand pipes—but that presented architectural problems. I designed a plan and anonymously submitted it through Princess Metternich. It was adopted. When Emperor

Louis-Napoléon commissioned the new opera house, I created a design for the underground levels, which included elaborate mechanisms beneath the stage area. The princess passed my plans to the emperor, who gave it to Garnier. My designs were adopted, and Garnier asked me to oversee the construction of the lower levels."

"Did the elaborate mechanisms include any trapdoors?"

"Yes. A number of them." *So, she seeks to verify whether I used trapdoors the way Leroux claimed I did.* "You realize I designed the trapdoors in the *new* Garnier opera house, but it was not yet completed when the war and siege occurred."

Undaunted, she presses, "Were you as familiar with the trap doors in the *old* opera house? The Salle Le Peletier?"

I gaze directly into her eyes. "Yes. I know every inch of that building."

"Is there anything you gave Princess Metternich that could be verified?"

"No, it would not have been proper to give her a gift." *That is a lie, but some things must remain private.* "But there is something she gave me which may be of assistance to you. I retained all the invitations and notes she sent me."

She peers at me, astounded. "You have correspondence from the princess?"

"Of course. How else would she have contacted me?"

"Were those at your boarding house? Wouldn't they have been discarded when you didn't return?"

"No, the invitations were kept in the metal box under the Garnier."

Realization flashes across her lovely features. "And you hadn't retrieved the box yet when the Communards...captured you? So it's still buried there?"

"Yes. Unless someone has found it by happenstance."

Her eyes widen again. "So, what else was in that box, Erik?"

"For one, the contract with Garnier and also the contract with the directors of the Paris Opéra concerning my fee."

"That sounds very promising." Abruptly she stops and studies me with a distinct air of skepticism. "However, Leroux mentioned a 'fee' that was, uh, requested of the opera directors, but it was not in a contract. Exactly."

"What did Leroux claim it was, *exactly*?" I bait her, knowing full well what Leroux wrote.

"Well, the fee appeared to have been added after the fact to the Opera's Book of Instructions that was given to the new directors. The fee clause was handwritten in scrawled red ink and required a monthly payment of 20,000 francs." She tentatively says, "Please tell me your document is not like that."

I break into a caustic laugh. "Rest assured, it is a contract, neither scrawled nor a belated addition to the Book of Instructions."

"What was the contract for?"

"My professional services. For sketches of backdrops, as well as posters for the various operas. Even sketches for costumes. Eventually, I also provided music to be played during the intermissions. At first, I left my work on the directors' desks at night. They used my ideas for over a year without paying me. Then one night I placed a contract for my services on their desk. My letter explained that for them to continue receiving my designs, I required a salary. They declined to sign the contract, so I terminated my services."

"But they eventually changed their minds?"

"Oh, yes. Two months later, a notice appeared backstage requesting a meeting with the person who had been leaving 'suggestions' on the director's desk. When I met with them, they recognized me as the musician whom the conductor had refused to hire."

"Didn't they ask how you'd been able to get into the opera house to leave your designs?"

"They asked. I did not answer." I smirk. "And they did not press the point. We signed a five-year contract, beginning June 1866. My fees were set at two thousand francs each month."

"Not twenty thousand francs per month as stated in the book?"

"Of course not. Two thousand was quite a handsome amount. The average worker earned only about one hundred francs a month. Along with the income from my work on the new opera house, I lived very comfortably and saved a considerable sum. My money is also contained in the box I buried under the Garnier."

"We need those documents. Could you draw a map with the location of the box? We'll try to find it." She walks over and hands me a pad and pen, then watches over my shoulder as I draw the map. "Is there anything else in your box I should know about?"

"Yes, a gold medallion. My foster father gave it to me. It is embossed with my family's crest. Whatever privation I experienced, that gold piece was never used to buy food or shelter. It was the only connection to my true identity. And that I finally discovered when Raoul took Christine to dinner the first time." My voice lowers to a hiss. "That is when I saw the crest on his carriage. His family crest. *And mine!*"

"Your older brother was Philippe and your younger brother, Raoul?" she blurts out.

"Indeed, they are my brothers, but I am the eldest. I was firstborn."

"You are the *Count* de Chagny?"

"Yes. We have my birth certificate and baptismal record. Did Collin not provide them?"

She stares at me, stunned. "No, he didn't."

Why was she not told my identity? What game is being played here?

"Thank you." Her voice breaks. "This concludes our conference."

Her face is set in resolve. Now *I* am stunned. Why is she dismissing me? I gather myself and make my way to the door. She arrives at the same moment and again our hands reach the doorknob together. She pulls hers back and whispers, "I'm sorry."

I open the door, and she heads toward Collin's office like a gale on the horizon, not hearing my last words. "So am I."

40 | ULTIMATUM

KATHRYN

Erik and I arrive at the door simultaneously, and our hands touch on the doorknob. Recoiling, I pull mine back. Is his the hand of a cold-blooded murderer?

"I'm sorry," I mumble and escape down the corridor. Ryan follows me, and George jumps out of the way as I steam past. I go straight to Collin's office and stop impatiently at his assistant's desk. "Harold, tell Collin I need to see him. Now!"

After informing Collin on the intercom that I "wish" to meet with him, Harold adds in his clipped British accent, "It appears urgent." Collin says to send me right in.

As Ryan opens the door for me, he asks under his breath, "Want me to come in with you?"

"No thanks, I can take Collin's head off by myself."

"No doubt." Half laughing, he adds, "But I'm here if you need me."

Collin is walking around his desk as if to greet me.

"This isn't a social call." My tone stops him cold.

He motions to a chair in front of his desk. "Make yourself comfortable."

I remain standing and come straight to the point. "Erik just informed me that he's an heir to the de Chagny line. The eldest son. The *Count*."

A look of comprehension flashes over Collin's features, but he quickly glues on an emotionless façade. "Yes, that's true."

"His birth certificate wasn't in the documents *you* gave me."

Unblinking, he meets my gaze. "I'm aware o' that." He walks over to a wet bar. "Would you like a drink, then?"

"No. I would like some answers."

Stalling, he pours scotch and takes a drink. "All right, wha' do you want to know?"

"Why did you withhold crucial information? Are you trying to undermine the case?"

"Why would I do tha'? We all want Erik acquitted. We're counting on it."

"But the fact of his being the eldest brother constitutes evidence and a strong motive for his killing Philippe. The prosecution will no doubt find out as well. Did you actually think that could be kept secret?"

"No, sooner or later Erik was bound t' let you know. And you're right. The PTB will probably dig until they uncover tha' and turn it over to the prosecution."

"So why didn't you tell me? Or give me the birth certificate?"

Stalling, he walks to an antique humidor cabinet. His office is windowless, devoid of the usual views of the Sound. Makes me feel claustrophobic. "I was afraid t' tell you," he finally says.

"Afraid?" I ask skeptically.

He opens a tobacco tin labeled "Dunhill, My Mixture." A pang of recognition and sadness sweeps through me. Anne used to specially order that for him. "Certainly," he says, "I was concerned about you."

"About me or just my reaction? Do you care about *anyone* anymore?"

"O' course I care." He avoids my gaze. As he turns the rack to select a pipe, I notice something unusual. There's no meerschaum—the pipe with a wolf's head carved from grey stone that Anne and I found after scouring London tobacco shops. It was Collin's anniversary gift, and he loved it.

As he selects a pipe, I comment, "I don't see a meerschaum in your collection."

His hand freezes as he breathes out, "No." Placing a small amount of tobacco into the pipe, he presses it down with his thumb. He repeats that until it's filled, then with pipe in hand, scrutinizes me. "So, Kathryn, what's on your mind?"

"Why aren't you being honest with me?"

"Whatever you want t' know, you only need ask."

"Really?" I retort. "After not hearing from you for three years, you call and ask to take me to dinner. But that was only a pretext for meeting with the Wheatons and asking me to take this case. You also neglected to inform me a bodyguard would be living with me and following me everywhere. Since then I've learned my 'confidential' conferences with Erik were being monitored by your people. Now I discover you've knowingly withheld incriminating evidence. How can I trust *anything* you say?"

"I'm sorry."

"That's not an answer. The point is, *why should I trust you*? Why didn't you give me Erik's birth certificate?"

He stares at the unlit pipe. "The reason you weren't told about Erik's family was because I thought you'd react exactly as you are right now. I know you very well. Anne and you were so alike. You'd both defend a victim, to your dyin' breath."

"So, you've been stacking the deck? Masquerading Erik as a victim?"

Collin takes a matchstick, striking it and circling the fire above the tobacco. Unhurriedly, he puffs several times, drawing the flame into the pipe. "If you'd known up front Erik was Philippe's brother and shunted aside, wouldn't you have thought him guilty o' murdering for revenge? Would you have even considered taking the case?"

"We'll never know because you didn't trust me enough to give me that choice. Whatever I would've felt then is no longer the point. Now the issue remains, how much information are you still hiding from me? I can't prepare the case properly if I don't have all the facts. That means every*thing* related to Erik or this case."

He puffs thoughtfully on the pipe. "There's no other information or document we have about Erik that has no' been given to you."

"That was a carefully phrased disclaimer. But you neatly sidestepped whether there's anything related to the case you haven't told me." I give him my ultimatum. "Let me make this perfectly clear—if there's *anything* related to Erik *or the case* you haven't told me, as soon as *it is disclosed*, I will consider that a material breach and file a motion to withdraw. That is, if I even decide to stay on the case now."

He picks up a tamper and pushes the tobacco down, stalling for time while he considers his answer. Taking a puff, he slowly blows out the smoke and gives me a sideways glance. "Well, there's something we have no' been entirely forthright about."

"You don't say." I don't even try to disguise my sarcasm.

He flinches. "At the meeting of the Foundation, you heard Howard tell why Erik was brought from the past. When you met wi' the Wheatons afterwards, you made it clear you found their explanation, uh, questionable. You didn't believe their reason then, and you don't believe it now, do you?"

"No, I don't."

"Actually, we didn't even explain the reasons to Erik until a couple days ago. He may inadvertently share tha' with you at some point as well." He eyes me soberly. "And tha' may not be the best way for you to learn how high the stakes are."

"What stakes?"

"The stakes for winning or losin' this case."

My stomach sinks. "I'm listening."

"I told you tha' we've traveled to the past. As ever-curious humans, we also went into the future." He looks down at his pipe and adds sullenly, "But we only went there once because of wha' we found."

I feel nauseous. "What was that?"

His voice goes flat, like he's numb. "It was bad."

"How bad?"

"Very bad." His eyes take on a dark, haunted look. "It was a ghost world. They did no' find any humans still alive. At least not in Europe, where they went. Perhaps there are pockets o' people somewhere in the world, but there was no response to signals sent out. Maybe some are still alive, but don't have means o' receiving or transmitting communications."

I want to end this discussion and leave—forget what he's just said—but I feel something urging me to stay. Like someone pleading. *Maybe it's Anne.* "So, what caused it?"

"We destroy the waters, both the fresh water and the oceans. Then there's a combination o' other things, mostly man-made, tha' result in famine and wars and a final plague."

"A plague?" With dawning realization, I ask, "Wouldn't the people who went into the future be contaminated too? Wouldn't they bring it back with them?"

"Yes, it was possible tha' it could be brought back and unleashed. So a difficult decision had to be made—tha' it would be too dangerous for them to return."

"What are you saying? That they didn't?"

"Exactly." His jaw clenches. "The people who went t' the future made the decision."

The horror of this is sinking in. "What happened to them?"

"They're still alive. We receive their transmissions each week."

"You mean none of them have died?"

"No, and it's been over two years. Our microbiologists theorize tha' the virus or bacteria—they don't know which it is—may have mutated over a period o' time and become innocuous."

"So, you'll be bringing them back?"

"We don't dare. The other possibility is tha' the plague is latent and the full-blown disease won't manifest for years." Collin shakes his head and puffs out a long cloud of smoke. "We can never bring them back. But the time-travel lab sends packaged food, clothing, medicine, and equipment. And seeds. They've found a place along the Mediterranean where the weather is relatively mild, and there's still wild game available. Now they're beginning t' plant and grow crops."

"How many are there?"

"Twelve. Six men and six women."

"Adams and Eves," I say under my breath. My brain reels at what Collin is telling me about the future, and my heart hurts for those people—caught in time, never able to return to their homes, their families, their lives. "What's being done about this?"

"The Wheatons shared the information with a handful o' trusted friends. The proposal from tha' group was to form the Foundation for Worldwide Action and fund as many projects around the world as possible to address the causes of the eventual apocalypse."

"So everyone on the board of directors knows about this?"

"No, actually they don't. The Wheatons and the members o' that original group agreed it would be devastating to release all the information—except to carefully chosen people. We only disclose it on a need-to-know basis. The danger is too great leaks could occur, and if the truth were released to the public, tha' could cause panic. When we discussed it with Erik, he was given only part of the picture, so you see, he and most of the Foundation's directors have selective information about what will happen in the future."

"*'Selective information'?* Isn't that a euphemism for lying?"

He snorts in protest. "That's not very charitable. 'When *I* use a word, it means just wha' I choose it to mean—neither more nor less.'" He punctuates the Lewis Carroll quote with a cloud of smoke from his pipe.

"And dealing with you makes me feel a lot like Alice in Wonderland! You're getting good at smokescreens and not just the ones you blow with your pipe." All my doubts about him, about this unbelievable story, spew out. "This tale about the future better not be another one of your ploys to manipulate me into staying on this case. Are you able to prove what you claim?"

His eyes narrow as he scrutinizes me. "Yes, as a matter o' fact, I can."

41 | REVELATION

Collin

Kathryn's going to regret demanding the proof. I *still* have nightmares about it. "We did no' want to believe it either, but then we started receiving the transmissions. Would you like to see some o' them?"

"You can actually show me that data?"

"I can." *And will.* I'll do whatever it takes to keep her on the case. Erik's getting more difficult to deal with, and he's let slip that Kathryn is the only one he trusts. By all the feedback I'm getting, he cooperates more with her than anyone else. If she quits now, there'll be hell to pay. I open the safe behind my desk and get the Qrystal which contains the Wheatons' secret project. Settling into my office chair, I again invite her to sit down.

Hesitantly, Kathryn takes the chair in front of my desk, and I place the Qrystal between us. Exhaling a resigned puff of smoke from my pipe, I begin. "The team transported into the countryside in southern France. When they arrived at a village, tha' was the first shock." I enter the code and project a hologram. The hilltop view overlooking a town shows a pack of dogs but no people. Vines cover decaying buildings and invade broken windows. Everywhere, the husks of rusting cars.

Kathryn shifts uneasily. "How do I know this isn't staged? Or a CGI creation?"

As expected, she'll need lots of proof. "Many towns were just like that. Devastation everywhere." I display one picture after another of towns and villages, all taken from a distance, all devoid of human life. "People had fled the cities. As you can see, the countryside was littered with abandoned vehicles and the remains of encampments. The towns and cities showed signs o' fighting and looting. Many buildings were burnt to the ground. Our group got as far north as Paris. It was mostly in ruins." I bring up the Paris skyline. The Eiffel Tower tilts to one side, balanced precariously and awaiting its own demise.

Then I begin pulling up the videos of what they found when they entered the towns—unburied skeletons. Everywhere.

"Oh my god!" Kathryn moans, but watches in shock for barely a minute. Then she says, "Enough!"

I turn off the hologram and wait.

Rubbing her forehead with her fingertips, as if trying to wipe away the horrific images, she asks, "What caused it?"

"We do not know for sure. The remaining records and data the team found indicate a number o' possibilities, a perfect storm o' combined causes. For one, chemicals and pollution devastated the land and the oceans."

"What kind of chemicals?"

"You name it. Tens o' thousands have been developed over the last couple centuries. The vast majority are never tested for either short- or long-term effects on humans, plants or animals. The laws don't require that type of testing before they're used. So, the chemicals get dumped into sewer systems or washed by rain into freshwater sources, like lakes and rivers. Or buried where they seep into underground water and wells. Then, there's the pollution from mining and oil drilling. And o' course there's the contamination of underground water by the chemicals used in hydrofracking for natural gas."

"But all that has been going on for a long time. By 2006, it was disclosed that fifty percent of China's two largest rivers was unusable for humans or even crops because of contamination by chemicals and pollutants. China has been importing freshwater ever since. I drafted some contracts for the sale of Canadian water to China when I worked for the international law firm."

"You're right. Even back in the 1900s, polluted or contaminated water caused half the deaths worldwide. In the future, it's going to get worse, much worse, and cause immense migrations. And o' course that ends up in wars." I puff on my pipe. "Could you use a shot o' scotch now?"

"No. But I'll have some wine."

As I go to the wet bar to pour the wine and another scotch for me, I continue. "Then there's the chemicals we eat. Chemical fertilizers and pesticides are sprayed on the crops, and other chemicals are dumped in water which then are absorbed by plants or ingested by livestock. Either way, they wind up in the food supply. As you know, cancer rates have skyrocketed. In 1900, only one in every *thirty-three* people got cancer. By 2000, it was one in *two* for men and one in *three* for women, and it's only gettin' worse. Statistics show neurological diseases like Alzheimer's and Parkinson's have tripled in the past century. Chemicals in our food and environment are likely the main culprit."

Handing Kathryn her wine, I settle back in my chair and take a gulp of scotch. "And other dominos will fall as well. The team sent to the future found a few databanks still sufficiently intact to access. They sent back a lot o' data to the scientists working in the Wheatons' inner circle..."

"Wheatons' *inner circle?*" She glances sharply at me.

"Yes." I give her a wry grin. "The ones who are given more than the selective information." Tipping my glass to her, I state, "Welcome to tha' *very* select group."

She frowns. "It's an honor I'd rather not have."

"You demanded t' know. And you must never mention it unless you're certain the person already knows, and there's absolutely no discussing it outside these walls."

"So, what did the Wheaton scientists conclude from the information sent back?"

"Crop failures get worse. Although there will be several causes, often that's due to bioengineering." I pull up a slideshow of headlines and research articles. "Notice how many articles focus on the lack o' variety within each crop species because o' bioengineering."

She leans forward to read the headlines as the articles flash past. "My grandparents had a farm in Ireland. I remember how upset they were when the government allowed genetically modified seeds to be planted. Those plants cross-pollinated with the plants in neighboring fields. That happened to my grandfather's field crop. Even the heirloom seeds my grandmother used in her vegetable garden eventually became contaminated."

"Ultimately, bioengineering results in losing a wide variety o' natural crop seeds. There are far fewer genetically modified varieties than used to occur in nature, and many o' the natural seeds went away through disuse or contamination. Genetically modified varieties are weaker than natural ones, but there is also the problem of using monoculture crops commercially, such as the yellow Cavendish bananas we used t' eat. Remember those?"

"Of course. Used to eat bananas for breakfast. Loved them," Kathryn replies.

"Well, those were monoculture which means they were all grown from the same plant, so there was no biodiversity t' create resistance to a newly emerging fungus. A virulent fungus started spreading from Malaysia around the world. When it eventually arrived in Central America, all the Cavendish bananas were destroyed by that epidemic. As the bioengineered or monoculture varieties fail, increasingly there are no' natural varieties available to replace them, so mass starvation occurs." I show her news articles reporting food riots, then famines and war on every continent.

"The same thing happened during the Irish potato famine in the 1840s. The people had become dependent on the potato and when it failed, they had nothing else. Not far from my grandparents' farm was a memorial to the million people who died during those years." She exhales sadly. "Anne and I would place flowers on it every summer. But what about the seed bank in Norway? Isn't that supposed to be where seeds are safely preserved?"

"The Norway bank is a depository where countries can voluntarily preserve seeds as backup to their own seed banks. However, each country controls the seeds it deposits, and the worst famines will often occur in countries which had no' saved their native seeds. In other cases it appears tha' growing conditions had changed so much, the native seeds were no longer viable. From the articles sent back, it appears the bank proved either too little or too late. So history repeats itself."

I shut off the hologram. "As you can also see from the articles, the bioengineered plants are weaker so fungicides and pesticides are incorporated into the seeds. Tha' not only causes further problems with the food, but probably also caused the final demise o' bees, along with many other species."

"The bees? They've been on the edge of extinction for some time."

"Correct. Bees used to pollinate at least a third o' the food we eat. Remember all those fruit pies we enjoyed as children? The apples and pears and peaches. All the berries? It's rare t' see them anymore. The Wheatons still have beehives and fruit trees because all their farms are isolated. They're trying to preserve and reintroduce them wherever possible. The loss o' bees is one cause for increasing crop failures and famine we're already witnessing. Tha' is why we're sending bees as well as seeds to the team in the future."

She takes a long drink of her wine. "But isn't that sending them the same bioengineered seeds and contaminated bees? Doesn't that perpetuate all the problems?"

"That's why we've gone back to 1935. We're sending seeds and bees from there."

"You've thought of everything, haven't you?" she asks.

I toss down the rest of my scotch. *Little does she know. Need to change the subject.* "But destruction o' the oceans also contributes to famine. You know wha' plankton are, don't you?"

"Yes, they're the tiny animals or plant organisms that float on the ocean's surface."

"Right, but they remove carbon dioxide from the air and produce seventy percent o' the oxygen on this planet."

"I thought trees produced most of the oxygen."

"Trees produce a lot, especially the rain forests—wha' is left of them. But plankton produce even more and are a major food source for the fish and ocean mammals. Problem is, no' only chemicals have been dumped into the oceans. They've become garbage dumps. You've probably heard about the mass of garbage—three times the size o' Texas—which formed in the middle of the Pacific years ago and just keeps growing. There are others like it in all the oceans. All tha' junk and plastic eventually degrade and release chemical contamination into the ocean which is ingested by the plankton—and by all the fish for tha' matter. The garbage, along with the chemicals and oil spills, is killing off the plankton. That's a critical loss to the food chain. Here, let me show you some more videos the team found."

I reactivate the hologram to show scenes of garbage floating on the ocean as far as the horizon. Dead, colorless reefs attest to the consequences. Covered in oily sludge, whale and dolphin carcasses sickeningly litter beaches. Kathryn's beginning to look a bit green around the gills herself. "Some parts o' the ocean already contain dead zones," I point out, "and in other places, ninety percent o' the fish are gone. The scientists predict there'll soon be nothing living in the oceans."

"Many countries rely on the ocean to feed their people."

"O' course, and when the fish are gone, more famines, uprisings and wars." I get up and pour myself another scotch. I need it. "The scene will be set for wha' appears to be the final blow—a Carrington event."

"What's that?" she asks, her voice strained.

"An enormous solar storm tha' gives off a CME—coronal mass ejection—so large it can burn out the satellites in orbit and even blow out the giant transformers our electrical grids rely on. It's named after Carrington, the scientist who identified the CME in 1859 which blew out telegraph wires and systems across the United States. But tha' was before everyone relied on electricity. It's long been known another CME as large could occur any time. In the future it finally happens and the electricity goes down, no' just in one place, but all over the country." I pause to let that sink in.

"Think about it," I say, continuing. "No electricity t' pump gas at the stations, so no trucks can bring food supplies to cities. No electricity t' pump water to deliver to homes. No electricity to keep refrigerators or freezers going, so tha' food is lost within days. No electricity in hospitals. No electricity anywhere. And the records found in the future indicate tha' governments still hadn't prepared for a Carrington-sized CME by having backup transformers on-hand and ready to put the electricity back online. When the electricity is down, you canno' build new transformers and equipment overnight—it takes months. So the electricity stays down for a long time, and most people, especially those in the cities, have no food and no water. You can imagine wha' happens then. In the United States, they'll still be using nuclear reactors, and those only have back-up energy supply t' last one month. The reactors start to melt down and—"

"I get the point," she interrupts.

"So, there will be total chaos. Then the final catastrophe hits—a bacterial or viral plague spreads around the world. People's immune systems are too weakened and provide little resistance."

"Where does the plague come from?"

"We're no' certain, but the team in the future found reports about terrorists breaching a biotech research lab when the electrical systems go out. It happens so fast, the scientists don't have time to find the cause or a cure. That's the final nail in the coffin."

"How far in the future does all this happen?"

"Many o' these problems have already begun, as you know. But the final blow is about twenty-five years from now."

"So soon!" Kathryn stares blankly at her wine glass. "Can't this be prevented?"

"The Foundation for Worldwide Action is doing wha' it can. But you know how the world operates," I reply bitterly. "Corporations like Powers, T'ang and Bianchetti have long since bought off the politicians. Businesses take their short-term profits and governments ignore the disastrous, long-term consequences. We forget this is a livin' planet. If we kill it, we kill ourselves. So to answer your question, we don't know if it's too late."

Her face has gone ghostly white.

"Are you all right?" I ask.

"Now that I know all this? No!" She takes a gulp of wine. "But how on earth does this connect with Erik and the case?"

"The Wheatons and the original core group created the Foundation. They hoped their projects would be enough to change the future. But that isn't assured."

"So, the Wheatons developed a backup plan, a Plan B, is that it?"

"You could say that." Taking a deep breath, I drop the next bomb. "If the world's doomed on this time stream, the logical solution is to create a different time stream. Using the knowledge we have of wha' went wrong the first time, Plan B is to go back and change the course o' history. Hopefully, humans will make different choices and survive—if we don't screw it up again."

There's dead silence as she tries to wrap her mind around my disclosures.

"Just how do you go about creating that?" she finally asks.

"You heard Dr. Hua explain tha' when we travel to the past *and change it*, a new time stream is created, forking off from the original. When we went back and saved Erik from execution, we made a significant change. Tha' created our new time stream."

"But how will you go back to that particular time stream instead of the current one? Or even a third, unknown one?"

"Good question. Just know we can, but tha' part of the technology is confidential. All I can disclose is that we are able t' target a particular time stream and arrive at a specific place within a two-hour time window."

She blinks in disbelief. "And Erik—somehow he's part of this plan?"

"He certainly is. We analyzed wha' would be the optimal date t' begin our new time stream and chose 1871. The Civil War in America was over, the French-Prussian War in Europe had just ended, and it was forty years before World War I began. The last decades of the 1800s were a cauldron o' economic, scientific, and social change. It was a period of advances—the foundation for our modern world—but many problems we're dealing with now also began then. And we needed someone from tha' culture who knew his way around t' help us, to serve as our front man, if you will. We developed four criteria for choosing the person.

"This I'm dying to hear."

"First, he must be a genius, and we felt it had to be a man because o' the prejudices and limitations on women in the 1800s." She frowns but bites her tongue.

"The second criterion was tha' his intelligence must be *creative* so he's capable o' thinking outside the box. We needed to bring him to our world for a period o' time, so he had to be open to our technology and social changes and able to comprehend the plans we want to implement in the past."

"Erik fits those. What else?"

"Third, he must not be overly connected to his family or his social and political environment. This person needs t' be independent and have no loyalties tha' might undermine the interests of our, uh, agenda."

"That certainly describes Erik."

"The fourth was particularly important. The person should have personal connections to the upper echelons o' society and power. Lady Margaret hired an investigator who discovered Erik's birth records and those verified he was born to a noble family. Erik is the heir to a title tha' comes with a prominent standing in society along with a substantial fortune. More to the point, he is a friend o' Princess Metternich, one of the most influential and politically connected people in Europe. A persuasive argument was made tha' Erik fits all four criteria."

"I'll bet Mrs. Wheaton was the one who made that persuasive argument."

"Correct." I take a puff, savoring the smoke. One of my few remaining pleasures.

"That explains her vehement belief that he's either innocent, or if he committed the murders, he must've been justified. She was defending the person she proposed."

"It's true, Lady Margaret does seem to always take Erik's side."

"So, just how will Erik fit into the Wheatons' agenda?"

"We've already sent a group of our people back t' 1871 France, and they're investing substantial sums. Tha' will create a fortune to fund this first project and others to follow. A château outside Paris is being purchased. Erik will be portrayed as the owner—a man who made his fortune in mining and business investments in America. The château will serve as a front and base of operations for the people tha' go back with him."

"What was Erik's reaction to all this?"

"Favorable." Truth be told, Erik's like a caged lion, biding his time and willing to use his fangs if necessary. That's why we need Kathryn.

"The people who go back with Erik—what will they do?"

"Tha' is where I come in. I'll work with them to alter the disastrous trajectory mankind is now on. My job is t' analyze the political, scientific, and social turning points."

"Political? Like averting wars?"

"Yes, but we'll also try t' change political and social resistance to movements tha' were quashed or programs instituted too late which could have made pivotal differences." I study Kathryn. Time to land the final blow. "Pivotal differences to possibly insure mankind's survival."

"So, your plans depend on Erik going back with your people. And *that* depends on his being acquitted." She stares into space for many moments, then breathes out. "Heaven help me! What have I gotten myself into?" She finishes off her wine. "Do you have anything else to tell me?"

"No. I think tha' about covers it."

"Good." She stands, swaying slightly. "I'm going home."

"You're still with us, aren't you, Kathryn?"

"I don't know. You've implicated me in your intrigues without my knowledge or consent. I have to sleep on it." As if escaping, she hurries to the door. Without looking at me, she tosses back, "Call me in the morning."

Hell. Not what I wanted to hear. I stand at the door and watch her flee. Then I catch a flash of black down the corridor. I can't see him, but I know he's there.

"I'll take care of this," Ryan says calmly as he grabs a towel and cradles my hand with it, catching the blood. He sits me down at the breakfast bar. I wait, dazed, while he gets his medical bag.

Carefully, he examines the embedded glass. "Looks like it's all in one piece," he reassures me. When he uses tweezers to pull it out, the pain is sharp, and I clench my jaw. He gently pats away the blood with a gauze pad and asks, "Feel any more glass in there?"

"No. Feels like you got it all."

He holds the pad on the wound until it stops bleeding, then cleans it and applies a butterfly bandage. Deftly, he wraps my hand in gauze. When he finishes, he smiles. "You can have your hand back now."

"Thanks." I ease off the barstool and walk robotically into the kitchen. There, on the countertop, broken glass mingles with blood.

Ryan walks up behind me. "Don't worry about that. I'll clean it up." His voice sounds like it's coming from the far end of a tunnel. Swaying, I lean against the counter for support. "Are you all right?"

I can't speak. Uncontrollable tears pour down my cheeks. The room seems to fade into nightmarish images. Of the future. Of all that is broken and will be lost. I begin to sob as everything comes crashing in on me. Ryan takes me in his arms while I cry on his shoulder. He tries to comfort me, but what has been done cannot be undone. Collin has told me the truth about the future and the responsibility I carry in this Humpty Dumpty world. How can I ever put *that* back together again?

42 | SHATTERED

KATHRYN

With Ryan at my heels, I rush down corridors that feel like a labyrinth. *Have to get out of here.* I stop at my office only long enough to lock up my QRYSTAL. Desperate to escape, I hurry to the elevator and hit the call button, then wait impatiently.

I get on the elevator and lean against the back wall for support. Looking up, I catch sight of a half-hidden shadow across the corridor. *Erik!* His face stony white against the black mask and his mouth set in a taut line. His eyes are piercing, questioning. Numbly, I return his gaze but give no hint of an answer. Then the doors close.

I sink into the seat of the car, overwhelmed. Just want to shut out the world. Ryan says nothing the entire drive. I close my eyes, but sleep and peace elude me.

When we get home, I go straight to my room and dress for bed. Too restless to sleep, I decide some hot tea might help. Slipping on my robe, I go to the kitchen. Ryan is making a sandwich. He looks up, surprised. "Going to bed already? It's only eight."

I glance at the clock, then out the windows toward the bay. The sky's so overcast and dismal, it seems much later. Somehow I've lost track of time.

He smiles sympathetically. "Can I make you a sandwich?"

Through a haze, I watch him slather mayonnaise over a sourdough roll. My stomach turns. "No, thanks." I reach into the top cabinet for a cup, but my hand grazes a glass, knocking it down. The glass hits the countertop and shatters. A shard spears my palm, and I cry out in pain as blood streams down my arm.

43 | HOURGLASS

Sunday, June 24
Seattle

RYAN

I'm just flipping the last pancake when Kathryn comes into the kitchen and stops dead in her tracks. "Ryan, you're cooking?" The expression on her face is the payoff for putting on an apron and making breakfast.

"Yeah. Don't want you using your hand today. Doctor's orders." I plop a couple big, steaming pancakes on her plate.

She stares down at them. "You sure make a *mean* pancake." Then she breathes out a sincere, "Thanks."

I grin back. For once I'm not just the annoying bodyguard.

When we settle into our places at the breakfast bar, she gasps. "Strawberries! Where did you get *strawberries* from?"

"George sent them."

"Why would he do that?" she asks, still staring at the delicacies.

"I don't know. He had them delivered specially for you from one of the Wheaton farms. Maybe he noticed you had a bad day yesterday. Not much gets by him."

She picks up one of the strawberries and studies it. It's large and perfectly ripe. "It's more likely that Collin is behind this." She bites into it and turns quiet as she eats.

I'm also feeling concerned about how she reacted yesterday to her meetings. I don't know what Erik said, but it triggered a fury I hadn't seen in her before. Then she came out of Collin's meeting looking shaken to the core and nearly had a breakdown last night. I'm wondering if Collin told her the truth about the future when my QRYSTAL goes off. Kathryn stops eating and frowns, like she knows who's calling.

It's Collin, asking to talk to Kathryn. I hand the QRYSTAL over, and her face goes grim as she listens. "Yes, I've decided to continue," she replies with a deadened voice. So he must have told her about the future and apparently gave her an out. Gutsy woman, she didn't take it. "We'll be there about one," she says, ending the call.

"Let me guess, we're going to Land's End?" I ask, disappointed.

"Yes. Change of plans. Mr. Wheaton leaves on business tomorrow. Lexa was in charge of our response to the motion about bringing people from the past as witnesses. Since she's stuck in London, I'm preparing it. Mr. Wheaton only has today to go over what he wants."

It's Sunday and she promised to work just half the day, then get some rest. She needed that. She's even got dark circles under her eyes. In gloomy silence we eat. After breakfast, I take her to the Quaker meetinghouse, then drive her to Olympia for her conference with Wheaton. The entire trip she's silent, absorbed in her thoughts. Ever since she broke down last night, I keep thinking I should switch from bodyguard mode and bring up my concerns as a doctor.

Lying in wait at the elevator, George tells Kathryn, "Monsieur Mercier requests a meeting with you in the grand piano room." Caught off guard, Kathryn's face goes blank, but she recovers quickly and says to let him know she'll be right there. What happened between Erik and her? She stops by her office to pick up the QRYSTAL for Erik's case, then we head for her meetings.

Pounding music from the Steinway piano assaults our ears long before we get to the grand piano room. Sounds like thunder. I can always tell Erik's mood by the way he plays. This warns of a storm ahead. Erik stops playing the second we enter. He turns around on the piano bench and watches Kathryn walk down the steps. When she reaches the lower level, he stands and bows stiffly as she sinks onto a couch.

I remain on the upper level, but on alert. Concerned about Erik's bad temper, I turn on my earbud to monitor the situation. I'm relieved he sits back down on the piano bench, putting a safe distance between them.

"I trust this meeting is not inconvenient, *Ms. Copeland*," he sneers.

"What do you wish to discuss?"

Erik looks away and brushes a hand across the top of the keys. "Collin has informed me you intend to remain my lawyer."

"That's correct."

"Despite your misgivings?" Erik's tone cuts like a knife.

"Misgivings?" Kathryn's voice is strained.

"You ended our meeting abruptly. Clearly you were"—Erik turns and glares accusingly at her—"*displeased* to learn I am the elder brother of Philippe and Raoul de Chagny."

Kathryn clears her throat. "I wasn't displeased."

"What exactly would you call your behavior?" Erik's unrelenting.

I'm trying to figure out why this has become such an issue between them.

"I was surprised. You know I hadn't been given that information."

"The question remains," he says, pressing the keys and sending a grating chord into the air, "now that you know I am the Count de Chagny, how does that affect your opinion of me?"

"You remain my client, of course."

"That is not what I mean," he shoots back. "Do you now believe I killed Philippe? That I was capable of killing my own brother out of some sense of outrage or revenge?"

"I'll answer you honestly. I don't know what to believe." Her back is to me, so I can't see her face, but her voice is steely. "I sincerely hope you did not. But as your attorney, I need to inform you that you're not obliged to tell me."

"You always speak forthrightly with me, so I will reciprocate." Erik gets to his feet and towers over her. My body tenses, preparing to race down those steps. "I did *not* kill Philippe." Then his voice lowers to a snarl. "He did nothing to me personally to deserve that. If I were to kill one of my brothers, it would be Raoul. I even had the opportunity, but..." He doesn't finish the sentence. "So, does that satisfy your concern regarding this matter?"

After a pause, Kathryn replies sincerely, "I believe you, Erik."

He inhales sharply. I don't think he expected that. Next thing I know, he's bounding up the steps and striding past me, out the doorway. I sprint down to Kathryn. She's just sitting there, frozen, and staring at the piano. "You okay?" I ask.

"I think so."

"Want to take a few minutes before you meet with Wheaton?"

"No, let's get this over with," she mumbles.

George is waiting in the corridor and leads us past the library and into the windowless waiting room. He does a retinal scan and opens the hidden door. Disguised as part of the paneling, the door slides open, exposing the elevator. Kathryn looks around nervously. "What is this place, Ryan?"

"It's okay. We're going to a SCIF—a sensitive compartmented information facility. That's an area within a building that is totally shielded and secure, restricted to select people."

"You mean an *inner sanctum* for the Wheatons' *inner* circle?"

I half chuckle. "That's one way to put it."

As we descend deep into the ground, Kathryn is silent. This confirms my suspicion that Collin told Kathryn about the future and the Wheatons' plans. Only those with inside knowledge are permitted here.

When the elevator opens onto a small room with a steel door, she hesitates. George quickly steps in front of a retinal scan and stares it down with his sunken eyeball, causing the door to slide open. Still, Kathryn gazes doubtfully down the long corridor that comes into view. I gently touch her shoulder. She takes a deep breath and finally steps forward, following George.

At the turn in the corridor, we come to a sweeping wall of glass which permits an unobstructed view into a cavernous room with banks of screens covering the walls and countless workstations. Transfixed, Kathryn stops and watches the scientists and programmers going about their work. I know the feeling. I felt the same way the first time Collin showed me this room.

"Those aren't security monitors, are they?" she asks.

"No, they're special quantum computers. This is the time-travel lab. You know about the team in the future now, don't you?"

"Yes. Collin told me yesterday and you saw the effect last night."

"That's what I figured."

"But all those people. I've never seen them around the mansion. And, there were no extra cars in the garage today. How do they get here?"

"There are several underground garages—one for the scientists, one for employees and security, and another for deliveries. We park in the garage for the Wheatons and their guests."

"I thought the time-travel lab was at Wheaton Industries in Seattle."

"The research, development and manufacturing are done in the other Wheaton Industry locations. The computers and scientists involved in time travel are here. And that's confidential. Don't disclose it to anyone."

She studies the engravings in the glass wall, seeming to puzzle over the "HG Laboratory" etched next to the logo of an hourglass.

"So HG stands for hourglass?" she asks.

"Yes, but that's also Mr. Wheaton's first and middle initials, so it's a double entendre."

"It's interesting that something as primitive as an hourglass represents the world's most advanced technology." Under her breath, she adds, "But there's no doubt about it any longer—I've definitely arrived in Wonderland."

Before I can reply, George interrupts in his polite but pointed manner, "Mr. Wheaton and Lady Margaret are waiting."

At the last door, George again eyes the retinal scanner. When Kathryn steps inside, some of her tension seems to go away as she surveys the room whose indirect lights cast a soft glow on murals depicting the Pacific Northwest. Potted trees are scattered between tables and chairs made of heavy driftwood. The room gives the feeling of being surrounded by nature instead of a carved-out chamber eighty feet below ground.

"Not quite what you expected, huh?" I ask.

We thought this was just a conference with Wheaton, but it looks like a meeting of the clan. Diane's chatting with Collin, and Jarrod and Tom are here, too. Erik is the only one missing.

"Thank you for coming on such short notice," Wheaton says to Kathryn. I give Jarrod a questioning look. He points with his chin toward Diane. Yep, something's up.

Diane smiles her toothy grin as a prelude for whatever problem she's about to unload. "I appreciate each of you being here on Sunday. I'll try to keep this brief. I feel we need to address a problem that's turning serious. Erik seems to be withdrawing more these past several weeks. Have any of you observed that? Or any other behaviors that have flagged your concern?"

"Yeah, he's become more reclusive, more moody," Jarrod says.

"When did you notice the change?" Diane asks.

"It started when we were told criminal charges would be filed."

"But didn't his behavior take a turn for the worse after the court appearance?" Tom asks.

"Yeah." Jarrod shakes his head. "He was angry about not choosing his attorney."

That grabs Kathryn's attention. "But I told him he had the right to choose his attorney."

"Yes, tha' you did," Collin replies, "but he had no' made his decision by the time he was arraigned. Lexa had to step in on short notice. Erik resented it."

The air between them is charged. "Was it his decision for me to represent him?"

"Yes," Collin declares testily, "it was."

"But he's gotten more difficult since then," Jarrod says. "Since he escaped from Kathryn's office, he's gone missing several times. Then he'll just reappear as if nothing happened."

"At least wherever he goes in the mansion," Wheaton says, "he can't escape."

Kathryn turns her glare on Wheaton. That sure hit her the wrong way.

"I'm concerned he's withdrawing into himself. Several times he's remained in his room all day," Diane says. "He's been skipping most of our counseling sessions."

George clears his throat with a rather loud "ahem." Mrs. Wheaton smiles up at George and asks, "Is there something you wish to add?"

"Yes, ma'am. When he remains in his suite, I serve his meals there. He eats very little."

"I've also heard that." Diane frowns. "These are all symptoms of depression."

"Why not just give him an antidepressant?" Wheaton asks, annoyed.

"No, Howard, I don't casually give drugs for depression," Diane replies adamantly. "Those often create far more physical and psychological problems than they solve. Particularly in a case like this, which appears to be caused by the situation."

"What do you expect?" Kathryn speaks up. "He's about to be put on trial and could spend the rest of his life in prison. And he's already being confined like a prisoner."

I glance around the group. Kathryn hit a nerve. Everyone looks distinctly uneasy.

"Perhaps Kathryn got to the heart of the matter." Diane nods in agreement. "He's accustomed to controlling his own destiny. So, what are we going to do about this?"

"Collin, when you told Erik about our plans for the new time stream, what was his response?" Mrs. Wheaton asks. "Was he favorable about working with us?"

Collin rubs his chin. "Basically, he did no' reject our proposal. He called it an interesting proposition and asked some questions. Said he was favorably disposed."

"That sounds like so much double-talk if you ask me," Wheaton says cynically.

"Who can blame him? Isn't he always being given choice-less choices?" Kathryn retorts.

Wheaton frowns at Kathryn, but she doesn't flinch. Something dawns on me—maybe Kathryn relates to Erik. Maybe she's feeling the same way since being drawn into this clash of wills between Erik and Wheaton. The two men reflect each other's intensity like opposing mirrors that magnify endlessly, just like that torture chamber in Leroux's book.

"Are you proposing Erik needs to be given some freedom and choices?" Diane smiles with approval at Kathryn, taking off some of the heat.

"I have an idea," Mrs. Wheaton says with her soothing confidence. "We have a lodge in Alaska. We could ask Erik if he'd like to go there." She turns to her husband. "Has Erik ever seen a whale? Fished for salmon? Kayaked on a crystal lake? If he has never experienced that, how can he care about preserving it or working with us toward those goals?" She turns to Kathryn. "Would that give him a choice? And enough freedom?"

"Why don't you ask *him*?" For the first time today, Kathryn smiles.

44 | CHOICE

Dr. Adler

"Why don't you ask him?" Kathryn's words hang in the air.

"What's your assessment?" Howard asks me, disgruntled.

I've observed that Howard has been short-tempered recently, also exhibiting signs of stress. But he has the freedom to come and go, and a variety of options to deal with his stressors. Erik doesn't. "Erik's mental and emotional condition has clearly been deteriorating. In my professional opinion, he needs an opportunity to get away from the constraints of Land's End."

Howard looks at his wife. She nods almost imperceptibly. Turning to Tom, he demands, "What about security? Can you ensure his safety? And that he'll return?"

Characteristically, Tom takes a little time to consider his answer. "We can fly to Alaska and back at night. Create a smokescreen so no one will know he's gone."

"Based on what those men said when they waylaid Erik after he escaped from the office," Jarrod speaks up, "the PTB probably wouldn't interfere or jeopardize his safety."

"Yes, they made it quite clear they want their show trial," Howard says, not hiding his resentment. "Collin, what's your opinion?"

"Erik's been a bit thorny. A change o' scenery might do the trick."

"All right, go ahead," Howard orders, then abruptly stands. "Ms. Copeland, let's work in my office."

As Kathryn walks by, I notice her mouth is pinched and tense, also a sign of stress.

After Howard's office door closes, I voice what everyone's thinking. "So, who wants to talk with Erik?"

"Diane, you're the perfect person," Lady Margaret says to me.

Jarrod stands and grins at me. "I'll go with you."

"This is a security matter now. I've got work pilin' up," Collin says, and departs. Glad to wash his hands of this, I suspect.

"I'll go with Diane and Jarrod," Ryan volunteers.

"Good," Lady Margaret says, smiling. "Tom and I will discuss the security issues. If Erik agrees, let him know we'll go over the plans at dinner tonight. George, please escort them through the secured doors."

Our intrepid delegation sets out with George in the lead. Ryan falls in beside me. "You'll be going on the trip, won't you, Diane?" he asks.

"Mostly likely, in case I'm needed."

"I was just thinking—there's no doctor on the island. Maybe I should go too."

"You've got a good point. Since I've been practicing psychiatry for the last two decades, my medical skills are a bit rusty. But what about Kathryn? Does she have a backup bodyguard?"

"Sure, Jim's been assigned, but she's never met him."

"You mean you haven't taken any time off? Why?"

"Kathryn's got enough problems without two bodyguards popping in and out of her life."

I study his expression. Perhaps there is more to why he remains so dedicated to her safety. Unexpectedly, George takes us right past the grand piano room. Something's wrong. Erik spends every Sunday afternoon there. "Isn't Erik at the piano?" I ask.

"No, ma'am. Monsieur Mercier is in his suite." *Interesting.* George was busy attending to our meeting. How did he keep track of Erik's whereabouts? Lady Margaret doesn't allow security cameras throughout the mansion, but my hunch is she doesn't need those. She has George.

At Erik's suite, George pushes the intercom and stands in front of the camera.

"Yes, George?" Erik's deep voice resonates with irritation.

"Dr. Adler, Dr. Kirkman, and Mr. Pearce wish to visit. Would that be convenient?"

There's a long silence. Just as I'm beginning to have misgivings, Erik opens the door and invites us in. He's wearing a black silk lounging robe over trousers and shirt. Quite striking and Victorian, just like his room. Lady Margaret let Erik choose his furnishings from their French antiques at the penthouse. He invites me to sit on a side chair near a marble fireplace with a Degas hanging above the mantle. The famous painting features a ballerina en pointe, but a man in a black suit stands behind the stage's curtain, his face hidden. *Who was this man Degas painted?*

Erik motions for Jarrod and Ryan to take the settee, then seats himself on a regal, high-backed chair. Gracing the tables are elegant carvings—in particular, one voluptuous mermaid of aged ivory.

Looking around, I note that the room has a split personality. This half, an elegantly furnished sitting area, neat as a pin. The other half, a mélange of chaotic, creative energy. An antique desk is strewn with papers and piles of hardbounds. A long oak table in the center of the room serves as his work area, covered with sketches and a sculpture in progress. Boxes of charcoals and various carving tools litter the top. Over by French doors to the balcony, a music stand sags under piles of sheet music and a violin case leans against a chair. The only thing the two sides of the room have in common are candelabras.

I glance up at the skylights that Lady Margaret had installed while Erik was in the hospital. The shades are pulled back, letting in soft daylight. I wonder if he uses only candles at night. Perhaps that's why he's been spending so much time alone in his suite. He can block out the modern world with all its strangeness and a looming trial. Perhaps this has become his sanctuary, like his rooms under the opera house.

Erik folds his arms and asks bluntly, "To what do I owe this honor?"

"We just wanted to stop by for a visit," I reply, but his eyebrow dips skeptically. I try to strike up a conversation. "I didn't know you were so busy with sketches."

"George has not kept you informed?" Erik replies acridly.

"No," I reply. So he thinks everything he does is being watched and reported. Uneasily, I realize he's probably right. The conversation stalls.

"Dr. Adler has a proposal." Ryan breaks the awkward silence. "I think you'll like it."

Erik's expression doesn't change, yet his energy intensifies so dramatically, I can feel it. "Indeed?" He scrutinizes me.

"Yes. A trip so you can have some time away from Land's End. To Alaska. The Wheatons have a lodge there."

"*Alaska?*" His voice is tinged with incredulity. "How long would it last?"

"Probably several days," Jarrod replies as his elbow slides off the high armrest. He curses under his breath and moves over a little, trying to fit his bulk on the delicate settee. Erik watches, amusement glimmering in his eyes. Jarrod notices and a look of realization comes over his face that Erik's putting him on the settee was not accidental.

"When would this occur?" Erik asks.

"The dates haven't been decided yet," Ryan replies, "but soon."

"And we'll be going by private jet and seaplane," Jarrod explains.

"It'll be great," Ryan adds. "We'll fish, hike, even do some kayaking."

"You are going along?" Erik asks.

"Probably. As the doctor for the trip."

Erik's eyes narrow at Ryan. "But what of Ms. Copeland? You are her bodyguard. Does that mean she will go as well?"

"We haven't talked about it yet," Ryan replies, "but she needs some time off too."

"If Ms. Copeland were to come on the trip, would you have any objections?" I ask Erik. "This is an opportunity for you to get away from legal matters."

"No," Erik replies abruptly, then resumes his mask of indifference. "No objections." He rubs his thumb over his gold ring, deep in thought. Finally, he looks up and states, "Yes, I'll go."

"Good." As we stand to leave, I tell him the plans for the trip will be discussed at dinner. On our walk back, I say under my breath to Ryan, "That went better than expected."

"I figured he'd take any opportunity to break out of these walls," Ryan whispers smugly. "We all need time out of this pressure cooker. Kathryn too. When she's not working on this case, she's working on a dozen others. And yesterday Collin told her about what's happening in the future. It hit her hard. Don't you think she needs time off too?"

"Perhaps, but I have no authority over her."

"Couldn't we at least bring it up? Suggest she come along?"

I consider this possibility. Erik says he doesn't object to Kathryn coming. Maybe spending time with her outside professional conferences will help him feel more comfortable talking to her, make it easier to open up about his past. "All right, I'll recommend it. It might be good for everyone."

Back at the conference room, Lady Margaret's smile broadens when she learns that Erik agreed. She informs us that we'll leave Thursday after sunset and return Sunday night. Ryan suggests that Kathryn be invited, then looks to me for support. After hearing my observations and reasons, Lady Margaret agrees without hesitation.

While we wait for Kathryn and Howard to rejoin us, I notice Ryan keeps glancing at the office door. Is he concerned Kathryn will balk and refuse to go? She's always been the one who defended Erik's right to choose, but now I wonder if she will go merely out of duty, perceiving this as her own "choice-less choice."

45 | CHOICELESS

Thursday, June 28,
Seattle

RYAN

"Kathryn." I lean over the desk and peer down at her. "We gotta go."

She raises her palm in protest. "Give me a minute. This motion just came in."

"You said you'd quit at six. It's fifteen after. We've got places to go, things to do."

"I'm almost finished. I've got to leave instructions for Barb." She uses her smile on me.

"All right, you've got five more minutes. If you're not done by then, I'm picking you up and carrying you out of here."

She returns to her work with no more arguments. I sit on the edge of her desk and stare at my watch—give her every second of five minutes. "Time!"

"Just another minute?" She tries her smile on me again. I get up and start walking around her desk. "Okay, okay. I'm done." She pushes the send button on her laptop and closes it.

In chilly silence, she follows me through the empty office. Barb and Eileen are already gone, and Lexa's still stuck in London. Kathryn's irritation at being roped into the Alaska trip radiates all the way to the car. She doesn't consider this a vacation and only agreed to go because of Diane's persuasive prodding.

When I don't head straight to her condo, she asks, testy, "Where are we going?"

"Shopping. We need clothes for the trip."

"I don't. I have jeans and Irish wool sweaters."

"That's what I figured. But it won't do for hiking and kayaking in Alaska. Tom gave me a list. We're shopping for Erik too."

The sports equipment at the store is sparse, a luxury most people can't afford any more. Luckily, the clothing is better stocked. I show Kathryn the list: wicking pullover and zipper-front shirts, waterproof ripstop pants, hiking jacket, hiking socks and boots.

"Good grief," she sputters. Grinning, I help her track down the items. According to Tom's note, Erik also wants buttoned shirts. Kathryn spots some hand-knit Irish sweaters and insists we buy him a black one. *Yeah, all Erik needs is some more black clothes!* I grab a couple shirts for myself, and as the cashier's totaling up the damage, I check the time and groan. We're running late.

As soon as we get home, Kathryn throws all the shirts and pants into the washer. I try to stop her, but she declares they need to be washed before they're worn. I point out they're *new*, so why wash 'em? I lose the argument when she starts the machine. The only sound as we eat in icy silence is the whirring of the washer. When dishes are done, she tosses the clothes into the dryer, and I check the time. *Eight forty-five.*

"We're pushing it," I tell her. "We're scheduled to leave Land's End at eleven. Everything's timed so we'll arrive at the airport in Ketchikan while it's still dark. And there's only a small window of darkness in June, from midnight to about three." She gets the point.

We hurry to our rooms and pack whatever wasn't stuffed into the laundry. When the clothes are dry, we fold everything in record time and put all of Erik's things in a duffle bag. While she packs, I stuff my *clean* shirts in my bag and head for the door. Exasperated, I glare at my watch. *Nine-thirty. Cutting it close.*

But when Kathryn gets to the door, she drops her bag and exclaims, "*My ficus!* It's very delicate. It can't go dry!" She dashes to the kitchen and fills the watering can. Then she rushes over to the monster tree that monopolizes the window facing the Seattle skyline. Personally, I'd chuck it out the window for blocking the view. She quickly waters the pampered plant and gives me a sheepish smile. My anger dissolves, but I have to push the speed limits all the way to Land's End.

When the elevator opens, Tom's staring at the door, Jarrod's pacing, and George is nowhere in sight. Jarrod grabs Erik's duffle bag and rushes away. Steering us back into the elevator, Tom uses his override code to take us to the secured top floor and hurries us past the rooms where security guards watch banks of monitors.

We go into the lounge area and hand our bags to an attendant, then join Diane in front of the windows. Kathryn stares out at the large, black Sikorsky. "I've never flown in a helicopter before," she says, half-stunned.

"Don't worry. Compared to military helos, this is a luxury model."

As the bodyguards arrive, I make the introductions. Then Dave saunters in. Kathryn jumps up and rushes over to him. "Where've you been?" She smiles warmly.

I watch dumbfounded as Dave gives her a bear hug and grins. "Right here, working for the Wheatons."

"You said you were going out of the country on a job. I didn't hear from you after that."

I look from Kathryn to Dave. What does *that* mean? I go down the list. Bodyguard? Friend? Something else?

"I was worried about you," Kathryn chides. "I thought you dropped off the planet."

"Sorry, I've been a bodyguard for Mrs. Wheaton and that's a non-stop job. Should've let you know."

Kathryn gazes up at Dave. "Well, there's no one like you and there were times I really needed you. The bodyguard I hired to help with my clients just doesn't fill your shoes."

Ah, he was her bodyguard. Before the reunion goes any further, the announcement to board is made, and Dave joins the other bodyguards. I hurry Kathryn and Diane across the landing pad. The lights have been dimmed to avoid drawing attention, so the Sikorsky's black hulk blends eerily into the darkness of night.

Inside, I direct Kathryn to the first set of seats. She takes one by the window, and I sit across from her. On the other side of the aisle, Diane gazes out the window, toward the waiting room and says, "Ah, here comes Lady Margaret now."

"I didn't know she was coming with us," Kathryn says.

"Yep, as a cover," I explain. "Everyone was told this trip is for her and Diane. Only security knows Erik's coming. George'll cover by taking meals to his room and making excuses."

We watch as Mrs. Wheaton approaches the helicopter along with Jarrod and a blonde bodyguard I don't recognize. He must be new. I look back toward the waiting area, but still don't see Erik. What's keeping him?

Mrs. Wheaton smiles at Kathryn as she takes the seat facing Diane. Jarrod lowers his large frame into the seat next to Kathryn and grins down at her, pleased with the arrangement. The other man sits next to me. "This seat's taken," I tell him. "You need to sit in back with the other bodyguards."

"I prefer this seat, thank you." The sonorous voice is slightly mocking. He turns his head and I catch a glimpse of the other side of his face.

Kathryn gasps. It's Erik.

46 | SOARING

ERIK

"Un-damn-believable!" Ryan peers at me. "That mask really blends into your face. And that blonde hair! I couldn't tell it was you at a distance. Like you just arrived from Sweden. But isn't Erik a Scandinavian name?"

"Truly. My family descended from Norsemen who invaded France in the Middle Ages."

"You mean the Vikings?" Jarrod asks.

"Indeed." I keep to myself that one night I let myself into a library at the Sorbonne and looked up the de Chagny crest. Learned about my Norseman lineage and the family tradition that the name Erik was always given to the eldest son. That was when I fully understood my identity.

"Great disguise, isn't it?" Ryan asks Kathryn who has been strangely mum.

"Leroux wrote about a masque ball," she replies thoughtfully. "Perhaps you're experienced with disguises?"

Experienced? I am a *master*. "Always the lawyer, Ms. Copeland?"

"I'm sorry. I didn't mean it that way."

"Erik told me he designed his own costumes," Jarrod blathers.

I glare at him. Evidently, I should be more circumspect about what I confide to him. But it is true that the Paris Opéra often hosted *bal masques*, and Princess Metternich invited me to the lavish ones at the Austrian Embassy. Those were the only occasions I could circulate freely in society. Since all hid behind a mask, for that evening I was like everyone else.

"Perhaps even a Red Death's costume?" Kathryn pursues.

Curse Leroux. "Perhaps."

Jarrod leans back and stretches. "Just what costumes did you wear, Erik?"

So, Jarrod is taking up Kathryn's cause. I, too, can play this game. "I posed as Blackbeard. A matador. A French captain." With an intense glare, I add, "And once, Don Juan."

That put an end to her questions. She shifts nervously and looks away.

"Want my window seat?" Ryan asks me.

I accept and change chairs, sitting opposite Kathryn, but my long legs consume an inordinate amount of space. Self-consciously, she moves her knees to the side. Most awkward, a single woman surrounded by three men. And she is attired in trousers that disclose her shapely legs. Shocking in my culture. I look out the window, mindful not to stare.

The vibration intensifies while blades overhead whine, spinning ever faster. When we lift above the ground, my stomach knots. As we rise ever higher, I peer down, intrigued by the rapidly diminishing stone buildings of Land's End. A surge of power thrusts us forward, into the darkness of night. My heart skips a beat at the sensations of racing above the earth and the sights below of water reflecting moonlight between black forests

"Incredible," Kathryn declares.

Indeed. Like nothing I have ever experienced. In my time, only ungainly balloons took men aloft. Those carried government messages and private letters to the outside world during the siege. For this experience, I can almost forgive the Wheatons for all their schemes. *Almost…* Just as I get accustomed to the many sensations assailing me, the helicopter descends and lands smoothly next to an immense building that Jarrod refers to as a hangar. Not far away, the Wheatons' private jet awaits, engines roaring.

As we ascend the steps of the regal flying machine, Jarrod says, "Beautiful, huh?"

"Undoubtedly," I concur, admiring its long, sleek body which glistens in the hangar's dimmed lights.

The interior is lavishly furnished with pairs of padded leather chairs facing each other along windows framed in highly polished wood. Not long after we are seated, the plane skims along a paved surface, then turns and stops. Whining engines rise to a fevered pitch, making me both anxious and excited that I will soon be suspended high above the clouds.

The plane is unleashed and my stomach rises to my throat as lights on the ground speed past. Within moments we are airborne, and my breathing nearly stops as we mount into the night sky toward the stars. Then a wing dips to one side—suddenly the sensation of floating. I grip the armrests as the plane turns in a wide arc. When it smooths into its course, I stare out the window at the myriad lights that illuminate the unending cities like a galaxy of stars.

"Cognac?" George's voice intrudes on my enjoyment of the world below.

I turn and find him hovering beside me. "Why are you not at the mansion?" I growl.

"The plane returns to the secured hangar in Olympia tonight. I will be back in time to serve breakfast to your rooms." His lipless grin is almost smug as he delivers my cognac and Jarrod's orange juice, then departs. I have not yet decided if George is a blessing or a curse in my life. At least he will not be in it for three days.

As I sip my cognac, I savor everything. Gazing out the window at moonlight casting an eerie glow on the clouds, I feel suspended in a dream world. Below, the occasional lights of small towns outline their boundaries like bastions against the surrounding darkness. Observing the world from this lofty perspective makes me feel like Zeus peering down on his creation.

My seat faces the back of the plane, so I gaze down the aisle. The lights have dimmed, and almost everyone is sleeping. My eyes come to rest on Kathryn, curled up and already deep in slumber. Watching her seems almost improper, but it is difficult to look away. She looks so peaceful, like a goddess, with hair cascading across her cheek and graceful neck.

It is unimaginable to me that everyone is so accustomed to this experience they can sleep through it. I do not want to miss any of the extraordinary sights and sensations. George returns with a tray of cheese, fruit, and croissants. He hands me earbuds, and I choose a Chopin sonata, luxuriating in this cocoon of unexpected pleasures. The two-hour flight passes too quickly. When our imminent landing is announced, Kathryn stirs and stretches. I look away.

"That's the Tongass Narrows." Jarrod points out the window. "Part of the inland waterway along the Alaskan coast. The airport's on the west side, Ketchikan on the east.

The wheels touch ground with a soft jolt, then the plane races smoothly along the ground. I sigh in relief. A number of bodyguards escort Lady Margaret, Dr. Adler, and Kathryn from the plane. Then

Jarrod, Dave, and the remaining bodyguards surround me. As we hurry to a path that goes to the Narrows, I wonder if they are protecting me or assuring I remain under their control.

We cross the gangway to a small dock where two seaplanes bob gently on the water. Soon we are skimming above the waters, headed into a twilight sky, not quite dark and not quite sunrise. The vistas capture everyone's attention as the seaplane soars above primeval forests and mountains. Ryan whispers in Kathryn's ear as he points out something below, and she laughs. I bristle and look away.

As I look at the terrain below, my image reflects in the window. The short hair is startling. I am accustomed to my black hair being combed back from my forehead and touching my collar in the back. The blonde wig reminds me of Raoul's golden hair, so I could barely force myself to wear it. I peer at the flesh-colored mask mirrored in the window. It does not dominate my face like the black one. For once I examine my features. The jaw and forehead are not unpleasant—quite similar to Raoul's, except his face is unblemished and handsome.

Soon, Lady Margaret points out their lodge glimmering eerily below through mists of fog. The plane skims along the water and settles down smoothly, gliding to a long dock where boats are berthed. We disembark and follow a stone pathway toward the lodge constructed of rustic logs and surrounded by a spacious deck. All three floors are visible through the wall of windows that covers its façade and rises up to an arched roof. Most of the bodyguards head for a building situated between the forest and lodge.

We are greeted by a native woman, one of the Tlingit Indian caretakers of the lodge. She conducts us through the living room with its soaring, three-story ceiling and up an open stairwell. Lady Margaret bids us good night, and the Tlingit woman escorts me to my door. My room is dominated by a hand-hewn pine bed. I fall onto its thick quilt and toss aside my wig and mask. Above me, tall clerestory windows frame verdant forest. Captivated, I watch fingers of pink and orange sunrise spread behind the canopy of trees. But I cannot keep my eyes open.

A knock on my door brings me out of deep slumber, and a voice calls out that breakfast will be served in half an hour. I quickly shower and shave. A note on the mirror lists the clothing to wear today: waterproof pants, pullover shirt and jacket. The constricting clothes mold to my body, so unlike silk cravats and waistcoats over loose linen shirts, worn with superfine wool suit coats and pleated trousers. Adjusting to modern suits has been difficult enough, but these clothes feel most odd. I don a flannel shirt with buttons, determined to wear something that feels like real clothing. Thankfully, I need not wear the wig today. I put on the flesh-colored mask and inspect my appearance. I look alien—like the rest of them. Scowling, I grab my jacket and face the day.

When I arrive at breakfast, Lady Margaret seats me between Kathryn and herself. "Sir Kenneth called and said that the inspector has given permission for Lexa, Josh, and Blake to leave England," Lady Margaret announces with a pleased smile. "They're flying home today."

"Thank goodness," Kathryn sighs.

Although adept at sparring with Kathryn or evading her inquiries, I feel at sea when attempting casual conversation. I am relieved when the meal is over and everyone goes down to the kayaks. Jarrod and I get into one of the strange little boats that remind me of a genie's lamp. We push away from the dock and glide effortlessly over the water.

As we pull even with Ryan and Kathryn, Jarrod shouts, "Race you to the first bend." Everyone paddles furiously and for several moments we remain side by side. Then Jarrod and I redouble our efforts and pull away. "Ante up," Jarrod gloats when they catch up.

"What?" Kathryn sputters. "We didn't make any bet."

"We'll set it after the fact." Jarrod grins slyly. "And I know just the thing. Kathryn has to have dinner with Erik or me tonight. We'll toss to see who wins."

"Nope," Ryan says smugly. "She's already agreed to have dinner with me tonight."

"How about Saturday night?" Jarrod retorts.

"Sorry." Kathryn grins impishly. "Saturday night is Mrs. Wheaton's dinner party."

"Okay, dinner on Sunday. We don't leave until midnight." To my surprise, she agrees, obliging herself to dine with Jarrod or me. I am not sure which prospect is more unsettling.

Our entourage travels along the shoreline. Lush rainforest covers the hillsides, and on occasion we skim beneath the long branches of gigantic trees. Great blue herons stand in shallow waters along the shore, poking their long beaks into the river to catch fish.

With hushed voice, Kathryn says, "There, on the bank." All heads turn and spot a doe warily guarding fawns at the riverbank. As Kathryn's kayak floats in front of mine, I take in the view, entranced.

47 | MARVELING

Friday, June 29
Alaska

Kathryn

A silver streak leaps out of the water. I yelp as a cold splash hits my face.

Ryan laughs. "That salmon almost landed in your lap, Kathryn."

"Probably headed for a hot date," Jarrod calls out.

"Typical guy, then," I sputter, wiping my face.

As a river otter lazily floats by on its back, Erik stops paddling and watches. His eyes glimmer with something I've never seen before. He's actually enjoying himself. Maybe the trip's just the thing to bring him out of that dark shell. I know I'm already relaxing.

"Looks like a good fishing spot." Dave points to a sandy beach ahead.

"I'm more interested in lunch," Jarrod says.

We land the kayaks on the shore and bring out the satchels of food and drinks.

As Erik chooses a beer, Dave grunts in surprise, "I've never seen you drink beer before."

"I drank it when I lived in England." Erik adds pensively, "A long time ago."

"Yeah, what's it been? Two hundred years?" Jarrod says, chuckling, and Erik puts on a wry smile. I give him a sympathetic look.

After passing out the sandwiches, I head for the small hill above the beach. At the crest, I remove my jacket and lounge back on it, soaking up the warmth of the sun. Ryan and Jarrod join me while Erik and Diane picnic with Mrs. Wheaton. Dave and the other bodyguard grab fishing poles and head up river. Lunch conversation turns into a debate about grizzly versus black bears. Jarrod's certain that if you meet up with a grizzly, the tactic is to play dead. Ryan argues that's done when confronted by a black bear. Jarrod calls down to Mrs. Wheaton for her opinion.

"Play dead when cornered by a grizzly," she says, "and don't make eye contact."

Jarrod gives Ryan a smug look. "I grew up on a cattle ranch in Wyoming, and we had grizzlies." Then he states bitterly, "But not anymore. No more cattle or grizzlies."

"What happened, Jarrod?" I ask.

"They discovered natural gas, but Dad wouldn't sell rights to do hydrofracking. Didn't matter. Other ranchers sold out, and it wasn't long after the fracking began that the cattle got sick and died." Jarrod chucks a rock at a tree. "Then Dad got cancer and died three years later. The grizzlies are gone now too."

"I'm sorry, Jarrod. So sorry," I say. He looks away, deep in thought. So that's the reason why Jarrod is invested in the Wheatons' schemes.

When we're done eating, Ryan asks if I want to go fishing with them. "Nope. I just want to read." They get their gear from the kayak and talk Erik into joining them.

I gaze up at the spruce branches overhead and pull out my pocket-sized hardbound of *The Prophet* by Kahlil Gibran. The day my Grandma gave it to me, we were picnicking on her farm in Ireland, surrounded by a grove of Sitka spruce just like these. My last trip to the farm comes to mind. It was bittersweet. Mom and Dad had moved back after Grandma passed away. I learned that memories are to be cherished, but you can't go back. I brush away a tear. Life lies ahead, not in the past. I can still hear Grandma's Irish brogue as she read this book to me. With the warm sun on my face and branches swaying in the breeze, I curl up on my side and begin reading.

"Kathryn." The voice seems far away. I'm on a cloud, floating. "Kathryn!" I ignore the intruder, but someone shakes me. My eyes pop open. Ryan's kneeling next to me. "Wake up, Sleeping Beauty. We gotta go." I blink, trying to bring myself back to this world. The other one was so peaceful. Ryan holds out his hand and helps me up.

Down at the beach, Dave and Jarrod display their impressive strings of fish. "While you were snoring, we were catching your dinner," Jarrod boasts.

"Snoring? I wasn't snoring."

"Yeah," Dave joins in, "like a chainsaw. Thought it was going to scare away the fish."

My sleepy mind searches for a comeback. Erik catches my eye and subtly shakes his head *no*. So, they *are* pulling my leg. "Maybe I just scared them onto your hooks," I shoot back, grinning my thanks to Erik. His mouth quirks up in humor.

On the journey back, we spot a bald eagle perched on a cliff. It lifts off effortlessly and circles overhead. By the time we arrive at the lodge, everyone's tired but exhilarated.

Going straight to my room, I get in the Jacuzzi and stretch out my legs. The hot water eases the muscles strained from hours in the kayak. Finally, I slip into linen slacks and an Irish wool sweater, then hurry down to the main floor and out to the deck. Only one table is set. Only Ryan is there.

"You look lovely," he says with a smile, "worth the wait." With a flourish, he pulls out my chair, then pours some wine.

"Just a little, please. I don't drink much."

"Yeah, I've noticed. But I promise not to take advantage."

"If you try, I'll just sic my bodyguard on you."

"I'd be in real trouble then. They say Ryan is one mean guy."

"He has his good points."

"Oh yeah? Name one."

"Ummm," I stall. He folds his arms, waiting. "He makes great pancakes."

"That's some high praise." He laughs and so do I.

"I like it when you laugh," he says. "Needs to happen more. Tell your bodyguard to see to that." With a rascal grin, he adds, "He needs to be good for something more than pancakes."

"Oh, he is. He makes me take time out from work."

"Bet he's gotta twist your arm, though."

"I used to take long drives in my Vette to relax, but I got grounded." He grimaces apologetically, so I quickly add, "Oh, I blame Collin, not my bodyguard."

"He'll be glad to hear that." Ryan gazes at me over the rim of his glass. "He'd like to be friends."

"I thought he was already a friend."

"Maybe I didn't say that right. At your Quaker meetings *everyone* is called *friend*."

"Well, *friend*, you said it just fine." I smile. Maybe it is time to set aside the professional relationship for a while. "Enough about my bodyguard. Tell me more about you. You mentioned that your father was a colonel in the Air Force. So where'd you go to college?"

"Dad was stationed at the base outside Spokane, Washington, and I went to college there, at Gonzaga. We're Catholic, and it's a Jesuit university with a great basketball team."

"Do your parents still live there?

"Dad died in one of the wars and Mom never got over it. Wasn't long before she followed." He clears his throat. "So where are you from?"

"I was born in Burnham-on-Sea in England. Dad's family lived there, but Mom's Irish."

"Irish? Is your mother Catholic?" His face lights up.

"Yes, but my father's family is Quaker, and Mom adopted that faith. When Dad graduated from Oxford, he got a position as a professor at Johns Hopkins, so we moved to Maryland. That's where I grew up. Mom was a librarian for the university's collection of hardbound books."

"So, that explains all those hardbounds in your condo."

"Uh-huh. Grew up around them."

"It's a new experience for me, but I'm enjoying it. Johns Hopkins? Did my residency there after medical school at the University of Washington. Did you go to Johns Hopkins?"

"Yes, for my B.A. in East Asian studies, although I spent one year at Oxford—family tradition. My law degree is from Harvard, then I moved to Seattle."

"I'm three years older than you. That means by the time I was at Johns Hopkins doing my residency, you'd already left for Harvard. Right?"

"Sounds about right." I take a sip of wine.

"And after law school, you ended up in Seattle where I'd gone to med school." He shakes his head. "Seems we kept missing each other. What made you move to the West Coast?"

"Because of my degree in East Asian studies, I worked for a law firm in Seattle that specialized in trade law with Asia. It was a good job, and I got to travel to China. But after several years with the firm, I realized it wasn't my cup of tea and left."

Ryan groans at my bad pun just as the Tlingit woman brings the appetizers. He takes some smoked salmon and eyes me keenly. "So, why'd you give up a good-paying job?"

"I guess it began at my Quaker meetinghouse. With so many people flooding into Seattle and not being able to find jobs, we started giving free meals every weekend for the homeless and unemployed. But they needed so much more, so we began offering free counseling."

"And I'll bet they also needed legal advice."

"Yeah. Women needed protective and support orders for themselves and their children. Homeless teens needed protection and counseling. Many of the men had post-traumatic stress from their military service and needed proper care and disability benefits. So, I started giving legal advice and, after a while, felt that was where I really needed to be. Corporations can afford attorneys, but those people can't. By then I'd saved enough money to open an office."

"That took some guts." He tips his glass to me.

"That's not the usual reaction I get to my leaving a good job. Thankfully, I've been able to build my practice with a variety of clients. Those who can pay the fees support the overhead. That allows me to help those who can't. You see why I do my work, don't you?"

"Yes, I do." Leaning back in his chair, he takes a deep breath. "After med school, I chose to join the Army and asked to be sent on a tour of duty in the war zones. Between tours I'd be stationed at a hospital in Germany that was the first stopover for the men returning from combat. You know, even if they didn't come back physically injured, they'd be psychologically wounded, usually for the rest of their lives. That's when I contacted Diane. She helped me develop a comprehensive PTS program."

I study him in a new light. "So you're the doctor Diane developed the program with."

"Yes. But it isn't always enough." With pain in his eyes, he continues. "Like my brother. He was also an officer in the Army—a family tradition, I guess. He came back from the wars with serious PTS, and his wife divorced him. He used alcohol to deal with it and couldn't hold a job. Then one night, he pushed his car to the limit and it crashed. He died instantly."

"Oh, Ryan." I reach over and take his hand.

"I've lost my appetite," he says, looking away. "Would you like to take a walk?"

"Sure, we can have dinner later."

We take the pathway that borders the forest and stroll down to the lake. Ryan holds my hand as we climb a narrow path to the rise overlooking the water. When we sit down, he doesn't let go. It feels good. It's been a long time since a man has held my hand this way—since my engagement was broken.

We watch the midnight sun slowly sink behind the trees. Ryan tells me about his brother—pranks they played, secrets they shared, things they learned from each other. I share with him my summers on my grandparents' farm in Ireland and stories about Anne, who was like my sister—how we used to search for ancient Celtic ruins, how we'd glory in the circles of rock and the famous Mound of Tara. Anne was already taking pictures, and I would tell all about the history as we toured the ruins. Sometimes Ryan and I laugh so hard, our eyes fill with tears.

"I was reading *The Prophet* today. There's a line, *'The selfsame well from which your laughter rises was oftentimes filled with your tears.'* "

He squeezes my hand. "That's true, Kate."

"Why'd you call me Kate?" I ask, taken aback.

"Just slipped out. I always think of you as Kate for some reason."

"Only one other person ever called me Kate...and that was Anne."

"Sorry. I'll call you Kathryn if you prefer."

"No, it's okay. You can call me Kate." I look down at his hand, still holding mine. "It's getting dusky. Maybe we should go back to the lodge."

Ryan calls the kitchen and asks if we can still have dinner. By the time we get back, plates overflowing with salad and salmon have been served and candles lit.

"Just what I imagined"—his eyes spark at me—"a candlelight dinner."

"You're incorrigible."

"I think you've told me that before."

"I suspect I'll tell you again."

48 | NAVIGATING

JARROD

"Raise." Erik says as he pushes five chips to the center of the table. Three players fold.

"Jarrod, it's up to you," Dave says, throwing down his cards. My pile of chips is dwindling and the pot's good-sized. But Erik's had the devil's luck and never telegraphs his hand. Surely he can't beat my three jacks. I push my chips forward. "Call."

Erik coolly nods and spreads out his cards. Three tens, then he shows the next card—a five. I sigh in relief. Then comes another five. "Damn," I grunt.

The others groan as Erik gathers his winnings. Dave slaps my back. "Good try."

"You're pretty slick with cards." I give Erik a sharp look. "Leroux didn't mention that."

"Leroux did not know everything about me." He smirks as he creates five neat stacks of twenty-dollar chips. Out of the blue, he slides one stack to each of us. "It is late. Past my bedtime," he announces as he gets up. "Good evening, gentlemen."

It's ten and still light. Erik usually stays up until midnight. What's going on? I watch him go up the open stairwell of oversized logs. Then it dawns on me. "Is there any other staircase to the third floor?"

"Nope," Dave replies as he deals. "But the balconies have rope ladders for fire escapes."

"Hell!" I throw my cards down. "Gotta go." I race down to the main floor. Out on the deck, the table that was set for Ryan and Kathryn has been cleared off, and they're nowhere in sight.

I take the path that winds around the house and look up at Erik's room. He's on the balcony, and the next thing I know, he's tossing out a rope ladder and climbing down. It twists and sags under his weight, but he manages easily, like he's done it a thousand times. Probably has, on the flies at the opera house. I hide behind a spruce as he noiselessly walks around the lodge. He checks out the deck where Ryan and Kathryn were eating, then takes the path bordering the forest and heads toward the lake. Staying in the cover of trees, I follow.

Abruptly, Erik fades back into the forest. That's when I spot Ryan and Kathryn sitting on a hill. I position myself where I've got them all in my sight. Watching Erik lurk in the shadows reminds me of what Leroux said about him being a phantom and haunting the people in the opera house—just like he's doing now.

It's not long before Ryan and Kathryn walk back to the lodge. I notice someone has set the table for dinner. Hidden in shadows, Erik follows but stops not far from the deck—trapped. He can't take the path to his room without being seen. The minutes crawl by as they eat, oblivious to two men spying on them. When they go in, Erik hurries back and deftly climbs the precarious ladder. I stay outside until his lights go off, then return to the lodge and send a man to stand guard the rest of the night.

When I wake up, my stomach's setting off emergency sirens. I hurry down to the deck and find wild-berry muffins and coffee already set out. I fish out a large muffin and take a bite. Washing it down with coffee, I grab another.

"Hey, leave a few for someone else," Ryan kids as he pours himself some coffee.

"First come, first served." I chuckle. "How was your date with Kathryn?"

"It wasn't a date. We were just having dinner." His smile says otherwise.

"That's the worst poker face I've ever seen. If you'd been playing with us last night, Erik would have cleaned your clock."

"Lose much?" Ryan grins wickedly.

"I'd rather hear about your dinner."

Drinking his coffee, he stares out at the hill by the lake. "It was nice."

"It's gotta be better than that. You spent the entire evening with her."

"We had dinner. Walked to the lake. Sat and talked."

"After all that, didn't you at least get a kiss?"

"That's not any of your business," he replies, but he won't meet my gaze.

I need to know how serious this is getting, so I keep pressing. "Come on, surely a kiss?"

"I planned to," he says, exhaling raggedly. "But just as I was saying good night at her door, Erik comes out of his room."

"You're kidding."

"Nope. He sauntered right by us and went downstairs. Made Kathryn nervous, so she kept looking toward the stairs, instead of at me. Then he comes back a minute later with a mug of coffee. By then my opportunity had passed, and she went into her room."

I give Ryan a sympathetic grunt but don't let on about Erik's late-night hovering. Is Erik watching over Kathryn to save her honor in some nineteenth-century sort of way? Or is it more personal? That could complicate all the problems we're already having with him. And it complicates my life since I'm in charge of the security team that goes back to France with Erik.

At breakfast, I catch the way Ryan looks at Kathryn. I better win that bet with Erik over who has dinner with her on Sunday. Don't need Erik developing an attachment to Kathryn too.

When we go up to our rooms to grab jackets for the day's trip, I stop Erik at the second floor and say offhandedly, "Want to settle that bet?" I point to the game tables. "How about a cut of the cards? High card wins." Erik agrees, so I shuffle the deck. He cuts and has me pick the first card. Grinning, I hold up a queen.

He puts his hand over the deck—for just a second longer than I think necessary. He cuts near the bottom and turns up the card. A king. "Damn, how do you do that?"

"As I said, Leroux did not know everything about me." He smirks. "Perhaps it's magic." Then he gives me that formal nod of his and goes up the stairs. Do the Wheatons and Collin know what they're doing, putting him at the center of their plans? Just who will end up calling the shots?

After breakfast all the bodyguards join us, and we board the seaplanes. Mrs. Wheaton explains we're headed northwest to Sitka on Baranof Island and launches into a summary of the local history. Erik keeps stealing glances at Kathryn and Ryan in the back seats. Beginning to worry me.

At Sitka we fly over the harbor and get a great view of the Three Sisters Mountains in the distance. The seaplanes land near a dock where a private yacht is waiting. The bodyguards closely surround Mrs. Wheaton and Erik, getting them safely aboard. I order a couple men to remain and guard the seaplanes.

The boat engines roar powerfully and waste no time taking us into coastal waters. Erik and I go to the front and zip our jackets against the cold wind but can't resist the exhilaration of standing at the bow. After a while Ryan and Kathryn join us. She laughs at a sea otter floating along on its back while munching on a snack. "They're really adorable," she exclaims, looking up at Erik and smiling. "But I hope we get to see some whales today." Then she turns back to watch the otters, her dark eyes filled with excitement and long hair blowing wildly in the wind.

Kathryn totally misses the look on Erik's face as he watches her. But I don't. And now my suspicion about Erik's feelings are confirmed. He's a goner, just like Ryan. Hell, I'm feeling like the captain on the deck of the Titanic—and an iceberg just showed up on the horizon.

49 | FALLING

ERIK

As Kathryn exults in the antics of the otters, she is standing so close, just inches from me. It would be easy to touch that black silken hair, cup her face in my hands and succumb to those infinite eyes. The thought makes me shudder. I slip away to the other side of the boat and gaze out toward the horizon.

Jarrod joins me at the railing. "Beautiful, huh?"

"Yes," I reply, taking in the Pacific.

"No, Erik. I don't mean the ocean." I glance over and catch him appraising me. "Kathryn isn't part of the Wheatons' plan. She's not going back."

That is what I wanted to know. Dreaded to know. I turn my back on him and walk to the stern. *Need to be alone.* I stare at the ocean broiling almost hypnotically in the wake of the boat. When did it happen? When did I become conscious of my feelings for Kathryn?

So different from how it happened with Christine. From the first time I saw Christine, I was enraptured and fell under her spell. My feelings drove me to make contact. Indirectly, of course, and I knew of a way. Bordering her dressing room was a hidden corridor to allow trysts with the singers. I stood there, spoke soothingly and offered to train her voice, to perfect it, so she could rise to the highest levels. When she invited me to enter her room, I desperately desired that but held myself back. I knew she would be frightened by my mask. Still, I pressed her for an answer and she accepted willingly. With Christine I was patient, gentle—not at all like I was with Kathryn. For three months, I endured that dark, reeking passageway to teach Christine and mold her voice. When she demanded to see me on the night of her successful debut, *our triumph*, I could wait no longer. But when I stepped through the hidden door behind the mirror, she gasped. Although she usually averted her eyes and rarely gazed on my face, she did not question the mask. She wanted my attentions, yet I always sensed her fear lurking just below the surface.

With Kathryn, I steeled myself to reject her—turned my back on her, even unleashed my anger about being forced into public exposure. I thought the guillotine loomed as my possible fate, so their foisting a woman lawyer on me was infuriating. Unfathomable. With every fiber of my being, I attempted to drive her away.

But Kathryn would not go. When I had one of my episodes, she withstood it and never flinched from looking at my face and the mask. I even tried to intimidate her, berate her, dismiss her heartfelt words. I gave her no quarter, but she stood up to me with that quiet courage. With her intellect and wit. And those eyes—always full of compassion. Try as I might to rebuff her, she gave me a choice and always told me the truth. Perhaps that is when I began to fall.

Her eyes—beautiful beyond even the elegant women who inhabit the rarified atmosphere of the Opéra. But unlike them, Kathryn seems oblivious to her own beauty. I began falling, uncontrollably. Like standing at the edge of a cliff, admiring the breathtaking splendor. Then the ground gives way beneath the feet, like an act of nature. One has no control over it. It happens and one falls, flailing and reaching out for something to grasp, to break the plummet. But there is nothing to hold on, so one keeps falling.

"Erik."

Her voice behind me. Tensing, I turn slowly to face her but say nothing, for fear my voice may give away what I feel.

"Why are you over here?" Her smile is beguiling. "I was chattering about the otters, then I turn around and you're gone. Won't you stop disappearing? At least for this trip?" I give her a thin smile. "Come back over here with us, won't you?" Her eyes are inviting, sincere.

With a curt nod, I follow her. She has me stand next to her at the railing as she points out the things which excite her. Mountain peaks in the distance. Sea lions sunning themselves on flat rocks. I begin to see with new eyes. The world seems richer in color, brighter in hue, somehow pristine and perfect. Exultant, she suddenly points toward the horizon. "A whale!"

The long body of a whale skims the ocean's surface. The captain shouts that it is a humpback and steers the boat toward it. When we get closer, a small whale is spotted which the large whale protectively flanks. I admire their graceful display, spellbound as one breeches in a high, powerful arc. As the immense tail slides below the ocean, Kathryn looks up at me, her eyes bright with wonder, almost ecstasy.

The large whale surfaces near the boat and swims alongside, its large eye examining us. Conscious intelligence is unmistakable. Incomprehensible that the women of my century use baleen bones as corset stays. How could anyone who has witnessed these magnificent creatures ever justify killing them?

The whale moves perilously close to our boat, then dives. When the massive tail is about to slide under, it slams on the surface of the ocean. I clasp my mask tightly to my face as a wall of water explodes over us. After the initial shock, everyone laughs. Towels are brought, and we use them to dry ourselves, but no one leaves the railing.

With wonder, I watch the pageantry of the whales and Kathryn's joy. I do not want this moment to end. Every image is recorded in my memory to sustain me the rest of my life. Then the whales dive under the ocean and do not resurface. Kathryn and I continue to search the horizon, hopeful, but they never return.

The boat turns back toward land, and we spot birds bobbing on the waves. Their white chests and black wings make them appear formally dressed, yet garish yellow beaks with red tips give them a whimsical quality.

"They're puffins," Lady Margaret informs me. "The natives made parkas with their skin and wore it feather side in.

"Indeed?" I try to imagine such clothing.

"Puffins spend all winter on the Pacific," she says, "and only visit the land in the summer to breed."

Kathryn and I watch them dive and use their webbed feet to propel themselves under the water. She giggles when a puffin runs across the ocean's surface like a ballerina en pointe. Then its wings catch the air, and it lifts off, using the flapper-like feet to change direction landward.

The yacht anchors at an isolated dock. Taking knapsacks which contain our lunches, we follow a well-worn trail steadily uphill. Mountains with lacy clouds hanging between their peaks loom far in the distance. The forest here is lush, and we cross a stream, balancing carefully on boulders while water rushes beneath our hiking boots. The sun is warm and the air cool, replete with the moist, verdant smell of trees and moss.

After an hour, we come to a small lake. Lady Margaret and Dr. Adler suggest we rest and have lunch, but I spot a waterfall.

"I wish to explore upstream," I announce, so Dave and I start to hike along the rocky bank.

"Can I go?" Kathryn calls out, running after us.

"Of course." I turn around and smile, waiting for her to catch up. Then I see Ryan following not far behind. I should have suspected.

I lead the way to my destination—a ledge above the waterfall. We have been climbing for some time when I notice markings on a boulder. I push aside the vines, revealing numerous carvings on the rock. Dave explains they are native petroglyphs as I run my fingers over an engraving, a bear's claw, feeling kinship with the ancient artist.

We reach the rock shelf above the falls and peer over the ledge at the water cascading into a pool far below, sending up a misty spray. Kathryn stands close to me, transfixed, as we gaze over the treetops to the ocean stretching into the horizon. Again, I store away the memory.

We join the others for an amiable lunch and too soon trek back to the boat.

On the return trip to Sitka, I drink in the ocean's many-faceted greys and blues with cormorants and seagulls flying overhead. Standing beside me at the bow, Lady Margaret asks what I enjoyed the most. "The whales," I reply, keeping to myself my memories of Kathryn.

"That was very special, wasn't it?" she murmurs. "And rare. There are very few of them left, you know." Deep sadness sweeps through me at the very thought.

As we board the seaplanes, our pilot approaches me. "Would you like to ride in the copilot's seat?" she asks, her English accented with the distinct lilt of the Tlingit.

Surprised by the offer, I reply, "It would be my honor." Settling into the seat next to her, I watch, intrigued, as she maneuvers the plane to the middle of the watercourse. We skim over the harbor, picking up speed and heading into the waves, which gives the unnerving impression of water rushing toward us. When the plane lifts off, my heart sinks into my stomach. Rising steadily, the plane soars above the ocean, then turns eastward. This vantage is engrossing. "Thank you, uh, Mademoiselle...?"

"It's Jennie," she replies.

I decide to offer my name as well. "I am Erik."

"Yes, I know." She smiles disarmingly. "I've read Leroux's book."

"I see." Unsettling that my life is *literally* an open book. Hastily, I change the subject. "May I inquire, how did you become a pilot of seaplanes?"

"Maybe it's because I'm from the Eagle Clan. My father and uncles and their families are the caretakers of the lodge. I was always hanging around the planes and bumming rides. Mrs. Wheaton said she'd pay for flight training if I passed all the written exams. I aced them, and she kept her promise. When I got my license, she bought me this plane, and I have my own charter business."

"Indeed?" I find Lady Margaret to be something of an enigma.

Jennie proceeds to regale me with tales of flying, both humorous and harrowing. Marveling at her stories and the sights of majestic lands below, I regret the flight coming to an end.

We dine outside tonight, so I shower quickly and don a black Irish sweater, then hurry down to the deck, impatient to see Kathryn. I wait anxiously, watching the door she will come out. Finally she arrives with Ryan.

"I picked that sweater out for you," she unexpectedly informs me. "I hope you like it."

"I do. Thank you." My mouth goes dry, and I can think of nothing more to say. Still, I feel irritated when Ryan escorts her away.

Gradually everyone arrives, and Lady Margaret again seats me between Kathryn and her. As Pinot Noir from the Wheatons' winery in France is poured, she asks each of us to propose a favorite toast and requests that I begin.

I sweep my glass around the table. "Santé."

Next, Lady Margaret offers, "Cheers."

Ryan holds up his glass. "Here's to the heath, the hill, and the heather, the bonnit, the plaid, the kilt, and the feather."

"What bar did you learn that in?" Dave asks.

"That came from my grandfather," Ryan retorts. "He was full-blooded Scots."

The toasts proceed around the table until Kathryn gives the final toast as we all hold out our glasses. "Go mbeirimid beo ar an am seo aris. That's an Irish toast," Kathryn explains, "that I learned from *my* grandfather. It means 'may we all be alive at this time next year.' "

Lady Margaret's hand trembles as her glass clinks against mine. I study her, wondering what is amiss, but refrain from making a comment. She quickly recovers and bids us to enjoy the dinner of grilled salmon and corn. The corn is served still attached to the cob and covered with butter and spices. Primitive, but rather delectable.

After dinner, we move to the lower deck and lounge on comfortable chaises. Several bodyguards browse music selections on a screen. Soon earsplitting music fills the air. To my surprise, Jennie invites Ryan to dance—apparently acceptable in this culture. Dismayed, I watch as they gyrate wildly to raucous music. After several grating pieces, Kathryn walks over and peruses the music screen, choosing a melodic song with a fine male voice. When she returns, I express my gratitude for her selection.

"I'm glad you like it," she replies with a smile that beguiles me. Just then Ryan interrupts and asks her for the next dance. Taking Kathryn in his arms, he holds her against his body in a manner that would be unacceptable at a *bal masque*. With effort, I cloak my discomfort as they dance slowly. And too close together.

The next song is also agreeable, no doubt another selection of Kathryn's. Jennie approaches our group, presumably to invite Ryan to dance once again. Instead, she asks me.

Startled, I stand to address her. "I regret that I am not familiar with this manner of dance." The truth is, I have never danced, never had lessons. And one cannot dance at the bal masques of Princess Metternich without being a skilled, polished dancer.

"No problem," she says undeterred. "It's easy. I'll teach you."

I feel everyone's eyes on me. I would be on display, the object of amusement with each misstep. "Thank you for the courtesy of your invitation, but I must decline." She smiles graciously, and I am relieved when Ryan intercedes and asks her to dance.

Kathryn seamlessly picks up our conversation, but I remain ill at ease. Soon, I make my excuses and leave. In my room, I read until Kathryn's voice is heard in the hallway, bidding Ryan good night. Then I turn off my light and drop into a restless sleep.

The morning knock on my door awakens me from a disturbing dream, one where I am running endlessly but never certain what I am trying to reach. I push that out of my mind. Just anxious for this day's outing to begin. We will be flying in the seaplanes again, an experience I have come to love.

At breakfast, I overhear Lady Margaret inform Kathryn of a development regarding my case. Apparently through his contacts, Wheaton arranged for his men to obtain access to the lower levels of the Garnier in Paris. Based on a map I had drawn, they searched for my buried box. Lady Margaret says they could not locate it. Apparently, they found the rooms beneath the Garnier to be confusing and dug many places without success. Kathryn is disturbed by the news and asks her usual array of questions. As for me, I am not the least surprised and make no comment.

Anxious to begin the day's outing in the Misty Fjords, after breakfast we go straight to the seaplanes. Again Jennie offers me the copilot's seat and I accept.

My long legs fit tightly in the cramped space, but I do not mind. Preoccupied with discerning the function of each gauge, I am caught off guard by Kathryn's voice behind me. "Enjoying yourself, Erik?" I turn and discover her eyes glimmering at me.

What a remarkable question. No one has ever asked me that before. Upon reflection, I reply, "Indeed." Her lips break into a smile. I pretend to study the gauges, but all I can think about are those eyes. No hint of the formal lawyer in them or in her voice.

Soon the plane is skimming the water. "Misty Fjords, here we come!" Jennie says over the engine noise. "Do you know anything about it?" I shake my head. "It's over two million acres of national park. You can only get around it by boat, kayak or plane."

Shortly after we have become airborne, she points to a herd of white mountain goats and heads the plane toward them, descending rapidly. My stomach is in my throat as we fly over the running animals, sweeping so low I can see their flowing hair and curved horns. When she passes over them a second time, I grin with exultation.

For two hours, majestic panoramas spread out below us—at first, rugged mountains and expansive valleys with glaciers of snow and ice. Then the landscape becomes almost ethereal. Clouds float between towering peaks and waterfalls pour down ragged cliffs. We spot deer climbing mountain paths and brown bears standing in rivers, swatting at salmon.

At one point we circle above a massive cylinder of rock. "That's New Eddystone Rock," Jennie says. "It's a pillar of basalt from magma that rose out of a volcanic vent."

Finally, a clearing with a small dock comes into view. The other seaplane is already there, and Jennie brings ours to rest beside it. Bodyguards await with knapsacks, which we don to begin our trek.

The forest is pristine, as if no man has ever trod here or touched this place of wild beauty. Squirrels chatter at us from trees, and when a fox streaks out of its burrow, Kathryn smiles with delight. A fine, misty rain begins to fall, so I zip up my jacket, suddenly appreciative of the waterproof clothing. We have been traveling for some time when Dave halts us and points to a ridge far above where a lone moose stands. The large, gangly animal raises and lowers its impressive antlers while grazing.

After climbing for an hour, we reach a clearing with a huge, flat rock suspended above a stream. The sky is overcast and misty rain chills slightly. I help pile wood on the rock to create a bonfire. As everyone gathers around the leaping flames for warmth, I imagine the native people circling fires in a like manner, perhaps on this very rock.

Jarrod hands me a metal utensil that unfolds, creating a long handle with tines. He spears two sausages, and I hold them above the flames, watching as the skin crackles and chars. The aroma of roasting meat soon fills the air, igniting my hunger.

When cooked, the sausages are placed in long rolls. Jarrod passes me two bottles, but I stare at them with deep suspicion. Chuckling, he says, "It's just ketchup and mustard. They're not hot or spicy. Most people use both on hot dogs."

Hot dogs? I regard the sausages uneasily but decide not to ask why they are called *dogs*. The possible answer is unsettling. During the siege of Paris when food became scarce, I was reduced to eating horse meat but *never* dog or cat as others did. Since Kathryn uses the sauces without distress, I apply cautious amounts of both, but take a bite with no small misgiving.

"How is it?" Kathryn asks me with an impish grin.

"Quite edible," I reply, relieved that my mouth is not on fire.

Jarrod breaks into a laugh. "From you, that's a compliment."

The meal is a leisurely repast of hot dogs and fresh fruit. I avoid the "chips" and "salsa." Afterward, everyone chats while enjoying the warmth of the fire. I lean back on my elbows and take in the mountain peaks through a haze of contentment. Just as I am making a mental picture, Lady Margaret sits down next to me.

"Howard and I always come here for a picnic when we visit the lodge," she says wistfully. "Sometimes we camp overnight."

"It has a wild beauty. I wish I could stay here longer and sketch that mountain."

She studies me thoughtfully. "So, you have enjoyed your time in Alaska?"

"Indeed. This has been," I pause, choosing my word carefully, "unparalleled."

"I'm glad to hear that." She smiles warmly. "And when you play your music, remember these trees. They are Sitka spruce, and their wood is made into the finest pianos. These are the heart of the Steinway, as well as the violin you play at Land's End."

"Truly?" I gaze in awe at the towering spruce. Somehow it seems fitting that such magnificent trees create sublime music.

On the return hike we spot a mother grizzly lumbering along. Her two cubs playfully roll down the hillside, trying to keep up with her. As I take in the magnificent panorama, a bittersweet feeling takes root. This is the last excursion. Tonight we leave.

When the seaplane circles above the forest, I spot the rock where we picnicked and keep my eyes fixed on it until it disappears from view forever. With all my soul, I do not want this to end, but the flight is over too quickly. I feel a wave of sadness as the lodge comes into sight and the plane settles on the lake, the water rushing toward us.

On the walk to the lodge, Lady Margaret bids us to do as we please the rest of the day. She says a buffet will be served all evening. I have not yet discussed dinner with Kathryn. Does she remember the wager or know I won? How can I broach the subject?

I retire to my room to shower and dress for the evening. Again I don the black sweater Kathryn chose for me. The bodyguards are playing cards, but I decline to join them and continue down to the main floor. Pouring myself a cognac, I step out on the deck and discover Kathryn sitting on a bench, absorbed in a book. No one else is in sight. I cannot believe my good fortune.

"May I join you?" I venture.

It seems I have called her back from another world, but she smiles warmly. "Of course."

Casting about for a topic, I begin prosaically, "Lovely weather this evening, is it not?"

"Yes." She gazes at the forest, wistful. "I hate to sit and let the rest of the day pass me by."

Do I understand her meaning correctly? "Would you like to go for a walk, then?"

"I'd love that," she murmurs. My heart skips two beats. "Do we need a bodyguard?"

"That should not be necessary. We will stay on the island and not go far."

"Wonderful."

I motion for her to precede me down the stairs. *"Indeed."*

50 | TRACKING

Dave Waulker

"Another bad hand, Waulker?" Jarrod smirks as he deals me three more cards.

I groan. The cards didn't help and it's looking grim. Then my QRYSTAL goes off. "Mercier and Copeland just took the path into the forest," a security guard informs me. "They're headed for the northern end of the island."

"Thanks. I'll take care of it." I look over at Ryan. "Kathryn and Erik decided to take a walk. They went into the forest."

"Crap!" Ryan says, starting to get up.

"I'll go, Ryan," Jarrod says, already on his feet.

I grab Jarrod's shoulder and stop him. "Nope, let me go. They've got a head start, and I'm the tracker." Hurrying to the gun case, I unlock it and grab a hunting rifle, then rush down the stairs and jog to the trail.

The rain has turned the ground muddy, so their footprints are deep and easy to follow. Looks like security was right, and they're headed to the other side of the island. Probably felt a little walk was safe. But the river there is shallow and bears sometimes cross over. And I'm not just worried about the four-legged critters. There's also the two-legged kind. The security guards here say no one can get through the monitors and sensors on this island, but I'm not so sure. Foolproof contraptions just beg to be outwitted.

Saying I should follow them because I'm the tracker was bull too, but Jarrod's already spent one night following Erik around, and Ryan's feelings about Kathryn aren't difficult to read. Watching her with Erik is the last thing Ryan needs—because I can also read Erik's feelings toward her. When he looks at her, he smiles—and Erik's not in the habit of smiling.

And Kathryn, well, she's just going about her business, like always. I doubt she's got a clue these men are working toward locking horns like bull moose. Barb told me Kathryn had been engaged once, to some hotshot attorney in the corporate law firm where she'd worked. Kathryn wanted to start her own practice and help people. He didn't approve and thought she was throwing away a big-time career and big-time money. But Kathryn follows her heart. Takes care of everyone except herself.

I peer into the dark shadows of the forest. Something doesn't feel right, so I break into a run. Won't feel easy until I have them in my sight. When I get to the other side of the island, I stop at the ridge. Erik and Kathryn are sitting on a bench at the water's edge, talking. Erik's holding Kathryn's hand and not paying attention to anything else. But I keep scanning in every direction. Can't get over that feeling we're being watched. But who? And where?

51 | SPELLBINDING

ERIK

Kathryn and I stroll unhurriedly as she takes in the beauty surrounding us. And I take in the beauty of Kathryn. Her black hair flows around her shoulders as she turns to observe everything—tiny flowers shielded by a fern, a porcupine lazily sauntering along a fallen tree trunk, two butterflies circling each other in delicate dance.

At a fork in the path, we stop and peer down the other trail into dark forest. "Ryan told me it goes to the other side of the island," she says.

"Would you like to find out?" I ask, challenging her.

"Yes." She smiles mischievously. Within several steps, we are swallowed by the encompassing trees. The fertile smell of damp earth and moss hangs pungently in the air. Lush ferns cover the ground and ivy trails up towering pine. "It's like being in a primeval forest," Kathryn sighs. "Like stepping back in time, into a magical place, isn't it?"

"Yes." Then a memory flashes through my mind, taking my breath and causing me to halt abruptly.

"Are you all right?" Her concerned voice floats to me through an encroaching fog.

Taking deep breaths, I pull myself from the brink, and Kathryn's worried face comes into focus. "A gypsy at the carnival spoke of a magical place in my future. Of something that would happen there."

"She was a fortuneteller?"

"Yes, and one night she stole the key to my cage and helped me escape."

"I didn't know that."

"One of the few things you have not asked about," I tease as we proceed down the path. "She brought my meals and occasionally smuggled a little extra food. She would apply her herbal remedies on my back whenever…" The memory still pains me. "She would also read my palm. Many of her predictions have come true."

"So you believe in palmistry?"

"I do. In fact, she taught me the art, though I do not have her level of skill. She also had second sight." I decide to open a small window into my life. "Princess Metternich occasionally asked me to read palms at her soirees. One can discern many things—the future, secrets."

"Really? I've never had my palm read. Would you…read mine?" Her smile is irresistible, so I agree. Impishly, she asks, "The magical place the gypsy mentioned—have you found it?"

"I am not certain."

"And you're not going to share the rest of her prediction, are you?"

"Always the questions." I look into her upturned face and quash the impulse to brush her hair back, to touch her cheek. Perhaps the gypsy woman's parting words may come to pass.

At the far end of the island, we find benches facing upriver, where we had traveled by kayak. The beaver dam is visible from here, and as we sit down, Kathryn points excitedly to an eagle's nest lodged near the edge of a cliff. Two bald eagles lift off gracefully and fly over the river, searching for prey. We watch, entranced.

"Weren't you going to read my palm?" she asks, holding her hand out expectantly and breaking the spell.

For a moment I stare at her hand before reaching out and touching it, taking it in mine. My heart pounds as I run my fingertips over the soft flesh at the base of her fingers. "These are called the mounts. Yours are rounded and full. That means you are strong, energetic. The mount under your index finger represents Jupiter. Yours is rounded, showing leadership." I refrain from divulging it also denotes a sensuous nature, and that it is not dissimilar from mine.

"Note the shape of your fingers—slightly pointed with smooth knuckles. You are sensitive to the thoughts and feelings of others, very insightful. Perhaps you have the gift of second sight?"

"Do you mean psychic abilities? No, not that I know of."

Certainly hope she does not. I quickly move on. "The tip of your index finger is even with the bottom of your middle fingernail—that shows you possess confidence but also an openness to consider opposing views. The middle finger represents Saturn. It extends beyond the nails of the adjoining fingers, so your relationships have equanimity. Your middle finger is long and straight. You are steadfast in your commitments—and your love."

"I see." Her voice breaks slightly. "What does the ring finger represent?"

"Apollo. The tip of that finger reaches the bottom of your middle fingernail. You are diplomatic and have strong powers of perception. Also good discernment in style and taste." With a sly smile, I add, "And romance."

"What does the little finger mean?" I notice she changes the subject most adeptly.

"Mercury, how you communicate." I chuckle. "The tip of yours is even with the first joint of Apollo. Most definitely reflects your nature."

"And what is that?" She regards me, half-curious, half-challenging.

"Perceptive. And impeccably honest and forthright."

She breaks out laughing. "So you've noticed?"

"Indeed, I have been the recipient." I cannot suppress a grin. "And that finger curves slightly toward your ring finger. Denotes someone who forges her own path."

She sighs. "For better or worse, that does seem to be true."

"Your thumb shows you have a strong will. I have most definitely observed that. But you are willing to be reasonable. See how the thumb's middle phalange is shaped like an hourglass? You exhibit tact and sensitivity." She blushes.

Next I run my finger along the line in the middle of her palm that curves around the thumb. "This is the life line. Yours is deep and long, indicating good health. You would make a formidable opponent. I will take more care to stay in your good graces in the future."

"Does that mean you'll answer my questions more readily?"

"Apparently, it would be wise for me to do so. We shall see," I smirk. "Here—note how your life line goes over to the left of your palm? That means you will travel far. To other countries, other places."

"Well, I was born in England, grew up on the East Coast of America and work on the West Coast. And I've traveled in Asia, so that seems to fit."

"But I have never seen one like this. Since it extends so far into Neptune, perhaps you are a visionary. See this? A mystic cross in your palm."

"No, I'm just an ordinary person." Gazing into her eyes which have such depth and compassion, I am aware there is nothing ordinary about her. She blinks under my scrutiny. "What else do you see?"

My breath catches at the sensation of her silken skin as I trace the line which crosses her palm above the life line. "This is the line of mind. Yours is long and curved, disclosing an ability to perceive possibilities. Notice how it splits into a fork on the left, the sign of a lawyer or a writer. Perhaps it was destined for you to become a lawyer. The gypsy told me our hands reveal our innate nature and soul—destiny if you will. But that is only a possibility. Whether it manifests depends on the individual's actions."

Circling overhead, an eagle cries out. We look up just as it dives and snatches a fish which struggles wildly in its talons, but the fish is doomed and cannot break free.

"The gypsy also said that fate is the unexpected outside force which crosses our path and changes our destiny. Fate is beyond our control."

"A wise woman," Kathryn murmurs.

We watch as the eagle returns to its nest and feeds the eaglets. Then, realizing her hand is still held in mine, she asks awkwardly, "Do you see anything else?"

"Your line of mind is also deep and clear. You possess the ability to hold your own in a debate." With a sly grin, I add, "A most reassuring quality in my lawyer." She chuckles.

"Notice this line between the line of mind and the mounts of the fingers? The heart line. Yours is long and curving, a romantic when it comes to love." She coughs nervously. "Yours begins next to the base of Jupiter, the index finger. You care deeply about people, about family. You will make a good wife."

She withdraws her hand. "But I've never married and it's not in my plans."

"You can plan such things?" Now she has taken me by surprise.

"Of course. My work consumes all my time, and it's a little late to be starting a family."

I am stunned. This beautiful, brilliant woman. So full of life. Yet she precludes the possibility of love. Refusing to accept such a destiny, I take her hand once again.

"There is more." I point to an *X* on the mount of Jupiter. "This shows you will have a good marriage, a passionate one." She tries to pull her hand away, but I hold firm. "And beneath your small finger, this line has two lines radiating from it. There will be two children. Perhaps your destiny is still before you."

"And perhaps fate has already intervened. I was engaged once." With a sad voice, she adds, "But it didn't work out." Her revelation startles me. She too has a wounded heart. When I gently fold her fingers into her palm and release her hand, she murmurs, "Thank you. Very interesting."

"Have I offended you?"

"No. Of course not. I asked you to read my palm." But she draws one foot onto the bench and wraps an arm around her bent knee, leaning her cheek upon it. Upriver a beaver emerges from its dam and busily gnaws on a sapling. Kathryn seems to watch it, but clearly her thoughts are elsewhere.

Did I touch a sensitive place? Does she escape from her own losses through her constant attention to the lives and needs of others? Maybe we have more in common than I realized. Our lives are filled with accomplishments, but we have had no one to share them with. For me, it has been beyond my control, but for her, it is a choice I do not understand. I would never choose to go through life alone. It has been thrust on me by fate, by the curse of my face.

Becoming uneasy at her silence, I decide to draw her out. "You seemed quite absorbed with a book earlier."

"It's special. My grandmother gave it to me."

"You are fortunate to have such a gift—and to have known your grandmother."

"The book was written by a poet. Would you like me to read from it?" she asks softly.

Having revealed too much already, I look away, unable to meet her eyes. "I would."

She pulls a small, tattered book from her pocket and begins to read about the wisdom a holy man shares with his people before he departs. Kathryn's gentle voice caresses the simple but profound prose. Like a finely cut gemstone, each chapter contains a facet of human endeavor, reflecting the struggle and the triumph.

When she reaches the last page, it saddens me for this special reading, this special time, to be over. "I will always treasure this gift you have given me." Embarrassed, her face reddens. I suppress a grin. She has no qualms about jumping into a fray but blushes at a compliment. Another paradox. A charming one. "May I see the book?" I ask.

When she hands it to me, I hold the well-worn volume like a Swarovski crystal. *The Prophet,* written in 1923, I note. Turning the pages with care, I commit my favorite passages to memory. When I hand back the book, I glimpse her other palm. Taking her hand in mine, I scrutinize what I find there and rub my forefinger gently over a recent wound. "Were you injured?"

She shrugs dismissively. "It's just a small cut. I'm really clumsy."

"What happened?" I ask calmly, covering my unease.

"I broke a glass last week and cut my hand."

My heart skips a beat. I release her hand quickly lest she begins to ask her probing questions.

She glances at her watch. "It's almost dinnertime. Who won that bet?" she asks with a smile. "You or Jarrod?"

"I did," I admit. "Is that agreeable with you?"

Her smile broadens. "More than agreeable."

The response catches me off guard. Hiding my elation, I reply, "Shall we go back, then?"

As we follow the path, Kathryn seems absorbed in her thoughts. Suddenly, she shrieks and tumbles toward me. I catch her and lower her to the ground. Her foot is twisted, caught beneath a layer of pine needles and mud. I push them aside and discover her foot is pinned beneath a rock.

She moans out, "See? I told you I'm clumsy."

"This was not your fault." I dislodge the stone and carefully lift out her foot. "May I examine it?" She nods, so I pull down the sock, revealing a bruised and swelling ankle. "You should not walk. Would you consent to my carrying you?"

"All the way to the lodge?" Her pained eyes grow larger.

"That is not a problem for me." I say hesitantly, "If it is not for you."

She breaks out in a nervous laugh. "I haven't been carried since I was a little girl." She stares at her foot, considering. "But all right. Let's give it a try."

I call out, "Dave, we require your assistance."

Kathryn looks around, startled, as Dave emerges from the forest.

"How long have you known I was there?" he asks.

"You have been watching us from the ridge since just after we sat down." I smirk. "Jarrod and you are fine trackers but could use some pointers in concealment."

Dave chuckles. "We haven't had your practice." Kneeling next to Kathryn, he asks, "How ya doing? Hurt bad?" She grimaces. "So, what can I do to help?"

"Inform Ryan," I reply, "so he can have his medical paraphernalia ready." As Dave communicates with Ryan on his gadget, I ask Kathryn, "May I pick you up now?"

She nods tentatively, so I place my arm around her waist. She is so light, lifting her is effortless, and to my surprise, she puts her arms around my neck. Her touch disconcerts me. When she rests her head on my shoulder, the silken hair I have so longed to touch brushes against my neck and cheek. Overcome, I breathe in the fragrance of her hair and feel her tiny waist beneath my hand. Dave walks ahead, vigilant as ever, and I carefully navigate the muddy path, all the while overwhelmed by the sensations of Kathryn in my arms.

When we arrive at the lodge, Ryan directs me to place her on a couch. Removing her shoe and sock, he runs his hand around her foot and ankle, then up her calf. I watch, distinctly annoyed that he is touching her. "It doesn't appear to be broken," he says, "but we'll scan it when we get back." He bandages her ankle, then places it on a pillow and covers it with a bag of ice. Handing her pills and a glass of water, he says she must remain on the couch.

"I'm so sorry, Erik," she says. "Could you take a rain check on the dinner?"

"Rain check?" I ask, confused.

"That means we'll have dinner another day."

"Yes, that will be satisfactory," I reply, pushing down my disappointment.

Jarrod grabs my arm. "Come on, Erik. Better luck next time. Let's go eat."

I do not want to leave Kathryn's side but force myself to follow Jarrod. As we dine on the deck, I keep gazing at the entrance to the forest trail, longing to relive our time together—hold her hand in mine again, hear her voice as she reads, feel her warmth in my arms. Just as I am yearning to go back in time and retrieve those hours, time speeds up.

I eat little and follow Jarrod upstairs. In a fog, I pack. When we board the seaplane, Kathryn is already reclining on a seat with Ryan attending her. Jennie offers me the copilot seat, and I slip into it, dazed. Everything around me seems like a dream. As we lift into the dusky sky, tinges of orange and red bleed from the dying light on the horizon.

We circle the lodge, and I look down for the last time. Three days ago, I knew nothing of this place. Now I do not want to leave. There were occasions when time did not seem to exist. Now it is truly gone. Forever.

Kathryn's voice reading a passage from *The Prophet* comes back to me: *"Yet the timeless in you is aware of life's timelessness, And know that yesterday is but today's memory and tomorrow is today's dream."* I gaze longingly at this unforgettable place, feeling poised precariously between a memory and a dream.

52 | DAGGER

Ketchikan, Alaska

Lady Margaret Wheaton

Diane flashes me a smile. "Well, except for Kathryn's accident," she says, "the trip turned out very well. Bringing Erik here was just the ticket. He truly seemed to enjoy himself."

"Everything went better than I could have imagined," I reply, gazing at Ketchikan's lights below. And Diane's right about Erik. Sometimes I even caught him smiling. I doubt he's ever experienced anything like it, either the beauty of untouched nature or the camaraderie.

As Jennie settles the seaplane gently on the water, I sigh with relief that soon we'll be safely home. Howard and I were worried the media or the PTB would get wind of our trip. Thankfully, that didn't happen.

When we pull up to the dock at the Ketchikan Airport, bodyguards search the area, then give the all clear. Kathryn is taken first to the waiting jet. As soon as we get the signal she's settled in, we quickly walk up the ramp from the dock to the tarmac, surrounded closely by bodyguards. I look around, nervous. This is the most exposed and dangerous part of the trip.

At the top of the ramp, Erik grabs Jarrod's arm. "Look!" He points to a post with an airport sign. A red envelope is pinned to the sign by a dagger.

"Close ranks!" Jarrod calls out. The bodyguards press in from all sides, grabbing Erik and me and virtually hauling us into the plane.

"What do you think it was?" I ask Jarrod as I sink breathlessly into my seat.

"I don't know," Jarrod replies, then turns to Erik. "What do you think?"

Erik's jaw clenches. "It was my *custom* to leave notes of warning around the opera house. I used red envelopes. I surmise it is for me."

My mind races through the possibilities. "So you think the PTB found out somehow about our trip?"

Jarrod rakes his hand through his hair. "It certainly has the earmarks of their handiwork. If the media or paparazzi knew Erik was here, they would've hounded us."

"We should see what it says," Erik states acridly. "Is it not wise to know one's enemy?"

"Yeah, I think we should get it," Jarrod says. I agree, so Jarrod puts on gloves and motions to several of the bodyguards. They draw their guns and race with him to the signpost. He pulls out the knife and grabs the envelope, returning to the plane without incident. As soon as they board, Jarrod orders the pilot to leave the luggage and take off immediately. Our seat belts are barely latched before the plane begins to taxi.

Jarrod places the dagger in a plastic bag, then holds up the envelope. *To the Phantom* is scrawled ominously in florid black letters. Diane looks at me, alarmed.

Erik's eyes narrow to menacing slits as he holds out his hand.

"Put your gloves on first," Jarrod tells Erik, "just in case there's some toxin embedded in the paper. Besides, we'll want our lab to check for fingerprints."

Erik pulls on his black leather gloves. Taking the red envelope, he scowls at the writing as he reaches into his pocket and takes out what appears to be a silver fob. Almost magically, a narrow cutting edge slides out like a penknife. Jarrod seems surprised to see it. Erik deftly slices the envelope and removes a single page. As he reads, his mouth curls into a dangerous scowl. The back of my neck prickles.

Seething, Erik hands the letter back. Jarrod frowns as he reads the note, then holds it up for Diane and me to see. The words are scratched in the same black ink, like gashes on the red paper:

We trust you enjoyed your excursion—
It will be your last

53 | STRATAGEM

Monday, July 2
Land's End

Collin

"We're doing everything we know," Tim tells me, pointing to the purposeful chaos of HG-Lab through his office window, "and a few things we've never tried."

"Something had better work. This sure as hell's the last thing tha' we need right now." I'm wondering just what else could go wrong.

"See the group surrounding Dr. Hua? Those are our best quantum physicists," Tim replies in his unflappable manner. "They're brainstorming. If anyone can figure out what went wrong, they can." Reassuring words, but I wonder if the sweat trickling down his temple is a better indicator.

"Good." I turn to my assistant. "Harold, stay here and keep me informed o' any news."

As I leave Tim's office, I'm remembering the superstition that bad things come in threes. I sure hope that's all. First, the team sent to Paris to retrieve Erik's box came back empty-handed. Then the threatening note for Erik. And now, this crisis at the lab. Preoccupied, I shove the lab door open, right into George.

He stumbles, his paper-thin eyelids fluttering in surprise. "Pardon, Dr. McKay."

"My fault," I mutter. George wobbles, so I grab his arm. "Do ya need to sit awhile?"

"No, I am quite fine." He tugs his jacket down and restores his dignity. "I must escort the people to the meeting." He scurries toward the elevator, and I head straight to the underground conference room where Lady Margaret is waiting.

As soon as I enter, she asks anxiously, "What's the latest?"

"The communication system is functioning again." I lower myself wearily onto the couch next to her. "The people in the future finally got a message through. They said tha' the canister arrived red hot, and when it cooled enough to open, the seeds had been destroyed."

Already marred by dark circles under the eyes, her face goes ashen. "What if that had happened while Howard was transporting?"

"The lab also got a message through to Howard letting him know he'll have t' wait for the all clear. Received his response a few minutes ago. He's fine."

"They'll solve this, won't they? Howard will be brought home, *right?"*

"The lab's working feverishly on the problem," I say, trying to console her, "and Tim is confident tha' they can solve it. The physicists are checking within the system as well as for external causes or interference."

"They suspect possible sabotage by the PTB?"

"Everything has t' be considered."

She gazes down at her wedding ring. "How's Howard taking his being stranded?"

"He said he'd use this extra time t' work with our investment team back in 1871. He's also occupying himself with refurbishing the estate."

"Were they able to take possession of it already?"

"The last hereditary heir died just before the war and Commune uprising, so the estate's been sittin' there vacant. The government considered it an albatross, and they need the money for war reparations they owe Prussia. They bought the story tha' Howard is the agent for a wealthy Frenchman. Howard already hired the architect, and since he's stuck there for a while, he plans t' oversee the initial renovations."

"I can just see him rolling up his sleeves. Howard worked with the architects to design Land's End and our Alaskan lodge, you know. As an undergraduate he studied architectural engineering. But with his aptitude for quantum physics and computers, he switched fields because he felt quantum computers were the wave of the future. Still, his heart has always been in architecture."

"Would ya like to see a picture of the estate?" She nods, so I pull up the hologram.

"The front section appears to be medieval," she observes approvingly. "From the stonework, I'd guess fifteenth century, built as a defensive castle. Notice the battlement with crenellations and towers in front. But the other three wings around the courtyard are constructed of bricks, no doubt added in later centuries."

As we examine the stately building, I tell her, "Howard said he discovered something about the medieval fortifications tha' may come in handy."

"I wonder what that could be," she says, examining the building with renewed curiosity.

The buzzer goes off, signaling that everyone has arrived. I put the QRYSTAL away and brace myself for this meeting. George holds the door open for Kathryn, who enters slowly, favoring a bandaged foot and using a cane. She's accompanied by Ryan and Lexa, with Tom, Jarrod, and Dave close behind.

"Wha' was the doctor's verdict, Kathryn?" I ask.

"Just sprained. Shouldn't take long to mend."

"That's good news," Lady Margaret says. "And Lexa, so glad to have you back."

"Not nearly as glad as I am to be here," she replies with a grin. "The inspector took perverse pleasure in having us return to Scotland Yard to grill us. Sir Kenneth finally got him to back off and let us leave."

Once everyone's settled, I get straight to the point. "This meeting is called to discuss our options now tha' the team we sent to Paris could no' retrieve Erik's box. Kathryn, are the documents in tha' box absolutely critical to the case?"

"Yes." She flinches. "It contains letters from Princess Metternich—also his contracts with Garnier and with the directors of the Paris Opéra. Now that we don't have the evidence from England, those are even more crucial to prove Erik was in Europe and not Persia. And the contracts could help disprove some of the allegations related to the murders."

"I was afraid tha' would be your opinion. The problem is, he buried the box five years before the Garnier was completed. Rooms were added in tha' part of the cellar, so it's impossible to determine now which room Erik meant on his map. There's only one way in my thinking to find it—go back to 1871."

The silence in the room is matched by the frozen expressions.

"You mean go back into the past to search for it?" Tom asks skeptically. "The men we sent last week said the building's a maze, especially the cellars. They couldn't even be sure they were in the right area."

"You were there before," I say to Jarrod, "couldn't you find the location?"

He hesitates. "They're right about it being a maze. The difficulty is that the current architectural schematics we have for the building are not the same as the original designs. Frankly, we could have the same problem and not find the right spot. There's only one person who knows exactly where it is."

"You canno' be proposing tha' Erik goes with you?"

"I hate to admit it," Jarrod replies, "but that's probably the only way to find the box."

"What if Erik decides to do his disappearing act?" Lexa blurts out.

"How many men would you need to keep Erik from gettin' away?" I ask Jarrod.

"I think we could do it with three," he replies, none too convincingly.

"To my mind, it'll take four," Dave says, folding his arms, "so we can surround him."

"If the men are going back to find the box under the Garnier," Kathryn interjects, "maybe they could also go to the director's office at the old opera house. Erik said there was an underground passage between the two opera houses. They could look for more documents there. I'll provide a list."

"Documents?" Jarrod snorts. "I'm no attorney. Wouldn't know what to look for."

"Lexa's with the group accompanying Erik when he's returned to the past," I point out. "Wha' do you think about going back and helping find the documents, Lexa?"

"I'm game," she says without hesitation.

"Yes, that would be good," Kathryn says, giving me a cold glare. Maybe not the best way for her to find out Lexa is part of the Wheaton project.

"It appears we have no choice." Lady Margaret pretty well sums it up. "But before we go any further, we should ask Erik his opinion about this venture." She asks George to bring him.

"How has Erik been since he saw that note at the airport?" Kathryn asks.

"His sullen mood's back," Jarrod replies. "He's been in the music room a lot, working on the new piece." That comment opens up a discussion about Erik's behavior which has again taken a turn for the worse.

"By the way, Jarrod, what was the silver tool Erik used to open the envelope of that threatening note?" Lady Margaret asks unexpectedly.

That takes me off guard. *What on earth is she talking about?*

"I asked Erik about it and he told me it's a fob, but I've never seen anything like it," Jarrod replies. "Ryan, did you find a silver gadget on him at the hospital?"

"Yes, when he was prepped for surgery, he had what looked like a silver fob in his pocket. We returned it to him along with his gold ring," Ryan says. "It had some kind of knife?"

"Yeah, like a pen knife," Jarrod explains.

Ryan seems puzzled. "But it didn't look like it opened."

"What did it look like?" Kathryn asks.

Ryan rubs his chin thoughtfully. "It was about five inches long and covered with filigree engravings. There was no indentation that indicated a blade was inside, though."

Alarmed, I ask, "Should tha' really be in his possession?"

"No, I don't think that's a good idea," Tom says, shaking his head. Jarrod agrees.

"I saw it," Lady Margaret says, "and I don't think it's anything to worry about. Can't you disarm a man who's holding a gun on you?" she asks the bodyguards.

They all agree, but look damned uneasy.

"Well, then, why is a small penknife inside a fob anything to worry about," she states, more than asking.

The buzzer goes off, so there's no time to argue the point further. George enters with Erik who's still wearing the flesh-colored mask. Erik surveys the group and halts, immediately wary. Lady Margaret invites him to be seated, but he declines and remains standing, aloof as usual.

I inform Erik that we weren't able to find his box under the Garnier. He doesn't react—like he's not surprised. Maybe he drew the map so we couldn't find the box. So is it chess he's playing now? And is he already several moves ahead? As I relate that Kathryn feels the documents are critical evidence, he listens impassively. When I propose we use time travel to retrieve it, still no reaction. But when I ask if he would agree to go along, his eyes register something akin to triumph. My suspicion deepens.

"I would be willing to assist in the retrieval of the documents," he states matter-of-factly.

"Would it be possible," Kathryn asks, "to also go to the director's office at the old opera house? Lexa would be with you and could check for other documents to use at trial."

"Yes, that could also be done," he replies with an unnerving assurance.

I cut to the point. "So you'll go, then?"

"Indeed. Is there anything further?" Erik asks without taking his eyes off Kathryn.

"No, tha' about covers it," I reply. "Thanks."

He begins to leave but stops at the door and glances back over his shoulder—at Kathryn. I recognize that look. It's the way I used to look at Anne when she left on one of her assignments. He hesitates, as if torn, then disappears down the corridor. My stomach churns. Once HG-Lab gets the time transport into service, the team can leave on this mission. But until they bring Erik back, I doubt the queasy feeling in the pit of my stomach will go away.

54 | MANEUVERS

Friday, July 6
Seattle

Collin

When we pull into the garage beneath Kathryn's condo, Sam scans the area and calls Jim, giving the all clear to bring her to the armored van. Kathryn's still using the cane and walking gingerly on the injured foot. When she gets in the van and says, "Good morning, Collin, my Qrystal for the case, please," her tone is clipped and all business.

"At your service," I say with a grin. As she takes the Qrystal, she bites her lip like she'd love to tell me what I can do with my service. Jim catches my eye and shakes his head slightly. So, Kathryn's a bit testy today. I wonder if it's because she just met her alternate bodyguard for the first time. She probably would've preferred Ryan being with her this first day of court, but he's part of the team that is taking Erik back to 1871. He'll be back in a few hours. If all goes well.

People and news vans cram the street leading to the Criminal Court of the Americas. Sam swerves the car, barely missing a crazy paparazzo. Police have cordoned off the garage entrance but wave us through when Sam flashes our pass. Because of the case's notoriety and the media chaos that happened at the arraignment, only the attorneys and their retinues will be allowed in the courthouse when the trial is in session.

The security guard takes our International IDs and reads the chips with his scanner. "I've got Ryan Kirkman and Jarrod Pearce on my roster, not James Banich and Sam Garza."

"Kirkman and Pearce are out of town," Sam replies, "so we're the replacements."

"I need authorization." Taking our IDs, he goes to the security booth and phones someone. He takes all of ten minutes before he returns the IDs. "Okay, you're all approved."

As we drive through, Sam mutters, "I sure hope they're that thorough with everyone."

"Yes, especially since they've flat-out refused to work with our security team," I grumble. "We tried again last night, but the head o' court security is cocksure they can handle this." But Tom and I aren't so sure. Not with the PTB heavily invested in the outcome of this trial.

Inside, we're processed through the security station, then directed to an elevator on the other side of a modern, antiseptically white lobby. I felt uncomfortable in the crowded courthouse the day I tracked down Kathryn, but this lobby is completely empty and downright spooky, a lifeless void. As we enter the elevator, I try to shake off the eerie feeling.

On the seventh floor, we find Courtroom 79 at the far end of the corridor. The room's not large, with only five rows of seats for spectators. But there'll be no spectators since Erik waived his right to a public trial. The last thing he wanted was the prying stares of strangers. Only reporters and a court artist will be allowed—the media creature must be fed, after all.

When Kathryn reaches the attorney's tables at the front of the courtroom, the two men at the prosecution table interrupt their conversation and pointedly stare at the cane. One stands and offers his hand to Kathryn. Distinguished-looking, from his steel grey hair to hand-tailored suit, he's got the attitude of a man who gets his way. "Jack Spires," he says, "and I assume you're Ms. Copeland."

Kathryn shakes his hand and introduces me. When the other attorney stands and extends his hand, I recognize him as Charles Pennell, a legal pundit on the PALnet talk news shows. He's got a bald head with a high forehead and pronounced cheekbones that hover above a pointed chin. Reminds me of the gargoyles that peer down from medieval cathedrals. His lips curl back in a condescending smile. My Scottish Highland upbringing wars with my professorial veneer as I fight the impulse to wipe that sneer off his face.

Without further unpleasantries, the two attorneys take their seats. I sit with Sam and Jim behind the bar. Bodyguards also sit behind Spires and Pennell, but everyone else wears press badges. The court artist studies Kathryn, then begins sketching her. The picture will be all over the news, her anonymity gone forever.

The court clerk enters from a side door and takes her place just below the judge's bench. Several bailiffs lounge at the side. This is the opening volley, so there'll be no jury today. We'll just be dealing with the prosecution's motion to bring witnesses from the past, and the judge makes that ruling.

A bailiff calls for everyone to stand as His Honor takes his perch above us. His ink-black robe contrasts with thinning, white hair. He glares down at the attorneys through wire glasses suspended on a hawk-like beak. Quickly getting through preliminary formalities, he directs the prosecution to proceed since they filed the motion.

"Mr. Mercier is charged with numerous murders and crimes against humanity," Pennell begins. "No statute of limitations exists on those crimes, and he has never previously been charged or tried. Since this is a criminal trial, the level of proof is the highest—beyond a reasonable doubt. Unfortunately, the only living witness is the defendant himself, and he can choose not to testify." Pennell launches into the legal issues surrounding the documentary evidence. He meticulously details how most of it could be challenged and considered hearsay. Then he asserts there's only one solution. "Because they have potential first-hand knowledge concerning the various murders, the prosecution requests five people be brought from the past as witnesses: Armand Moncharmin, a director of the opera house; Christine Daaé; Raoul the Viscount de Chagny; Madame Giry; and the Persian known as the Daroga."

Instantly, Kathryn is on her feet. "Objection. The Daroga was not named in the motion."

"I hereby make a motion to add his name as a witness," Pennell responds. "The Daroga was not listed because we didn't know if he could be located. The trial hasn't begun yet and defendant's attorneys still have time to prepare their cross-examination for him." *This makes me nervous.* Erik claims he never went to Persia and didn't torture anyone, but can the Daroga refute that?

Kathryn calmly asserts, "Leroux never stated the name of the person known as the Daroga. That is his title as a government official. Even if a man were found in Paris with that title, how would we know it was the same individual referred to by Leroux?"

Waving a file, Pennell peers at Kathryn with eyes an unsettling golden hazel. "We've obtained a letter written by a ParshAn Amjad to his nephew in Marseilles. Mr. Amjad had held the position of Daroga in Persia. The letter was dated 1910, a relevant date since Leroux published his book that year. Mr. Amjad writes that he met Leroux and discussed matters concerning his home country and the Phantom of the Opera. The descendants of his nephew inherited some of Mr. Amjad's possessions, including letters written by Christine Daaé. We were therefore able to identify the Daroga and have now also succeeded in locating his residence in Paris. A detailed evaluation by handwriting experts has authenticated all these letters."

"Motion granted," the judge rules without allowing further rebuttal. "ParshAn Amjad, also known as the Daroga, is added to the list of requested witnesses."

Pennell's voice turns conversational as he continues to address the judge, like he's talking to an old drinking buddy. He asserts that time-travel technology could be used to bring the proposed witnesses to the present in the same manner as Erik. After a long-winded monologue about the need to reach the truth regarding the charges and in the "cause of justice," he concludes those five people must testify.

In a well-reasoned argument, Kathryn explains that time travel is in its infancy and details the risks to the witnesses, including mental and emotional breakdowns. She further clarifies that time travel focuses on the person at a specific date, time, and place, but that the specific whereabouts of the witnesses is not known. After a persuasive, logical rebuttal, Kathryn requests the motion be denied.

Spires stands and dramatically holds up more files. "Your Honor, the letters written by Christine Daaé are dated ten years after the murders. From those letters we can locate her and her husband, the Viscount de Chagny, on a specific date. We've also traced Monsieur Moncharmin to a hotel and the Daroga to his residence on specific dates." With a shrug, Spires says, "However, we are still attempting to locate Madame Giry."

"Madame Giry may have been killed during the Commune," Kathryn interjects.

"Then we could bring her from a time just before her possible death," Spire rebuts coldly.

"Bringing these witnesses to the present could have other serious consequences," she forcefully replies. "They will be exposed to our modern culture. Returning them to the past with that knowledge could contaminate the time stream and result in many unintended consequences." I'm aware this is one of Howard's main concerns.

The judge turns to Spires and asks, "Do you have a response?"

Spires is ready. He proposes that the witnesses be brought for only one day. "We further propose that a professional hypnotist give each witness a hypnotic suggestion upon arrival," he adds, dropping a bomb. "The suggestion will be that everything they see, whether clothes or buildings or furnishings will appear normal to them. When they leave, they will be given another hypnotic suggestion to forget everything they experienced. The hypnotist assures us that, at the very most, the witnesses would only remember their trips to the future as fanciful dreams. All these objections by the defense appear to be its attempt to exclude crucial testimony."

Like a carefully crafted mask, the judge's face is unreadable. Is the fix already in?

Undaunted, Kathryn counters that the witnesses must arrive and depart at the time-transport laboratory. Thinking quickly on her feet, she says, "That creates additional problems. Couldn't the prosecution later allege that improper hypnotic suggestions were given to the witnesses when they arrived that biased their testimony in favor of the defendant? What about the trip to the courthouse? Wouldn't they see the modern city? Even if they weren't able to remember that afterward, such exposure might create culture shock or emotional trauma."

Pennell is undeterred. "We propose that prosecution and defense attorneys accompany each witness from the transport lab to the courthouse. That ensures neither side has the opportunity to talk to the witness or influence the testimony. The vehicle's windows can be curtained so the witness can't see the city." He assures the judge a hypnotic suggestion can be made that everything the witness sees will appear as it does in the nineteenth century. They've handily concocted a way around every objection we could raise. Definitely not looking good.

I'm aware Kathryn has another logistical argument, but she can't use it. HG-Lab is beneath Land's End, an hour's drive away. But Howard wants its location kept secret, so if we're ordered to bring witnesses from the past, a second time-travel lab will have to be constructed at the Wheaton Industries Research and Development Lab in Seattle. Kathryn hammers all the dangers of time travel and paints a disturbing picture of the potential trauma to the witnesses. Her argument should give pause to any thoughtful person—or judge.

She's barely seated before the judge rules in favor of the prosecution. He also rules that the procedures for the witnesses are to be as the prosecution proposed. The judge slams his gavel and ends the hearing, exiting the courtroom without further comment.

Grinning, Pennell struts past us and leaves. Spires briefly pauses at our table and hands several files to Kathryn. "Copies of the letters of Christine Daaé and the Daroga. We've just completed verification of their authenticity. Those are also enclosed. We'll be submitting them at trial. You're welcome to send experts over to our offices to examine the originals."

"Our office will be in touch to set up appointments for our experts," Kathryn replies. The mutual mistrust is now fully acknowledged. Spires gives a derisive chuckle and walks off.

Back in the van, Kathryn says she'll return to Land's End with us since she wants Dr. Adler's input on the letters right away. Her expression doesn't hide her disappointment about the judge's ruling.

I try to take off the edge. "You did wha' you could. The judge had his mind made up before he walked in."

"I agree. But there's never been a motion like this before. Since there's no precedent, how can we prove bias? We can't disqualify a judge without cause, and his ruling against us doesn't constitute valid cause. This confirms our decision to have the case heard by a jury."

As she reads the letters, I keep mulling over what happened at the hearing and how the judge rubber-stamped everything the prosecution wanted.

Distractedly, Kathryn looks up from the papers. She seems troubled.

"Wha' is it?" I ask.

"Christine's letters contain statements that contradict what Erik told me."

"Can you tell me wha' they are?"

"Sorry, can't say. Attorney-client privilege."

"But you canno' just say tha' and give me no clue. Could you point out a passage that's bothering you?" She opens a file and points to a paragraph. Leaning over, I read:

He took me to his music room. Like the sitting room, it was carved out of the cold stone. Tapestries covered the walls except for one, which was covered by the pipes of a floridly carved organ. Red velvet curtains hung like a canopy above something I could not discern clearly. I ventured closer. That's when I realized it was a satin-lined casket! Can you understand my horror? I asked what it was doing there, and he told me he slept in it. I fainted.

55 | TIGHTROPE

Friday, July 6
Land's End

JARROD

"Ready, Pearce?" Nolan slaps my shoulder on the way to his station. He may be the whiz kid of HG-Lab, but Nolan irritates the hell outta me. Always announces the initiation of time transport like it's the lift off of a rocket. Thinks it's exciting. Probably because he's never done it.

My nerves are even worse this time. I almost wish Tom hadn't divulged the problems with the system earlier this week. Wheaton did make it back all right and the scientists decided it was unusual sunspot activity, but I still wonder if it had more to do with unusual *human* activity. That's why I decided to go first today. If something happens, it'll just be my hide. I chuckle grimly—*fried to a crisp of course.*

I glance around the lab. Everyone's here except Josh. And everyone's on edge. Except Erik. He's dressed to the hilt in his black morning suit, cloak, fedora and gloves, and hasn't said a word. Just watches the rest of us like he's biding his time. For what? His chance to escape? We've done everything to make sure that doesn't happen—scanned him with a metal detector, and removed his watch and that interesting little fob. Did a thorough check, even found some matches and took them. And he's sure not going to like what Collin and Tom ordered me to do when we get there.

I decide to test the waters. "Erik, you were unconscious when we transported you. It's a bit nerve-racking near the end, but don't panic. You'll get through fine. Any questions?"

Erik shakes his head indifferently.

"Good." *But it's not good.* I need him invested in coming back. "This'll be over in about six hours, and we'll be back in time for dinner. So you won't miss your conference tomorrow with Kathryn." His eyes narrow, as I keep prodding, "You're gonna use that rain check and have dinner with her, aren't you? I know I would." His eyebrow dips menacingly. That should give him a reason to return. I was concerned about Erik's feelings for Kathryn complicating matters, but on second thought, it could actually end up being an insurance policy.

Josh arrives, cussing and struggling with his cravat. "I'd rather wrestle a Brahma bull," he groans.

After watching from the sidelines, Erik steps forward and removes his own cravat. Deftly manipulating the silk, he demonstrates the technique, elegantly tying and pinning it.

"You can do it, Josh," Lexa goads, which starts the coaching and heckling. Josh is all thumbs with the unwieldy silk. Erik watches, smirking, but after a battle, Josh gets it done.

When Tom hands me an oil lamp and wooden matches, I grumble, "What could it hurt using a flashlight? We did last time."

"Collin's orders," he replies unapologetically. "This time you're venturing outside the Garnier. In case you're stopped, can't take the chance anything modern is found on you."

"Quit belly-aching, Jarrod." Self-confident as always, Ryan folds his arms over his chest. "I'm stuck with a medieval medical bag that's got glass bottles and a needle that'd scare the hell out of you. Better hope I don't have to use it."

"Countdown in five minutes," Nolan calls out. "Tom, it's time to take your place."

That means it's also time for me to take my place in the transport chamber. I enter holding the lamp and matches, feeling as ridiculous as a bear in a bar. Then I wait. Take deep, regular breaths. Brace myself. Finally Nolan begins the countdown, ending with his annoying, "Blast off!"

First the greenish haze, then the lab dissolves before my eyes as eternity engulfs me. Nothing here. No earth or moon. Not even stars. Just the feeling of being alone in the universe. A faint whistling sound and pressure on my eardrums are the only sensations. *Calm down, Pearce. People are keeping track of you somewhere*. I've done this before, but anxiety that something may go wrong this time turns to cold fear.

July 23, 1871

Paris, France

Just at the precipice of panic, a stream of colors shoots past me and coalesces into green fog. Then total darkness. I quickly strike a match and light the lamp. Its glow flickers eerily off arched stone ceilings—the underbelly of the Garnier. I press the QRYSTAL transistor embedded in my ear lobe, signaling my safe arrival. Nightmarish gloom surrounds me outside the circle of light. How could Erik live in places like this? It gives me the creeps just waiting for the next person. The layers of clothing begin to feel suffocating, and I keep checking my pocket watch.

Over forty minutes pass before the greenish fog coalesces and Dave emerges. He steadies himself, trying to reconnect with physical reality. "You all right?" I ask.

"Yep." He shifts his shoulders uneasily in the suit. His long hair is tucked under a hat.

"What would your Sioux ancestors think if they saw you in that get-up?"

"They'd think I look as silly as I feel," he snorts.

I hand him the oil lamp and send the signal. This time it takes even longer, over an hour for Josh and Lexa to arrive. Lexa's badly shaken and wobbling. Josh grabs her by the waist to steady her. "Whoa." He whistles. "What's this? It feels like a cage."

"It is. It's a corset," she quips. "And take your hands off me! Now!"

Josh steps back and gives her a smart salute. "Yes, Ms. *Alexandra*. Just tryin' to do my duty." Lexa gives him a withering glare.

This time the wait is only ten minutes. When the green fog announces the arrival of Ryan and Erik, I order Josh, "Keep your derringer on Erik. If you have to use it, shoot to wound not kill."

Lexa frowns at my order and the handcuffs I take out of my waistcoat. Erik arrives with the dazed look of readjusting to three-dimensional reality. Before he can get his bearings, I slip a handcuff over his wrist. He sneers as I attach the other cuff to my wrist and snap it shut.

"Sorry, Erik." I explain simply, "Orders." Seething anger spews from his eyes.

Ryan looks around the chamber and finds a niche to hide his medical bag. It was agreed to leave it at the arrival location, since he needs to keep his hands free just in case Erik gives us any trouble.

"So, which way do we go from here?" I ask Erik while stowing the key to the handcuffs safely inside my vest, just in case pickpocket is one of Erik's talents.

He points to the right with the handcuffed arm, jerking mine along with it.

Holding up the lamp, Dave leads the way with Ryan and me flanking Erik. Keeping his derringer on Erik, Josh follows with Lexa. We walk through the Garnier cellar in hushed wariness. This place has all the charms of a crypt.

Suddenly, Lexa shrieks and halts.

Ryan and I look back. "Just a rat," Josh says with a cocky grin.

"I'm okay," Lexa states, giving her skirts a serious shake. "I doubt you'd have that silly grin if you had to worry about rats running up your legs under layers of skirt!"

"Rats *and other creatures here*," Erik states coldly. "Be on guard."

What does he mean by *other creatures*? Probably just playing mind games, but I scan in all directions, ready. Erik doesn't hesitate at any twist or turn of this maze. Although I studied the architectural blueprints for this lower level, I'm already lost. And my gut keeps giving off warning signals. What if there isn't any box? What if he's leading us into a trap? I read all about the torture chamber in Leroux. Erik told me he designed the lower levels of the Garnier. I scrutinize the floor ahead of us, wondering if trapdoors have telltale cracks. Or do they swallow you up with no warning? This feels like a cat and mouse game, and I'm pretty sure I'm not the cat.

We enter another tomblike room. "Stop," Erik hisses.

Dave holds up the lamp. The light barely reaches into the shadowy corners. Erik raises his handcuffed arm as if asking to be released. "Must pace to find it," he utters acidly.

"All right. I'll pace it with you." No way I'm uncuffing him.

He scowls but leads me to the far corner where he begins pacing along a wall, counting off thirteen steps. Then he turns ninety degrees and paces nine. He stops and declares, "Here."

"Josh, do the honors," I direct. He hands the gun to Ryan and takes a trowel from his jacket. Kneeling down, he starts to dig. He volunteered for the job, just in case Erik has something else buried there—like a gun or knife. Josh keeps digging deeper with no result. He stops and peers up at Erik. "You sure this is the place?"

Erik nods and motions to go deeper.

Josh attacks the ground again. After a couple more minutes of dirt flying, the trowel sends out a metallic clang. Digging feverishly, Josh uncovers a metal box and lifts it out.

Reaching out his free hand, Erik says, "My fob." I hand it over, and Erik kneels in front of the box. With my hand still cuffed to his, I'm forced to bend down. Everyone gathers around and peers over Erik's shoulder, wondering what's in this box we came so far to retrieve.

Erik's thumb rubs a section of the fob and a small, crooked pick pops out—totally different from the blade that he used on the envelope. I wonder what else that little gadget has hidden in it.

Erik inserts the pick into the lock and turns it. The lock clicks audibly, but the lid sticks when he tries to open it. Turning the box on end, Erik strikes it with his fist. This time it creaks open. I hold my hand out. Erik hesitates, but returns the fob to me. It occurs to me that could be used to open the handcuff, so I give the fob over to Dave rather than returning it to my pocket.

We all lean forward to get a look at the contents. On top are two thick stacks of French banknotes. He holds them up, showing that one contains hundred franc notes, and the other, five hundred franc notes. Next, Erik pulls out a pile of envelopes with an embossed crest. He shows them to Lexa.

She takes in an audible breath. "The letters from Princess Metternich!"

Erik points to bulky parchment documents in the bottom of the box. "The contracts."

Lexa breaks into a smile. "Kathryn will be happy to get those."

At the mention of Kathryn, Erik's hand clenches around the banknotes. I shoot Dave a questioning look. He nods. Something's up.

Putting down the money, Erik holds up a large, gold coin.

"Is that your family crest?" she asks.

"Yes," Erik says simply. I've noticed he's a man of few words today. Then he leans over and closes the box.

Josh quickly fills in the hole while Erik brushes dirt from his trousers. When Josh finishes, he takes back the derringer and picks up the box.

"The next order of business is to locate the director's office at the old opera house." I give Erik an appraising look. Don't really trust him. "Lead on, Erik."

We follow Erik's directions through the jumble of rooms. When we reach the top of a long, sloping ramp, Erik tells us to stop at an open doorway. Dave holds the lamp high, and I peer into a small room with no doors or windows. Dave gives me a skeptical frown.

"Erik, what's going on?" I demand.

"The tunnel between the opera houses." His voice drips with offense at my suspecting him.

"Where? There aren't any doors."

He glares at me with disdain and points to the far wall.

I scan the brick walls. No openings. "All right. Show me." I tell the others to wait in case it's a trap. I follow Erik, one hand securely cuffed to him, the other holding my derringer.

He goes to the far corner and puts his hand between two bricks. Sliding his fingers in, he pushes up and a latch snaps. The entire wall pivots, swinging open. I stare into a dark, dripping tunnel. Erik puts on that smirk as I call to the others, "Come on through."

Once we're inside the tunnel, Josh begins to shove the wall shut, but Erik tells him to leave it open. The tunnel reeks of stagnant water. We trudge through a claustrophobic passageway, our shoulders brushing against rough walls, sometimes being forced to bend down or go single file. Whenever rats scamper across our path, Lexa muffles her squeals.

Where three tunnels converge, Erik guides us to the left. After some distance, he stops in front of another open doorway. "To the old Paris opera house," he states.

Dave lifts the oil lamp and sheds light on a circular stairwell carved out of the rock. It winds upward, out of sight.

"See what's up there," I order Ryan.

He takes out the box of matches and lights one. Going cautiously up the stairs, he disappears around a turn in the stairwell. We listen to his boots scraping against stone, then the sound of a door opening. Ryan calls down, "It's a storage room."

Single file, we climb the narrow stairs and enter a cavernous room. It's crammed. Light from our lamp reflects off backdrops and piles of stage props. Could this be the storage room Erik told me about? The one he played in as a boy?

Erik points across the room. "The Opéra's offices. Through there."

Could Erik be on the up and up? I give him an apologetic nod as we begin our trek through a jungle of theatrical paraphernalia. The lamplight reflects eerily off statues, creating ghostly shadows. Then Dave holds the lamp high, illuminating a forest of costumes on racks jammed against each other, row after row. Yep, just like Erik told me. Ryan and Dave plow in first, and I follow with Erik trailing just behind. The bulky costumes cram in from both sides, choking me with the dust and smell of sweat from heavy velvets.

An unusual drag on my handcuffed wrist alerts me. Something's wrong! I spin around but can't see anything through the crush of costumes. I tug my arm. The other handcuff appears, holding only Erik's cloak.

"Erik's escaped!" I yell. "Cover the doors!"

Josh's boots pound the floor as he fights his way back to the door off the stairwell. After a loud crash and cursing, he shouts, "Got it covered."

Ryan shouts that he's got the other door up ahead.

Holding the oil lamp high, Dave begins thrusting clothes aside like a snowplow.

"Careful with that lamp, Dave," Lexa shrieks. "You don't want to start a fire in here. This place doesn't burn down for two more years."

"What do you mean?" I demand.

"This building burned down in 1873," Lexa says, panicked. "Let's not start changing history by setting it on fire now."

"Hell no! But we need more lamps!" I call out, "Ryan, Josh, any lamps by the doors?"

"There's some over here," Ryan hollers back.

Ryan lights two lamps, and Lexa and I grab them. We begin our search through the costumes while Dave scours the backdrops and props. But Erik's nowhere.

"There's no way he could've gotten out the doors," I fume.

"Maybe a trapdoor?" Lexa says, beginning to search the floor.

"Right! Cover every inch of the floor," I order. "Lexa, Dave, you take the prop area. I'll check under the costumes." I yank off my cravat and suit coat, and drop to the ground. Leaving behind the lamp, I crawl along the dusty floor, virtually swimming through an ocean of costumes. The feathers are the worst, getting in my mouth and up my nose.

Then my hand catches on something cold and hard. A grate! Heaving it off, I look into the opening. It's pitch-black. I can't even see a wall, but the smell of rank water assaults me. "Get me some light!"

Dave shoves the clothing aside and hands down a lamp. When I lower it into the opening, the light flickers off tunnel walls. The truth sinking in, I sit back up and stare into the gaping hole.

"He's gone?" Dave snorts, wedged between a red gown and clown outfit.

"Hell, yes, he's gone!" Angry, I shove the grate back and slam it with my fist.

We regroup beneath the columns of a Roman forum. I take in their stunned faces. "We're not giving up!"

"I agree. Where do we go from here?" Dave asks.

"I vote we go out into Paris and comb the city," Josh declares.

"Paris is huge." Lexa stares at Josh as if he's lost his mind. "Two million people and more buildings and streets and alleys for him to hide in than we could ever search."

"Logically, you're right, Lexa," I say, walking back and forth between two columns. "But I don't care if it takes the rest of our lives, we'll damn well find Erik."

"We may have a more immediate problem. It just occurred to me that we took his matches," Dave says, grimacing, "so he went into those tunnels blind."

Lexa gasps. "He could get lost down there. He could die!"

"We've got no time to waste. I'm leaving you three here to search for Erik. Dave, you're in charge. Go out into Paris and get whatever supplies you need to search these tunnels. Find some tunnel workmen who know this section. Hire them to help out with the search and don't come back into these tunnels without them."

"But Erik knows these tunnels. Maybe he'll find his way out." Ryan says with something less than confidence. "I could start searching for him in Paris. After all, we've got his money here in that box, so that limits his options."

"The money! Oh hell!" I stop dead in my tracks and bark an order at Josh, "Open the box."

He sets it down and tries to open it, but it's locked. "How about that fob? I sure could use that pick."

Dave hands me the fob. I rub my thumb all over the engraved silver surface, but nothing happens. Everyone watches in disbelief.

"You sure you're doing that right?" Josh asks.

I glare at him, then rub both thumbs in every direction over the maddening fob. Still, nothing happens.

"Josh, give me that trowel," Dave says impatiently. He kneels down, and with a powerful shove of the trowel's blade into the lock, the box pops open. We all lean over and take a look inside.

The banknotes are gone. All of them.

Lexa inhales sharply.

"That conniving, blackhearted snake," I breathe out.

Josh drawls out a long, impressed, "Daaaamn."

"Did anyone see him take it?" I ask.

"I didn't see a thing," Ryan says. "But all of us were standing behind him when he closed the box. Come to think of it, that hat he was wearing blocked my view."

"And with a little sleight of hand…" I swear under my breath. It galls me that Erik didn't have any trouble getting out of the handcuffs when he wanted to, either.

"What's this?" Lexa takes something out of the box and holds it up. It's an envelope with Mrs. Wheaton's family crest. "Looks like Erik left us a note." Her hands shake as she pulls out a letter and reads the elegant handwriting, "These maps will take you to the manager's office at the Paris Opéra and back to the Garnier."

Below the writing are two maps. The first shows where we transported into the Garnier and the path we took to get here. The second map details the way to the director's office from this very storage room.

"Erik had his escape planned all along," I mutter, "down to the last damned detail. That devil played us like a fiddle."

"Jarrod, you're pacing again. What are your orders?" Josh badgers.

"Dave and Josh—search in the tunnels. Ryan, you start searching the city. I'll go back with Lexa to face the Wheatons. First, we need to find the director's office and hope these maps don't get us permanently lost. We've got work to do."

56 | CHECK

Friday, July 6
Land's End

KATHRYN

As Collin and I walk from the limo to the elevator in the parking lot, Christine's letters—and the disturbing things she said about Erik—keep gnawing at me. Especially the part about her being terrified when she saw the coffin in the middle of Erik's room and was told he slept in it. I shudder. Erik assured me there was no coffin there. He even laughed at me for thinking that.

There are other discrepancies between Christine's letters and what Erik told me. But Christine's version corresponds to what Leroux wrote. Is that because Leroux based his book on her letters? So who is telling the truth? What if Erik lied about the coffin? And other things?

Totally preoccupied with my thoughts, I don't notice where I am until the elevator door opens on the main floor. George is waiting for us, with thinly veiled doom and gloom on his skeletal face.

"Wha' is it?" Collin blurts out. "What's happened?"

"Mr. Wheaton and Lady Margaret require that both of you meet with them immediately," he croaks out.

"O' course. Lead on," Collin says, with an uneasy glance at me.

My mind races through the possibilities. Did the team return without finding any of the evidence? Or did something happen to them? Then it hits me. Erik! Did he escape?

George takes us to the small room with the elevator to the lower levels. I begin to fear the worst. No one speaks as we descend into the earth, but Collin's expression turns grim. We follow George down the corridors as if this were a walk to the gallows. When we pass the HG-Lab, I glance through the wall of glass at the scientists and programmers. A tense stillness seems to hangs in the air.

After the final retinal scan, George opens the door to the underground conference room and steps aside for Collin and me to enter. We immediately take stock of the situation. Mr. and Mrs. Wheaton's faces are strained with roiled anxiety. In front of them stands a small group of people, all focused on Lexa who is talking animatedly. She's still wearing her 1800s dress, its many layers of skirt rumpled and the hem stained with mud. Jarrod stands next to her, tense and controlled. There are familiar faces—Tom and Diane—and several I have never seen before. Collin and I slip quietly into chairs at the back, while George fills Mrs. Wheaton's wine glass and hovers over her like a protective specter.

"So, after Erik escaped," Lexa says, apparently well into her narrative, "we found that he had taken his money from the box. But he left us two maps, one to the director's office at the old opera house and another back to the place we arrived in the Garnier."

My stomach twists into a knot. Just as I had feared.

"After we went to the director's office," Jarrod says, "I ordered Dave, Ryan and Josh to stay behind and begin to search the city for Erik."

"We succeeded in retrieving the documents Erik said were in his buried box. All those have been brought back, as well as some records that were found in the director's office." Lexa puts a game face on and tries to reassure Mr. Wheaton. "Everything we found will help greatly at trial."

"I see, and just whose trial would that be? Erik's?"—Mr. Wheaton fumes—"Or mine?" Glancing around the room, he seems to notice Collin and me for the first time. "Ms. Copeland, please come forward."

Uneasy about being made a target with no notice or preparation, I take my place on the firing line between the nervous Lexa and a deadly serious Jarrod.

"Ms. Copeland, as lead attorney, what is your assessment of the pending case if we are unable to retrieve Erik and bring him to trial?"

"The International Criminal Courts have no policy or jurisdiction to try Erik in absentia. He must personally appear in court for his trial to proceed."

"Well that lets Erik off the hook, but not me," Mr. Wheaton snarls. "Isn't that right?"

"Unfortunately, true. For you to retain custody of Erik pending the trial, you paid a five million dollar bail. That would be forfeited. The court also ruled that you would be held in contempt of court if Erik does not appear for trial."

"The money is nothing! What happens if I'm convicted of contempt?" Mr. Wheaton presses.

"This is a criminal case, so the court could deem your contempt of court to be criminal rather than civil."

"What does that mean for Howard?" Mrs. Wheaton blurts out, her voice trembling slightly.

"If Mr. Wheaton is convicted of criminal contempt, that would come with a prison sentence."

"How long?" Mr. Wheaton says between clenched teeth.

I look over at Lexa. "This is more your field. What do you think?"

"The statute allows for a minimum six months in prison, but the court could order an indefinite length of imprisonment until the contempt is ended."

"You mean *ended* by producing Erik for trial?" Mr. Wheaton asks, his anger barely controlled.

"Yes, that's what it means."

"There is an additional complication," I interject.

"And what would that be?" Mr. Wheaton nearly snarls like Erik.

"The Court could also choose to file charges against you, alleging accessory after the fact on all the criminal charges currently filed against Erik."

"Why?" Mrs. Wheaton asks.

"Because Mr. Wheaton was in control of the time travel technology used when Erik escaped. Mr. Wheaton could be considered an accomplice to Erik's actions and also be held criminally responsible."

Mrs. Wheaton reaches out and takes her husband's hand in an anguished grip.

"And what happened in court today?" Mr. Wheaton asks me. "Did the judge issue his ruling yet?"

"The judge ruled from the bench that the witnesses are to be brought to trial," I reply.

"Kathryn used every argument she could," Collin says, interrupting. "It was pretty apparent tha' judge had his mind made up before he walked into court."

"But what about the issue of shock to the witnesses? What about possible contamination of the time stream?" Mr. Wheaton presses.

"The prosecution proposed using hypnosis," I explain. "Each witness is to be brought for one day only and will be hypnotized so that they perceive everything as normal to the nineteenth century. The attorneys are to be present at all times and the cars that take them to the courthouse are to have shuttered windows so they don't see the city."

"The judge rubber-stamped those proposals," Collin adds, "and everything the prosecution wanted. None of the facts or arguments Kathryn presented made a difference."

"What have we gotten ourselves into—bringing Erik into our project?" Mr. Wheaton says bitterly. "We should have chosen someone else."

Mrs. Wheaton leans closer to her husband. "No, Howard," she says so softly I can barely hear it, "he was the right one. Trust me." Her words seem to have no effect on her husband.

"If you are tried and convicted either o' contempt or as an accessary," Collin speaks up again, "the PTB will use all their propaganda machines to fully discredit you, Howard. They will inflame public opinion and get enough of the population to demand tha' the time travel technology be removed from your control. Once the government has taken the technology, it will be handed over to the PTB. It does no' take much imagination to guess wha' will happen then. The PTB billionaires will plunder wha' is left of this world and use time travel for their own escape into the past. They'll leave everyone else to fend for themselves. And we all know how tha' ends."

No one speaks while Collin's analysis sinks in. Lexa is clearly dismayed, while Jarrod seems to be biting his tongue. Tom remains calm, enigmatic, and Diane is deep in thought. I recognize a scientist from the lab, but the other men are unfamiliar to me. Based on what Collin just said, evidently everyone here is part of the Wheaton inner circle.

Mr. Wheaton's mood changes. He seems to go coldly calm. "So, Jarrod, what are the chances of finding Erik and bringing him back?" Mr. Wheaton throws the question out like a gauntlet.

"The first problem is whether he got trapped in the tunnels. We took the matches he had on him, so he's down there without any light. The men are getting supplies and hiring tunnel workers to start the search there."

"But the tunnels below Paris are a maze!" Mrs. Wheaton's face pales. "If he gets lost—if you do not find him—he may not make it out alive."

Jarrod doesn't respond. He doesn't have to. Everyone knows the consequences, and not only for Erik. That could also be "game over" for Mr. Wheaton. And everyone.

Jarrod clears his throat. "As Lexa said, Erik took his money, so he has enough funds to leave Paris. But a man with a mask stands out. Given enough men and enough time, we'll track him down."

"Finding him is one thing. Keeping him under your control until you get him back seems to be quite another," Mr. Wheaton says, almost seething.

"It's true, despite our taking every precaution, he escaped. We took his fob, his matches and anything he could use to get out of the handcuffs, but he had the advantage of being on his home turf. Once we capture him, we'll get him away from those opera houses and tunnels as fast as we can. We'll use the transport location near your château outside Paris. Since Collin has ordered us not to use any future technology outside the château, we can't use the anesthesia we knocked Erik out with when we rescued him from the Communards. But I swear—when we catch him, we'll make damned sure he can't escape his bonds."

Alarmed, I exchange uneasy glances with Lexa and Diane.

"But we need more men," Jarrod reiterates.

Mr. Wheaton asks Tom, "Can you send another security team from here?"

"Yes, and why not use some of the security people who are already stationed at the château?"

"I was thinking about that." Mr. Wheaton addresses one of the men I don't recognize. "Send a message back to the accounting team at the château and have them provide any funds that Jarrod needs for this search. And for as long as it is needed." Looking back at Jarrod, he grimaces. "At least we have the advantage that no matter how long it takes you to find Erik in the past, he will be returned through time travel to a date prior to the trial. And I don't care how long it takes, how many men, or how many trips to other countries, if need be. I'll grant that Erik is cunning, but I've also seen you in action. You've saved our lives on more than one occasion. So bring him back, Pearce!"

Jarrod responds with a curt nod.

Mrs. Wheaton looks over at me. "In the meantime you and Lexa will proceed with preparation for trial, won't you?"

"Of course," I reassure her. But I can't help wondering if that trial will ever happen.

Collin remains behind with the Wheatons and Jarrod to discuss strategy, so I leave with Diane and Lexa. As we follow George down the corridor, I tell them about receiving Christine's letters in court. They're surprised the letters have surfaced and anxious to review them with me.

"Why don't Lexa and you stay at Land's End tonight, so we can get started first thing in the morning?" Diane suggests.

"I vote for that. I'm exhausted. I need a hot bath, food and a soft bed in that order," Lexa replies.

"And I doubt any of us could concentrate on work today," I point out.

"Truly. His escape is our worst nightmare," Diane says, "but perhaps I am not so surprised. Erik is known for his skill as a magician and escape artist, and as Jarrod said, he was in his element."

"He told me he knew every inch of the opera houses. I've had a feeling ever since the trip was planned that something could go terribly wrong."

"Yeah, and I don't envy Jarrod having to find Erik." Lexa sighs. "I've been in those tunnels. And I grew up in Paris. It's another labyrinth. Mr. Wheaton and Jarrod seem to feel confident they will eventually catch him, but I'm not so sure."

"I don't think Erik can be found if he does not want to be," Diane says.

"And even if they do manage to find him, I doubt they can bring Erik back if he doesn't want to come." I feel torn between the two sides—commiserate with Erik's desire to escape, but understand the chaos this creates for everyone else.

"Did you hear what Mrs. Wheaton said to Mr. Wheaton?" Lexa asks Diane.

"No, I was too far away."

"When Mr. Wheaton said he wished they had not chosen Erik for their project, she disagreed. She said that he was the right one."

"And she asked Mr. Wheaton to trust her," I add.

"Interesting," Diane muses. "What is it she knows to make her so sure about Erik and his motives or even what he will do? But I have observed that she always defends Erik."

"You aren't implying some sort of romantic connection, are you?" Lexa asks.

"No, not at all. Erik's attitude toward Lady Margaret has always been very formal. And Lady Margaret and Mr. Wheaton are devoted to each other."

"Still, her defending him seems above and beyond the normal." I have always wondered about that. "She also clearly didn't like Jarrod implying they would use brute force to make sure Erik does not escape—and frankly, neither did I."

"I think that was the elephant in the room all of us women were noticing," Diane says. "It is *very* disturbing that when Erik is found, Jarrod will not hesitate to bring him back by force."

"Exactly!" Lexa blurts out.

I nod my agreement. No doubt Erik will put up a fight if they try to force his return. After all, what could possibly make him choose to return to a trial? Why would he want to be ensnared by the Wheatons' web of control? I know how he feels. I feel trapped, too, by these people with their desperate schemes. I long to escape from this place and return to the life I had before. But I can't escape the future that is already set in motion. No one can. So I will stay and do whatever I can. And hope.

As we pass the HG-Lab, I look through the glass façade at all the scientists focused on their quantum computers and endless arrays of screens. I'm struck by something ominous about the hourglass logo etched next to "HG Laboratory" on the wall of glass. How many times have I walked past, never before noticing the sand? It's falling in a fast stream down into the bottom half of the hourglass. But there is almost no sand left in the top. Almost no time left at all.

57 | DESTINY

July 23, 1871
Paris

Erik

Pain stabs up the leg broken by the Communards—reinjured in the drop from the storage room. Blindly, I limp through the nightmarish clutches of the tunnels. *Curse Tom!* He took my matches.

With one gloved hand in front of my eyes and the other scraping on the rough-hewn stone of the wall, I decipher its embedded code. Soon Jarrod will discover how I escaped. I trust he is not foolish enough to follow me. I have traversed this maze for years, learning its secrets, but without that knowledge, a person would surely perish in its tangles. And without matches to light my way, even I may succumb.

But the fear of dying in this tomblike tunnel clashes insanely with the exhilaration that I am free! *Free!* Uncontrollably, my mind keeps reliving the escape. The lock on the manacle offered no challenge. As planned, the sea of costumes shrouded me while I slipped off my cloak, secured it in the manacle and dropped to the floor. As I crawled away, the fedora hat and mask were tucked safely into my waistcoat. With painstaking care I snaked around the gowns dripping with beads and avoided any telltale noise. Inhaled the ancient dust, but choked back a cough.

Then Jarrod realized I had escaped and bellowed to the others to cover the doors. My blood ran cold as I slithered across the floor. I began sweeping my arms in wide arcs, trying to find the grate, my sounds masked by the din of their panicked search.

For what seemed to be endless terrifying moments, I was still there, still in the room with them. Had they moved slowly, quietly, they may have heard some small sound I made. Instead, they thundered about in a frenzied hunt. Then Ms. Simmons warned everyone not to set the building on fire. I still wince at the thought of my beloved opera house, my home, being engulfed in flames.

My own frantic search ended when my hand brushed against the grate which had often provided a trusted escape route. As I lifted the cover, my pursuers were scrambling loudly for more lamps. I lowered myself into the abyss, hanging on the rim until my body stopped swinging. Yanking the grate back into place as I let go, I landed with a thud, rolling to break the impact.

I sat there on the slimy ground, stunned. Over my ragged breath and pounding heart, I listened to the chaotic noises above. Despite the pain in my leg, I thrust myself to my feet and looked up at the light filtering through the grate's filigree pattern to get my bearings. That is when the full weight of my gamble crashed down on me. I had to turn my back on the direction which I always took to the Garnier and to my rooms. Jarrod and the others would soon be returning through that passageway. I had to hazard going in the opposite direction—into tunnels I had not traversed in many years. Tunnels I did not know well. A shudder went through me as I took one last look at the light coming through the grate. Was that the last light I would ever see?

Even as I relish my triumph, I cannot ignore the extremity of my plight. I may be trapped by my own escape. Trapped in endless night. Should a black cat cross my path, I would not know the difference unless it cried out as I stepped blindly on it's tail. I laugh madly. For me and the imaginary cat. But for now, there is only the sound of my boots against stone and the occasional splash of stale water.

Suddenly, no wall beneath my fingertips! I have come to an open cavern. The most perilous part of my journey. Taking a deep breath, I remove my gloves. Pain shoots through my leg as I kneel and begin to search the cold stone. Desperately, my fingers trace the worn surface of the pathway, trying to distinguish it from the rougher cavern floor. I dare not stray into the cavern, or I am lost—like the godforsaken man whose bones were later found mere steps from a door that would have led him out.

With painstaking care, I inch forward through the black void. Endless moments pass yet I still do not reach a tunnel. Have I already veered off the pathway? The thought spreads icy terror through me.

Seconds after their scraping noises warn me, I feel the sharp claws of rats scurrying across my hands. I swat them aside and they scutter off, leaving me again in deathly silence.

What if I encounter the *other creatures*? I have nothing to protect myself except my voice. Heart pounding, I move on. All sense of time is lost as I crawl across the ground.

But I refuse to turn back. Jarrod would not allow me to do what I must. His putting manacles on me banished any doubt about their intentions. I am but a pawn that they would shackle like a slave for their own purposes. And why should I return to the future to face a trial with an uncertain outcome? If I were convicted, I would be imprisoned, unable to play my music. For me, worse than death. At least now I have hope. I have my savings and all the fighting in Paris has now ended. I can leave the city and carry out my plan of settling in the countryside. I chuckle darkly. *That is, if I get out of this tomblike hell alive.*

Water! I hear it dripping just ahead. That could be from water falling into a cistern. I reach out, flailing through the pitch black air.

My hand brushes against a cement surface. Is this a buttress built to support the middle of the cavern? Or have I crossed to the other side? I stand and walk forward, slow and tentative, my hand tracing the cement. After a short distance, the surface changes to hewn stone. A tunnel wall! I have put the cavern behind me.

With renewed hope, I follow the sound of dripping water. In the distance a dim mist seems to appear. But I can see it! That means there is light. I quicken my steps. Heart pounding in my throat, I begin to make out shapes. Finally I reach the stone stairwell that goes down into a cistern. Far above, daylight filters through a street grate where water drips slowly down many stories into the cache of water. I am loathe to leave this small sanctuary of light, but I must. Again I plunge into night, praying that workmen's stairs are nearby.

I grope along the wall—desperate now—nearly mad.

But luck may not be with me. Limestone was not quarried in this part of Paris. A few caverns here in the ancient heart of the city were created as places to hide from invaders, and others were used for storage—like the three carved-out rooms which I claimed for my home.

There are not many tunnels here and only a few stairs built for the workmen of the Inspection des Carrières. If I have to cross another cavern, I may not be so fortunate next time. I could still become lost. Time seems to come to a standstill as I claw my way forward.

Suddenly my hand brushes against wood. The workmen's stairs!

Conflicting emotions flood through me. Shock. Exultation. Amazement. My hand shakes as I grab onto the railing and begin my long climb to the surface, reminded with each step of the last time I ascended the stairs. That trip was to end in my death. Bile rises in my throat at memories of the beating and pain and despair. I had lost everything—everyone I had cared for, and even my own hope for life.

But fate intervened. I was taken to a future world of unimaginable wonders. Yet despite all the clever inventions, all the so-called progress, the tentacles of corrupt power still hold the world in its grasp. Even the Wheatons have their schemes. Are they trying to save the world? Or ultimately making their power play or planning their own escape?

Yet there was Kathryn. I can see her face as if it were hovering over me, watching me with those dark, infinite eyes. But I must not think of that.

I want to find Adèle. Her diary ended that horrific day the Communards forced her to identify my remains in the basement of the Garnier. But then she had returned to her room during the bombardment. I must find out what happened to her. And little Meg. What of her?

And Christine—where is she? Does Raoul still protect her? If he did not survive the fighting during the siege, is Christine now abandoned?

I have much to do. And this time, not only my money is in my hands, but also my destiny.

**Look for the continuing saga, Qrystal Fate,
which will be available in early 2018.**

I am stunned. This beautif

precludes the possibility of love. Refusing to accept such

her hand once again.

"There is more." I point to an X on the mount of Jupiter. "I

you will have a good marriage, a passionate one." She tries t

hand away, but I hold firm. "And beneath your small finger

Marilyn
(509) 230-8024

CPSIA information can be obtained
at www.ICGtesting.com
Printed in the USA
FFOW03n1637050318
45444206-46175FF

9 780692 968659